THE CALL

"When asked what he was fighting for, General Washington, in writing to General Thomas, said the object was 'neither glory nor extent of territory, but a defense of all that is dear and valuable in life.' He must have been an umpire. That's what umpiring is about."

— Doug Harvey

1

THE TRYOUTS

1977

Tim filled the doorway of Margie's bedroom, duffel bag over his right shoulder. She glared at her twin brother's blond surfer-dude hair and pretty face, marred only by a twitch in his jaw. Thanks to a few carefully picked arguments over the last few days, she'd caused that tension and, until that moment, had been proud of her handiwork.

"Last chance," he said.

Margie returned to the book she'd been pretending to read. She felt guilty for being so mean to him lately, but she'd had her reasons. The highlight of baseball camp was the major league tryouts. He'd signed up and, sixteen and male, met all the requirements. No doubt some scout would notice his killer fastball and draft him, and then it would be sayonara, sister. Maybe it would be easier to say goodbye if she was good and pissed at him.

He looked like a dumbass standing there, mouth gaping, hoping she'd change her mind.

"Seriously? You're not coming?"

The trip would mean a tedious three-hour drive from Saugerties to some college campus in the bland, empty middle of New York State. Then, after watching a zillion boys take their shots at a future in baseball, one she was denied, she'd be trapped with her chain-smoking mother all the way home, while she went on about her prodigal son. "Yeah, uh. No."

He attempted a conciliatory smile. "I'll tell 'em you're the only one who gets to catch for me."

"Pathetic, John-Boy."

"Bargie," he whined.

She snapped the page. "Even more pathetic."

He huffed a short sigh. "Fine, then. I'll be back in two weeks. Stay out of my room."

"As if I'm going into your den of iniquity."

"My den of what?"

"Never mind. See you on your baseball card." But despite their mother's squawking that they had to get on the road, the shadow in her doorway didn't budge. Margie glanced up—big mistake. He had that same sad, lost look on his face when they were five and Mom took his favorite blankie and put it in the washer.

It always undid her, and he knew it, so when she tossed her book aside and got off the bed, he grinned.

She let him have his little victory, then pointed at his duffel. "Other side, Righty. Don't mess with that arm. Have I taught you nothing?"

He rolled his eyes but, as she grabbed her baseball cap and followed him to the car, transferred the strap to his left shoulder.

* * *

Scattered across the sparkly outfield grass, teenage boys stretched, took practice swings, shagged flies. Men with clipboards circulated among them. Families and friends had been banished to the bleachers, where Margie and her mother sat bathed in Coppertone and drinking cans of almost-cold soda. Her mother was jabbering her ear off about what "they" were looking for in a young pitcher, as if she had a direct pipeline to Major League Baseball's scouting strategies. Then she mused about the all-you-can-eat buffet they'd passed in the dining hall on their quick tour of the complex.

"I don't know if that shrimp was fresh. It looked frozen to me. Do you think it looked fresh?"

"Mom." Margie popped another can of Fresca and slipped the pull-tab into the hole, a practice that gave her mother apoplexy about her children accidentally swallowing one and slicing their digestive systems to ribbons. "We're hundreds of miles from the ocean. It's probably frozen."

Her mother went off on the buffet. That of course they couldn't judge the quality of the food from what the college would be serving for lunch; they probably put out their best for the families, and once she and Margie left Tim there, who knew what slop her golden boy would be forced to endure?

Margie had once seen Tim eat a two-day-old sandwich he'd left in his locker in junior high school, and he'd been fine, so she wasn't worried about that. What concerned her was Tim himself. He didn't look good. His shoulders slumped forward; his gaze darted like he was searching for something familiar to ground him.

Margie handed her mother the soda. "I'm goin' down there."

"You can't just—"

She mumbled excuse-mes to a variety of parents and trotted down the concrete steps to the field, tucking her blond ponytail into her ball cap on the way.

Nobody stopped her. In her jeans and baggy Saugerties Sawyers T-shirt, she could have passed for a boy if nobody looked too closely. She grabbed a catcher's mitt from a pile of equipment and kept walking toward him.

"Oblonsky!" she called out. "Show me what you got."

He grinned when he spied her pounding her fist into the pocket, but his expression faded, as if afraid she'd be arrested any moment and dragged away to an imagined gulag deep in the bowels of the college's athletic department.

"You said I could catch for you. Let's go."

She'd never been on the field of a stadium that big before. Settling in was tough, with all the chaos around them, the smack-talking boys and the barks of the coaches, the cheers from the stands. Soon they fell into their regular rhythm—him setting, winding up, and pitching; her winging it back and crouching for another one. As easy as if they were in the backyard on a summer evening.

"So what do they do?" Margie overhanded the ball back. "They watch, make notes, or do they actually come over and talk to you?"

"I guess both."

A random ball rolled toward them. A voice called out, "A little help there, pretty boy?"

The guy waiting with his glove out was smirky and acne-scarred, the vibe of entitlement as obvious as his Rod Stewart haircut and the gold chains around his neck. Margie scooped up the ball and powered it back to him, a clean strike. The guy caught it but stood there for a second, looking stunned. She might have apologized to Tim for a return that hard, but not to this guy.

Then a voice growled, "Kid. Blue T-shirt. What's your name?"

"Oblonsky," both twins said at once.

The guy scanned his clipboard. "I only see one of you here. Timothy. Pitcher." Tim pointed to his own chest. The guy nodded, made a notation on his chart, then turned to Margie. "I saw that throw. Nice arm. What's your story, ace?"

She couldn't fight the blush firing up her neck and into her temples. "I'm, uh…"

Tim mumbled a few words—they were twins, paperwork went missing, late entry—but his excuses weren't smooth enough or fast enough. Margie already saw recognition dawning in the man's narrowing eyes, his tightening lips.

"All right, missy," he said, not exactly gulag-mean but not too nice either. "That's enough, now. Only registered players are allowed on the field. That's the rules, you understand?"

Margie could have crumpled into the turf, but she wouldn't give him the satisfaction. "Yeah. Loud and clear." She flipped the mitt to the ground and stomped back to her mother. Out of the crashing wave of noise that closed over her head, the last words she picked out were, "Okay, Oblonsky. You're up."

2

THE IDEA

1980

While she waited out a pitching change in the bottom of the sixth inning, Margie eyed a row of fans sitting on the third-base side. She was choosing which kid would get the next foul ball that came in her direction. The team frowned on giving too many balls away—"This ain't the majors," the equipment manager often reminded her—but that was a stupid rule. Baseballs were cheap, and it was good for business to toss a souvenir or two into the stands. Even though this was only a Class A Short Season game, and it would just be a gimme from a ball girl, what kid wouldn't be jacked up to get a baseball from a real ballpark? What kid wouldn't be waiting by the field gate after the game for a player to sign it?

Plus, messing with the crowd made Margie's job more interesting. When softball season ended, her coach had put in a good word for her with the local minor league organization. They needed ball girls and batboys, and they preferred to use hometown college athletes. Everybody won. The team got free help, the schools got free advertising, and the kids got a sweet reference for their résumés.

Well, almost everybody won. As much as Margie loved baseball and appreciated the opportunity, sitting around hoping to snag a stray ball could be damned dull. She missed playing—softball or baseball. The pickup games that usually filled her summers were a relic of her childhood. Now Tim was gone, too, drafted into the minors. But he got to play, not just trot around chasing foul balls as a public relations move.

The pitcher finished his warm-up throws, and the batter stepped into the box. Margie stared down the visiting team's catcher, imagining herself behind the plate in full gear. On the first pitch, the batter connected and the ball sizzled up the third-base line: foul. Heart leaping, she made a run for it. But the third baseman snatched it up before it could reach Margie. He flipped the ball back to the pitcher. She shrugged at the kids in the stands and sat on the rolled-up infield tarp, where she waited for another opportunity.

During orientation, she'd been told to keep her distance from live play. But sometimes Margie couldn't help shadowing the home team's third-base coach. He was a slightly paunchy, round-shouldered man named Bill who owned a local car dealership. According to rumor, he'd been a decent college shortstop. He never told Margie to get lost, so she kept watching him. The signals were interesting. He'd tug on his cap or touch his chin or sweep a hand across his chest. Her softball team used similar gestures, but she mentally catalogued a few new moves to try next season. The third-base coach even filled her in on the finer points of the game. Maybe he got bored, too. While the teams were changing sides, sometimes he'd point to a player and say, "Watch this guy, number eighteen. Bet you a Coke that if he gets on, he's stealing."

That night, her body jumped with nerves from the first pitch. Timmy was starting for the Bellingham Mariners in the Pacific Northwest League. She was bummed that she wouldn't get to see his first official start. But the lineup had only been decided that morning, and she and her mother couldn't get a flight.

"Don't sweat it, Bargie," Tim had told her on the phone. "I don't know how long they'll keep me in. I'd hate for you guys to spend all that money and come all the way here to watch me pitch for, like, one inning."

One inning. As if. He'd probably pitch their lights out and leave them crying. She paced along the third-base line, eyeing the plays, the signals, snapping with adrenaline when the ball cracked off the bat and the field went into motion. Still, she hadn't mentioned Tim to anyone, not wanting to jinx him. Maybe the third-base coach noticed her anxiety, because he paid more attention to her than usual, calling her over to explain things or tip her off to watch the next batter.

"Margie." He cocked his head toward the guy on first.

The runner led the league in stolen bases. He danced around to distract the pitcher. It was working; the lefty looked rattled. He'd thrown three straight balls, one in the dirt that, thanks to the catcher's quick hands, didn't go wild. After the manager trotted to the mound to buy time and settle the kid down, Lefty pitched a mean strike. The batter connected, dribbling the ball into short right field. The runner on first sprinted toward second. Meanwhile, confusion reigned in the outfield. The center fielder booted the ball, finally got control of it, and made an ill-considered side-flip to the second baseman, who dropped it. This gave the lead runner the confidence to try for third base, even though the coach wasn't giving him the green light. As the second baseman set to throw, Margie held her breath. The runner was fast; the play would be close. Time seemed to slow, dividing the impending play into its component parts: ball in the air, runner's sliding foot, third baseman's glove moving into position, the umpire scrambling to get a good angle on the action. The ball kissed the leather glove. The third baseman applied the tag a split second before the toe of the runner's cleat hit the base. Then the ball bobbled out of the webbing. The fielder scrambled for it, scooping it back in, holding the glove over his head as if he'd made the play clean.

The umpire called the runner out.

"But he was safe!" Margie blurted.

Bill flashed a look at Margie, like maybe he was pissed at her for trying to interfere. But before she could apologize, Bill charged up to the umpire. Eyes bulging, he said, "He dropped the ball! The runner was safe!"

The umpire put his hands up as if trying to calm the coach. The runner stabbed a finger toward where the third baseman's glove had been. The third baseman was pleading his case. Then the home team's manager came out, pointing and yelling and trying to pull his players away from the ump, who told them all to shut up and go back to their positions. But the runner was too wound up to stop. Despite the arms trying to yank him off the field, he yelled some words the umpire didn't like: "You fuckin' blind asshole, I was safe. What the fuck's wrong with you? He dropped the fucking ball, you blind son of a bitch!"

The gesture the umpire made next was unmistakable. The runner was thrown out of the game. Then the situation devolved further—more shouting, more cursing, more players ejected. Margie, wide-eyed, heart pounding, couldn't tear herself away, couldn't get her feet to move.

Only when she felt two strong hands pull her back by the shoulders did she hear Bill calling her name. Only then did she realize what she'd set in motion.

"I'm sorry, I wasn't trying to get in the way! It's just…" She turned to face the coach. But he didn't look angry. In fact, he was almost smiling.

"Don't be sorry, Margie. You're the only one who got it right."

* * *

Bill landed with a groan on his metal folding chair and pushed a glass of soda in Margie's direction.

"What's that for?" She chomped the last forkful of her dinner. Her mother wouldn't have approved of the oversalted chicken breast that had probably been frozen, nor the way Margie was inhaling it. But she'd been racing around getting ready for the start of a new school year, and the end-of-season awards banquet was the first chance she'd had to eat all day.

"That game against Cortland," Bill said, "when you told me the big right fielder wasn't gonna steal and I didn't believe you."

She grinned. "Now, see, you said you were gonna buy me a Coke. Everything's free here."

"You're too damn smart, kid." He leaned back in his chair and surveyed the tables spread across the Knights of Columbus hall, filled with teenage boys in ill-fitting suits who were chowing down like they'd been stranded on a desert island for a month. There probably wasn't enough oversalted, previously frozen grilled chicken in New York to feed this crew. From the jokes and the high fives, you never would have known they'd finished the season in the cellar. Maybe they were just happy it was over. Margie thought she'd be happy to see the last of her ball girl uniform, the last of that tiny stadium, but she was already missing it.

"So, tell me," Bill said. "How'd you know that the kid wasn't gonna steal?"

Margie shrugged. "I don't know. Body language, maybe. He wasn't set; he wasn't all coiled up. Like he wasn't even thinking about it."

Bill crossed his arms over his chest and nodded slowly. "You got some good instincts."

She blushed at the compliment, couldn't help a fluttery smile. Her high school coach had told her the same thing. Coach also said she had a good eye and was probably one of the best catchers the school had ever seen. Then a loud guffaw from somewhere in the room drew her attention to the tables of boys. Boys who could look forward not just to next season but the season after that. And maybe a minor league contract, like Tim had. In that moment, playing softball felt so…useless. It was fun, but it was a big fat tease with no future, at least not one that she wanted. She'd already gone round and round about it with her brother. He said she could shoot for the Olympics, then coach for a college team. If she still wanted to keep playing, she could find a weekend league.

But despite her good eye and her instincts and Tim's rosy picture of her athletic prospects, it wasn't enough. She wanted to tell Bill that, but it felt so pathetic, and she didn't want to be a wet blanket on everybody's Big Night. Guys were laughing and flirting with the waitresses and talking about next year. Next year, she'd have an associate degree and a bunch of trophies gathering dust on her bookshelves. Maybe she should ask Bill if she could work for him. At least being out in the fresh air talking to people sounded better than being stuck in some soulless, suffocating office all day, like her mother.

"You think I could sell cars?"

Bill cut a glance at her, took his time answering. "Heck, I could always use a sharp kid. But I'm wondering if you're selling yourself short."

Margie puzzled over what that meant. He motioned her closer. "You love baseball. Anyone who talks to you for five minutes can see how much you love it. You know the rules. You've got a good eye…"

"And…what? I'm a girl. They're never gonna let me play." *But if they won't let me play…* "It would be pretty sweet to be a coach. You'd have to have some kind of baseball experience first. Like you, right?"

He tapped a finger against the table. "Or. You could become an umpire."

3

THE ROOKIE

The white powder sat in neat rows on the back cover of some crap disco album. Nerves skittered down Tim's arms, tingling the tips of his fingers, already going numb from the death grip he had on his bottle of cheap beer. Led Zeppelin thumped from the speakers, and people talked way too loud. In high school, and in college before he got drafted, he'd snuck a few beers on a weekend, maybe shared a joint or three, but never the night before a game. He knew what booze and pot did to him; he enjoyed the gentle lull that smoothed the edges off a rough week, a bad outing, and that seemed like enough. He knew how much he could do and still function the next day.

Mostly.

"Ha, Blondie's lookin' at it like it's rat poison." Enrique Alvarez shot a toothy grin around the living room, chock-full of secondhand furniture, baseball players, and girls—the same girls who came to all the parties.

When the Bellingham Mariners were at home, the parties were always at Enrique's place, which made sense. The big right fielder's signing package came with enough rent money for an actual apartment, not a tiny room in a boarding house. Tim tagged along to Enrique's, most of the time. He liked to think he was a go-along, get-along type, but he had a couple of strikes against him: he was the new kid, and he was a pitcher. He didn't want to look like a diva, so he partied. But he was beginning to wish he'd stayed behind.

Enrique nudged Tim's arm. "Come on, man, lighten up."

Easy for you to say. I don't know what this shit will do to me.

As if he'd gleaned his thoughts, the right fielder said, "You don't even have to play tomorrow."

True, he wasn't starting, but he could be called in at any time. He didn't want anything messing with his pitching. Too much was at stake. He'd been a third-round draft pick, and a lot of eyeballs were on him. Some talked like he was supposed to be the next Nolan Ryan.

"Trust me, pitchers do this all the time," Enrique said. "It helps their performance."

Tim's eyebrow hooked up. Enrique then told him about a Cy Young winner, one of Tim's idols, who did coke before every game, sometimes even slipping into the clubhouse for another hit between innings. He had a hard time believing that at first, but Enrique had been around. He was from Cuba, where boys come out of the womb playing baseball, where he'd been one of their superstars. Nobody really knew how old Enrique was—he claimed his records had been destroyed when his family defected—but he knew a hell of a lot about the majors for someone who was only in his second season of Class A ball.

Rick, the second baseman, leaned over, pressed a finger over one nostril, and hoovered up one of the lines. The cute redhead sitting between Tim and Rick started giggling at a joke only she seemed to know, then took the album cover from him and snorted like a pro. Tim's nose itched just from watching them. The act looked so unnatural, as alien to him as sticking a hypodermic full of whatever into his veins. Drinking and smoking were familiar to him. This? Weird. And maybe a little dangerous. He'd resisted the first time it was offered to him, at his high school graduation party, because his friends who had already done it were looking kind of messed up. Talking too fast, moving too fast. Fast and slow at the same time. He got the skeeves at the idea of being out of control, so at the time he'd made some excuse and gone out on the patio to talk to some girls.

"Seriously, you'll dig the rush," Rick said. He sniffed and rubbed at his nose, flashing him a big grin as the redhead passed Tim the album cover and squeezed his thigh, her hand climbing higher. Tim sucked in a breath and twitched in anticipation of where that hand was going.

She leaned closer and breathed in his ear. "Do it, gorgeous. Do it and meet me in the back room after. You think the coke's a rush, just wait."

Yeah. That was enough. Tim bent to the album and copied what Rick had done. The coke tickled and burned, but thank the whatever gods that he didn't sneeze and look like an asshole. Someone then handed him a shot and he downed it. Everyone laughed and high-fived, like it was funny as hell that they got the new kid. He sat back and waited for something to happen. Nothing. Maybe it didn't work on him. Maybe he should have taken more. But then he felt like someone had thrown a switch inside his head, riveting him to attention. Colors pulsed; the intricacies of the Zeppelin song flittered along his nerve endings. The redhead stroked his thigh, her fingers dancing across his crotch as she got up and sashayed out of the room.

Tim followed.

4

THE ACADEMY

1981

Margie had never been to Florida before. When she and Tim said it might be fun to take a family vacation there—they were twelve, it was 1973, and Disney World had just opened—Dad railed on about the tourists and the humidity and the disgusting insects as big as your fist and the lack of decent pizza. End of discussion. Then, after he grumbled back to his recliner and his beer, the twins eyeballed each other, suspecting the reason behind their father's disgruntlement: he'd been a bullpen catcher for the last decade of his career, and every season he'd spent stuck out there started with spring training in Florida. All of his disappointments and regrets were wrapped up in those thousands of miles of shoreline. The boot of the Sunshine State had kicked his sorry, sorry ass.

As she flopped onto the outfield grass to eat yet another greasy takeout lunch with her two hundred and ninety-nine umpire-training classmates, many of whom refused to talk to her, Margie wondered what her father might have told her before she got on the plane to the land of his discontent. He would have clapped a big hand to her shoulder and said, "Kid, bring your own food." Then he would have given her a fly swatter.

She'd been so tempted to drop his name in camp, give them a hint about the baseball in her blood, tell them about the day her father snuck her—and not Tim—into the bullpen at Yankee Stadium. Whitey Ford had tugged her ponytail and shown her how to throw a fastball. But she knew she couldn't say those things. A lot of people thought she'd strong-armed the school into letting a woman attend, or that the owners were trying to make good-guy points with the media for being "open-minded." And a lot of her classmates didn't like it.

Some of the instructors didn't like it, either.

A whistle blew, rattling her from her thoughts. Trainees scrambled to ball up food wrappers and assemble in the outfield. They'd spent the morning studying the rule book. Afternoons, they worked on making calls. It looked so simple on TV: ball, strike, safe, out. From watching hundreds of ballgames with her father, she knew there was performance in it, a kind of choreography. So she got it when the instructor said that you didn't just make the call—you had to *sell* the call and look confident while pumping a fist or sweeping an arm. She'd grown up admiring the smooth, deliberate class of old-school umps like Doug Harvey rather than the showboating styles of some of the younger guys.

But twice that afternoon, she'd been tagged for not keeping her thumb tucked in when making a fist to call a strike. Rude remarks from the trainees followed. She ignored them. But it was hot as hell for a January day in Florida, she'd already done ten laps around the field for the infractions, the burger and fries weren't sitting well in her stomach, and one of the guys had tried to trip her. It took all her strength to keep from returning the favor.

She'd promised herself she wouldn't lose her temper during the six weeks of training. As the first woman admitted to Big Al's Umpire Training Academy, she had to stay calm, and cool, and work twice as hard as the guys. She was okay with that because she loved the game so hard it hurt, but sometimes—

"Oblonsky! Thumb!"

Crap. Margie spun toward Rocky Anderson's voice. Beefy and red-faced, Anderson stood not six feet away, arms across his chest, pit stains growing down the sides of his polyester golf shirt. He'd had a hair up his ass about her from the start; he'd been a major league umpire since the Brooklyn Dodgers left Ebbets Field, and he thought only the candidates he personally anointed should be allowed in. That didn't include women. From the way he continued to glare, not much had changed since the first day she'd walked into orientation and he'd called her "honey" and told her where to set up the coffee.

He squinted so hard she thought it must have been giving him a headache. Then he lifted a corner of his mouth and said, "Are you deaf? Is that your problem?"

Don't show a damn thing. Don't move a muscle. "No, sir. I'm not deaf."

"Or do you have some kind of physical affliction that prevents you from articulating that particular joint?"

"No, sir. That particular joint articulates just fine."

A couple of guys guffawed.

"Mind your own fucking business," Anderson barked at them. Then he waved them off. "Five laps."

Margie cringed, and for a second considered running along with them as a show of solidarity before common sense took hold. *Head down.* She couldn't make her thumb behave, but they were being jerks; let them take the punishment. She sure as shit wouldn't expect them to do laps alongside her if she'd screwed up.

By the end of that afternoon, she was sweating like a hog and wobbling on her feet. And she still had to walk a half mile to her motel. The on-site housing was single-sex only, and they wouldn't let her stay there. She'd nearly tackled her mother to keep her from getting on the phone and arguing with the school about it. Fearing repercussions, they quietly offered her a stipend toward "making her own arrangements." With that, she found a motel that gave her a decent monthly rate. The crappy air conditioning and stench of mold were a bonus.

She was starting to see her father's point about Florida.

She gathered up her gear, preparing to make the trek back to her room and enjoy a long, hot shower. As she was stowing her rule book, a knot of guys walked past. She caught the words "thumb up her ass" and flung down her bag. As she took two strides toward them, a firm grip tightened around her upper arm.

Margie turned, expecting Anderson, already biting her tongue. Standing in front of her was Big Al himself, the guy who'd started the umpire school. The guy who'd let her in. He wasn't all that big, despite his name—maybe that part was a joke or something—but still he looked like someone you didn't want to cross. His mouth was tight, his weathered eyes trained on hers. She was about to blast off that she would have been justified in taking those assholes down, but he cut her off with four calmly enunciated words, four words she'd hear many times throughout her training: "In my office, please."

She said hi to Hector the custodian when she passed him in the hall, then waited in a folding chair in Big Al's office, the backs of her thighs sticking to the metal. A few minutes later, Al walked in and plunked a Styrofoam cup of water before her. Even though it was lukewarm and smelled faintly metallic, she downed it in two gulps.

"I'm sorry about that, before," she said finally. "It's been a long day."

"You can't let it get to you. This"—he tapped a surprisingly groomed finger against the desktop—"is the least of what you're probably gonna face out there."

She nodded. "I can handle it."

He leaned closer, taking a measure of her. "I pushed for your application. Don't turn me into a liar."

Her spine stiffened. The question she'd feared the answer to— *Am I some kind of bullshit affirmative action charity case?*—lodged in her throat. Instead she asked, "Do you think I belong here?"

His face hardened, and that tapping finger pointed straight at her. "Are you questioning my judgment on who gets into this institution?"

Margie blushed. "No, sir, I just…"

"Look. I saw a qualified candidate; I got that qualified candidate in the door. I took some heat for it, but that's my job. What you do after that is up to you."

Taking heat would be her job, too. Margie was only the third woman in recent history to try to become a professional umpire. In 1972, the first, Bernice Gera, quit after working a single game, and the second didn't make it much further. So why should Margie think anything would get any easier for her now?

"I'll level with you," Al said. "Some of my instructors thought your application was a put-up job. You're here to show them they were wrong." He cocked his head toward the field. "And all those other hopefuls out there? They don't sign your contract. But you might find yourself partnered with any one of them, and it's up to you to figure out how to make that arrangement work." He stopped a moment, sipped his own water, cringed, and set the cup down. "Fuck, that's god-awful. How do you drink this shit?"

* * *

As Margie rounded the right-field corner, Wes Osterhaus fell in beside her. His wiry limbs matched her stride, his pale, freckled cheeks pinking from the exertion and the Florida sun. In their morning classes, Wes sat Catholic-school-straight in the chair in front of hers, bobbing his head at the instructor. He always had the right answers, and a hundred other questions. The instructors had been patient with him, but more and more they said, "Let's talk during lunch," or told him to go look it up in the academy's library. The "library" was a dingy, cinderblock-walled equipment room that smelled of sweat and old coffee and contained two metal folding chairs, an old TV, and an erector-set bookshelf of manuals and videotapes. Sometimes Margie passed the room on her way to Big Al's office and Wes would be sitting there alone, staring at the screen, scribbling notes on his pad. She felt bad for the guy. He was smart, that much was clear, and he was one of the few people in camp who would talk to her. She overheard a couple of trainees calling him "Oster-cize," and she wanted to kick them.

"Nice day for a run, huh?" Margie said.

"Technically, no." Wes said some stuff about dew point and relative humidity that left Margie's head spinning. Then he trailed off, and on the left-center warning track he said, "Forty-eight."

"Excuse me?" Margie wiped the sweat off her brow with the back of her hand.

"Sixteen percent of three hundred." He nodded toward the group of guys practicing on the field. "That's how many candidates will get recommended for evaluation after we're done. Fewer still will get minor-league assignments."

She smirked. "I think you're gonna do fine."

He nodded toward Rocky Anderson, who was berating some guy until he hung his head. "But that instructor is lowering our chances. He's doing it all wrong."

Her eyebrows hopped up. "Whaddya mean, wrong?"

"Positive reinforcement has been shown to help long-term learning better than negative reinforcement."

"You got English for that?"

"Okay, right," he muttered, as if giving himself a reminder to dumb-down his vocabulary for the masses. "Your strike fist. If he said, 'nice job' when you tucked your thumb in, instead of making you do laps when you get it wrong, research says you'd learn better."

"What, you saying I'm never gonna learn?"

"No, Margie, I believe you will." He paused a moment and added, "Because you remind me of Doug Harvey. He's the best umpire in the game."

She grinned. "Really? Doug Harvey?"

"Yes. The way you make your calls. The way you know the rules."

Damn. "You wanna race?"

"Not especially."

She knocked an elbow into his arm. "Aw, come on. Race me to the on-deck circle. Loser picks up the beer tonight."

"That's negative reinforcement. And besides, I don't drink."

"Okay. Winner gets to pick the game tape in the library later."

"See? Now I'll do it," he said. "Because you're offering me a learning opportunity."

He took off. She took off after him. For the first time in Margie's life, a boy beat her in a footrace. Probably because she let him.

* * *

Margie studied her rule book, participated in class discussions, kept her thumb tucked, and finished her training and evaluation with the second highest score in her class.

Wes finished first.

During her last advisement meeting, Big Al pushed a piece of paper across the desk. It was a list of names, organizations, and addresses. "Write to these people. Send your creds. Then wait. It could take a while."

Margie sucked back a groan. How she'd gotten in still made the back of her brain itch sometimes, but at least the academy wasn't guilty of overinflating her expectations.

Al also made a couple calls and signed her up to work a few local junior college games. They didn't pay, but she needed the experience. It was good timing, too. Her room was settled through February, she still had some cash for food and incidentals, and as much as she hated Florida, she didn't relish the thought of a New York winter without Tim, in addition to the anxiety of waiting.

So when the money ran out, with her two suitcases, her professional volume of the rules of the game, her diploma, and her official academy windbreaker and baseball cap, Margie flew back to the land of decent pizza and normal-sized insects. To live with her mother, and wait.

5

THE OFFER

"And you accepted?" Her mother's painted eyebrows arched to the heavens. "What the frig is wrong with you?"

Unable to even register her mother's comment at first, Margie stood in the kitchen doorway, clutching the letter in her hand. It was too soon to get an offer. She hadn't even contacted any of the people on Big Al's list yet. She couldn't help thinking it was a gimme. But what if this was her only opportunity and she didn't bite because she couldn't trust that it was real? She wanted it to be real. She wanted to jump up and down and scream. She couldn't reach Tim, and she needed someone to be excited for her. This person wasn't going to be the woman who had given birth to her, apparently.

Pat Oblonsky shoved the spatula through her famous meatball casserole with so much force that the cow's mother must have felt the pain. "East armpit nowhere. You're gonna end up like your father, God rest his soul. Blowing your knees out in obscurity."

"It's three months of single-A ball in the Bighorn League, for Chrissakes. I'm not going to Mars." Her mother gave her a quick, baleful stare, to which Margie shrugged and answered, "It's a start."

"Calling games for high school kids."

"Mom. It's not high school. Well, okay, some of the players are pretty young. But I gotta start somewhere. I gotta pay my dues. What, you think they're gonna airlift me straight from umpire school right to home plate at Yankee Stadium? Even if they did, how do you think that would look?"

Mom's hand froze on the spatula, her lips pinched together, her chin bobbing with determination. "It's not too late. I could call some of your father's friends. I can lean on the right people, get you into those tryouts, like Tim—"

Holy Toledo, did her mother have a stroke while she was in Florida? Margie snapped the letter in front of her. "*This* is what's gonna happen. I just spent six weeks working my ass off for this. I graduated second in my class, this is my shot, and I love this game. You know how I love baseball."

"It's my fault," her mother said. "I shoulda pushed you. You hit decent. You're a good catcher. We can take that friggin' world by storm."

Oh, good God. This again. "Mom." Margie blew out a breath. "You couldn't get Dad out of the bullpen, what makes you think—?"

She pointed the spatula. A glob of meat flew off and landed on the linoleum. Margie snatched a paper towel from the roll and bent to pick it up. "Because he wouldn't listen to me. 'Marty,' I said. 'Get the hell out of there. Finish your career with some respect.' You know, I think he liked being the bullpen catcher. I think he liked being around all those tomato plants out there."

Maybe the bullpen was the one place Dad could go where nobody yelled at him or tried to change him. Then it occurred to her. Despite her bluster, or maybe because of it, Pat Oblonsky couldn't control her husband. Tim had been out of the house for almost a year. Margie was her last chance. She would have bet her Big Al's Umpire Academy golf shirt and matching windbreaker that her mother would have liked nothing better than to manage a baseball team.

She shook the letter at her mother. "Mom, I'm takin' this job."

The tone was louder than she normally used with her, and she felt bad about that, but not bad enough to apologize. Sometimes it was the only way to get her mother to listen to her.

The angry words hung in the kitchen, along with the aroma of beef and tomato and onion. She lofted the crumpled paper towel into the trash.

"It's gonna be damn hard," her mother finally said. "If you're gonna work so hard, you should at least have a shot at some glory. This..." She waggled the spatula toward the letter. "It ain't no glory. Who the frig remembers the umpires?"

* * *

Tim called back later that night. After a bit of whooping and hollering, at a notch lower volume than it might have been if she hadn't argued with her mother, she grabbed a beer from the fridge.

"So what's your strategy?" Timmy said.

Margie unscrewed it with the hem of her T-shirt and tossed the cap onto the table. It skittered across the surface and landed with one lip off the edge. That meant score, all those times they played table hockey after dinner. Man, she missed him.

"Like I said. I'm gonna go to the Bighorn League and ump. Whaddya mean, strategy?"

"Well, they're gonna know you're a girl, for one."

She slumped into a chair and imagined him across from her. "So what? They gotta know that already. I got hired, I can do the job, they're gonna have to get used to it."

"You can't be that naïve. Bargie. You ever been to Montana?"

"Sure. Lord it over me that you've been everywhere. What? They got prairies and buffalo and cowboys, right?"

"Not quite. But let's just say it's a little more conservative than New York. Especially some of the baseball guys. Especially about what women should and shouldn't be doing."

She knew that. She'd had nightmares about that. About the boos, the catcalls to get back in the kitchen, to go home and have babies. Like they did to Bernice Gera. Like Mom said they did to her, at first, when she became the first female executive in her office. *We all gotta go through it*, Mom said. *And then you gotta go through it some more.*

"Maybe they won't notice," Margie said.

He laughed. "You'll have a big ugly uniform and a mask, Barge, but I doubt even you're gonna get away without somebody noticing for long."

6

THE ROPES

It was the morning of her first official game, an early afternoon start in Billings, Montana, and Margie had already thrown up twice. She leaned her cheek against the cool porcelain of the vanity, catching her breath. Good thing most of the other rooming house tenants had left for the day, or else there'd be a lineup of fists pounding on the bathroom door. One of the women who lived in the house, a ballplayer's girlfriend, had already decided Margie was the enemy, that she'd become an umpire just to meet men. Margie had nothing against men. But this accusation was one of the more ridiculous things she'd heard lately—and she had a strong hunch it wouldn't be the last.

Eventually she got to her feet, spots still dancing before her eyes, rinsed out her mouth, and gave herself a long, hard look in the mirror. She'd never been much for makeup; it was a pain in the ass, all that putting on and taking off. But for her first game, shouldn't she make some kind of effort? Would everyone get on her harder for looking girly, or would they bust her for not?

"Screw it," she told her reflection. She tucked her blond ponytail into her cap, swiped on some lip balm, and headed out.

But she needn't have worried, because nobody seemed to notice.

Just as well. When she got to the ballpark, she was so nervous that at first she could barely remember her basics.

Her partner, an old sourpuss named Warren Durning, didn't even talk to her. Margie chose not to take it personally. Maybe he needed time to get accustomed to having a girl on the field. She worked the bases in a fairly routine game, a smattering of singles and fly-outs and walks, the calls at first and second easy and clean. The scoreless game ended with a walk-off home run, and Margie made sure that runner's foot hit every base on his way around the diamond.

When he landed on home, it was over. It was done. Her first professional game was in the books, and as she left the field, feeling taller and stronger than when she'd arrived, not even Old Sourpuss could spoil her good mood.

* * *

A reporter from a newspaper in Boise, Idaho, wanted Margie's story. She came home from her second game to find his phone message tacked to the bulletin board in the lobby. She and Durning were working a game close to home the next day, and if she wanted to talk to the reporter, she was to meet him at the diner near the stadium after the game. As she stood in front of the message board, puzzling over whether she should meet him, a couple of the girls brushed by her. One was the charmer who'd accused her of getting into baseball for the boys, and she mumbled something about Margie's "unflattering uniform" as she walked away. That didn't help calm her nerves. Large winged things were doing kamikaze maneuvers in her stomach.

Later that night, she called Timmy.

"Bargie!" His voice sounded strange, and she could barely hear him over the shouting and laughter and Led Zeppelin in the background.

"Bad time?"

"Naw, wait, I'll take it in the hall."

Tim had just started his second season with Bellingham and was renting a room. But while he got to live with his teammates, she shared a house in Helena, Montana, with a combination of students taking summer classes at the local college and women like the one she'd met, who'd tagged along with the players and coaches.

"So, what's up?" Tim said, the party muffled behind him. "How's Big Sky Country?"

What she'd seen so far had been beautiful, but she didn't anticipate much time for sightseeing—unless she counted the hours she'd be spending in the car bouncing around the eighteen stadiums of the Bighorn League. "It's gorgeous. But I got a problem."

She explained the situation, and then he said, "Yeah. They talked to us about how to do an interview. Be respectful, stuff like that. Give credit where credit is due. Try to stay positive. Talk about your family. They love when you talk about your family."

Margie couldn't imagine why a reporter from Boise would track her down only to talk about her family. Unless it was to ask if her family thought she was completely nuts for doing this.

"Bargie. This is a good thing. You'll do great."

Then someone yelled his name, and he said he had to go. After they hung up, Margie leaned against the wall for a moment, thinking. Then she smiled. She never would have imagined that out of the two of them, a rookie ump who'd worked exactly two professional games and a budding superstar with a blazing hot fastball, she would be the one a reporter wanted to talk to first.

* * *

Warren Durning, solid as the Black Hills of South Dakota, stood with his feet shoulder width apart in the green grass of short center field. He cleared his throat and said, "Okay. Here's some things you need to know."

Margie stood blinking before him. It was the first time he'd spoken a full sentence to her directly. While she was absorbing that, how someone who was supposed to be her partner could have gone two whole games barely speaking to her, he went into a litany of bullshit stuff she'd already learned in the academy. Why the sudden interest? Did he think that since she'd made it through the first two games, odds were better that she'd be sticking around, and now she was worth the benefit of his knowledge? Or at least his attention?

She decided to give him the benefit of the doubt. He'd been in baseball forever. It should have been reassuring that Big Al chose to partner her with a veteran—if indeed the assignment was Al's doing—but so far, nerves had her second-guessing a few of her calls while her heart sometimes pounded so hard in her ears she could barely hear anything else. After Durning had gone over his list, which included the chance of rain and a variable wind blowing toward right field, he said, "Oblonsky. One more thing."

Margie's stomach churned. At least she'd only thrown up once before leaving the boarding house, and she considered that a major accomplishment. The big man shifted his weight from one giant black-shod foot to the other.

Stupid. What am I afraid of? What can he do to me? I already have the job. He's just a guy. You've met lots of guys. He reminded her a little bit of her mother. What did they call that, the male equivalent of a queen bee? He'd done his time. He was owed his due. Margie gave him that. She'd been addressing him as "Mr. Durning" and never challenged a single one of his calls.

"I don't like it," he said.

She focused on his thick salt-and-pepper eyebrows. "Don't like what, Mr. Durning?"

He gave her a sour squint. "Jimmy Olsen up there, third row behind the visiting team's dugout."

Yikes. He's here? Margie didn't dare look at the reporter. It wasn't easy to avoid him; there was hardly anyone in the stands.

"He asked. What was I supposed to say?"

Durning crossed his arms over his massive chest. "You say 'no comment.' You got nothing to say about baseball off the field. That's not your job, rook."

"But he came all the way from Boise, and—"

He held up a nicotine-stained finger. "Yeah. He told me. Just before you showed up, he came out here asking if you'd talk to him after the game. Like I'm your secretary." His eyes bored down on hers, and the kamikaze planes in her gut crashed. "This is your problem. Don't make it mine."

* * *

Margie tried her hardest not to look at the reporter, even during the inning changes or when a new pitcher was taking his warm-ups. She watched every move those players made. She made sure the runners stepped on each base, clean and legal. She eyeballed every checked swing, every tag, every batted ball that went anywhere near the foul line. Durning was right. Not only did she have a job to focus on, if she caught a glimpse of Dave Marquette, the aforementioned "Jimmy Olsen," she thought she might throw up again. So when a skinny kid hovered near her booth at the diner after the game, she almost choked on her water.

He introduced himself, his voice cracking, and asked permission before he sat across from her. Then he started fidgeting with stuff on the table, which sort of helped Margie relax, knowing he was nervous, too.

"First of all"—Margie leaned forward—"I don't bite."

"Oh," Dave Marquette said. "That's a relief."

Margie gestured for the waitress, who left two menus. "First job?" she asked.

The kid nodded.

"Mine, too. So, I've never been interviewed before. How does it work?"

"Uh. I ask questions. You, uh, answer them?"

She would have called smart-ass on him, but he seemed genuinely innocent in his reply. After examining his face for a moment, she settled back into the booth. "Okay, shoot."

"What's it like being one of the first female umpires to work a professional baseball game?"

Margie reined back the urge to roll her eyes. *Stupid question.* Then she steadied herself with a deep breath. "It's a privilege and an honor. I only hope that I can make a positive contribution to the sport and make my colleagues who put their trust in me confident that they made the right choice."

The boy nodded and scribbled furiously on his pad. He asked a few more canned questions that could have been from a list he'd memorized, and questions that he could have easily answered with ten minutes of telephone research—nuts-and-bolts info like where she'd gone to school, her softball stats, how she'd done in the academy. But she mustered up her patience and answered every one. It wasn't like she had anywhere else to be except her dull room at the boarding house, under the scornful eyes of the women who thought she'd come to Montana to steal their men. Last night, while they were dressing up to meet their guys, giggling and borrowing each other's clothes, Margie was studying her rule book...and she was a bit envious. She'd never really dated a lot—certainly not as much as Tim did; girls hung all over him—but now she didn't even have a choice. During the season, baseball came first.

"How have they been treating you?" Dave, who said she could call him Dave, said. "Any, um, problems?

"Fine. But I'm not surprised. We're all professionals here. I've been treated with the same respect my other colleagues have enjoyed." *Liar, liar, pants on fire.* But she damn well would not tell the Boise Daily Post Bugle Gazette Journal Whatever about the guys in the Missoula dugout catcalling and grabbing their crotches and making kissing noises. Or the evil looks her own partner gave her. And the silence. The silence was the worst. If guys got in her face, called her names, she could do something about it. The silence could have been anything. The silence hid things.

Jimmy Olsen just nodded. In that moment, Margie realized that Dave Marquette was not a very good reporter, or at least was not one yet.

* * *

Dave Marquette's lame-ass story—Tim called to read it to her—got picked up by the Associated Press.

"What the hell?" Mom said, having seen it in the Kingston *Daily Freeman.* "He had a tiger by the tail and he writes that he never expected an umpire to look so pretty? Shoulda told that putz to take a friggin' stab at a rolling donut."

Margie nearly dropped the phone at the volume of her mother's voice. Mom would have made a kick-ass ump. She wouldn't have taken crap from anyone. She definitely wouldn't have gone into the ladies' room between innings to calm down after a player sliding into second called her a "fucking useless blind fucking bitch" for saying he was out.

She would have been within her rights to eject him, or at least issue a warning, but Margie just took it. Durning called her into his "office" after that game and gave her a talking-to that included various metaphors about giving inches and taking miles. "Stand your ground now with these guys," he said. "Else they'll be questioning everything you do."

After that, the phone calls from the press really started coming. Margie didn't know how they got her number. The Boise guy, that would have been easy enough. But these were from the big guns. The *Los Angeles Times.* The *Chicago Tribune.* *60 Minutes.* Sixty-freaking-Minutes wanted to talk to her. For what? Six weeks in an umpire academy and ten outings in Class A Short Season ball? It felt ridiculous. "You talk to all of them," her mother said. "Margie. This is an opportunity of a lifetime. For all of us."

Us? All of us? She must have missed the memo that she was doing this for all of womankind. "Mom. You don't get it. Yeah. If I were catching, I'd make the news. If I were Timmy, I'd make the news. But umpires aren't supposed to be the story. We're supposed to be invisible. We only get attention if we make lousy calls."

"You take that attention," Mom said. "Screw 'em. What, you can't make good calls *and* talk to reporters?"

Margie groaned and hung up.

In the end, she turned them all down.

But that didn't seem to matter.

The silences grew more pointed. She'd suit up and come out and conversations would stop. She understood why. Players could talk to the press all day long. Umpires, not so much.

Durning was watching. At least once a game, he'd call time, pull her aside and give her shit about one of her calls. She let the first one slide; it was a judgment call and maybe she'd missed something. When it happened again, she knew she'd gotten the call right and asked to talk to him after the game.

"What did I tell you?" he barked. "Your focus is here." He stabbed a finger into the crappy old desk in the crappy spare office Margie had been given as her own personal clubhouse. The room smelled like rotting leather and liniment so old Babe Ruth might have used it at some point. "Your focus is here, on this game, on whatever play is going on, and not out in the stands wondering if some reporter is watching."

Margie threw up her hands. "I never—I turn them all down. Every call I get—"

"It comes back to me, you know," he grumbled. "You refuse, they go to work on me. I got other things to do. You want to be some women's libber leading the charge, I'm sure you'll do a better job of it without the distraction of calling games."

That shut Margie up. For a moment. "You can't fire me."

"No. I can't. But piss me off enough, and I'll have you reassigned."

Margie wondered where they could stick her that was more out of the way than western Montana, but she declined to voice her opinion. That night, Timmy got the brunt of it.

"Fucking asshole," she said. "I didn't ask for this. It's not like I'm parading *60 Minutes* through the stadium."

He paused. Margie didn't like that pause. It hung in the damp Pacific Northwest air, full of I-told-you-so's. But maybe, just maybe, Mom's golden boy was jealous.

A small part of her enjoyed that a little too much.

7

THE WORD

It was a fact of being female that Margie would have to spring for her own room when she and Durning went on the road, but why he refused to drive with her and share expenses was a mystery. She asked, and he gave her some bullshit answer about how it might look to be traveling together, and then she stopped asking. Just as well. Driving the many miles between stadiums was a painful hit to her budget, but it spared her Durning's sour company.

It was also a fact of being female that Margie never knew where she'd be suiting up when she first visited a new stadium. Getting pissed off about that seemed like a waste of energy, so she decided instead to let the surprise of it amuse her. For that afternoon's game, her assigned "boudoir" was basically an oversized equipment closet that looked like it hadn't been cleaned, much less used, since World War II.

The maintenance guy mumbled an apology about the accommodations as he unlocked her door. "Not a problem," she said. "Take a chainsaw to those cobwebs and this place could be oh-so charming."

But he'd already shuffled off down the hallway. Margie shrugged and made herself at home, taking down the *Playboy* calendar and clearing off an old weightlifting bench and a small filing cabinet. Apparently the closet shared a wall with the visiting team's clubhouse, because she could hear a few voices close by. Some of them sounded older than players—coaches, maybe—and they were talking strategy, how they were going to handle that day's pitcher.

She tuned out and continued putting on her gear, not wanting any of her calls to be influenced by their discussion, but as she was strapping on her chest protector, she heard one guy say, "I tell ya.

Hiring *her* was bullshit. A fucking bullshit put-up job."

Her heartbeat went to the races, the air freezing in her lungs.

"Just some whore they dragged in off the street...looking for attention...bitch is only in it for the fucking women's libbers..."

"Nothing but a lame-brain, no-talent cunt..."

The last word landed like a fist in her gut. No one said that word in her house. Not even as a joke.

Maybe this was why.

It made her feel dirty and small. Like she had no right to even exist in their world.

She sucked in a deep breath, standing straight, glaring at the adjoining wall as if she could melt it, listening as they kept on with their crap. Each voice she committed to her memory. If she heard any one of them talking shit to her during the game, she'd bounce him and bounce him hard.

The knock on her door broke her trance. She hadn't even realized the voices had gone silent.

"Miss Oblonsky." It sounded like the maintenance guy who'd let her in. "Time."

* * *

Fortunately, the game popped with action, and Margie was able to settle in and put the incident behind her. Her first-inning nerves eased off after the second batter, and she fell into a nice groove.

Until the sixth inning. She called a guy out trying to steal third; the play looked clean to her, the tag sweeping down a good beat before the runner's foot reached the bag.

But then the visiting team appealed it—one of their coaches claimed the third baseman had missed the tag and the ball had come out of his glove.

Before she could say a word, Durning was calling him safe.

What the... Why is Durning overruling my call? He's not allowed to do that!

She stomped toward him, ready to do battle. In the academy, they'd taught her it was bad form to challenge your senior partner on the field. But Durning was dead wrong, and she'd had the better angle on the play. What the hell was his problem?

His eyes were laser black through the wire cage of his mask. "Back to your position, rook."

"He was—the tag—"

"Back. To. Your. Position."

She opened her mouth but shut it again when she noticed him trained on something over her right shoulder.

She turned. The visiting manager had stepped out of the dugout, arms crossed over his chest. The guy was glaring hate beams at her, like he was daring her to challenge the overturned call.

Her stomach trembled. She already had a strike against her with Durning for bucking him in public.

She'd been about to back down, telling herself that knowing she'd been right about the call would be enough.

But it wasn't enough. "You got a problem?" she said to the manager.

He didn't move.

"Then get off the field."

He didn't move.

Margie's pulse thumped in her ears. She'd never thrown a player out before. "You wanna find out what happens if I have to ask you again to get off the field?"

He stared at her a moment longer, and then, smirking, he stepped back.

* * *

After the game, Margie hit the cocktail lounge next to the motel. It was dollar beer night, and that put a smile on her face. She needed something to blunt this day, and a couple bucks were about all she could spare.

She was nursing her second beer at a table in a dark corner when Durning and a few other guys lumbered in and made themselves comfortable at the bar. They downed hard liquor in fancy glasses and looked all fat and happy.

One of them was the visiting team's manager.

Bastard.

Two beers weren't cutting it. Margie dug into her pocket, hoping she had enough change left for a third. The least Durning could do for overturning her call was pick up her tab. He was retired, had a pension, wasn't even doing this for the money. Damn sure he didn't have to wash his unmentionables in a crappy boarding house sink.

Then someone in his group told a crude joke, and one particular laugh made her want to punch something. Him. The manager. He was the one who'd called her that awful word. Her hand tightened around the bottle, mainly to keep herself from springing up and bashing him over the head with it. Timmy would tell her to suck it up. Her mother would say, "Baseball guys cuss, what the frig did you expect?"

But it'd been a bad day, she had thirty-two cents to her name, and she didn't want to listen to anyone.

She downed the rest of her beer, slammed the bottle to the table. The noise, or something, caught Durning's attention. His beady eyes bored into her. In his face, though, she read "stay away."

That was enough to make her pause. Two slow, deep breaths later, she decided there had to be a better way than going apeshit on this guy. There had to be a better way, one that wouldn't involve losing her job. To make that better way happen, it was important that she leave this place right now, go back to her room, and cool off.

Unfortunately, that involved passing them on the way out the door.

She tried not to look, but some train-wreck craziness couldn't stop her from giving them a glance. Then the guy grinned at her. The guy who'd called her a cunt merely grinned at her and said, "Good game, honey."

Her hands tightened into fists. "Yeah. Yeah, it was a good game. And while I appreciate the endearment, maybe it would be best if you kept that to yourself. Wouldn't want anyone to get the wrong idea, that you have warm and fuzzy feelings for me or something."

He lifted a hand. "Hey, I didn't mean anything by that…"

"Sure you didn't. I bet you say stuff you don't mean all the time. Like in the clubhouse that's maybe two feet away from the room the female umpires change in."

His face slackened.

She patted his cheek and smiled. "Hope you have another good game tomorrow. Because I'm working the plate. Honey."

When she got back to her cheap motel room, she took her

THE CALL

frustrations out on her bedding. After a few hundred deep breaths, feathers still settling into the thin, filthy carpet, she called Tim.

"I just murdered one of my pillows," she said. "And I don't think my per diem is gonna cover that."

"Do you feel better?"

"No."

"I'll wire you twenty bucks. Kill another one."

They shot the shit for a while, and he made her laugh, and she started to feel a little better. When they were done, she opened the drawer of the particleboard nightstand and underneath the Bible found an old notepad and a ballpoint pen.

It was about time she took Big Al's advice and drew her own line in the sand. At the top of a new page, she wrote "Margie's Rules."

One: You call me out during a game and say any shit that I don't belong there, you're done.

Two: You say I should be home in the kitchen having babies, you're done.

Three: You call me a cunt, you're done.

* * *

After tossing and turning for a while, and thinking about destroying another pillow, she'd barely fallen into something resembling sleep when her phone rang. Worried that it might be her mother, she batted a hand out for the receiver.

It was Roger Sutton, the league president, which gave her a different kind of cramp in her stomach. "Sorry for the early wake-up call, Margie."

She sat up straight, pushing a hand through her hair. "Mr. Sutton. Is there a problem?"

"You're reassigned."

"I'm...what?" Shit. Durning. She sucked in a breath. "Okay, so after this series I'm going where?"

He cleared his throat. Yeah. That wasn't a good sign. "Pack your bag, Margie. You're in Boise for a seven o'clock start."

He gave her the address and hung up. Part of her wanted to jump out of bed and dance. She wasn't fired. She was still in the Bighorn League. And she wouldn't have to work with Warren

39

fucking Durning anymore.

After a shower and cup of coffee, she packed up, wrote an apology note for housekeeping promising a really big tip next time she was in town, and headed to Idaho.

8

THE ALLY

She'd been so rattled about Sutton's phone call, the questions she hadn't asked, that she missed her exit and had to backtrack twenty miles to get onto the highway. Whatever new hell awaited her, courtesy of Warren Durning, she didn't want to make it worse by being late to her new assignment. Fortunately, she'd worked this stadium before, so she knew where to park and which entrance to use. Unfortunately, the unused office that served as her impromptu changing area was locked, and she had to go find the dude with the key. As she was waiting for him to fetch his giant ring, she peered out toward the field, looking for her new partner.

She didn't see him. Only some fans who'd arrived early, a bunch of players tossing the ball around, a big blue sky, and a few light, puffy clouds. *This sucks. It sucks to be flung around like that ball, thinking you're going to work a game in one place only to be told to pack your stuff and go somewhere else.* Yes, that's what she'd signed on for; she knew she had to pay her dues and go along to get along, but it still sucked. What sucked worse was that she wasn't going to get paid for another two weeks. She hated that she hadn't had enough to leave a tip for the housekeeping staff, and she was feeling really bad about the pillow. Maybe she could have a temper, but she wasn't that person, like a rock star, who tore up hotel rooms. The maid probably had to work extra hard to get the feathers out of the rug. Bad enough to have a crap job without making it crappier. And Durning had probably talked Sutton into sticking her with some hard-ass even worse than him. Maybe she shouldn't have shown Durning up like that. She reminded herself that next time she worked that stadium, she'd leave extra for the maid. Maybe even bring a new pillow. Instead of Margie's Rules, maybe she should be writing Margie's Apologies. She sighed, dragging up what she could of her patience and flexibility, forcing it if she had to, when she felt a tap on her shoulder and spun face-to-face with a familiar grin.

She beamed like someone had just given her the night off and beer money.

Her new partner, suited up and ready to go, was Wes Osterhaus.

* * *

She'd already learned from their academy days that Wes was a precise and careful umpire. He knew his rule book, but he also knew his weaknesses—rare in a guy his age—and he was not just willing but eager to work on them. Watching that in action as his partner made Margie smile, wiping out most of the sting of Durning's bullshit. Wes Osterhaus was in control of that plate, consistent with his strike zone, politely cautioning players who got out of line, even going to her when he wanted a second opinion. She took mental notes for when she'd be working the plate the next game. Unlike Durning, she knew Wes would never keep her from working the plate when it was her turn.

After the game they went to a local diner—he was buying. The waitress walked away with their orders, and Wes pulled a notebook and pen out of his gear bag.

"What's that?" Margie said. "You wanna interview me or something?"

A corner of his mouth turned up. He'd probably seen that horrible story. "I'll leave that to the reporters. No, I like to go over the calls after a game while everything is still fresh in my mind, especially if there was something controversial." He paused. "My former partner found it annoying. I said it was an opportunity to learn, but he said it was a waste of good time he could spend back at the motel getting drunk."

If the guy had wanted Wes reassigned because of that, then he was the biggest asshole on the planet. "Well, the hell with him. Bring it on." Margie grinned and leaned back. "Let's have a learning opportunity."

He tapped the pen against his first point. "The call at home in the top of the sixth inning." The incoming runner from third had collided with the catcher, and the ball had come out of his mitt. Wes's view was apparently blocked, so he'd signaled for Margie's confirmation that the catcher had held on to the ball long enough. They hashed it out for a bit, and he agreed with her take on it, and she said, "Thanks for asking me out there."

"That's what we learned in the academy. That you have a crew for a reason."

"Durning didn't ask me shit."

Wes nodded. "Yes, when I heard you were assigned to his crew, I wondered how long it would last. It's not going to work like that with us." He gave her the odds—the percentage of Class A umpires promoted to Double A. Then to Triple A. The numbers got smaller as the rungs got higher. "We're making it to the majors," he said. "But it won't be easy. We have to keep learning, from the game and from each other."

Their meals came, and Wes put his notebook away.

He passed her the ketchup. As she drowned her french fries, she said, "So. You had to eject someone yet?"

He blushed and appeared to be studying his plate for the answer. "Once."

Shit. She'd punch anyone who talked crap to him. "Was it hard?"

"No. He violated the rules. He kept arguing about a pitch that I called a strike. I asked him to stop arguing, and he wouldn't stop. Then he called me a…name I won't repeat, so the rules say I can eject him."

"I haven't done it yet. I wanted to, yesterday. I should have. The guy deserved it. But then I wondered if I was only pissed because of some stuff he said about me off the field. Like my being here was bullshit."

"There've been some interesting scientific studies about human instincts and how often they end up being right."

"What, my instinct that I would have tossed him because I was already pissed?"

"Or the other way. That you said you should have ejected him because the guy deserved it."

"And that would have given *him* a learning opportunity."

"That's when we have to make a judgment call. Those are always the hardest. But we can help each other with those."

"I'm looking forward to it."

Wes set down his fork and eyeballed her like a close play. "Well, okay. Here's one. I don't know if I should be telling you this, but maybe it will help you learn. You're getting a reputation."

Her stomach sank. "Crap. Let's have it."

"The players tell me you have a good eye, that you're a good umpire."

She snorted. "Not all of them, I'd imagine."

"Some of them, and a few managers, too," he said. "But something's funny about that, though. They tell me in secret. Like they don't want anyone else to know that they think you're good."

"Yeah." Margie finished her Coke. "That's funny as hell." Funny how women could do most anything these days—the president had promised to put a woman on the Supreme Court, and she'd heard a female astronaut might be going up on the space shuttle—but stick a woman on a baseball field and the crazy comes out. "So what am I supposed to learn from that?"

"That not everyone out there wants to see you fail."

She grinned and dug back into her meal. Then she made a promise to herself to always have his back. Not because of what they learned in the academy, and not because of the rules. But because he'd had faith in her from the start, and that meant one whole hell of a lot.

9

THE BATTERY

His old man might have shaken his head and muttered "Florida" when the Cincinnati Reds picked up Tim's contract and sent him to their double-A affiliate in Orlando. But Tim couldn't have been happier. He had to find a new place to live. He had to get acquainted with a whole new set of teammates. But those were minor compared with the thought that kept dancing through his head: *I'm on my way up, I got this.*

He'd been an official member of the team for exactly twenty-four hours when he got word that he'd be starting the next game. Talking with Margie the night before had helped some, but when he got to the stadium and began suiting up, the jitters hammered him hard.

His fingers shook as he laced his cleats, took them off, rearranged his socks, and put his shoes back on, just to have something to do.

His new manager must have been watching him, because he came over and said, "Son, why don't you go out to the bullpen and start loosening up? Ask for Phil. He's probably the only one out there."

Only one guy was out there—a scruffy bullpen catcher who looked like years of Florida sunshine hadn't been kind to his face.

"Hey, kid." Phil flipped Tim the ball. "Let's dance, huh?" Later Tim learned that Phil called everyone "kid" because the players were in and out so fast he didn't bother remembering their names.

As usual, the tension made him throw too hard. Phil told him to go easier, and he tried, but it wasn't helping. After a few more pitches, he saw a guy ambling up to the bullpen gate. He recognized him as the team's starting catcher. Big guy, about as tall as Tim but wider, more linebacker than quarterback. Square face, cheeks kind of chipmunky. Overall he reminded Tim of a big, goofy dog. What was his name? Malone? Monroe?

The catcher leaned his meaty arms on the railing at the top of the gate.

"Got something to say, kid?" Phil tossed the ball back to Tim. "Or is this a social call?"

"Mind if I spell you for a while?" The catcher opened the gate and stuck his mitt out.

Phil smirked and threw the guy the ball. "Knock yourself out. I gotta take a whiz anyway."

"Coach sent you?" Tim said.

"Nah." The catcher took off his mitt, shook Tim's hand, and gave him a big friendly smile. "Dan Monroe. Saw you in the clubhouse before and thought I'd say hey officially, before the game. You hanging in?"

Tim shrugged. One thing he'd learned is that you don't snow your catcher. Tell the coach whatever, but the catcher knows how you're doing. For real.

Dan patted his arm. "Yeah. Come on. Toss me a few."

He settled into a crouch where Phil had been. Soon they fell into a rhythm, and a couple starts later, they became a good team. Or, as the manager put it, "a damn effective battery."

Even though they had Phil to warm up the pitchers, Dan still hung around while Tim was getting loose. He told jokes or basically talked about nothing—anything to settle Tim down when he was tweaked about a start. His easy manner brought Tim back every time.

One day, while Phil was busy, Dan caught warm-up for Tim, and they got talking about umpires and strike zones. Dan asked him to throw a pitch inside, then showed Tim how a catcher could sometimes reel one into the strike zone by the way he positioned his mitt or moved his body.

"Yeah, Margie told me about that."

"Girlfriend?" Dan flipped the ball back.

Tim snapped his glove around it. "Sister."

Dan stood. "Wait. Margie…Oblonsky. The umpire?"

Tim nodded. "We're twins."

"Cool." Dan crouched for another pitch. Tim tested his slider.

Not bad. "I read something about her in the paper a while back. How's she doing with it?"

"Pretty good, actually." He caught Dan's return. "She has to take a lot of shit, but she's tough."

"Bet you gotta be. But I think that's great, though. Good for her. Don't see any reason why a woman can't get the job done." He grinned. "Might be better than some guys I've seen."

"From what I've seen?" Tim threw a fastball that landed square in Dan's mitt. "She's a hell of a lot better." He reminded himself to give her a call after the game. She'd been having a rough time lately, and she might enjoy hearing that not everyone wanted her gone.

10

THE JUICER

Margie borrowed Wes's binoculars and leaned forward, resting her arms on the railing in front of her seat, third row up on the first-base side. She'd been watching the umpires, seeing if she could pick up any tips. Traveling around the Bighorn League, she and Wes didn't get to see too many other umpires in action, and this was a brilliant opportunity. When their afternoon game had been called because of rain, the two of them looked at each other with one thought: road trip. Some of their colleagues would have hit the bars. Not the "one-two punch," a nickname Big Al had given them after they'd graduated first and second in their class. No, for Wes and Margie, a day off meant hightailing it to the closest higher-league game, then deconstructing the calls all the way home. They couldn't find a triple-A matchup, but they did see a double-A game on the schedule, a seven o'clock start, so they could make it in time.

Number twenty-six, working the plate, just called a batter out looking at a third strike. "He's got some panache, the way he sells that call," Margie said, zooming in closer on the umpire. *Pretty cute, and he does some fine justice to that uniform, too.*

"See the way he keeps his thumb tucked?" Wes said.

She rolled her eyes. "Thank you. I never get tired of hearing about my friggin' thumb." Margie gave Wes the binocs and settled back in her seat.

A player, a big lug, stepped into the on-deck circle. He hadn't been in the starting lineup.

"Holy Christmas," Wes said. "That explains why it took three phone calls to get these tickets. I thought he was still on the disabled list. I guess they sent him down to the minors to recover."

Margie sat up straighter. "What? Who? Dude on deck?"

"Dolph Edwards."

"Damn." She gave the guy the once-over and didn't like the look of him. She hadn't liked the smell of the whole story when she read it in the newspaper. "So, what do you think? The 'back injury.' Legit?"

Wes shrugged. "I met a guy who played with him. He said Edwards had gone to some secret rehab."

"Some secret, then." In the academy, Big Al warned them that at least a dozen big leaguers he knew about were using artificial hormones to bulk up or try to recover from injuries faster, and he alerted them to the signs. It wasn't illegal, Al said, but it made some players more aggressive. It was totally wrong to do that shit, in Margie's book. She didn't believe in unfair advantages. And she ought to know, being on the receiving end of people just imagining that she'd had one. "Looks like he's juicing."

Her partner nodded. "I've heard some rumors about that. And about some other things. But I don't know if they're true."

Margie knew about the other things. Some she'd read, some she'd heard from Timmy. Edwards was a hothead, probably from the steroids. He played hard, sometimes dirty, but on that account, he seemed untouchable. He did all kinds of shit—knocking down infielders on the base paths was his MO—and nobody called him on it. Even when the occasional ballsy umpire tagged him for it, he'd argue and get his manager involved and make a big stink about it in the press. Then the whole incident would magically go away.

"He got something on these umpires, or what?" Margie watched Edwards take a few practice swings and step up to the plate amid a mix of cheers and boos.

"That's anyone's guess," Wes said. "But if it's true, I don't like it. I don't like it one bit."

Edwards knocked a dribbler into left field and he pulled up at first. Margie had a good bead on him. He looked out of breath. His face was puffy, his eyes practically bulging out of his head. "Yep," she said. "Juicing."

"Would you call him on it?"

"I don't see how we could. You remember what Big Al said. It's not illegal."

"No. I mean, because of that. If you saw a player you thought wasn't clean, anyone playing under the influence. Would you take a closer look at anything he did on the field?"

She thought about that for a minute while Edwards twitched and danced to get the pitcher's attention. He was a definite flight risk. Bill, the car salesman third-base coach, would owe her a Coke. "I might. Depends on the situation. It's hard to take it out of context. Why, would you?"

"I have," he said, after a pause. "How do you think I ended up with you?"

Her eyes widened, and she was about to spin back to him when the guy at the plate hit a grounder to the third baseman. It looked like a routine double-play ball, especially since the batter wasn't known for his speed. The third baseman made the scoop and threw to second. The second baseman, who'd been caught flat-footed, wasn't touching his base. He was probably hoping to get the out on a "neighborhood rule" call, sometimes granted in double plays. But as the second baseman was setting up to throw to first, and definitely would have caught him, Edwards flung his body sideways and plowed into the second baseman. The throw to first went wild.

Margie and Wes leapt to their feet, waiting for the ruling. Her right hand twitched with the almost automatic reflex to make the "out" sign, and she grasped the railing to stop it. The base ump should have called Edwards out for offensive interference and then called the runner behind him out, too. It was a clear violation, a clear intentional attempt to disrupt the fielder. The ump was right there. He had to have seen Edwards veer out of the base path while the second baseman was trying to make the throw. But no. Instead of calling Edwards out for interference, with exuberant gestures, he declared both runners safe.

"What the—?" Wes muttered, as the manager for the home team came out to argue and the plate ump just…stood there.

Margie spun toward Wes, who looked equally befuddled. "That was interference. What the hell, dude?"

Both managers were arguing now. And both umpires. While Edwards, that self-satisfied dick, stood atop second as if he owned the damned thing. Margie glared at him. And in that moment, she decided. If she ever worked a game he was in, she wouldn't let him get away with that kind of shit. Forget Margie's Rules. If he even looked at her funny, she was going to bounce his ass.

* * *

After about fifteen minutes of silence in the car—Wes was driving—Margie got into it again. "That was bullshit," she kept repeating. "Complete and utter fucking bullshit. My grandma could have called that interference."

"I know. It's…" Wes sounded weary. A lot older than any nineteen-year-old kid had a right to.

She watched his profile flash in the flicker of the highway lights. "So what did you mean back there, that's how you ended up with me?"

He sighed, straightened his arms at the top of the wheel, flexed his fingers. "Apparently, I turned the wrong guy in. You remember how Big Al said nobody should be bigger than the game? That if you see it, you should call it? I saw it, and I called it. And my partner, someone I should have been able to trust, told Roger Sutton that I needed to be taught a lesson."

"What, so working with me is supposed to be some kind of punishment? I'm a fuckin' sweetheart." Then she realized. Maybe Durning thought Sutton had given him the short straw by setting him up with Margie in the first place, so her dick of a partner was looking for any opportunity to pawn her off on someone else. What a coincidence that Wes had landed in the doghouse just when Durning wanted her gone. Sutton probably thought he was being the big man, solving everyone's problems with the reassignment, and she and Wes would have to lump it for being rookies, for being kids, for graduating one-two in Big Al's academy, like they needed to be taken down a peg.

She leaned toward the window, rested her head on the glass. "It's all fucking bullshit."

Wes grinned. "Yeah. Only, maybe we'll have the last laugh. Little do they know that we actually make a good team."

"Fucking great team."

"One-two punch," Wes said, and high-fived her across the seat.

11

THE REPORTER

Fitz hadn't wanted the assignment, but when he heard Dolph Edwards was off the disabled list and back to his old tricks, he started sniffing around. The pieces didn't add up, and nobody was talking. That only made him want to dig deeper. He called some connections, guys he'd known from journalism school and his early beats. One of them had a kid brother who'd interviewed a lady umpire just hired on from the academy. Fitz, who considered himself knowledgeable about the game, was astounded to realize he'd never heard of her. The kid had said, off the record, that she'd been "a little scary," which made Fitz laugh. If it were true, then God love her. Umps ought to be scary. Good ones, anyway. And if any woman was going to break in, she had to be scary like a demon. Scary like his grandmother, with her rosary beads and evil eye. Nobody lied to Nonna. Not if you wanted to live.

Then one of those old connections said he'd seen that same lady ump at the game, not officiating, but as a spectator. A damn vocal spectator, sitting third row first-base side with Wes Osterhaus, another rookie umpire, who someone claimed was her current partner in the Bighorn League. Fitz got back on the phone and rattled a few cages. It turned out she and Osterhaus were tops in their class in Big Al's Umpire Academy but only got paired up a couple weeks earlier, due to some kind of midseason switcheroo.

Interesting.

He drummed his fingers against the crappy table in his crappy motel room. Was it worth it, all this running around, to chase down what might be nothing? It wasn't like he needed the cred, the byline. A buddy at a Flushing weekly had floated his name out for a column; a little radio station in New York wanted a nighttime sports guy.

Damn, how he wanted to return to the city, after all these years of chasing down "local boy makes good" stories, covering college ball and every last freaking thankless thing. He was ready to stop moving for a while. And his scary old nonna wasn't getting any younger.

But something about this story had him hooked. A few calls later, he knew where to find her, and soon, he popped on his fedora, slid back behind the wheel of his beat-up car, and headed to Big Sky Country to see what he could see. If nothing else, he looked forward to a scenic ride and a chance to meet the very scary Margie Oblonsky.

* * *

She was still at the stadium when he pulled up to her boarding house. At least that was what the landlady said. She gave him the stink eye and looked him up and down, as if deciding if she was going to let him stick around. Perhaps she'd swept a few reporters off her front porch. Or maybe a would-be boyfriend or two. He'd seen a picture; Margie Oblonsky wasn't half bad, if you liked the sturdy type. That could have just been the persona, though. She wasn't smiling in her photo; not too many umps smiled for the camera, in his experience. He guessed they didn't have much to smile about. The pay sucked, the hours sucked, the travel sucked, and everyone kept yelling at them. They had a lot in common with sports writers, if you got right down to it—both of them were in it for the love of the game, the thrill of being involved.

"You can wait out here." The woman pointed to the stairs. Her chest pushed out with what Fitz could only call pride. Like the woman had a celebrity in her house or had some other reason to feel protective. That made sense. She looked like the mama hen type. Miss Oblonsky was barely twenty, lived with her mother in the off-season. Her father, a major-league utility catcher, had died of a massive heart attack when she was fourteen, and her twin brother was a promising double-A pitcher with a blazing fastball; scouting reports pegged him as one to watch. Most single-A umps lived out of a suitcase, dragging their asses from motel to motel, yet Oblonsky had taken a room in this house for the season, like she wanted the security of a home base between road trips. Maybe the landlady considered her a kind of lost pup.

He asked the woman a couple of questions she didn't answer. She merely squinted up at him and pointed to the stairs. He sat. Finally, after letting him twist in the wind for a while, she brought him a glass of ice water, but she still wouldn't talk to him. He was about to pack it in—or head over to the ballpark, a move that would surely get Oblonsky's hackles in a bunch, because word was also that she hated publicity—when a boxy, pale-blue sedan with Connecticut license plates pulled up to the curb. A redheaded kid was driving—Osterhaus, no doubt—and then a tall, fit woman unfolded herself from the passenger side.

She stopped his train of thought for a second. Not that Oblonsky was a knockout, not in the classic manner of thinking. His father's generation might have called her a handsome woman. Her hair was dishwater blond, tugged into a messy ponytail. Her cheeks were flushed, probably from the heat or all the fresh air and outdoor living. Maybe what struck him was how her eyes narrowed at the sight of him. He imagined how those eyes would be fearsome, locked in a battle with some hard-ass manager. The landlady knocked one sturdy shoe into his right hip and muttered something that sounded like, "Get up, dummy, and stop staring."

He got up.

Like the landlady, Oblonsky also gave him the up-and-down. "What?" she said.

"Nice to meet you, too."

And then the squint. His smile dissolved. She gave a quick nod to Osterhaus, and the blue sedan rolled away. "Look," she said, and hauled herself up the stairs. "I just worked a double-header on two hours' sleep. And I gotta do my laundry and about a hundred other things before I hit the hay and leave for friggin' Idaho in the morning. So whatever you came for, let's get at it."

"How'd you like Edwards?"

The eyes flickered. Her mouth twitched a hair. "What are you talking about?"

"Think he's ready to go back up?"

"Ask his manager. I was only a spectator."

"Then you were at the game."

"Yeah, me and fifteen hundred other people."

"Ms. Oblonsky."

55

"Cut it with that crap," she said. "Just call me Margie."

He shuffled the sole of his shoe on the worn planks. "Margie. Fine. I'll come out and say it, then. Think the call was a put-on job?"

She paused a moment, then said, "No comment."

He grinned. "You do. You think something's fishy."

"I don't think anything," she said, much too quickly. Then, maybe realizing she'd tipped her hand, she shook her head. "Look. I watched a ball game. I was not there in any official capacity. You got a question about how the game was called, talk to the umpires who called it. Talk to the league. I got nothin' for you."

"I guess I got all I need, then." He pressed his lips into a smile. "Steve Fitzgerald," he said. "Most people call me Fitz."

"Nice to meet you, Steve," she said. "Now I gotta go wash out my delicates."

He'd seen the mental door closing, in the lack of expression on her face. Soon the physical door would close as well. "He plays dirty, doesn't he? Edwards. You think he plays dirty."

Her eyes, an indeterminate shade between blue and brown, shifted toward his. He backed up a step, pouring on some professional calm. "I'm not saying nothin' about nobody. Like I told you. Not my game, not my problem."

"But he could be your problem. If he ends up in your ballpark. You get sent up and he stays down? I heard a rumor that after this season, you'll be—"

"Listen, Fitz. Whatever your name is. I don't truck in what-ifs. If he's on my turf, I'll deal with him then. And damn sure I'm not—"

He waited. He smiled.

"Forget it." She waved a hand. "I'm not talking to you. Now, you can just crawl back into that hole where you've been storing that suit and...that *hat* and...and go talk to the players. They're the ones who should get the ink. Not me."

The door slammed in his face. Right behind her, after drilling him with a look that could have melted off his five o'clock shadow, went the landlady.

He sat in his car for a while, thinking, tapping his pen against his pad. She knew more than she cared to admit, but he understood her deal. A reporter doesn't become the story. Neither does an umpire. You exist in the service of those who hired you, and you don't rat your guys out. Sure, he had some reporter friends who weren't exactly on the up and up, and those names would die with him. He was pretty damned sure that, given the opportunity, Oblonsky would say the same. He started the engine and got back on the highway. *Okay*, he told himself. *Okay*. He tightened a fist and pressed it into his thigh, then lit another cigarette he took three puffs from before throwing it out the window. Damn things. Fine, he'd let the fight drop.

For now.

12

THE STORY

Margie hauled into the stadium early for the one o'clock start. Her private clubhouse, be it ever so humble, was already open, and a note was taped to an empty file cabinet one of the guys had moved into the equipment room for her to use as a locker.

Sutton wanted to meet with her before the game.

She crumpled the note and groaned.

People said Sutton was a decent guy. Margie didn't see it. Then again, she'd only spoken with him a couple of times on the phone, very briefly. Both times resulted in her having a crappy day, but still, maybe he'd been having one, too. She truly wanted to give him the benefit of the doubt.

But what the heck could be so important that he wanted to actually meet with her before a game? She tried to tell herself that he was coming out to the stadium anyway. Because that was his job, right? To actually watch a few of those games he was in charge of running the umpires for? Maybe he wanted to talk to her about next year, although something in her gut told her that wasn't the reason.

She suited up quickly and waited for him to show.

And waited.

And waited.

Finally, there was a knock on the door.

Sutton wasn't as tall as he'd sounded on the phone. In fact, he looked a little like a rodent with a bad perm. Maybe the prune face had something to do with the newspaper rolled up in his hand. For a second, Margie thought he was going to whack her with it. But instead, he sailed it onto the chair next to her file cabinet. It landed face up, the sports section. Margie swallowed. The headline read FOUL PLAY? in three-inch-high letters.

"Miss Oblonsky," he said.

She was still studying the newspaper. There was a god-awful photo of her, not that she gave a shit about that. It was the other photo that bothered her. Dolph Edwards, at his juiced up, snarling best. The byline was Stephen Fitzgerald.

That fucking bastard.

"Yes," he said. "I'm aware that everyone and his mother wants your story. I'm aware of the human interest angle, and we could not be so naïve as to think that wouldn't attract the media. It's good for baseball, or so the higher-ups tell me. But as for your opinions about your peers and the players? Save it for your memoirs. Save it for the goddamn rubber-chicken ladies auxiliary award-ceremony dinners. But don't do it in the middle of my season, where it could make all of us look like goddamn fools."

His silence was like another aroma in the room, mixing with the decades of sweat and liniment and rotting leather.

"We're sitting you out three games."

She looked up in question, but his face was unyielding.

Then she reverted back to what she'd learned at Big Al's School of Professional Umpiring. "Yes, sir."

He nodded crisply, thin lips pinched together, then left.

For God knows how long afterward, she sat on the wooden bench, staring at that awful story, hating both of those bastards.

On her way out, she kicked a wall. Then two.

She passed Wes as he came in to suit up. "It's a great day for a ballgame—" Then he spied her face. His mouth softened. "Margie. What's wrong?"

"Fucking Steve Fitzgerald, that's what's wrong." She kicked another wall. "Fucking reporters. Don't talk to them. Don't talk to a single fucking one. See you on Monday. Enjoy your sub. Whoever the hell they can throw in there on a half-hour's notice. You'll probably get the fucking mascot."

Then she turned and left him standing there.

All the way back to the boarding house, sweating buckets because she was still in her gear, she cursed Fitzgerald's name. She'd borrow enough quarters from all the girls in the place to get that arrogant son of a bitch on the phone and blast him back to whatever hole he'd crawled out of.

She smacked the door open, and Mother Superior was hot on her heels. That's what the girls called her. She'd been in the middle of sweeping the lobby area, and with the puss on her, Margie thought she'd shove her right back outside. Or at least carp about not slamming the door and if she'd been raised in a barn.

"Eh, why are you here?" she said. "On game day?"

"Not for me. I got suspended." She dropped her bag on one of the love seats and shoved a hand through her sweaty hair. "That reporter. Did he leave a card?"

Mother Superior's eyes narrowed. "Which one? I boot at least a half dozen out of here every week."

"Tall, glasses, wrinkled suit, stupid old-fashioned hat, kind of a snooty Ivy League look about him?"

The landlady snorted. "Him. Moony-eyed sad sack if I ever saw one. And no. No card. When I told him you weren't here, he said he'd wait."

Fuck. Margie's shoulders sagged. "Look. Can you help me out? I gotta set this guy straight. He said some things about me in the paper I didn't want him to. It's gonna take a few calls to find him, and I'm short right now. I'll give you extra when I get paid, for the long-distance bill. But it'll be a lot easier if I can use the house phone."

The woman looked to be thinking it over. She cut her eyes left, then right. "Okay, okay. Use the one in my room. Just don't tell the other girls about it." She paused. "And if you're done and want a little tea and talk, come get me."

Margie grabbed a pad and pen and started tracking down Stephen "Fitz" Fitzgerald.

The local paper yielded nothing but a suggestion to call the AP. After a bunch of runaround there, she was put in touch with the editor-in-chief at what they claimed was his hometown paper somewhere in Wisconsin. The guy snorted. "You're a day late and a dollar short, honey. Fitz just pulled up stakes and went back to New York."

Blood raced into her cheeks, and her temples pounded. Fucking nerve they had. Talking to her like she was some poor spurned girlfriend. "Listen, asshole. This is important. He's got his facts wrong, he can't—"

And then the phone was being ripped out of her hand. Margie

cursed as the receiver landed gently in the cradle. The dishpan index finger pointed. "Tea," the landlady said, eyes hard as steel. "Talk."

Margie followed her into the kitchen like a chastened puppy. She clomped her ass into a chair and let the woman fix her a dainty cup of tea. Then sat across from her. It was the longest damn uncomfortable minute of her life. Right up there with waiting for Sutton earlier.

"I get it," her landlady said finally. "You're angry. But you catch more flies with honey than you do with piss."

"Piss drowns 'em," Margie grumbled.

"Kill them with kindness and they'll never know what hit them. And they'll want to do you a favor besides. Or didn't they teach you that in finishing school?"

Margie lifted an eyebrow.

"Sweetie," the woman said. "Isn't this row you're hoeing hard enough without making enemies?"

Margie shrugged. "Enemies come with the job. My job is calling the game and not letting them get away with shit. Show them who's boss on the field."

"Yeah." The landlady sniffed. "On the field. Off the field, don't give them any ammunition."

"Sounds like you know a little about this."

"This ain't my first rodeo."

"You definitely know a lot of clichés."

"Smart-ass. Look, you're a good girl. A little rough around the edges, but that's what they call personality. Okay, I'll tell you. I fell for a ballplayer once." She waved a hand in the direction of the Helena Hornets stadium, about a mile down the road. "Spent most of the season over there, hoping he'd notice me. Then he did. We were married thirty years. Traveled all the hell over the place, had a life. When he kicked, I got nostalgic. Took what he left me and bought this place. At first I just took the boys in, you know. They're so young, never been away from their mamas. Then one of them, he was married. High school sweethearts, and she was knocked up, and he didn't want to leave her home when he got drafted. No money for a hotel, couldn't find no one to take them in the whole season. So I did. She told a friend. Soon I had more girls than boys calling me. And I decided to make this a girls-only house. Y'all need watching, too." She paused, tapping a finger against her cup. "Some more than others."

"You think I need watching?"

The woman laughed. "Calm down. No. I don't think that. I see a little of me in you, that's all. I see what I wanted to be before I met that boy."

Margie grinned. So did the landlady. And with a squint, the older woman said, "I used to throw one mean slider."

13

THE PRESSURE

Tim held his breath, waiting for the umpire to call the pitch. Waiting for the fist pump that never came. *You could eat your lunch in the time it takes this ump to give the word. Come on, dude. Give it to me already.*

"Ball!"

He groaned. Two balls in a row. Three if you count the hanging curve he'd served up leading off to this guy. He'd been lucky the batter had chased it and missed. He'd been so damn lucky.

A bead of sweat rolled down the back of his neck. He sniffed, wiped his forehead with his sleeve, knocked a toe into the dirt. Margie popped into his head, what she would say to him now. *Forget the crowd, forget the noise, forget the guys on base, forget the big mother of a guy on deck, forget your stats about to blow up. Play like we're home in the backyard. See the glove, hit the glove.*

Dan sprang up, tossed the ball back. Then went into his crouch and signaled for the heat. *Really? Three and one fastball; the way I've been throwing, you want a fastball?* He had to try another slider. Tim shook him off. Dan called time and got to his feet. Tim blew out a slow, even breath as the big guy ambled out to the mound. Usually just looking at Dan's goofball face chilled him out, but it wasn't working on Tim today.

Dan clapped his mitt against Tim's shoulder. "Timmy, relax, man, you got this."

Seriously? Relax? His stomach was climbing up his rib cage, expanding like it could explode inside him. Could that actually happen?

"Forget those last two. Blank slate. Just focus on this guy." He gave Tim an easy grin. "Not the blonde in the second row. She likes me better anyway."

Tim nodded, his neck stiff, his smile forced. *Easy. Focus.* But the way his pitches were landing today, he couldn't hit the Goodyear blimp if it were parked on top of home plate.

The umpire was getting antsy, wanted to resume play. *Yeah. Now he's in a big rush.* With one last tap of the mitt on his arm, Dan went back behind the plate.

Tim set to pitch from the stretch, something he hated doing; it messed with his rhythm not to go through his whole delivery. He stared down the alley, the tips of his gloved fingers pressed against his chin as if in prayer. He needed a prayer.

The second the ball left his hand, he knew. He knew in that way that your car door is about to lock shut with you on the outside and the keys in the ignition. The breaker wasn't going to break. It was a big fat hanging grapefruit, ripe for the slaughter, floating toward home in slow motion. The batter knew it. His eyes lit up like a five-year-old on Christmas morning, and the bastard had the nerve to smile.

When the guy made contact, Tim didn't even look back. He didn't have to. He knew the sound of a ball being launched into orbit, the sound of his stats exploding, the sound of the other team's fans cheering. He hung his head and breathed. And breathed. And breathed. He knew if he looked up he'd see the coach leaving the dugout, see his hand out, waiting for the ball.

Done.

* * *

In the clubhouse, there'd been talk of a party at some girl's apartment after the game. There was always a party. Tim didn't want to go. On any given day, anyone could have a crap game, but he didn't want to keep hearing about it. He couldn't bear one more guy coming up to him, patting him on the shoulder, telling him "great effort," and "shake it off." He just wanted to get stinking drunk and forget about it. Drinking in his motel room with lousy cable came in neck and neck with drinking at some party where his face ached from smiling, but after Dan gave him the business about winning as a team and losing as a team, the party prevailed. At least the party held the potential for getting laid, for some girl to think he was awesome on a stick for about twenty minutes. And sometimes, that was enough.

That night's therapy was the blonde from the second row, who indeed preferred him to Dan. Funny, for all his jokes, Dan rarely hit on any of the baseball girls. He said he was kind of old-fashioned, hoping to find his Mrs. Dan, and the guys teased him about it, but Tim sort of respected that. Didn't mean he was changing his own ways, though. Girls were everywhere, gorgeous and friendly girls who were really into pitchers, really into him, and as long as he used protection, didn't make any promises he didn't intend to keep, and all parties were willing, he didn't see anything wrong with that.

The blonde's name was Jennifer, and the party was at her apartment. He made a point of remembering the girls' names, because if the shoe were on the other foot, that would be damn humiliating, and he didn't want to do that to anyone if he could help it. She had a really cute Southern accent and a little overbite that was kind of sexy. She was also nice, and comforting, an actual fan of the game, not some poser making notches on her bedpost. He'd met her before, last time his team had played in Tampa, and he liked hanging out with her. She was easy company, the best kind.

"You all right there, Tim?" She stroked his shoulder after they'd finished.

"Yeah, I..." His head began to spin a little, and he rolled to the opposite pillow. "Just dragging, I'm sorry. A day game after a night game is kind of tough, even if you're not playing."

She gave him an impish smile. "Well, I got just the thing for you, then." From a drawer in her bedside table, she pulled out a baggie of coke, then put her finger to her lips. "Don't go tellin' the others, now, and we'll have our own little private party."

He grinned. Blow made him feel powerful. Fearless. Indestructible.

"Not too much, now, honey," she said with a wink. "We don't want to put you out of commission."

He pulled back the blanket and set up a line across her belly, her skin twitching as she giggled. "Don't worry," he said. "I know my limits."

14

THE RULES

Margie lay on her crap-thin boarding house mattress in the middle of the afternoon, working a baseball around in her fingers. She pressed into the red seams the way Whitey Ford—and then her father—had taught her. Fastball. Slider. It kept the bad thoughts from creeping in, at least for a while. The empty hours of her suspension were eating away at her, making her second-guess herself. Probably that was the idea. Maybe Roger Sutton was smarter than she thought—by taking her out of the game, he'd made her step back and think about what she'd done.

A learning opportunity.

But what had she done, anyway? Talked to a reporter who screwed her words around to make his own story fit together? That wasn't right. Yet her response to him hadn't been right, either. Calling said reporter to berate him could reflect badly on her, too. It reflected badly on the other umpires. It reflected badly on Big Al, who had confidence that she could handle herself under pressure and do her job. Al had probably recommended her for the Bighorn League in the first place, and maybe he'd even intervened to get her partnered up with Wes after Durning had dumped her.

She snuck out of her room and once again imposed on her landlady, and once again tried to find Fitzgerald. She ate some crow and made a more polite call to that editor-in-chief in Wisconsin. A female voice answered, said she was his assistant. Margie said that she was the housekeeper in the rooming house where Fitz had been staying—he had that rooming house air about him, same as her, so it probably wasn't a complete lie. She said that while she was cleaning up she found a couple things he might want, but unfortunately Mr. Fitzgerald hadn't left a forwarding address.

The line went quiet for a few seconds. "I'm not supposed to do this, but..." The assistant lowered her voice and rattled off an address in New York. She thanked the woman profusely, and the way she talked led Margie to believe that the assistant had grown fond of the moth-eaten reporter with the stupid hat, maybe even had a little thing for him. Then she took a deep breath and navigated a system of operators until she had a phone number that matched the address.

She stared at it for a long time, formulating the words she'd use. It wasn't as easy as she'd thought. A flat-out apology felt wrong, like she was being a doormat, letting him get one over on her. But if she called him out, wouldn't that just draw more attention to the issue? Like that thing she remembered from reading Shakespeare in tenth-grade English, about some lady protesting too much?

As she went back and forth, the anger snuck back in. About Fitzgerald. About the suspension. It wasn't her fault! If some jackoff wanted to make a name for himself in the newspapers, that was one thing, but he couldn't talk about her like that, as if she was some kind of gossipy sneak trying to bad-mouth a player in public. And then maybe she slammed the phone down too hard, because next thing she knew, the landlady was standing in the doorway, hands on her hips, looking none too pleased with her.

"You want to talk, I got some laundry to hang. A big, strong girl such as yourself, maybe you'd like to help."

It was the least Margie could do, given that the woman had been lenient with the phone privileges and understanding of an umpire's pay. She liked this boarding house, and if Sutton and Umpire Development decided to keep her in the Bighorn League next season, she hoped to stay here again. The house was perfectly positioned. Someone in Sutton's office had recommended it to her when she'd first come out. The majority of the stadiums were within a reasonable driving distance in several directions, so she didn't always have to stay at a motel. Which was a plus, because she hated them. The people who ran them were okay, and the housekeeping staff had her utmost respect, because that must be a sucky, sucky job, cleaning up after sweaty strangers who left God knows what on the towels and shredded the pillows, but most of the motels had the same look about them—the same generic carpeting, the same fake art on the walls, the same smell coming out of the clanking air conditioning vents. She'd rather have a shabby place that was sort of her own and even share a bathroom—it was pretty much the only part of her life, aside from living with her mother, where she had female companionship.

So while Margie hung out sheets and towels, she asked Mother Superior—whose real name was Jo—about the reporter. Jo listened while she worked, nodding every so often. Then she turned, bracing her work-hardened hands against her lower back. "Were they lies, what he wrote?"

Margie thought a minute. "If I'm being dead honest, I think Edwards is dirty."

"And you know that for a fact?"

"I got eyes," Margie said with a shrug.

"But this Fitzgerald guy. Did he print something different from what you told him? Did he commit... Oh, what the hell is that called? Libel or treason or some such?"

Margie laughed. Treason. That was a good one. Then she rewound her conversation with Fitzgerald on the porch. "Holy jeez. He asked me point blank about it. And I didn't correct him." She knew enough from watching TV and movies that you're supposed to say "off the record" or whatever when you wanted a reporter to keep a lid on something you said. She hadn't done that. But how was she, and Fitzgerald, for that matter, supposed to keep a lid on it? Wasn't that their jobs, reporter and umpire, to report the facts? The facts were that Fitzgerald had asked her a question. The facts were that Margie had reacted to that question, giving Fitzgerald a decent hint that she thought Edwards was up to something rotten. She'd let him leave without setting him straight. If he was a good reporter— wouldn't he be, if they wanted him to come to New York in such a big fat hurry?—wouldn't he have asked her more questions, or at least interviewed a couple more sources about Edwards before printing anything? Or was that why he bolted out of town so fast?

Should she talk to Timmy about this? Big Al? Maybe even Sutton himself?

They hung the rest of the wash in silence. Somewhere between snapping out a faded blue bath towel and grabbing another clothespin, she knew. Those rules she'd started writing in Boise. She had to make them stick. Big Al said that it was up to her to draw her own line in the sand. He said that to all his students. He could teach her everything he knew, she could study the rule book cold, but it was up to her to develop her own confidence, her own style, her own full set of rules of what she Would and Would Not tolerate. Whining to Sutton or her old teachers would make her look weak, like she couldn't hack it, like she couldn't make her own decisions. She didn't want to drag Timmy into this, either. Her brother had a lot on his plate, and she didn't want him wasting his pitching energy on her. So, there, on Jo's back porch, threadbare sheets flapping in the summer breeze and the smell of bleach and wet linen all around her, Margie Oblonsky added a few more rules to her list:

4. Curse all the fuck you want. Just don't curse at me. Or about my mother or my partner.

5. Nobody, and I mean nobody, is bigger than the game.

Dolph Fucking Edwards better watch his ass, because if he pulls that shit while I'm working his game, he's going to the showers.

With that guideline tucked into her head, she decided she'd leave Stephen "Fitz" Fitzgerald right where she'd left him—on the front porch of Josephine's rooming house with that stupid look on his face. Only next time, if some reporter wanted an interview, she'd be very careful about what she said. If she decided to talk to him at all.

15

THE WINTER

Margie didn't like the hesitation on the line after she'd asked Tim when he was coming home. That meant he wasn't, and that he felt guilty about it, and again she'd be stuck alone with her mother all winter. She'd only been back for two days, and her mother was already needling her with the questions about what would happen next season. *I won't know until January, Mom, that's when I know what will happen.*

Tim's voice came back weird, a little rushed. "Well, first, I'm doing winter ball in Puerto Rico. Work on my curveball. Then one of my teammates, his dad owns this swanky resort in the Keys, said we can stay cheap if we work there, you know, tend bar and stuff."

"Yeah. What do you know about tending bar?"

He laughed. "Been in enough of them. And you do it, so how hard could it be?"

She rolled her eyes. *He'll probably drown in tips. Good-looking kid, likes to charm the women. And he'd come to them with a spiffed-up curveball, of all things. How useful for a bartender.*

"You got any plans, Barge?"

She cast a glance around her bedroom, at the textbooks, the paperwork. Like Wes, she'd taken spring semester off to do umpire training, and her advisor had told her she could finish up in the fall. Class A Short Season was perfect for that; in fact many of the players were college students. Wes was excited to return for his own final semester of school because he was studying science and he loved science, but she wasn't feeling as enthusiastic. She just wanted to be finished. It was an unwritten rule of the Oblonsky household: college first, then do what you want. Of course, Tim only got halfway through his BA before he quit for baseball. Being a third-round draft pick versus two more years in school did that to a person, she guessed. Or else Tim was special or something. Either way, Margie didn't have a buddy in the Keys, and she felt someone should be home with Mom over the winter, chopping wood and helping her shovel out when it snowed. But she didn't want to be stuck there all the time.

"Other than classes and my bartending shifts? Who knows? Maybe I'll do a little skiing."

"You hate skiing."

"Shut up."

* * *

School, work, and chores distracted Margie from thinking too much about spring and October—a tough month in the Oblonsky household. That was when her father had died. Watching the playoffs and the World Series with Wes over the phone helped. They called each other after particularly interesting plays, and sometimes she shot the breeze with his sister Julia if he wasn't around. She thanked Margie for being so good with Wes. Margie didn't know what that meant, but it sounded condescending, like he needed special treatment. In her book, anyone who'd finished first in his umpire training class, was getting straight As in astronomy, and was doing a damn good job working the games and always looking for learning opportunities for the both of them, didn't need anybody's special treatment. She decided to let it go, not stick her nose in family business because, after all, Wes still had to live with her this winter.

Her mother, on the other hand, had her moments, usually after reading about such-and-such player who'd been traded or when she was trying again to quit smoking.

"Margie, you need to be more proactive."

"Mom, what are you talking about?"

"You know. Give 'em a little nudge once in a while. Let 'em know you're interested."

And then she'd say things about squeaky wheels and grease, and about women needing to shout louder than men.

"Mom. That's not how it works. You do your time, you hope to get noticed, you wait. They send you a letter in January, February, something like that."

Then Margie would call Tim. "You gotta come visit, at least for Christmas. I love her, but she's driving me nuts." He said he'd try.

Her mother had already gone upstairs to bed on Christmas Eve, but Margie had a feeling in that way of twins and stayed up in front of the fire reading a book. Soon, headlights crossed the window, and she jumped up to greet Tim at the front door with a big hug and a few sisterly insults about his Puerto Rico tan and his muscles and how long he'd been away. He set some presents under the tree and went to the kitchen, returning with two beers, handing her one and flopping down beside her. He looked happy.

"So how many girls did you flirt with on the flight?"

He cocked his head and grinned. "Bargie."

"I'm serious. I put money on this."

"Shaddap." He was actually blushing. Then he turned to her. "You hear anything about next season yet?"

"Stop, you're gonna jinx me."

"That's crazy. You're getting mad skills, Barge. Someone's gonna want you. If not Bighorn, then some other league."

"I tossed a mascot, Tim. Who's gonna want someone who tossed a mascot?"

He laughed, then stopped short because they didn't want to wake their mother. Not yet. "I gotta hear how that went down."

"It was, like, some giant penguin. Being a total jerk to me after a call didn't go his team's way. He just wouldn't shut up. Then he gave me the wingtip."

Tim shook his head, his shoulders twitching like he was trying to control a giggle fit. "That took some guts, though. I knew you had the guts for this."

She smiled. He was right, she guessed. She was learning. When players pushed, she pushed back. She stared a little harder on the field, was more emphatic with her calls. She stopped any nonsense quickly and ejected whoever needed ejecting. It didn't matter who it was—players, managers, coaches. The shortstop who tried to get out of a warning by asking her out on a date. The cut-ups in the home dugout who made kissing noises and talked about her ass when she worked near first base. The coach who yelled that she should be home, barefoot and pregnant. If they broke her rules, they got a warning, and if they didn't heed that, they got tossed.

"You ever get dumped from a game?" she asked.

"Only by my coach. Seeing what you go through, I got a healthy respect for umpires. I don't always like the calls, but I keep it to myself."

"Wish more of them were like you. Make my job a lot easier."

His grin was sly. "Aw, come on. It wouldn't be as much fun, then, would it?"

They started swapping baseball stories and, eventually, the laughter must have gotten too loud because Mom came downstairs. But all annoyance vanished when she saw her golden boy's smiling face.

* * *

Tim stayed three days, and Mom waited on him like he was royalty, but it was over too soon and her mother was picking at her for every little thing. Clothes on the floor. Dishes in the sink. Margie's plans for the rest of her life. She'd even put on her coat and followed Margie out to the woodshed, going on about how she should call headquarters and out-and-out ask for a better assignment and more money.

She tossed a just-split log onto the stack and turned to her. "You want me to go to Florida and tend bar with Tim next winter? You're makin' my choice real easy."

Margie chopped a lot of wood that winter.

Finally, the new year began.

She was shoveling the front walk on a sparkly post-storm afternoon when Art the mailman pulled up. After the first two weeks of January went by without a letter, she started dreading Art's arrival. Which was too bad because he was a really nice guy and his daughter had been on Margie's softball team in high school. He showed up for almost all the games, shelled out for pizza after, and sometimes they talked baseball for a bit if Margie happened to be out when he came by with the mail.

Instead of sticking the mail in the box and waving as he went on his way, he pushed through the gate and trundled up the walk. His smile was kind of sly, which often meant he was about to tell her a corny joke. He loved them. "You waitin' on something special, Margie?" he said. "You meet a guy out in Montana?"

"I met a bunch of guys, Art." She leaned on the handle of the shovel and forced a grin. "But there's only one I'm waiting to hear from."

He pulled a letter out of their stack. "Huh. It wouldn't be this, would it? Looks awfully—"

She almost gave him a paper cut yanking it out of his hands. Her legs went weak as she tore it open right there.

"You got some good news there?" he said. "You going back to Big Sky Country?"

For a second, she couldn't speak.

The door opened, and her mother said, "Hey, Art. Margie. Is that it?"

She spun toward the house, waving the letter in the air. "Mom. Mom. Mom. I'm going to the Eastern League. I'm goin' to the friggin' Eastern League!"

A wary look fell over her face. "That's good, right?"

"Mom, shut the hell up. Hell yeah, you know that's good. It's Double A. They're moving me up! Art! They're moving me up!"

He let out a whoop and gave her a big hug, murmuring *congratulations* and *atta girl*s and *I knew you could*s.

"All right, you, enough of that," her mother said. "My turn. My turn!" Mom grabbed her tight. Tighter than she had in a long time. Margie damn near cried.

16

THE PROMOTION

Spring Training 1982

The league required a detailed ejection report for every player an umpire threw out. While Wes was eager to hash out the calls with Margie after a game, he preferred to do his ejection paperwork on his own. And he believed in finishing it before he left the stadium. Margie liked to do hers, if there were any to be done, as part of her cooling-off process, usually over a beer or two back in her room. But Wes was her ride to the hotel in Tampa and her suitcase was in his car, so she did her ejections as they sat at a picnic table in the stadium's parking lot. Wes's mouth pinched as he filled out his forms. She worried about him. Like her, she knew he was stoked to get moved up to Double A after just one season, but she had a strong hunch the quick advancement was unusual and more would be expected of them, or they'd have to stay at this level longer, so that only added to the pressure. He said he was getting together with one of his sisters, who lived across the bay from Tampa in Clearwater. Maybe some family time would chill him out some.

She hated to rush Wes when he was having a learning opportunity. Not in the mood he was in, anyway. But she was running late and needed to give him a not-so-subtle nudge. "Hey, we gotta go. I gotta grab a shower and meet Tim."

He looked up, a bit dazed, squinting into the low-hanging sun. "I'm almost finished. I'm reviewing this again to make sure I have all the details in order. This one was a really complicated situation. I don't want to miss anything important."

It had been a complicated game. A tight play at first resulted in a run being scored and a hotheaded manager telling her she should go back to the kitchen, and what she could do when she got there. In the seventh inning, a baserunner, the batter on deck, and the third-base coach all got dumped for arguing a clean tag at the plate.

"Yeah, I hear you. I lost track of how many times number fifteen called us stupid motherfuckers. And it's only spring training. Imagine how tweaked he'll be by September."

That got a bit of a smile, and they headed back to the hotel.

By the time she'd showered, thrown on semi-clean jeans and a T-shirt, and then booked it over to the cocktail lounge, the place was packed. It wasn't hard to spot Timmy at the bar, though. He gave her one of his thousand-watt smiles and motioned her over. He was also a little drunk.

"One of my teammates wants to meet you," he called over the loud music and the voices. Then he gave a guy next to him a playful shove, pushing him free from the pack. Margie backed up a step as the guy regained his bearings and shot a good-natured retort in Tim's direction.

Timmy gave her a look like she should have known the dude, but for a second she couldn't place him. That wasn't unusual. Beyond the rules of the game, a huge document rife with legalese she'd studied chapter and verse from her first day of umpire school, she had to know players. She had to know a flick in an eye that foretold an attempt to steal a base. She had to know the tension in a forced smile that meant a player was going to see how far he could push her. For that, she took it upon herself to study facial expressions, body language…and that meant paying attention. Off the field, she often blanked on a guy until the gears kicked in. Maybe it was some kind of self-protective mechanism, preserving her memory for when she needed it.

The guy Tim had flung toward her stood there blinking, giving her an odd grin like she had something stuck in her teeth. She swept her tongue along her gumline, just in case, found nothing, and challenged him back with a glare. He was a good-looking guy in a comfortable sort of way. Big. Clean-shaven, a regular-joe haircut, golf shirt and chinos, and one of those broad, friendly Midwestern faces with smiling, light brown eyes crinkled from years spent outdoors. Maybe on some farm. She could almost picture him driving a combine.

He squared his shoulders and put out a hand. "Dan Monroe," he said.

Heat rushed up her face as she recognized the name from one of her ejection reports and from the lineup card. Dan Monroe. Dan Monroe was the goddamn catcher. She'd been standing right behind him half the goddamn game. Well, at least until the seventh inning, when he wouldn't stop arguing about that tag. She shot Timmy a fuck-you look for putting her in this position; he went all John-Boy Walton innocent on her. "You get why I dumped you, right?"

Dan shrugged, then cleared his throat. "You got a job to do, I got a job to do. I protect my guys, you toss me." Then that sort-of-cocky smile went a little shy. "So, uh, maybe you'll let me buy you a beer?"

Tim had vanished into the crowd. Typical. Probably chasing some girl. From what she'd heard, he had one in damn near every town he played. Mom would have a coronary. Fortunately for her twin, Margie's silence could be negotiated. She turned back to Farm Boy and shot him a crooked grin. "Let's see if I'm understanding this right. I dumped you and you're buying me a beer?"

"Hey, you're right." The shy smile widened. "*You* tossed *me*. You should be buying."

Seriously? He was probably making twice her salary. Then it occurred to her that he might have pushed her buttons on purpose following the play, knowing Tim was meeting up with her later. Pulling a little sympathy act. Well, he could forget that. She'd never dated a player before and wasn't about to start. "Nice try, I already filed the report." Tim had better watch his ass if she ever called a game he pitched, because she'd dump him, too. In fact, she was looking forward to it. She couldn't have anyone thinking she was playing favorites because he was her brother.

"Can't toss me out of the bar, though, can you?"

Drawn back by the hopeful tone in his voice and the twinkle in his eye, Margie raised an eyebrow. "I don't know. The night is young." Catchers, she thought, mentally shaking her head as he found a spot for them and signaled the bartender. Catchers had always been her weakness. And how wrong was it, really, to just *talk* to a guy?

"So let's have it, Big Dan. Stats, prospects, what?"

He laughed. It was a nice laugh. Manly. Not mean. A guy had to have a nice laugh. And something to hold on to, if she was of the mind to hold on to something. Those shoulders would do fine. Catchers' knees went, though. Toward the end, her father didn't have a pain-free day.

"You really want my stats?" The look on Dan's face intrigued her. His not-quite-there smile seemed puzzled, but his eyes held a touch of fear, like he'd had more than one nun slap his hands with a ruler for not giving the right answer. Wes had the same expression sometimes.

"You're serious." He cocked his head as if remembering, but Margie hadn't met a single minor leaguer who couldn't spit those numbers out on cue. A couple of them had laid them on her like some kind of pickup line. She waited to see how Dan would respond. Then his eyes brightened. He scrubbed a big hand against his big lantern jaw and said, "If you like 'em, can I buy you dinner, too?"

She shook her head. "You know it's against the rules to fraternize with the players."

"Fraternize? Who said anything about fraternizing? We'll take Tim with us. We all have to eat, right?"

"Fair point." She tapped her finger on the bar rail. "But I need some answers, Dan Monroe. I gotta know who I'm not fraternizing with here."

"Three ten against righties. Three eighty-two against southpaws. Went three-for-four today, before you tossed me; two clean singles, squibbed a double to left-center. I caught—"

She held up a hand. "They got any decent Italian in this town?"

17

THE RETURN

Heavy metal music pounded through the walls of the clubhouse in Binghamton, New York, and Margie bobbed her head and played a little air guitar while suiting up in the manager's office. She'd never been so amped for a game. It was the first regular game of her new season, her new assignment, and she was working the plate. She was so jazzed that she swore people could see the vibration lines outside her body. But she had to stay focused. Plate was tough and she had to keep cool—as she'd told Dan when he called the previous night to wish her luck. And staying focused meant concentrating on baseball right now, not Dan's laugh or his strong arms or how comfortable she felt talking to him. So when she and Wes took the field, she sucked in some deep breaths and let her instincts guide her. By the second inning, she'd settled down, and it felt like she could see faster. She could pinpoint where each pitch landed, had a good eye on the plays, was at the perfect angle to see and even admire the wicked breaking stuff of a young pitcher who looked to have a good future in the game. She and Wes worked together like a key in a lock, calling the plays and backing each other up, and it was going so smoothly she could hardly believe it.

Then came the top of the third. She'd just given the catcher a new ball when Chip Donofrio, the visiting team's shortstop, stepped into the on-deck circle. A shiver of "oh shit" went through her, but she tried to shove it away.

A few pitches later, the batter took ball four and trotted to first.

Donofrio sauntered up and flashed her a fuck-you look.

"Something you'd like to say, Mr. Donofrio?"

He had the balls to grin. "No, Miss Oblonsky. May we get back to the game now, please?"

Asshole punk.

During spring training, Wes told her that Donofrio and Dolph Edwards had a history. They'd been teammates at UCLA, roomed together, got drafted at the same time. The pair were best buds, apparently. Edwards had moved up the ranks faster—even though he was sent back down to Double A occasionally to rehab his frequent injuries—but they were still tight. Wes also told her that, given the relatively few teams in the Eastern League and the number of umpire crews working them, odds were that they'd be seeing a lot of Mr. Donofrio.

The man in question knocked some dirt around and got settled in the batter's box. He swung at the first pitch and missed, even though it was out of the strike zone. Margie could have bet the farm on that one. He looked like a first-ball hitter, all twitchy and impatient. She wondered if he'd tried juicing, too, although he was a lot smaller than Edwards. Maybe it didn't work on him. Maybe that's what made him so pissed off. Or that he'd been stuck in Double A while Edwards at least had made it up. Donofrio set again in the batter's box, leaning in, and the next pitch brushed him back. One and one. He shot a dirty look at the pitcher, who just shrugged. Then he stepped out and turned a hate beacon on Margie, as if she were in cahoots with the pitcher. Ugly shit was coming, she could almost smell it, but she glared back and held it on him. Still, he didn't break eye contact.

"Unless something's on your mind, Mr. Donofrio, I suggest you get back in that box."

She knew that return look well. It was a guy who wasn't going to let anyone show him up. He stepped back in. He took the next pitch, a clean fastball that nicked the outside corner. Margie did a one-count in her head and then pumped her right fist. Donofrio's eyes nearly bulged out of his face. "You're shittin' me, right? That was a fucking mile off the plate."

"Strike two," Margie said.

The next pitch was another brushback that missed; the next sailed over the catcher's head and the runner on first took second. After each pitch, Donofrio muttered some shit about the pitcher, that Margie should toss him for throwing at his head.

Margie bit back the sarcastic comment she wanted to slap him with, that maybe a hit upside his head was exactly what he needed. *Nobody but the guy who signs my check tells me how to do my job.*

Fortunately, the pitcher had the last word. The next pitch was a mean breaker, low and inside. She pumped her fist, selling the third strike and the out with all her heart.

"What the fuck? That's the same fucking pitch you fucking called ball four on the last guy." Then he dropped his voice. "You got it out for me? You hate men? Well, guess what, lady, none of us would even fuck you with someone else's—"

Margie shot toward him. "You're done. Out."

He started jumping around and screaming. His manager came out of the dugout, and Margie glared at him to step back. But he wouldn't. The manager kept arguing for the pitch, politely, that it was out of the strike zone, and that she should have seen that.

"I did see it," Margie said calmly. "I saw that it was in the strike zone. Then your player decided to make it personal, and I won't allow that."

The manager looked like he wasn't sure how to handle the situation. A few of these guys, especially the older ones, walked on eggshells around her. His mouth twitched. "Donofrio," he barked. "Apologize to the lady."

"I ain't apologizing for shit. And that's no lady."

Now the manager threw Donofrio out. But he still wouldn't leave, or shut up. "She shouldn't even fucking be here."

Margie got right in Donofrio's face, close enough to count his razor nicks. "And where should I fucking be, Mr. Donofrio?"

As she suspected, he backed down. But then the manager made the fatal mistake of trying to calm his player by muttering to him that it might be her time of the month. Just loud enough for Margie to hear.

"And you can join him!" She'd never heaved anyone out of a game so hard. You could have probably seen her arm-swing from the space shuttle. The smile, however, was only for herself.

* * *

After the game, Wes said he'd buy her a burger if she helped him with his ejection forms. He never asked for help with his forms, and she was never one to turn down free food, but something in his face told her not to question him. She nodded, and they met up at a nearby diner.

As she suspected, he didn't need help with the paperwork.

"I wanted to make sure we were on the same page." Wes tapped his pen against the Formica table as the waitress filled his coffee cup. He nodded toward the stadium. "You looked like you had Donofrio handled, but should I have done something? Had your back more?"

Anybody else would have gotten a lecture, but because it was Wes, she grinned despite herself. Not only was Wes a good umpire, he was a good guy, making sure she was all right without coming out and saying it. She knew she was lucky to have drawn him again. There were some great guys in baseball, but after working with Durning—

"Nah, you're right. Donofrio's a punk, but I put him down. But thanks. Now, if someone's doing something I can't see, and vice versa…"

"Right," Wes said. "That's a given." He paused a moment, his jaw working to the side. "I'm just glad I've got plate tomorrow. I'm not giving him an inch."

Margie smirked.

"What?"

"Maybe you look like a bookworm, but you're no pushover. Plus, you're a guy. So I doubt he's gonna give you any trouble."

Margie was right. Donofrio took every single one of Wes's decisions. The only thing he challenged that day was when she called him out on a close play at first. She'd glared at him long and hard and said, "Wanna try for two?"

He stood there with a big damn smirk on his face. Then he grabbed his crotch and his lips moved. Anyone who was even a beginner at reading lips could have made out what he said.

She tossed him. He went. She could tell he didn't like it, but she didn't care. She felt vindicated for at least that one small victory. She had to take them where she could.

18

THE TEMPTATION

After the shaky start, Margie's first season in Double A sailed along in a blur of stadiums, diner coffee, highway miles, and the occasional phone conversation with Dan, after eleven when the long-distance rates dropped and most of the other women had gone to bed. When he called her one night and said, "You doing anything for the All-Star break?" she was momentarily stunned. How had it become July already?

"Right now all I want to do is sleep."

"Tough day at the office?"

"Hell, yeah. Must have been the full moon or something. Brings out the crazy."

It was a slugfest with a lot of pitching changes, which meant a long, long game. Margie worked the plate and had to toss two guys. One didn't like that he hadn't checked his swing quickly enough to avoid a third strike call, and his fate was sealed when he said, "Who'd you blow to get this job, anyway?" Then her "friend" Chip Donofrio accidentally-on-purpose tried to knock her down while sliding into home, when Margie wasn't in his way and there wasn't even a need to slide—the throw home missed the catcher by a good three feet. Donofrio clearly could have seen from third base that the throw was going to be far off the mark. When she called him on it, he said she was a "fucking stupid cunt" for being in the wrong place at the wrong time, and when she tossed him for that, he threatened to file a complaint against her. She told him to go right ahead. Later in the game, when she handed the catcher a new ball from her pouch, a guy in the dugout said, "Baby, you can hold my balls all day long." Wes, standing near first base, got wind of that and stared him down. If that wasn't enough, somebody snuck into her changing room and left a dildo on the bench. Which made an even half dozen. But all she told Dan was that she'd had to dump a couple guys and the language on her ejection reports would make her mother blush.

"Sounds like you're ready for a vacation," Dan said.

She knew where this was going. It wasn't the first time they'd danced around the topic of when they could actually talk face-to-face again. With him in Florida and her working the Northeast, their schedules never aligned. Even if they did, if anybody saw them together… Margie raked a hand through her hair and reached for her half-finished can of Genny Cream Ale. Damn, how she wanted to be like the girls down the hall, all excited about leaving town with their baseball boyfriends for the break.

"And…now it sounds like maybe you're not ready," he added.

"It's not like that," she said. So many nights, after their calls, she wished she could say goodnight the right way, with more than just words. "I'd love to see you, but…"

"Yeah," he said. "That's a big old but. I hear you, though. We both got commitments. Maybe after the season's over, you think?"

She did think. She thought about it a lot.

* * *

Wes invited her to spend the break in Connecticut with his family. Her mother dropped not-too-subtle hints that a visit home might be nice, since Tim wouldn't be joining them—he and a couple of his teammates were going to the All-Star Game in Montreal. Two women from her college softball team were playing in their own amateur-league all-star game somewhere in Virginia and hoped she would come down to cheer them on. But Margie politely declined each offer. Most of the women in her house would be gone, and she was getting more and more excited about soaking in the peace and quiet, and the joy of doing whatever she damn well felt like doing. Even if that was nothing at all.

Her self-imposed downtime lasted exactly fifteen hours. She'd slept late on Monday morning, lingered over a nice breakfast while her landlady had gone out to get her hair done; then, as she was cleaning up, Margie noticed that a bulb over the kitchen sink was burned out. There were extras in the closet next to the pantry, so she replaced it. Then she saw that the pantry was a god-awful mess, one of the shelf brackets was coming loose, and a light switch in the laundry room wasn't working, so she tackled those, too. She didn't mind the work. Her rooming house for the season, smack dab in the middle of the Eastern League's stadiums, wasn't as homey as Jo's place, but she liked her new landlady, and when Margie was in town and had a moment, she enjoyed helping out. It felt good to fix something, have some control, even if it was just replacing a lightbulb. She was glad her parents hadn't raised her to be some fancy-ass girly-girl. No way she could have survived otherwise, wearing the same clothes day to day, staying in crappy motels when she was on the road, grabbing quick, lousy meals and making ramen noodles and boxed macaroni and cheese in various kitchens or in the hot pot she carried around in the trunk of her car.

Which reminded her that her car could use a good cleaning, too.

After she'd done that and gone out to the supermarket for a few fill-in items and more beer, the sun was fading into the trees and she still had energy to burn, so she went out for a run. It'd been far too long, and the rhythm of it soothed her. She stopped at her halfway point, a small park with a pretty view, admired a few early-rising stars—or maybe they were planets, she'd have to ask Wes—and headed back.

* * *

He was the last man Margie expected to find sitting in her front porch swing on a Monday night in July. As she approached the house, she blinked to make sure her eyes weren't playing tricks on her. They weren't.

"I thought you were going to Montreal with Tim. What are you doing here?"

Dan stood, gave her one of his cute goofy grins, and started down the stairs. She'd almost forgotten how tall he was. How broad those shoulders were. Damn, what a picture he made. Clean-shaven, starchy fresh in a golf shirt and chinos, a little nervous in an adorable sort of way.

He came close enough to make her insides tingle. He smelled nice, his aftershave subtle. Definitely he smelled better than she did after working around the house all day and then running eight miles. She backed up a step, fearing he might try for a kiss or a hug or one of those back-slappy man things, but he apparently read the situation, as any good catcher might, and let her have that small distance between them.

"Well," he said, quickly regrouping. "I could tell you something smooth and charming. Like I gave up a chance to go to the All-Star Game and drove twenty-two hours straight from Orlando just so I could spend time with the prettier Oblonsky twin. But you're too smart to fall for that."

She laughed. "You're right. I am." Although the way he said it worked, too.

"It's partly the truth," he said.

"Do I want to know the rest?"

He grinned. "The Baltimore Orioles picked up my contract. They're moving me up to their triple-A team in Rochester."

"Triple A! Dan, that's great! I'd hug you but I totally reek. So, you start on Thursday?"

Margie did the road atlas math in her head. Rochester was roughly two and a half hours north of Binghamton. But not that close to any of the stadiums she worked. And where did he have to travel? She wasn't even sure what league that put him in, but it wasn't hers, so that made her smile.

"Yep," he said. "Right after the break. So I said to myself, I could spend three days sitting in some smelly old rooming house in Rochester with a bunch of guys. Or I could stop in Binghamton to break up the trip, check into that little motel near the stadium, then see if Margie's around. You and the motel won." A blush crept up his cheeks. "Wow, that came out wrong. I didn't mean... I meant, if it's okay with you that I'm here. I know we agreed—"

"No. I mean, yeah. But..." Even though it was getting dark, she was suddenly hyperconscious of being outside with him. Anyone could have seen them together. Then she decided she was probably being an idiot. She would throw her own brother out of a game if he deserved it. She'd tossed Dan the first day they'd met. If they ever landed in the same league in the future, and Dan needed tossing, she'd toss him. Why should anyone care what she did in her free time, as long as it didn't reflect badly on the game and it didn't interfere with doing her job?

He glanced down the front of her sweaty running clothes to her sneakers and back up again. "Aw, shoot. I was so excited to tell you that I didn't even think to ask how you're doing. Good run?"

She was about to answer when something colorful over his shoulder caught her eye—a bouquet of flowers on the porch swing. The girly part of her sighed, and she was unable to resist touching his cheek. It was soft and hard all at once, like she imagined the rest of him, and she played off a shiver like the breeze had caught her by surprise.

"I'll tell you about it when I let you buy me dinner. Just give me a couple minutes to clean up."

He squeezed her hand. "I'll be right here."

* * *

Margie's heart hammered in her ears as she sprinted upstairs. She passed Anna, one of the non-baseball-related tenants, on the upstairs landing. The girl smiled in greeting, then her eyes narrowed. "Hell. Only one thing makes you move that fast. Must be dollar-beer night somewhere."

"Ha-ha, bite me." Margie was already pulling off her T-shirt.

"Or you got a guy." Anna followed Margie into her room. "Margie, you got a guy?"

"Right now it's just dinner."

"I'll bet." She peered out the window. "That him down there?"

Margie leaned close. Dan was pacing up and down the sidewalk. "Crap. Anna, could you do me a favor? I gotta shower. Can you get him inside?"

Anna started to smile dirty, and Margie smacked her arm. "Invite him into the living room. Jeez. Everything's goddamn pornographic for you, isn't it?"

"I don't get out much," Anna said.

Margie widened her eyes. "Please. He's a ballplayer. There's people in this town who'd make a whole hell of a stink about that guy hanging around this house."

Anna held up her hands. "Gotcha." She looked outside again. "Damn. You done good, Margie. If I had a guy like that, I'd want him in my shower, too."

She raced through her cleanup, forgetting how many times she'd lathered, rinsed, and repeated, getting soap in her eye, scraping the razor on her shin in her haste. Then she stopped. Took a breath. Why the hell was she even stressing over this? He wasn't getting to first base, let alone all the way around to the point where it mattered what her legs looked like. She couldn't date a ballplayer. How would it look?

It's just dinner. Cool your jets, woman. You've got the whole off-season to…

To what? Off-season he lived in Iowa; she lived in New York. During the season, they were running every which way and she hardly ever had any time off. How could they make anything happen other than talking on the phone when they could? Although it was really nice, talking to him on the phone…

Shut the hell up, she told that little voice of doubt. No, that big screaming voice of doubt. The one that told her to stay away from ballplayers. Especially cute ballplayers who brought her flowers and smelled good and smiled at her like she was something special.

It's just dinner. Just dinner with a friend.

Who'd driven twenty-two hours to see her. Who looked at her like a damn fool in love.

* * *

She knew he liked Italian food, and there was a place in town that would be perfect. It wasn't all that fancy, but it was open on Monday nights and it was decent. They stopped in front, looked into the window at the red plastic booths and paper menus, the empty cardboard boxes of pizzas stacked to the ceiling on a shelf over the ovens. Dan said, "You want to go here? You sure?"

Margie nodded.

He paused, shoving a hand in his pocket, twisting the toe of his tassel loafer into the sidewalk. They didn't look like shoes he wore all that often; maybe they pinched his feet. "Because, you know, I could do better by you. If you want," he added quickly.

Fussy fancy restaurants made Margie itch. She never knew which fork to use, and sometimes she knocked over water glasses and couldn't pronounce the dishes on the menu. She didn't want Dan spending that much on her. Since it couldn't be a real date, anyway. Nobody went to this place on real dates. If anyone saw them in there, they'd think nothing of it. A couple friends grabbing a slice. So why had she worn her best underwear?

"I like this place," Margie said.

They ordered a pie and a pitcher. She told him about how her season had been going. He told her about his. He asked if she knew a good place to watch the All-Star Game on Tuesday night, maybe a sports bar, if the town had one, and Margie raised an eyebrow. "In this town? Every other place is a sports bar." She thought a minute. Then leaned closer, splitting what was left of the pitcher into both of their glasses. Her cheeks warmed; being near him didn't help, and that aftershave was killing her. Two more seconds this close and she'd be touching him again. "We could go to my place."

His mouth dropped. She grinned, reached over and closed it for him, fingers lingering a moment longer than necessary on his smooth jawline. "I meant for the game, Big Dan."

* * *

On Tuesday night, the few girls who were home crowded around the big television in the living room, cheering for their favorite players. They took to Dan like he was their favorite teddy bear. He explained some of the plays to them, said what he knew about some of the players. During the seventh-inning stretch, he and Margie grabbed some cold beers from the fridge and went out to the back deck for some air. The night sky was thick with impending rain. Margie liked the way it smelled. It reminded her of home, the humid summer nights of the Hudson Valley. Which really wasn't that far away, maybe a two-and-a-half-hour drive door to door, but the weather always seemed different up here.

His sudden silence was unnerving her. She turned to him and said, "This isn't how you thought this evening would work out, did you?"

"I'm having a good time," he said.

She knocked a foot against his. "Why wouldn't you be? You got your own harem in there."

He laughed. "That's a ton of trouble in there."

"What's your living situation usually like?"

"Sort of the same. I keep thinking to find a better place, you know, an apartment instead of a room. But you know how it is. Never know how long you're gonna be living somewhere." He gazed beyond the deck to the decent-sized backyard, strewn with lawn furniture and picnic tables, lit up with a couple flood lamps on two corners of the fence. "I see why you like this place. Timmy talks a blue streak about your backyard, where you grew up."

She missed those days. Tossing the ball around with Tim. Being jerks to each other until Mom called them off.

"Is that why you stay here?" Dan said. "Umps I've met, they live out of their car, or a suitcase, going from one motel room to another. Must cost a bunch to keep paying rent here and sleeping on the road."

"It's not bad," she said. "My landlady's great. I do odd jobs when I'm around, and she cuts me a deal."

Then she realized it had grown quiet inside—no more chattering girls, just the rhythm of the play-by-play announcers, interspersed with commercials.

Dan must have realized it, too. "Everyone packed it in?"

She stepped back through the kitchen and into the living room. Only Anna was there, asleep in an easy chair in the corner.

They tiptoed out and sat in the front porch swing, where they talked for a long time. About baseball, about their childhoods. The highlights of the roads they'd taken to get to where they were now. She barely noticed the two of them drifting closer together. She barely noticed his fingers occasionally touching hers.

She cleared her throat. Suddenly she felt too exposed. Her gaze dropped to their intertwined fingers in the small space between them. His thumb caressed hers. Warmth began to spread through her body. Had it really been over two years since someone touched her like she mattered, since a man looked at her like he wanted to kiss her? She entertained the thought of going back to his motel room. Flinging off her fussy top and dress pants and even her good underwear.

But she didn't want to wait that long. She stood. Reached for his hand. With the other, she pressed a finger to her lips and pulled him inside the front door.

His grin went shy, his eyes focused on her mouth. "You're not going to toss me out again, are you, Margie?"

She laughed softly. "I was just doing my job, Big Dan. You get out of hand on the field, and I'll toss you again."

At the foot of the staircase, he stopped her, his arms circling her waist, his breath warm against her left temple. "And off the field?"

"We're gonna have to play that by ear." She tilted her chin up to kiss him; he met her halfway.

19

THE NOTE

As Margie and Wes drove back to Binghamton following an afternoon game in Corning at the beginning of August, her stomach started growling like a bear waking up in the spring. All she had in her room was a box of macaroni and cheese, and she couldn't claim to have much more in the kitchen fridge.

"You wanna stop at the diner, get something to eat?" she asked.

"No, thank you," Wes said after a long pause. "I think I'm just going to grab something quick near the motel and get to bed early." He'd been quiet for a while; that was unlike him, especially after such an exciting game where there'd been a lot of wild plays and she'd had to toss Donofrio yet again. As a bonus, his team was also playing in Binghamton the next day, a rainout makeup game that she and Wes were working. After that, they were heading to Connecticut to work a series in the eastern spur of the league. She glanced toward her partner, who was looking out the window at the stars, she presumed, and asked if anything was wrong. He said he was tired, but she had a feeling there was something he wasn't telling her. And another feeling telling her not to push.

After she dropped him off, she parked in front of her building and squinted toward the door. Something was taped to it: MARGIE in big black letters across a white envelope.

It couldn't have been from Dan. His team was in the middle of a five-game home stand in Rochester. And he'd never be so careless as to leave a message for her on the outside of the door. She cursed under her breath when it dawned on her that the note was probably from another reporter. A few others, not as dogged as Stephen Fitzgerald, had popped up here and there; a couple had even contacted her over the winter at her mother's, and Margie had ignored them. Eventually they got bored and disappeared when they finally figured out she wasn't going to talk to them. Maybe this new one had a burr under his saddle or was just slow to learn.

With a sigh, she snapped the envelope from the glass pane and stuffed it into her pocket. The place was dead quiet. Even the landlady had gone out, leaving her husband at the desk, but his idea of taking care of business was parking in front of the television in the living room and only responding when someone yelled for him. Nobody was yelling for him. Margie gave him a little wave and headed up to her room, her step livelier. Nobody around meant no competition for the pay phone, and she wanted to call Timmy and wish him luck for tonight's game.

But the guy who answered at his house said Tim wasn't there.

She was halfway down the hall when the phone rang again.

"Tim?"

"No, it's me." She smiled as Dan's warm voice, and the memory of being in his arms, flowed over her like water. "Margie, I got news." He sounded out of breath. "Timmy got called up to the show this morning."

While she was attempting to process that, and why Tim hadn't told her, Dan gave up the details. One of the starting pitchers for the Cincinnati Reds tore a rotator cuff, and they wanted Tim to fill in. He was pitching in Atlanta that evening. After a pause, Dan said, "So I should sign off. You probably want to give him a call like you do. My boy's probably pacing holes in the hotel carpet by now."

Then he gave her the number and let her go, but before placing the call to Tim's hotel, Margie fished out the letter from the reporter. Tim would get a kick out of it. He got so antsy before big games; maybe it would help chill him out a little. He'd especially liked the totally fawning one from some cubbie who'd likened her to a present-day Joan of Arc. That she was an "amazing lady" who was doing "amazing things for women and for the game" and he wanted to meet her and give her a hug. Because she was so amazing. She glanced around at the glamorous trappings of her life—her shabby room, her meager paycheck, her graying underwear hanging over the window rod—and laughed. "Yeah," she said. "Freakin' amazing."

But this new missive only contained these words: "You better watch your ass, you stupid fucking dyke."

She dropped it like it was hot, her mind swirling. Guys had cursed her before, made lewd comments and gestures, yelled at her—you name it, they'd done it. But if the shenanigans went beyond a certain point, she'd had recourse. She could toss them out of a game, recommend a fine, or confront them in other ways, like Durning's pathetic posse in the Bighorn League. They were bullies, which meant they were cowards, which meant that when you got in their faces they backed down.

This one felt different.

A shiver crept down her spine and settled in her gut.

She took a deep, shuddering breath to keep from puking. *Think, Margie. You might have recourse.*

Whichever dirtbag had written that note—and she had her suspicions—he'd crossed a line, made a distinct threat to her safety, and there were rules about that beyond her own personal code.

But she wasn't calling the league president. Not yet. She hadn't been on her new boss's radar yet and didn't want this to be their first encounter. At least not until she had a chance to work it out on her own. Damn sure she wasn't telling Dan, and double-damn sure Tim wouldn't hear about this, either. Both of them would want to bust some skulls.

She picked up the note as if it were dog shit and put it in her equipment bag. She'd give it to security before tomorrow's game.

There were a few pony bottles of Genny Cream Ale under her bed for emergencies. She popped one. It was warm and tasted like ass, but she didn't care. She finished that one and downed another. When her hands had stopped shaking, she called Timmy's hotel.

When he answered, she forced a smile and said, "Well, damn. I can't believe they put me through, now that you're some big hot shit major leaguer."

He laughed. "I left word that you and Dan are the only ones I'll talk to. Mom, though"—she heard the smile in his voice—"they're holding her calls."

"Your own mother." She shook her head, picturing his innocent blue eyes. "But I get it. She'd be calling you every ten minutes, giving you tips."

Timmy cleared his throat and imitated their mother's cigarette rasp. "Plant your back heel! You gotta get stable, get the fulcrum.

And for frig's sake, don't forget to shave. Don't make me look at your five o'clock shadow on national television and make me feel like I raised a bum. Your father, God rest his soul, he shaved every single damn day—"

"—and he never made it out of the friggin' bullpen!" Margie laughed. And for a while, everything felt right again.

20

THE MAJORS

Tim had never been treated like a big deal when he traveled for road trips; he'd toss his duffel into the baggage compartment and line up for the bus with the rest of the guys, all of them freshly shaved and showered and damp around the edges but still managing to look rumpled, hungover, a couple quarts low. For a moment he didn't know how to react to the sharp-suited guy at the gate holding a sign with his name on it. It wasn't even cardboard and handwritten, like in the movies. It was freaking official, the letters printed in fancy type with the Cincinnati Reds logo on the border. Tim pointed to the placard, then to his own chest, and shot a nervous, too-big smile.

"That's, uh, me?" he said. *Idiot. You're pitching in the majors. Show a little confidence.*

"Welcome to Atlanta, Mr. Oblonsky." The man's warm smile didn't do much to put Tim at ease. "Right this way."

"Don't I, uh, have to get my bag and stuff?" He was embarrassed that he didn't have proper luggage. Maybe he should buy some. He didn't know how to shop for things like luggage. *Where do you even go?*

"All taken care of," the man said.

Tim followed him through the corridors and out to the parking lot. He had a million questions. Were they going to the hotel or right to the stadium? Was he supposed to meet with someone from the team first? His manager had been short on information. It felt like mere minutes ago—actually it had only been a few hours—that he'd called Tim at his boarding house and said they were sending him to Atlanta for that night's game. They needed someone to fill in. They wanted to see how he fit.

"Car's coming for you in an hour," his coach said, and that was that.

He'd sat there dazed for a moment, still holding the receiver. Then he called Dan.

The big man whooped so loud Tim swore his windows rattled. Good thing Dan was in Rochester. Dude probably would have crushed him with one of his bear hugs, so hard Tim might have puked. His stomach had started going sometime during the call from the coach.

Fucking major league! Pitching against the Braves!

"You all right there, Timmy?"

"I don't know." Tim's voice sounded breathy and choked-off, like it was coming from somewhere else. Someone else. "It seems...wrong." He cleared his throat. "I mean, yeah, I've been having some good starts lately, pitches landing where I want them, but I can't help thinking why not tap someone from Triple A."

"Maybe you were just the closest. Or the most rested."

"Fuck you," Tim said.

He imagined Dan's grin widening. "You got this. Pitch 'em stupid, Timmy."

And then he was on a plane. One of those puddle-jumpers, since they weren't going that far. For a while they hugged the Florida coastline and he couldn't help but think of his father, how proud the old man would be. He kissed his fingers and held them to the window. He would have done it again right there, in the back seat of the car, but he felt self-conscious in front of the driver.

Apparently they were going to the hotel first. It wasn't too shabby. Palm trees lined the front of it, shaded by a canopy, and guys in cartoon uniforms settled luggage on brass-plated dollies. *I gotta get some luggage. And one of those fancy suit bags.*

"Your itinerary is in your room, Mr. Oblonsky," the driver said as they pulled to a stop. "Where you're supposed to be when. You got time to settle in, do what you need to do. I know you pitchers like to settle in."

"Yeah, uh, okay. Thanks." Tim sat there blinking for a second or two. Was he supposed to tip the guy? He reached for his wallet.

"The team pays me fine, Mr. Oblonsky," the driver said with a little grin. "Don't you worry about a thing."

* * *

The last and only time Tim had been to Fulton County Stadium was for the All-Star Game in 1972. He was eleven. Dad finagled tickets for the whole family, but Margie got the chicken pox and stayed home with Mom. His sister was so mad she punched him hard on the shoulder when he came home, but it was worth it. He'd gotten to see Hammerin' Hank Aaron belt one out of the park. Because it had been just the two of them, Dad took him into the American League's clubhouse and introduced him around. Dad knew everyone. They smiled big and shook his hand, as if he were some kind of hero. Tim couldn't help smiling just remembering that day. Like he'd gone to baseball heaven. Returning to the stadium ten years later as a player was a different kind of heaven; heaven and hell at the same time.

Had it always been this big?

Did the clubhouse have the same kind of reverent hush when you entered, like time had stopped for a second?

Holy shit, I'm going to puke.

Pull it together, man. Breathe. Find your locker, suit up, dig in.

He pushed through the doors into the chaos of men and conversation and music, some kind of disco funk pumping from the speakers. He swallowed a couple times, telling himself it was just a bunch of guys getting dressed for the game, that he was no big deal here—another body, another uniform. It started making him feel more comfortable, anyway. Nobody stopped what they were doing and made a fuss; guys barely even looked at him let alone talked to him, and that helped, too. That, he was accustomed to. He followed the line of benches and clean metal doors, reading names and numbers. Names he'd known and worshipped for years. Johnny Bench. Dave Concepcion, who he'd just seen play in the All-Star Game. Freakin' Tom Seaver was even with the Reds that season. Man, he wanted to meet Seaver. *Later, Tim. Later. Can't get all star-struck, now. Gotta focus.* Finally he found number forty-three, which was his, for tonight at least. It was one number from Hammerin' Hank, three away from his father's. Something squinched in his stomach then, and he thought about his discussion with Margie in the hotel room. After busting him about his return to Fulton County

Stadium, they talked about the old man, how he'd shown them pitches in the backyard. As they were winding down, she'd said, "He'd be proud of you, John-Boy."

"He'd be proud of you, too, Barge."

Then he opened his locker and saw his first major league uniform, and his thought-train skipped the tracks.

He could have cried. That thing damn near sparkled and sang the "Hallelujah Chorus." The intensity of the red and gray road jersey, the bright, sharp stitching, how carefully they'd fit the many letters of his name across the back: OBLONSKY in a perfect arc. He stared at it for God knew how long, until he was aware of someone standing close by, giving off an aroma of Juicy Fruit gum and aftershave. "Well, third-round draft pick"—the Spanish-accented voice sounded amused—"they might be sayin' you're all kinds of magic, but that uniform ain't gonna get on you by itself."

Tim spun. A stocky, fortyish Latino guy with twinkling brown eyes gave him an easy smile. "Name's Alejandro. I'm the bullpen catcher. Coach wants me to warm you up, so hustle it on and follow me."

The guy didn't move. "What?" Tim said. "You gonna watch me get dressed?"

Alejandro laughed and shook his head. "Trust me. You're pretty, *Oblondie*, but you got nothin' I'm interested in except that arm."

Tim reached for his jersey. He already had a nickname. That was good, right?

* * *

When he took the mound, Tim started getting jangled up again. Alejandro had gotten him calmed down a little and told him about the catcher who'd be starting the game, but neither of them would ever be Dan Monroe. Nobody would be Dan Monroe, but them's the breaks. He had some trouble in the first inning, settling down, finding his groove. He walked a couple of batters on some close calls, but then the catcher came out. He didn't joke around like Dan, but he was steady and direct and even gave him some good advice.

What happened next, Tim couldn't even believe.

He'd struck out two guys in a row. His fastball rocketed from his hand, landed exactly where the catcher set his mitt. His curveball tailed away, nicking the edges of the strike zone, and each fist pump from the umpire fueled him on. The noise of the crowd faded into the background.

He could do no wrong. Even his mistakes did no wrong—a batter swung and missed at a curve that didn't break enough; another that got away was saved when the batter got under the ball and popped it up, caught easily by the first baseman. He felt shining and powerful, on a high like he'd never experienced before.

Nobody talked to him on the bench when his team was at bat, and he understood that was tradition—because he was the new guy and because of the no-hitter. He didn't even want to talk. He kept a damp towel over his head and eyes and tried not to think.

Thinking was the enemy. Even thinking about thinking was the enemy. Sometimes the heebie-jeebies crept in, and his right eyebrow began to twitch, and he thought about Dan and Margie, what they'd say to him now.

The Reds made the third out, and it was time to go back to work. Tim flipped the towel into the bin and sucked in a deep breath. Took inventory. Everything felt fine, loose, as he walked back to the mound. He was kind of calm, actually, and the twitch had gone away, and he wondered if he should worry about that.

Was he too calm?

Then he heard his father's voice in his head: *Stop thinking so darn much, kid. See the mitt, hit the mitt, you got this.*

That inning he struck out the side. As the final pitch sailed low and outside and the umpire pumped his fist, Tim knew he had this. He knew.

21

THE ROAD

After replacing a few burned-out lightbulbs in the ceiling fixtures—the landlady's husband complained that an old knee injury prevented him from climbing the stepladder—Margie went back to her room. She cracked open another Genny, lifting a toast to her father like she always did, but this time she asked him to look after Timmy. Even though she'd gotten him laughing a bit, he still sounded nervous as all hell.

Fuckin' major league.

She took a long slug and wished him luck. Only two bottles remained in the flat under her bed, but she promised herself to stop at one, because while Timmy got to put on a fresh new uniform and pitch against the Atlanta Braves, she had to complete her ejection reports then wash her underpants in the sink. She'd tossed four guys during that day's game, but one of them she and Wes had double-teamed on. He'd made the official call, so that meant three forms were on her.

As she wrote out her reasoning for why the ejections were deserved, she started feeling a little better, more in control. At that point, she could go either way about the note. She didn't want to look like a crybaby. She considered that it was just Donofrio being a coward—he'd probably even gotten one of his buddies to tape it to the door—and to complain about him and act scared would only fuel his fire. Maybe he was trying to spook her out of filing the report. Maybe that was it, because he got tossed at least once a week, and it was making him look bad.

Well, if you don't want to get dumped, stop acting like a jerk. She was filing. She wouldn't embellish or flavor it with her personal emotions. She wrote down exactly what happened—what he called her on the

field, what he continued calling her even after she'd warned him—
and signed her name to the bottom. Then she went shopping. She
and Wes were taking off for Connecticut after tomorrow's game.
Three of his six sisters lived there, one had just had a baby and
another was expecting, and they had some time between games to
visit. From all he'd said during their travels, she felt like she knew
them already, and she wanted to buy a few presents.

* * *

She'd just trundled through the door with her shopping bags when
the landlady told her she'd had a call. The bottom dropped out of
Margie's stomach.

The woman's eyes widened. "Oh, it didn't sound like *bad* news.
Although he did sound rather important. Said to call his hotel room
as soon as you can."

Margie cursed under her breath. That was even worse.

Anna was using the upstairs phone. She was crying. It didn't
sound like a *hey-can-you-call-back* sort of conversation. So Margie
dropped her stuff off and cracked the second-to-last of her Gennys,
nerves dancing to the tips of her fingers.

Finally, the receiver clicked down. Anna stood wobbly-kneed in
the hall, about to crumple like a used tissue. Her eyes were huge and
wet, and Margie was the only one around. She couldn't leave her
there alone. She led her to the love seat in the upstairs alcove and let
her talk for a bit, although she didn't have any good advice for her
boyfriend problems, and finally her teary gaze rested on the note in
Margie's hand.

"Oh," she said. "I'm sorry. You needed to make a call."

Margie tugged in a deep breath and let it out, staring at the pay
phone with dread pooling in her stomach. "Not really sure I want to
make this one, but yeah. I gotta do it."

Anna straightened and gave Margie's forearm a soft squeeze.
"Well, make it then. And after, let's get the hell out of here."

Margie managed a weak smile and went off to call Mack
Abernathy, president of the Eastern League.

The hotel's receptionist put her through and he answered on the
fifth ring. "Well. Margaret Oblonsky."

108

"Please. Margie's fine."

"Margie, then. I'm glad we finally get a chance to talk. You can call me Mack. Everyone does."

The pleasantries were making her itch. "Thank you, Mack. But I'm kinda assuming you didn't call because you wanted to get to know me?"

He laughed. "Right to the point. They told me about you."

Oh, holy crap.

"I heard about the game today. Everything all right?"

She gulped. She hoped he didn't hear that through the phone.

"Everything's handled, sir. Sorry. Mack. And my ejection forms are already in the mail."

Pause. "That should be some interesting reading."

Pause. A bead of sweat dripped down the back of her neck. "My intention isn't to make interesting reading, sir. I mean, Mack. I just explain what happened. I'm just doing my job."

"Easy, soldier." He laughed again, then cleared his throat. "I heard it was kind of rough out there in Elmira, last couple of games, and I wanted to see if I could help."

Margie blinked. Somehow, his offer to help didn't make the block of ice in her gut melt any faster. "I've got this, but I appreciate your concern. I wasn't being a smart-ass, just then. Because I really do. Appreciate it, I mean."

She rolled her eyes and gently thumped her head into the wall.

"The thing is, Margie, there's another reason I'm calling, too. I got a situation."

"Yes?" Damn it. Why hadn't she bought more Genny while she was out?

"See, I got a guy in Erie, partner's gone for the rest of the season. It was a sudden kind of a thing."

One. Two. Three. Her left cheek twitched.

"So we're sending you out to Pennsylvania to work with him."

Four. Five. Six. Seven.

"Tomorrow, two o'clock start," Mack said. "That's not a problem for you, is it?"

Eight. Nine. Ten. "No, sir."

* * *

Margie squeezed her eyes shut, her hand still clutched around the receiver, back in its cradle.

"You need a tissue?" Anna asked.

Margie shook her head. Even though her whole face burned with the effort to hold back the pressure, she refused to give in to the tears. Even if Mack Abernathy couldn't see her, she wouldn't give him—any of them—the satisfaction.

Now she had two midseason reassignments on her record. Sure, Abernathy said that the guy's partner left him in the lurch. Stuff happened. But that's what the call-up list was for. Why bust up an established crew when you could call in one of the replacements?

It didn't make sense to her.

She'd go where they sent her, of course, because that was her job. She didn't always like it, but she knew the deal.

Yet she couldn't help but wonder about the timing, the reassignment coming on the heels of her increasing trouble with Donofrio. She couldn't stop herself from worrying about a rumor she'd heard at the academy: that getting bumped around was often a prelude to getting bumped out.

Anna's voice fell softer. "You need...anything?"

"Yeah." Margie cleared her throat, swiped the back of her hand across her eyes, then turned. "There's a couple shopping bags in my room. Would you mind—on your way to work in the morning—dropping them off with the security desk at the stadium? Tell him it's for Wes. He'll know what it's about."

The girl's eyebrows smooshed together in the middle, driving the guilt home. Yeah. It was a weaselly move, not going over there herself. If she were any kind of real friend, she'd pick up those bags and drive over to Wes's motel and say goodbye in person. But if she saw Wes, she was afraid she'd break. And she couldn't break. Not with another month left in the season. He'd understand. She hoped he'd understand. Maybe he'd have done the same thing. Nah. Probably not.

Anna touched her arm again. "You wanna get something to eat? Hang out? We could make margaritas, or—?"

"Sorry," Margie said. "Maybe another time. I gotta be in Erie tomorrow afternoon. I gotta be on the road so friggin' early."

"Sure." Anna sucked in a deep breath, let it out. Then said, stronger now, "Sure. You have a safe trip."

Margie drifted back to her room and paced around the four small walls. Sleep would be damn near impossible. So she packed. She packed, and when it sounded like everyone had gone down for the night, she left.

The note was still in her equipment bag. Instead of turning it in, she decided to keep it. For motivation. Or, if it came to it, for evidence.

* * *

Nervous energy fueled the first fifteen minutes of her trip, her hands gripped like death to the wheel. By the time she got on the highway, her mind whirled with trying to connect the dots of conspiracy. She convinced herself that someone, maybe Donofrio or one of his asshole friends, knew how much she liked working with Wes and had engineered a situation to split them up—trying to get back at her, trying to send a message that they could screw her over, any time they wanted to, in case Donofrio's complaint reports weren't doing the job. As she drove, she worked all the angles, turning the situation around like a play she was deconstructing, until her eyes glazed over and she was jerking her head up, trying to stay awake.

Then she saw a familiar truck stop in the distance. The safe thing would be to pull off, and her body apparently had decided for her, putting on the blinker and easing into the turnoff lane. She parked in the lot and sat awhile, trying to settle her body down. Taking off on a four-hour trip so late in the evening had been a dumbass move; she knew that now. But she couldn't stay in the house a second longer. Her nerves had simmered down some; now she merely felt like she'd been punched in the gut. Like in softball, when a big player barreled into her while she was protecting the plate. And that she just had to lie there, staring into the puffy clouds, catching her breath, until someone put out a hand to help her up. The thing was, Margie never took the hand.

And she didn't want to start.

Well, to hell with Donofrio and the rest of them. Maybe baseball owned her contract, maybe they could send her wherever they wanted at a moment's notice, but she was in charge of how she reacted to it. It didn't have to mean that she was giving in or giving up. It sucked, but this was what she'd signed on for, and having a temper tantrum over a crew reassignment only gave her enemies ammunition. Eyes on the prize, like Timmy always told her.

At least she was still in the Eastern League.

At least she still had the potential to move forward, all the way to the majors.

That reminded her...she ought to call Tim. It was pushing midnight. The game was most likely over by now, and he might be out partying with his new teammates. She hoped they weren't being jerks to him, the new kid plonked into their roster last minute. He was lucky to have teammates, though. She was essentially alone, with just her umpiring partner, whoever that happened to be, and like Big Al said, if you got assigned someone who rubbed you the wrong way, you had to suck it up and figure out how to make it work.

She'd been lucky to have Wes. For a moment, she considered that maybe a change could be a good thing, in the long run. Nothing against her former partner—a lump thickened in her throat about the *former* business. He had all the basic ingredients for a great ump—smart, good instincts, evenhanded, firm but polite—and she could easily see him in the majors. But both of them needed more experience with the game. Maybe working together, for the better part of two seasons in two different leagues, was actually making them complacent. They had slid into an easier pattern lately, hadn't been dissecting the plays so much after the game, and the last time they'd bombed out of town to find a higher-league matchup had been...well, she couldn't remember.

Like Sutton and Durning's move to pawn Margie and Wes off on each other had turned into a plus at the time, maybe this new move would also have a silver lining. Maybe it would backfire on the people who thought this reassignment was supposed to be a punishment for Margie.

While deciding her next move, she bit at a fingernail and gazed off into the milky night sky. If she veered north onto 390 at Avoca she could be in Rochester in a hair over an hour... No. It was too late to visit Dan. Then she'd have to tell him what happened, and she didn't want to be the girl who runs to her guy with all her problems.

But she had two hours until Erie. She could go for it in one gulp, but that would leave her with nowhere to sleep and nowhere to clean up before the game. Yeah. Great first impression when she was trying so damned hard to act like getting reassigned didn't bother her. She glanced around the lot. There was enough traffic to make her feel sort-of comfortable, and she'd passed through here enough that some of the truckers knew her. She could catch a few winks here. First things first, though. She had to take a wicked piss, she had to get something to eat, and she had to see if there was any news about how Tim had done.

She hauled her ass inside and sat at the counter with the truckers, tipping her chin to a couple of them in greeting. Tammy the waitress gave her a big smile and grabbed two coffee mugs from the rack. "Hey, Marge. You and Wes want the usual tonight? He outside watching the stars?"

She shook her head as she plopped onto a stool. "Just one of the usual, thanks."

Tammy's smile dipped a hair. "He okay?"

Margie nodded. "Fine. Visiting family. His sister popped out another kid." Well, most of that was true. There was another baby, and Wes would be visiting after tomorrow's game.

Tammy seemed reassured. She liked Wes. All the waitresses liked Wes. He didn't flirt with them; he was just nice. He asked how their days were going, asked about their families. He showed them pictures of his nieces and nephews. He told them to go outside, when they went on break, and look for Venus or Mars or whatever. He'd learned all that in school, where all the stars and planets were, but he never sounded snobby about it. Waitresses brought him free slices of pie and extra french fries, and his cup of coffee was never empty. She envied his next partner. Whoever got Wes would never appreciate how good he had it, or how much worse he could have gotten.

While she was letting the best coffee in the world roll around her tongue, she nodded at a truck driver she knew. "Hey, Tony." He was a rabid Cubbies fan and always listened to games on the road. Deep in the Finger Lakes region, most likely they could only find New York games on the radio, maybe Philly or Pittsburgh or even Chicago or Montreal if they had a good signal, but she was betting he'd talked to some of his friends in other cities. "You hear anything about the

Atlanta-Cincy game tonight?"

He blinked at her for a couple seconds. "Yeah. I remember something about that. The Reds are lookin' sharp."

"Heard they had a new kid on the mound."

A smile spread across his face. "Yeah. That's what they were talkin' about. Just brought some kid up from the farm. Arm like a rocket. Struck out the side twice."

Margie grinned and dug into her meat loaf and mashed potatoes. At least she'd sleep a hell of a lot better, knowing that. She'd had a feeling Tim would get it done. He got tweaky before a big start, but almost always, he got it done.

After Margie finished eating and jawing around with some of the guys, Tammy set her up with a thermos full of coffee and a sandwich for the road, and Margie caught a few winks in the car. When she woke up a few hours later, some pink rays starting to peer over the horizon, she felt not quite a hundred percent, but a lot less crappy than when she'd hauled out of Binghamton.

She shoved a hand through her hair, then slugged some coffee while watching the sun rise, while the world woke up around her. "Well, Dad." She toasted him with the thermos. "Maybe I'm moving in a different direction today than I thought, but at least I'm still moving."

22

THE REASSIGNMENT

Margie didn't know jack shit about Doug French, the guy Abernathy had told her to look for at the stadium. If she hadn't run out of town so fast, she might have asked Wes if he knew about him. Wes had a good ear to the ground; Margie didn't know where he got his intel— "I pay attention," was all he'd said—but he knew stuff. Now she had to rely on her gut. It wasn't a bad barometer—when she didn't let her temper or her paranoia get the best of her, anyway.

The first time to a new stadium, Margie liked to get in early and case the joint. Walk the infield, feel the wind direction, the angle of the sun. It was a dumb quirk, and she was a little pissed that Warren Durning had given her the habit, but it made her feel more comfortable.

A guy out in short left, wearing umpire gray and blue, was apparently doing the same.

He hadn't seen her yet.

He looked fortyish, a little thick around the middle, and that didn't make her gut happy. It might not mean anything—there were a few older guys in her class at the umpire academy, looking to change careers or supplement what they already had, and they'd been nothing but respectful—but the ones she'd worked with so far had been long in the tooth and bitter. A fortyish ump in Double A might either be mad about not getting moved up fast enough or secretly worried that his best days were behind him, so Margie would have to watch her ass.

He was watching the sky. Hands on his hips, a hint of a smile, passing a cool, even gaze over the clean field, the choreography of the groundskeepers, the floating clouds.

She thought it was the right time to step up, but when she walked toward him, he turned, and that face changed. He looked like someone had just farted. She saw his lips move. She knew what he was saying to himself, and it wasn't, "Hot damn, I'm so happy I get to work with you!"

Margie sighed and marshaled up a professional demeanor. Instead of something ice-breaking like "Congratulations, it's a girl," she merely introduced herself.

He stared at her outstretched hand a moment and nodded, his formerly smiling mouth now a flat line. "Look," he said. "Let's get one thing straight right now. I don't like this. This"—he waved a hand across the field—"is no place for a woman. I'm here to do a job, and if you think that job's gonna be protecting you because you're on some kind of goddamn women's lib crusade, well, you can just think again."

Margie could have kicked him in the shins. She took another deep breath against the burning in her stomach, from him and the last swig of coffee from Tammy's thermos, and reined in her temper. He was testing her, that much was clear.

"I'm here to do a job, too, Mr. French. I hope you'll see for yourself that I don't need handholding."

He grumbled something noncommittal and said, "I got plate today."

"Understood. That's what Mr. Abernathy told me. You'd start on plate. Anything else I should know?"

He thought a moment, shook his head, then pointed at her. "You fuck this up for me, I'll have you busted back to T-ball."

Margie swallowed. He couldn't do that. But he could make trouble for her.

She'd seen trouble, a whole big pile of it. And this guy looked like he couldn't wait to start shoveling more on top of the heap.

23

THE WARNING

As the right-hander on the mound went into his windup, the batter called time and stepped out of the box. It was too late for the pitcher to stop his forward momentum, and the ball landed dead center in the catcher's mitt.

Margie called it a strike.

"No way!" the batter yelled over the sudden mix of outrage and cheers from the stands. "I asked for time."

Margie shook her head. "Even if I'd granted you time, Mr. Thompson, it was after the pitcher set. So that pitch is on you."

"It's bullshit. He hadn't set up yet."

"That's not what I saw, but by all means, keep arguing if you'd like to leave this game early."

Thompson's face was turning red, his eyes narrowed, and he pointed down to Doug French, standing next to second with his arms crossed like king of the hill. French smirked at her and shook his head, as if she'd blown the call, as if it was her fault the kid went to him for a second opinion. Only his manager could request that.

"Your partner there looks like he thinks you were wrong," Thompson said.

No. She would not let French show her up. Or let this kid get under her skin. "Last chance to get back into that batter's box," she said. "I suggest you take it."

Thompson gave Margie a smug grin and lazily stepped into the box.

Then the catcher requested time, which Margie granted, and trotted up to talk to the pitcher.

Fuck you, Margie thought at the batter, then speared French with a glare. *And you, too. So this is what it's gonna cost me, when you deign to let me work the plate? You second-guessing my calls in front of the players?*

According to the rules, they were supposed to switch every few games, but like Durning had, French hogged that dish like he was saving it for democracy.

"Only baserunners are allowed to steal home," she'd said to him when he'd refused to give it up five games in a row. He didn't find the humor in that; he merely gave her a hard look and started walking away. She called his name and he stopped, turned. "Look," she added, "I'm just doing whatever I can to learn how to be a better umpire, and that includes getting more plate experience."

He'd nodded and left the field, but apparently what she said had made a difference.

The next game, he gave it up, but lectured her afterward about what she "did wrong" and yelled that he didn't have time to train her.

"I don't expect you to train me, Mr. French," she'd said, sucking down her anger. "I just want a chance to do my job."

She figured doing that job well would be the best revenge. But no matter how good a game she was having, he still found a way to poke away at her.

She missed Wes. Not only was he a damn good partner, and she knew how lucky she'd been, but he was like a little brother. She hardly saw Tim these days, and her schedule rarely aligned with Dan's since he moved up to Triple A, so it'd been fun to pal around with Wes. Go get some cheap food at a diner after a game, go outside at night and look at the stars. Her stomach knotted when she remembered how she'd slunk out of Binghamton, and she kept putting off calling him to apologize. *When the season's over,* she promised herself. Then she'd put a lot of what she'd gotten wrong right. She had the whole winter to explain it to him. If he'd only listen. She grinned. What if they both got winter ball? That would be so much fun. At least it wouldn't be like working with Old Sourpuss.

Time was up and the players took their positions. Thompson took a few practice swings and stepped into the box; the pitcher wound up and threw.

She called the third strike, a clean beauty of a fastball right down Main Street that caught Thompson flat-footed.

Not even French could argue.

* * *

At least the reassignment had kept her in the Eastern League, so she was glad to still have the comfort of her home base. When Margie returned to Binghamton after one particularly excruciating series in Buffalo, during which she again had to do battle with that pain in the ass Donofrio, a police car was sitting in front of her rooming house. Her first thought was about Anna and the other girls, if anyone had tried to hurt them. Her landlady was on the front porch, watching Margie get out of her car, and the woman's facial expression was clear: the police wanted to talk to her. Her shoulders tensed. Her next thought was that something had happened to Tim. Then she saw the front window. Crap.

"I'll pay for that, I swear. I'm so sorry. When I get paid, I'll—"

An officer walked up to her. "You're Margaret Oblonsky?"

"Margie. Yes." She swallowed.

He smirked. An I-heard-about-you smirk.

"So what happens next, here?" Margie asked.

"That's up to you and the homeowner. Vandalism if it's a personal property crime, we write up a report. But if there's no one to charge..."

Margie shook her head.

"Does that mean no, there's no one to charge? Or is there something else you'd like to tell me?"

She was suddenly aware of neighbors on porches. Next, the reporters would be snooping around. "Can we talk inside?"

The few girls who were home scattered, but Margie was certain they hovered nearby, eavesdropping. Margie and the officer sat in the living room. He declined the landlady's offer of iced tea, but Margie eagerly accepted. Her mouth was so dry she could barely swallow.

When she was fourteen, a cop had come to the house to tell her mother that her father had died. He just went to work one day and never came home.

Margie took a long gulp, but still she found it hard to talk. The officer looked like a nice guy, gazing at her like she could be one of his daughters. But she couldn't let that sway her. If word of this got out—

"So, uh, if I tell you, is that the same as if you were a priest or a doctor or something? Is it, like, off the record?" She knew enough now to say "off the record."

"I work for the public safety, Miss Oblonsky—"

"Margie, please."

"If we have a vandal running around breaking windows, that's something we usually like to stop."

"You don't have to talk down to me like that."

"Sorry," he said. "But if you have information that could help, we would appreciate it."

"And you won't have to report it. Like, to the newspapers?"

He shook his head. "Not unless an arrest is made."

Margie started breathing normally again. Sort of.

The cop shifted on the couch as if not sure how to begin speaking with her. "So I'm finding it interesting that you thought right away that this was about you."

"Um. Well." Should she say anything? She cut her eyes to her equipment bag. It would be so easy to hand him the note. She tugged in a deep breath, sighed it out. "I'm an umpire, Officer. Pissing people off comes with the job. You might know something about that, right?"

He gave her a baleful look. Margie shrugged. "But it's true, right?"

He skipped by that and took out a small notebook and a pen. She eyed it like it might bite her.

"Just in case something is relevant. And yes. I've been to a few ball games. You think an unhappy fan might have done that little renovation out front?"

That worked. "Yeah. There've been a lot of them lately."

"Renovations, or unhappy fans?"

Margie leaned closer. "Look. My mom lives downstate. She thinks I never should have taken this up. I don't want her to read the papers and worry about me. I can take care of myself pretty good, but I'd rather her not hear about stuff like this."

He eyeballed her for a couple of seconds, then pressed a business card onto the table with a sharp snap. "If you ever have the desire to enlighten me further, you can give us a call."

When the officer left, Margie found the landlady in the kitchen. She apologized for the window. Not only did she offer to pay for a new one, she'd call the repair people. The woman's mouth still turned down at the corners.

"It's just a thing," the woman said with a sniff. "A window, it's just a thing. It's not a person."

"But it could have been a person," Margie said. "Someone could have been sitting on the sofa there, and…"

"This was attached to the rock." The landlady pulled a crumpled piece of paper from her apron pocket and held it out to Margie as if it were something she'd fished from the garbage. "I took it off before…"

She opened it. It was another love note. Half the words were misspelled, but the implicit threat to watch her ass still tied her insides into knots.

"I'll…I'll find a new place to live. I don't want to bring this on you, you've been so nice to me and—"

The woman held up her hand. "Where you gonna go? They'll still find you. The reporters, the crazies…they'll still find you. Do I like having my windows broke? No. Do I like my tenants upset, cops coming around? Not especially. But you're in a tough spot, and we girls got to stick together."

The landlady returned to whatever she'd been cooking on the stove. "So I didn't tell the officer about the note. Up to you if you want to keep it that way. But maybe if you don't mind, you could sweep up the glass?"

It was the least she could do.

* * *

After Margie cleaned up the broken glass, she went to her room, cracked a Genny, and completed her ejection reports. Always a good time.

During his at-bat in the top of the fifth inning, when I signaled that Mr. Donofrio was out on a called third strike, he asked where the pitch had been. When I said that the pitch was straight down the middle of the strike zone, he said I was "an incompetent blind cunt," in a voice loud enough to be heard in the dugout. When I warned him that his language was inappropriate, he said I was "a fucking incompetent blind fucking cunt," in a voice loud enough to be heard in the first row of the stands, and I ejected him. He said, "I'm filing a complaint," then remained on the field for approximately five seconds, staring at me. Then he took two steps toward me, and his hands tightened into fists, at which point his manager came out of the dugout and convinced him to leave.

She would have loved to add, "And my partner just stood there with his thumb up his ass the whole time." But the reports were supposed to be purely objective. God knows what Doug French was really doing.

Maybe it was time to have another talk with him, give him another gentle reminder that they were partners and needed to try to work together. They were off to a game in Holyoke, Massachusetts, in a couple days. That could be a good time. He didn't talk much in the car, but if she started the conversation with him there, at least he couldn't walk away from her like he did at the ballpark. Ugh. Holyoke. She didn't know if it was true, but she'd heard a rumor that Dolph Edwards had been sent down again for rehab. The California Angels were in a hot pennant race, and he was one of the hot players who'd gotten them there, but he'd been on the disabled list with a hamstring injury. If he was in Holyoke in August, it meant they were tuning him up for a return to the majors for the post season.

Well, whatever, she thought, penning her name to the bottom of the form and picking up another. She didn't care about DLs or stats or pennant races. She just called the plays.

* * *

Margie had never been happier to see the end of a game in her life. Not since her first outing with Warren Durning had she felt so alone out there. French continued to shake his head at her calls, at least once per game, whether she was right or not. That was total bullshit. He never backed her up when a player argued a decision, leaving her hanging out to dry with three guys in her face, yelling in two different languages. That day's game was exceptional bullshit. She was so fried that when she finally dragged her ass to her boudoir, an unused office about a thousand miles from the field, she lay down on the floor and squeezed her eyes shut so she wouldn't cry.

Maybe she could stay in there until everyone else left. Maybe nobody would notice if she packed her bags and went back home to live with her mother.

She heard guys rumbling around, joking, yelling obscenities to each other. The office probably backed up against some part of the locker room. Some of these old stadiums were like the catacombs. Start wandering down one hallway and who knew where you'd end up. The concrete against her back was cool and soothing. The noise waned; she heard a few names she recognized. A few were guys she'd tossed. She'd have to do the ejection reports later. French never asked for her advice. She wondered what his reports looked like. Come to think of it, she couldn't recall him once tossing a player. They'd given him plenty of reason. One dude swore a blue streak at him, told him he was a big fat fucking loser, right to his face. French just smirked at him and walked away. Margie had even asked him, afterward, why he let the guy get away with that.

"Easy," he said. "I don't give a shit. Let 'em spew. They get it out of their systems and we go on with the game. All this bullshit arguing slows the whole damn thing down."

At least he deigned to travel with her. He didn't say much, and he insisted on taking his car because he wouldn't be caught dead riding in something not made in the USA, but he wasn't a total dick about the expenses the way Durning had been. She thought he might soften up over time. He didn't have to like her, but they had to work together, so she assumed that things would eventually improve, or at least they'd develop a grudging acceptance of the decision Abernathy had handed down.

She was wrong.

The voices were getting fewer and fewer. Water dripped in the distance as the showers went silent, the whir of the blow dryers stopped.

A door opened and closed.

"So, she got plate in Holyoke tomorrow?" a man's voice said.

"Yeah." Margie's ears pricked up. It was French.

Silence. Water came on, fizzled off. "Look. I gotta know you're on board with this," the first man said. "I'm getting a lot of pressure to get him on the roster for the postseason. And I don't want anything screwing it up, you know what I'm saying?"

"Yeah," French said. "I hear you."

"And your little girl, there. I don't like her. She's got it in for him. He gets tossed one more time, that could be a suspension, and that kind of stuff is out of my hands."

The breath froze in Margie's lungs.

"Don't you worry," French said. "I can handle that situation."

"You do, I'll make it worth your while."

Margie sat up so fast her head spun, and she cradled her temples in her hands. Did they mean…? They had to have been talking about Edwards. Tomorrow morning, she and French were heading to Holyoke, where Edwards's team was playing the Bristol Red Sox. Did they really expect her to look the other way? What in the holy frig did "worth your while" mean?

She stayed as still as she could, not moving a muscle. As far as she knew, French didn't know or care where she changed. Just that she was on the field on time.

Two words pulsed through her head: call Abernathy.

* * *

"That's a very serious accusation, Margie," Mack said.

"I'm telling you. I heard what I heard."

Pause. "Perhaps you want to think a moment if that's actually what you heard."

"You don't believe me?"

Pause. "It's just that it's a very serious charge."

"Look. I don't go around ratting people out. He's my partner. You don't rat your partner out. I solve my own problems, Mr. Aber—Mack. You gotta make decisions on the fly sometimes on the field, and I know that I own all of those. I try everything I know how in order to work it out for myself first."

"Well, have you tried working it out with him? Asking him if it's indeed what you heard?"

Right. She was going to saunter up to Doug French, a guy who hated her from day one, and ask if he was on the take.

"That's what you would do, if you were me?"

"Yeah," he said. "That's what I would do."

* * *

While he drove, Doug French drank coffee from an old-fashioned green thermos. It reminded Margie of the type her father brought to work, to the job he hated, because it wasn't baseball, but he only got to hate it for a very short time. French nestled it into a beverage holder that looked more like a sling jury-rigged into a plastic milk crate that sat between them on the bench seat of his station wagon. Funny, he didn't seem like the station wagon type. She'd imagined him driving a crappy old pickup that smelled like dog and had a gun rack across the back window, but maybe he saved that for the off-season. He had a wife, or at least had at one point, because he wore a plain wedding band, but he never talked about her. He never talked much about anything personal. Which she thought strange for a while, especially coming off working with Wes, for whom nothing was off limits. Wes could go from growing up with his sisters to the science of how a slider worked to the constellations they could see that night to a girl he'd met over the winter and kinda-sorta liked, maybe. Worrying that if it got serious, who'd want to put up with his schedule? Margie had to laugh and shake her head about that one. She'd worried about the same thing. What she felt for Dan was way beyond the kinda-sorta stage, but so far, their schedules had them bouncing all over. *At least we'll always have Binghamton.*

She glanced over at French, studying his sharp profile, his tiny steel-blue eyes. He'd been in the military, and the habit of a short haircut had stuck. She didn't know how to ease gracefully into difficult topics. She'd always been a blunt girl. Good or bad, it made life easier for her when everyone understood, no saying one thing and meaning another. But "So, are you on the take?" wasn't something she dared say, although it amused her to imagine his reaction—the squeal of the brakes, barking at her to get out. They had at least twenty-five miles until Holyoke, and she did not relish catching another ride on the Mass Pike.

Was it an army thing? she wondered. The guy who'd issued the command to ease up on Edwards also sounded military, and maybe that habit of obeying orders—or at least siding with your brothers-in-arms—was one that also stuck. Or there was something else altogether going on that Margie didn't understand. It wouldn't be the first time. She didn't want to believe that there was any kind of organized effort to keep *the girl* in line. But more and more often lately, things just smelled wrong.

"Something on your mind, Oblonsky?" French suddenly asked, and Margie froze.

"I, um, not especially."

"Then find something else to do than stare over here. Givin' me the creeps."

Margie studied the pattern of the highway markers, one after the other.

"So, who's pitching today?" she said.

He shrugged. It was a stupid question. They knew which teams were playing and where they had to be. Most umpires had a passing knowledge of the rosters from previous games worked. That was about it. You'd hope to work a game when a particular pitcher was on the mound, one everyone talked about, but it wasn't like they were furnished with the lineups in advance. They often didn't see those until the exchange with the managers before the game. So Margie changed tactics.

"You think Holyoke will have that lefty up?" He was currently the team's ace.

"Wouldn't be the worst thing," French said.

"He's got potential." The small talk was killing her, suffocating her head, words flung round and round. "Last time I worked plate on him, the ball looked like it was heading too far up and outside, but then it broke right down the middle."

For a second Margie thought she saw him smile, but then he reeled it in, his eyes narrowing. Her heart hammered in her chest and she tried to sound casual when she said, "I heard Edwards might get called up for the expansion deadline."

"Jeez. Double up on the coffee this morning?"

Margie sank into her seat. "I was just trying to be pleasant company."

"Well, stop it. I'm driving here."

She didn't know what he'd done in Vietnam, but she supposed that if you could handle being in a war, you could certainly drive a car down a straight highway that wasn't all that crowded while someone else talked. Maybe there was something she didn't know about Doug French.

She let some silence go by. Counted highway lights. Five. Ten.

"About that," French said.

"What, driving?"

"Shaddap. I meant Edwards."

He paused, and Margie turned a little in her seat. Her hand tightened across her blue-jeaned thigh.

"Ease up," French said.

Margie's heartbeat thrummed in her ears. "Whaddya mean, ease up?"

"I mean, don't call him on every little picayune thing. It's like you got a personal vendetta against the guy, and it's not a good look for an umpire."

Margie let that settle for a moment.

He shrugged his right shoulder. "People talk. You're the one always going on about learning how to do a better job. So I'll tell ya. People talk. When the guys upstairs are looking to move us to the next level, they read the evaluations. They consider what those who've worked with that umpire have been saying. If you got a stick up your ass about a particular player, they don't look so kindly. Makes them think you're not giving equal treatment. It could make you look bad. Trust me. I've seen a lot of umpires held back because of...*personal issues*."

Margie stared at him, words clashing in her head on their way out her mouth. Fortunately a few got stuck hard enough to prevent the tsunami of shit she wanted to spew from getting free. The balls he had, calling her for not giving equal treatment! After he'd treated her like a total incompetent since the day they met? Margie took a deep breath. The goal here was not to antagonize him. The goal here was to figure out what he was up to, and take it from there.

"Equal treatment," she said. "That's a load. Yeah. I don't give equal treatment. I give what a player earns. When I'm on the field, I call the plays. If a guy follows the rules, we don't have trouble. If a guy doesn't follow the rules? Trouble."

French nodded, pinching his lips together. He tapped his left index finger on the wheel, as if it was helping him decide what to say next. "Margie." He said her name like he was trying to give fatherly advice. "Ease up on Edwards, okay? I can't tell you any more about that, but if you give a shit about getting into Triple A, moving up to the majors, you gotta let one go sometimes." He paused. "And this game, it would be a good time to let one go."

Was that a threat? "You're telling me to look the other way. That if he pulls any shit to let him get away with it?"

A muscle twitched in his jaw as he made a hard veer into the left lane to pass a slower vehicle, and Margie grabbed the door handle to steady herself. "This is bigger than your fucking high-ass principles, Oblonsky. Maybe you'll understand that one day."

"No."

French groaned and slapped a palm against the wheel. "Fucking stubborn..."

She crossed her arms over her chest. "If I see that he's safe, he's safe. If I see that he's out, he's out. If he breaks the rules, he gets what's coming to him."

French shot her a dark look, and his hand tightened over the leather cover, his knuckles going white. "Fine," he said, his voice pitched higher than usual. "You're on your own, then."

Margie flopped back against her seat and suppressed an urge to roll her eyes. As if she hadn't been on her own from the first day they met.

24

THE VIDEOTAPE

The graveyard shift bored the hell out of Fitz. Covering high school, college, and rookie-league games was its own kind of dull, but at least he hadn't been stuck in the newsroom. Out there, he'd had people to watch, drama to spin, the lead always dancing in his head for the next story. His two cents weren't always appreciated, and his editors often rewrote his headlines, but the work kept his mind active. Around every corner lurked the potential to find a diamond in the rough. He once picked out a kid throwing heat in a high school regional tournament, a kid with a cannon for a right arm who had catchers grumbling about how hard he threw. That was five years ago. The kid was currently pitching lights out for the Yankees, on his way to a Cy Young season.

Sitting in a radio booth with a microphone in the middle of the night was a whole different breed of dull. A dull that made his eyes burn, that numbed him all over and made him want to punch himself in the face just for variety. New York was a sports town, and he was working for a fledgling sports-talk radio station, so there were callers to contend with. But it was mostly crackpots and bored night-shifters who wanted to rail on about the dumbest things. Why players spit. The way they wear their socks. He did get the occasional caller who had something intelligent to discuss and couldn't get through to talk to the big guys during the day, but most of the time it was insomniacs, cranks, and oceans of silence. There was a sliver of a bright side to pulling the overnight. Because he only worked with one producer, a guy Fitz swore was a vampire, he didn't get a lot of supervision. Who the hell wanted to be in the studio at two, three in the morning?

During those awful, dead stretches, Fitz made his own fun. He'd get Trevor to rack up a canned interview or three and watch replays of games on the monitors. He'd talk about his fantasy baseball teams, spinning up scenarios of players past and present. DiMaggio. Bench. Pete Rose. He liked the scrappy guys, the fighters. The elegant, athletic god types—the Walt Fraziers, the Nolan Ryans—were like another species to him. He liked the guys who fought and scrapped and hustled. They were more fun to watch. A colleague back in Wisconsin, for a joke, made him a video of famous baseball arguments: bench-clearing brawls, old school managers kicking dirt on umpires. He understood the passion. If you live for the game, you're throwing your heart and guts into it. If you knew you got that tag down in time to get the guy out at home, in time to save the game, the series, the season, but the call doesn't go your way, you'd lay down your sporting life fighting for it.

The guy still sent Fitz videos, and it made sitting with the silent phones in the middle of the night more palatable.

The radio deal wasn't the *Sports Illustrated* byline of his boyhood dreams, but it was damn better than the life he'd been living. It was better than eating stale sandwiches in his car on the way to the next game while composing headlines that would be rewritten, while trying not to think about the rattle in his engine and how much it would cost to fix. And after the game, getting on the phone before midnight to file his stories, dictating them to the kid in the newsroom if he couldn't find a teletype, and who the hell had those in the middle of nowhere?

In high school, he'd been too skinny and sickly to play sports, so he'd messed around with radio, covering his school's basketball games, nobody caring that he hadn't known what he was doing. But he was in New York now, in the union, using the same equipment the big guys used during the day. The station owner liked his voice. He said it reminded him of "the guy on the next barstool," which was fitting, because that was often how he related to people.

So now he fielded the occasional call, read scouting reports, and watched games on the monitors. He had to know the hometown teams, of course. He kept up with other sports, like cramming for finals, but outside of baseball, the others didn't thrill him as much. Baseball had been the soundtrack of his childhood. His old man lived for the Brooklyn Dodgers, and part of him died when they left Ebbets Field for Los Angeles in 1957. He always took Fitz with him when he went to the ballpark. Dad liked to play announcer, calling the action like Red Barber and Vin Scully and, later, Mel Allen and Phil Rizzuto, when he reluctantly shifted his allegiance to the Yankees. Maybe that's where Fitz got his knack for boiling things down.

He glanced at the clock, which was always a bad move. Time seemed to be going backward.

"Sunday," he muttered to the vampire, who merely gave a belated shrug. "Who the hell listens to the radio on a Sunday night?" So far, he'd had three calls: one guy who had a bug up his ass about the Mets' new uniforms, a wrong number, and some crazy lady with the thickest Long Island accent he'd ever heard. She wanted a pepperoni pizza and wouldn't believe him when Fitz tried to tell her she had the wrong place. Then he stopped answering. The vampire was nodding off, so who would care?

Finally, he got so bored he started cleaning up the desk. The day guys didn't like anyone touching their setup, but the piles of shit were getting to him.

Under a poison pile of *Sports Illustrated*s, *New York Post*s, and AP wire reports was a videotape with a note on it. "For Fitz," it read.

Amused, he popped it into the VCR—pretty much the only piece of equipment the union allowed him to operate in this place— and sat back in his chair. It probably showed some donnybrook because the guys he worked with also knew about his thing for them.

There was a minute or so of dead space and some static jumping around, but eventually a baseball game appeared. The recording sucked. Maybe it was a bootleg from some small-town station that covered it. Stuff like that made the rounds.

He squinted as he started recognizing the situation. From the soft roll of mountains in the distance and the flags flying in the outfield, it looked like a double-A game, maybe the Eastern League. Then he grinned. "Well, there's my old friend Mr. Edwards," he said. The vampire stirred a moment, and his eyes once again slid closed. He knew that little foot-to-foot dance Dolph Edwards did on first, trying to rattle the pitcher. Trying to make trouble, draw a throw. Edwards was always a threat to steal, and he made plenty of pitchers nervous. Sometimes they didn't even attempt to stop him. They'd give him second rather than risk a quick pickoff move that the first baseman might not be able to catch.

The pitcher rifled a throw to first. Edwards dove back. The next pitch was a serviceable fastball from the stretch. The batter didn't swing, and the umpire called a strike. The batter said something that sounded like, "I don't think so." He couldn't see the ump's reaction, but the body language said he wasn't putting up with any nonsense.

Fitz's brow furrowed as he reached for his wire reports. When had Edwards been sent down to the minors? Last he heard, the California Angels had put him back on the roster, but maybe there was some kind of new trouble. "Well, bud," Fitz said, watching Edwards brush off his uniform, "looks like you're playing on borrowed time. Or somebody's looking out for you."

The pitcher threw a strike, and the batter didn't like the call. The camera switched angles, covering first, and Fitz gave the base ump a squint. He thought he recognized the burly gentleman as Doug French. He'd been kicking around the minors for a while and called a mediocre game at best—certainly not worthy of Fitz's fantasy team.

Edwards crouched lower, elbows braced on his thighs, hands brushing his knees. Fitz was dead-nuts certain he'd be running on the next pitch. Three and two, why not? Sure enough, when the pitcher went into his windup, Edwards tucked his head and went for it.

The hit-and-run was on, and the batter poked a grounder into right. The fielder, playing deep, had to charge in to scoop it up, and he made an off-balance throw to second. It had the makings of a double play, especially when, about three-quarters of the way to the bag, Edwards slowed for some reason Fitz couldn't fathom. Maybe he was unsure if the hit had been hard enough to get him over. Edwards looked like a sitting duck now, a sure out at second because of his base running indecision and the long reach of the second baseman's arm, now stabbing at the errant throw. But Edwards turned it on and charged the man covering second, trying to break up the double play and divert the throw to first.

What the hell? Fitz blinked. He had to back the tape up and watch again, because he wasn't sure he'd seen that right. Edwards dove at the last minute and slid wide, off the base path, barreling right into the second baseman, who'd been stretched to his limit trying to stay on the bag while throwing the ball to first.

The base ump, who was watching the batter running to first, spun around and called Edwards safe. But then, on the lower right of the screen, the visiting manager's arm shot toward the plate ump, asking for an appeal.

The plate ump called Edwards out. And the runner behind him.

Well, that made more sense. It clearly looked like interference. Nothing had been officially called yet. The announcers riffed for a moment about what had happened, pointing out that, upon the appeal, the base ump had signaled that he was deferring to his partner behind the plate. The announcers confirmed interference just as Edwards jumped to his feet to argue, screaming at the plate ump who'd called it. The hairs on the back of Fitz's neck stood at attention. The camera zoomed into the argument. Fitz gulped. He knew that umpire.

25

THE FORFEIT

Margie had been attempting to get Holyoke's manager off the field when the first baseball landed. She only saw it in her periphery in a lot of other movement—arms and legs and screaming mouths—but she had other things to concern herself with. The manager looked a few blood pressure points from a coronary, for one. For two, where the hell was French?

Yeah. That's right. He said I'm on my own.

Well, fuck him. She tossed a few more players. Nobody paid any attention. Some of the Bristol players and a few of the fans were attempting to break up the melee. A handful of security guys were on the field, too, which helped some. But the noise. The noise from the crowd, the noise from the screaming players and coaches and managers—she could hardly hear herself think. Then the second ball—it was commemorative baseball day, of all things—landed on the field. Then the garbage.

Four minutes had gone by. Five. Six. It was not safe to continue play, despite the warnings Margie had given, despite the announcers' call for calm. A threat of a forfeit only made the Holyoke fans angrier, only inflamed the face of the Holyoke manager.

She heard him spit something about their season being on the line.

"So get your guys off the fucking field already."

Then someone pushed her. She flew forward, smack into the Holyoke manager, who started bitching like a little girl that Margie had touched him.

Edwards picked up a bat, and with a menacing glare, took two steps toward her.

"That's it!" Margie called the forfeit.

As plate umpire, she had the right to make the call, although it would stick harder if she had some backup. Where was French? Where was he when the play went down, where was he while the manager was screaming, when the unknown agitator pushed her, when the baseballs and garbage started flying?

For her own safety, she had to get off the field. Maybe if she left, the crowd would be taken out of it. She would no longer be standing there, tossing players and fending off blows, the lightning rod for their frustration.

Luckily she spied a security guard. He reached for her, and she let him help her off the field.

"You need a ride?" he said, close to her ear.

She shook her head. French had all the motel info in his car. They'd come directly to the stadium. The office she'd dressed in locked from the inside, and she asked the guard to walk her there. She'd stick around until things simmered down enough to slip out. If French took off without her, she'd deal with that later.

There was a foam exercise mat rolled up in a corner. She spread it across the concrete floor and lay on her back, attempting to calm down. She could still hear the shouting, the announcer's muffled attempts to get the spectators to leave. Not her problem anymore. Once she called the game, she was no longer in control.

They would blame her. Sure as knowing that French had set her up, she also knew they'd pin the blame on her.

"This is bullshit." She got up, grabbed her equipment bag, and pulled out a few ejection reports. She didn't know how to write one for having essentially ejected an entire team. Maybe that was a different form. So on the back of one, she began writing point by point what led to her decision to call the forfeit.

She didn't notice time passing and barely registered the thinning noises coming from outside her room. Eventually, a soft knock broke through. Her stomach clenched.

"Yeah?"

"Ms. Oblonsky? Security. Everything okay in there?"

She looked up from her writing. Every single blank back of her ejection forms had been filled, and she was out of antacid pills. Everything was not all right.

"You see Doug French around?" she asked. "The other umpire?"

"Didn't see another umpire. There's something taped to the door, here," he said. "Looks like a phone message? You want that?"

All the air left Margie's lungs. "Let me guess. Call Mack?"

* * *

At least she knew the name of the motel where they were supposed to check in after the game. She had the guard take her there, but no reservation was listed in her name. She asked if Doug French was staying there, but the not very helpful woman behind the counter mumbled that she wasn't allowed to give out that information. Which was bullshit. Margie had called at least two dozen hotels where Timmy had been staying, and she'd been put through each time. French was ducking her. Big fucking military hero was hiding from a girl. At least she was able to convince the woman to let her call Abernathy from the desk phone. Maybe his office would put her up somewhere else until she could figure out how to get back to Binghamton.

"That was quite the show today." He did not, however, sound like he was amused by it.

She opened her mouth to explain. But didn't really know how to. "I had to call it," she said finally. "In the interest of everyone's safety. It'll be in my report."

"In the interest of everyone's safety," he said, "and your own, I think it's best that we sit you out the rest of the season."

"The rest of…" Her voice came out as a squeak. She cleared her throat. "Excuse me, Mr. Abernathy? Mack. If you could just let me explain—"

"It would be better to meet in person. Please call my secretary in the morning to set it up."

* * *

Damn. Fitz grinned and sat back in his chair, eager to see what happened next. He didn't know whether to start writing this up or make some popcorn.

Not budging an inch, Oblonsky glared as good as she got. The camera pulled back, wobbled a moment. The manager strode out, taking Edwards's side. Then both of them were yelling at her. Even Fitz could lip-read what Edwards said. Oblonsky whipped off her mask and tossed him out. No emotion on her face, just flat-out gave the signal. Then she tossed the manager. But neither of them would leave, or stop yelling and pointing. The other team's manager came out and backed up his second baseman, who continued to defend the call. Now all he could see was a ring of uniforms around Oblonsky, and where the hell was French? The camera wasn't on him. Fitz couldn't tell whose arm reached in and shoved Oblonsky, but by then, it was too late. Both benches emptied.

Heart racing, Fitz leaned forward to get a better look at the screen. Oblonsky was attempting to restore order, that much he could see, but her gesticulations weren't enough, and she tossed a few more guys. Edwards picked up a bat. Finally, security had to come out and help clear the field, but damn, it took a long time.

The announcers couldn't get a bead on what was happening, but one of them kept complaining that the call was wrong. Fitz disagreed, but to make sure, he backed the tape up again. And again. Oblonsky had been right. It was interference, plain as day. He froze the screen and checked the AP wire reports. When the hell was this game played? Surely if it had raised such a stink, he would have heard about it by now. Then he found the notice, buried under a pile of crap. Holyoke lost the game to the Bristol Red Sox on a forfeit because of security concerns and all the fighting. A couple suspensions had been handed down. The game had only been a couple days ago. He'd spent the afternoon helping Nonna do some things around the apartment. He'd felt guilty for working so much lately, so he stayed for dinner, coffee, watched one of her game shows. But damn. If he'd only known about this.

He grinned. He still needed a topic for his weekly column. It was a piddly-ass paper, one of those weekly shoppers in Flushing, but they needed to fill column inches like everyone else. And they'd wanted a sports page. So he'd taken the deal. When he agreed to it, he was doing a friend a favor. Maybe three people read him, including his parents, so he eventually started writing whatever he damn well pleased. Depending on the season, he wrote about what was hot. Who was an overpaid crybaby, who didn't get what he deserved, the unsung heroes of the game.

Maybe one of those unsung heroes could be Margie Oblonsky.

Maybe the world needed to know what she was trying to do.

Maybe, for once, she'd agree to actually speak to him on record.

Fitz advanced the tape and smiled.

26

THE MEETING

"Portland. I have to go to friggin' Portland and meet with this guy."
Back in Binghamton, Margie threw a few things into her bag while
Anna looked on, worry pinching her face.

"You want company?" she said.

Margie set down the socks she'd been balling up and let out a
long breath. It would have been nice not to truck all the way up there
by herself. All things being equal, she would have loved to call Wes,
but she didn't know where he was working. Even if he could get
away, would he want to talk to her, considering how she'd skulked
out of town? In her mind she underlined the item about Wes in her
apology list. "Thanks," Margie said. "But I think it's better if I do this
on my own."

Driving to Portland meant heading across the Berkshires,
skirting around Boston and up 95 through the down east portion of
Maine. But with her thoughts focused so hard on how she should
handle herself, she couldn't enjoy the scenery, and much too soon,
she was sitting in an office waiting for Abernathy.

The pleasantries were stiff, formal, and Margie's stomach was
eating itself from the inside out.

He straightened a few things on his desk.

She could no longer take the silence. "Mr. Abernathy. Let me
explain. I got it all here." She fumbled with her satchel, and papers
spilled out all over his floor. Her pulse pounded in her ears, and her
palms dampened as she leapt from her chair to corral them. And
damn him, he sat there and let her, his damn pencil tap-tap-tapping
against the top of his desk.

"Margie…" The word was a warning, an apology, a hand around
her shoulder showing her the door. "Please. Sit."

She found something deep in herself then, her nine-year-old self winging the ball back to Timmy in the backyard, pissed as hell that they wouldn't let her sign up for Little League. The first of many insults for loving baseball and being born a girl. "No," she said. "This is crap. I know my game. I go wherever I'm assigned. I work with whoever I'm partnered with. My evaluations were pretty good last year, so apparently I don't totally suck—"

"Margie."

Something in his tone shut her up. She sat in her chair. Clutched her fingers together atop her thighs. A cramp was starting in her lower back.

"You tell me, Margie." He opened a manila folder atop the desk and spread a few papers across it. "If you were in my shoes. If you had an umpire with this many complaints filed against her. And now this."

The words froze in Margie's throat. She swallowed. "I did what I had to do in that game, Mr. Abernathy. If you'd been there. If you'd been in my shoes…"

He picked up one of the sheets of paper, eyebrows climbing as he examined it. Margie saw that the page had "fuck" written on it about seventeen times. He squinted at her. "Can't leave her personal vendettas off the field."

"Is that from Edwards? Donofrio?" No. It couldn't have been. Neither of them knew words like "vendettas."

He turned the paper over, then sat with his hands folded on his desk, a mildly scolding expression on his face.

Getting pissed off wasn't going to work. This wasn't her turf; she had no home field advantage. Plus, if she went all hothead, it would be playing right into the accusations that women were too emotional for this job.

She settled her hands in her lap, crossed her feet at the ankle, and tightened them there, as if they could anchor her to a state of professional calm. "His slide was illegal. It was clearly interference; it was clearly an intentional attempt to interfere with the double play. After my partner initially called Edwards safe, Bristol's manager asked for an appeal. My partner deferred to me, and I made the call."

He tilted his head slightly, as if waiting for her to say something that pleased him. Her chest nearly burst with the strain of holding back the words she wanted to say to defend herself.

"Walk me through it again," Abernathy said.

Margie took a deep breath and started over. When she got to the illegal slide, and added that this wasn't the first time she'd seen Edwards do it, Abernathy's index finger shot toward her. "There," he said.

"What *there*, Mr. Abernathy?"

He almost spat the words. "Personal vendettas. I can't have that. I can't have that in my league. I don't like the way it looks. It looks like you're gunning for the guy."

"Because he's dirty."

Silence. Margie went on. "He doesn't look right. You ever get a good look at him? I've been reading up on players taking hormones, I learned about it at the academy. It makes them super aggressive and..."

Mack's mouth tightened like he'd been sucking lemons. "You're a doctor, now? You're just full of accusations. About Edwards. About your partner. We can't have this controversy. Umpires have to rise above. Beyond reproach. Maybe you need some time to think about this arrangement we have with you."

Then it dawned on Margie. "You're firing me."

He let out a long, slow breath. "It's out of my hands pending investigation."

"Out of your hands? You're the league president, you—"

His words were as tight as his jaw. "I'd suggest you choose what you're about to say with some care."

Margie dug her hands into the pleather meat of her cushion. "I played it right. Mack. If there was something I needed to work on, I worked on it. I improved at the plate. If I was given someone new to work with, I made the best of it. I had two partners who hated the fact that I existed, who resented being teamed up with me, and I stuck. I made the calls I thought it was right to make, I was promoted from Class A, and now I'm getting punished for it, for doing the best job I knew how? With all due respect, if there's something I'm not understanding, I hope you can explain it to me."

He tapped a stubby index finger on the table. "Look. I got a league full of umpire crews to run. And that responsibility's a hell of a lot bigger than one person, one career. You're what, not even

twenty-one?"

Margie didn't like where this was going. "I will be. Soon."

He put out his hands in a gesture of supplication, of a plea for her to be reasonable, whatever the hell that meant to him. Walk away and not make trouble for him?

"There you go," he said. "A whole life ahead of you. I gotta be honest, Margie. I expected better from you. And now...well, as of right now, I got nowhere to put you next season."

She waved a hand across the folder. "Because of this. Because I wanted to do my job right. You just got done telling me the league is bigger than one person. And now you're taking Edwards's word over mine. Because he puts more asses in the seats."

He didn't answer.

Margie cleared her throat, letting the silence build. Wondering if she should mention calling a lawyer. Wondering if her mother really did know Gloria Steinem.

"There's more," Abernathy finally said. "I'd hoped it wouldn't come to this. There were rumors. About you. Fraternizing with players."

Margie's mouth fell open. "Fraternizing with...?" She blinked a few times. Dan. Who would be complaining about Dan? They hadn't gotten together once since the All-Star break. And they were in different leagues. Different levels. She struggled with what to say, if anything, but silence felt like the better option at the moment.

He slid another complaint form from the stack. He picked it up and read. "Umpire made calls favoring her boyfriend's team..."

That's it. Margie reached for the paper but he wouldn't relinquish it. "Wait a minute. That was a spring training game I worked. One game. Do those complaints also say that I tossed Dan Monroe out of that game? Does that look like I'm favoring his team?"

He flipped through the forms. A fly buzzed on the windowsill. Margie wanted to crush it. "Who wrote those complaints?" she said through clenched teeth.

"That's confidential."

"If Donofrio or Edwards wrote that, it's crap."

He said nothing. Which made her think the complaints went wider. There were maybe five, ten more pieces of paper in that stack.

"Look. I don't give a damn which team wins. I'd toss my own

brother if he broke the rules." She paused. "I never even worked the plate for him."

"And that's definitely something we can't have here. It doesn't look good for you. It doesn't look good for the game."

"So move me," Margie said. "I'll go to another league."

"I wish it were that easy. It's—"

"Yeah. Out of your hands." She slapped her palms against the armrests as she got up. "Well, what now? I go home for the winter and wait for someone not to call me?"

The firm set of his mouth softened, only for a second. Something crossed his face then. She wasn't sure what it was. Like maybe he was on her side but testing her, seeing how much shit she could take. "Just…lay low," he said. "Try to stay out of trouble."

Margie stared at the folder on Abernathy's desk. Her hands were going numb, her stomach doing some kind of Latin dance maneuver. Players threatened to file complaints about her all the time. But it always sounded like bullshit to her. The last resort of a guy who'd gotten caught, the last resort of a bully who didn't like that she—or any umpire, for that matter—had the upper hand. She knew Donofrio sent in complaints, because he told her, every time. And she'd laughed. She didn't think they'd amount to anything. But that folder was looking so damn thick it made more than her stomach ache.

Mack had been calm. He listed chapter and verse why the evidence didn't look good. For her. For baseball. The suspension went through the end of the official season. It didn't cover postseason. It didn't cover winter ball. Or next year. She wondered if that meant they were keeping their options open. Maybe thinking, like before, that she'd behave if they gave her a time out. She wanted to ask about that, but she didn't dare. Her insides were flaming with the urge to curse and yell and sweep all those papers off his desk. To scream at him that she was doing the best she knew how, that she'd done all the things her teachers had asked, that her skills were improving, that she'd put up with the likes of Warren Durning and Doug French and Chip Donofrio and dildos in her changing room, all in the name of learning how to be a better umpire.

But that would be exactly what they wanted. They wanted her to play the hurt little girl, to prove that women didn't belong and couldn't be depended on to be the levelheaded dispensers of baseball justice. She sucked it all down and clasped her fingers together, trying to imagine an exit strategy that showed him she was willing to play ball but not willing to compromise her values, or her belief that nobody was above the game.

Not on his home field, though.

"Am I allowed to have copies of those?" Margie nodded toward the folder. "Like maybe with the names off, if they're supposed to be confidential?" If she was going to build a case for herself, she needed the evidence. From her mother's warnings over the years about getting everything in writing, she knew that she was allowed to at least ask.

His mouth pursed. He didn't quite meet her gaze. His short, stubby fingers tucked the paperwork together into a single stack and he closed the file. "Leave my secretary an address where you'd like it sent," he said in a monotone.

Margie nodded, holding it together. Feeling the pressure behind her eyes, the catch in her throat. She knew that if she spoke, she'd be betrayed by her anger, and she refused to show him that. She pushed all of her strength into an expression that was firm but respectful, into a smile that she hoped didn't look too fake.

"Thank you for coming, Ms. Oblonsky." Abernathy scraped his chair back as he stood. His eyes looked so kind, his smile so grateful. Maybe he only looked grateful because she'd made his life easier. That because she'd come here, it meant she didn't want to make trouble for him.

Apparently he didn't know her very well.

He stuck out his hand. His eyes about level with her forehead. "We'll be in touch," he said.

Margie watched the hand a moment before she shook it, remembering some tidbit from high school history about how the symbolism of an outstretched hand was meant to prove that the parties involved weren't armed. But Margie already felt the knife in her back.

She gave the secretary the address, although she didn't have much confidence that she'd ever see that package.

146

* * *

She barreled out of the boss's office. Then she saw him. Tall, rumpled, those weird oversized glasses perched on his beak of a nose. "Great. What do you want?"

"Always a pleasure, Ms. Oblonsky."

She kept walking, and Fitzgerald fell into step behind her. "You a glutton for punishment or something?"

"Maybe."

She spun back to him, then turned ahead. "All we been through, I suppose you might as well call me Margie."

"Be still, my foolish heart."

"Shut the hell up." She slowed a step. "Aren't you supposed to be in New York?"

"I had the afternoon off."

Margie pressed her fists into her hips. "And Mr. Big Shot New York Sports Guy leaves it all to chase around after my story."

"Don't flatter yourself. Who says I'm here for you?" He sniffed, waved a hand toward the Portland Sea Dogs stadium down the road. "There are fifty-some players here. Any one of them could be the story."

She glared. "Yeah. And how many of them do you see coming out of a meeting with Abernathy."

He grinned.

She pointed at him. "No. I'm not talking to you." Then she kept walking. He dogged after her. Part of her felt like reaching back and swatting him. As if she needed another meeting with the president. This time for getting into a scuffle with a reporter.

"You'll have to talk to me sometime," he said.

"And pray tell...Fitz, is it? Why the fuck is that?"

"Because I'm the only one who can prove you've been set up."

She slowed. "Get real."

He gestured to a small diner they passed along the quaint street. "Let me buy you lunch and I'll explain."

"Are you kidding me? After what when down in there? I can't be seen with you. My career's already in the toilet. I don't want to flush it altogether."

"Anywhere you want, then. Back in New York, if you want."

She checked her watch. It had taken her six hours to get here. She did the reverse math, and she could be back to...

Fuck that. She didn't have a game tomorrow. She could be any damn place she wanted to. "You drove up here?" she said.

He nodded, and she gave him an address.

27

THE SETBACK

Margie pulled into her mother's driveway as the sunset was fading into the trees behind the house. She probably should have called first, but she just wanted to get home. Her mother was mopping the kitchen floor. When she saw Margie's face the mop clattered to the linoleum. The hug was long and hard. Mom had to know. Her kids didn't come home until their seasons were over. She grabbed two beers and bade Margie sit at the kitchen table. The windows were open. Cicadas thrummed outside. The nights were turning cooler. Goosebumps prickled Margie's arms. Mom's face hardened more with every detail Margie chose to reveal. Minus the death threats, of course. And the broken window.

"Sons of bitches," Mom said finally, smacking her bottle on the table. "Friggin' son of a bitch friggin' cowards. Tomorrow morning. Tomorrow morning, we're calling the big guns."

"Mom…" Margie scrubbed a hand over her forehead, imagining the house filling with the entire staff of *Ms.* magazine. Gloria Steinem making another pot of coffee. "I never wanted this to be about that. What really pisses me off is that part of me feels like I'm being railroaded. Like someone set me up, like I was let into this party as a joke, that they were expecting me to fail. And when that didn't happen, they made sure of it."

The index finger came out. The eyes sharpened. "Margaret Elizabeth Oblonsky. Don't you think for one minute this isn't about equal rights." She grabbed a pad of paper from the junk drawer. "All right." She poised the pen over the page. "Here's what we're doing. I want names. I want names of all your partners, all those league presidents…"

"No."

The shoulders sagged. "Honey. All right." She pushed the pad a few inches away. "You've had a long drive. It's been a tough day. Sleep on it, and we'll strategize in the morning."

She tightened her fingers around the bottle. "A reporter's coming in the morning."

Mom's eyes narrowed.

"It's okay. I think."

Mom's eyes narrowed more. "Let me talk to him."

"Mom."

"You're too close to the situa—"

"Because I was there?"

"Exactly. Emotions get in the way. Believe me, I know what I'm talking about. If you don't want my people up here, I could be your, whadda they call that? Liaison?"

"Mom. I really don't think that's a good idea. If he sees that, he's gonna write it like I'm friggin' Joan of Arc or something. All I want is to do my job. And keep moving up, if I'm good enough or if there's ever an opening, get into the major—"

"Timmy," Mom said.

"What?"

Mom snapped her fingers, and her cheeks rounded with an impish smile. "We'll call Timmy. He knows the game now, from the inside; he's seen you work. From a player's perspective. He'll tell that reporter—"

"My brother. You're going to ask a New York sportswriter to talk to my *brother* for an unbiased viewpoint about my umpiring skills, which are being called into question for being biased. Yeah, uh…no."

"Timmy's trustworthy. He has those blue eyes, that innocent face, like your father."

"Timmy's…" Good God. Where the hell was Timmy, now, anyway? She searched her head for some kind of schedule. About a week left in the regular season for Double A. The majors had a bit to go yet. His pitching had had its ups and downs, and the last time she'd talked to him he'd had a decent outing the night before, but she'd heard that tone in his voice, high and reedy. That walking on a tightrope about to crap his pants tone.

Then it occurred to her. Fitz, even though he was kind of an asshole, was a decent reporter. He might have already talked to Tim.

Tim might already know what happened in Portland, and probably through the grapevine he most definitely had to know what happened in Holyoke. Everything had been going too fast and furious during that debacle for her to call him. Had he been trying to reach her? And Dan. Had he been trying to call her, too?

"When…" Her voice had climbed half an octave and broke. She cleared her throat and started over. "When did you talk to Tim last?"

Mom's eyes bolted upward as if the answers were on the water-spotted ceiling—Margie made a mental note to look into that over the winter—and shrugged. "A week, maybe. I don't blame him, he's busy."

Margie debated calling him now. No. He'd be at the ballpark. It killed her a little inside that he and Dan might know about Holyoke, both of them worrying about her, or be worrying more that they tried to reach her at the boarding house and she didn't get back to them.

"I'll call him later," Margie said. Mom produced a schedule from a kitchen drawer and smoothed it out lovingly on the table. It was stained with coffee and had been folded many times. Margie smiled. For the first time in a long time, she really believed that if *she* had a schedule like that, Mom would be treating it the same way. She hid the swell of emotion in her throat with a slug of her beer and, following the schedule, found the game he'd be playing. Mom had marked each of Tim's starts with a red dot. At least Margie was relieved that Tim wouldn't be starting tomorrow. Whatever shit was going on with her, she didn't want to throw him off his game.

"So what's going on with that ceiling?" Margie said finally.

"We had a downpour, few weeks back. And then that. I haven't had a chance to call anyone yet."

"I'll take care of it. Maybe the roof needs an easy patch. Or a gutter's clogged—"

"Margie. Honey." Her mother's strong, bony hand came down over hers. "You don't gotta do that. You just got home. Relax, for frig's sake."

Margie shook her head. She had to keep moving. Because when she wasn't moving, she started thinking. And she didn't want to think.

She'd replaced three burned-out lightbulbs and a fuse, and had fixed a floorboard in the laundry room that kept popping up. She

151

tried to feign interest in a sitcom her mother was watching, but it was all so ridiculous.

Finally, she figured it was time to call Tim.

All she got was a recording. She didn't know how to explain what had happened, at least in a way that would fit on the machine. All she could come up with after the beep was "I got suspended again. I'm at Mom's. Call me."

She hung up and stared at the receiver, willing it to ring.

Maybe Tim was somewhere else, and he'd heard about this, and he was trying to call her.

Most likely he'd be angry for her, his voice deep with brotherly protection. He'd talk about getting Dan and busting some skulls. He'd talk about plunking Edwards if Tim ever had to pitch to him. But she couldn't imagine her John-Boy innocent brother plunking anyone. So she'd say, "No, don't do that. Or if you do, at least make it look like an accident."

And maybe he'd laugh, and she'd feel a little bit better. She'd tell him that a reporter might be calling, and—

She grabbed the phone and redialed, waited for the beep. "It's me again. If a reporter named Fitzgerald calls, don't talk to him. Unless you talk to me first."

After she'd hung up, she started getting the oddest feeling about Fitzgerald. That maybe he really was on her side.

Yeah, right. If it was making him look good, he'd be behind her all day long.

There was one more call she needed to make, and she smiled when she finally tracked him down. "Margie." Dan's voice wrapped around her like one of his big bear hugs. "I've been trying to reach you. I heard about that game. Man, that sounded rough."

"You have no idea," she said. "Look, I really need to talk to Tim tonight, so I shouldn't tie up my mom's line too long. I just wanted to, you know, touch base."

"Well, thanks. I'm glad to know you're okay. Wait. If you're at your mom's..."

"Suspension city. For the rest of the regular season."

"Aw, that stinks."

"Yeah." She sniffed. "Yeah, it does."

"Hey. I'm in town three more games, then we got an off day before we head to Toledo. Wouldn't be much to drive down your way."

She wanted to see him. Hold on to him for a while, build some strength, soak up some comfort. But to drive all the way to Saugerties from Rochester and back, only to turn around and go to Ohio? That was crazy. And with that "fraternization" complaint, she couldn't risk it. "Thanks, but I don't want to put you through that."

"You're sure?"

"Uh-huh. End of the season's close enough. I think I'll keep."

He hesitated a moment, then said, "Okay. But you need anything, and I mean anything, you let me know."

28

THE BULLPEN

Bad news travels fast in a clubhouse, and the guys had tried to get him to come out to the bar. Buck him up a little. But the idea of it, all those pathetic smiling faces, all those claps on the back, made him want to shrink into himself and die. "We're putting you in the bullpen, Tim," the pitching coach had said. There were more words. *Best thing for the team. Took a good look at the roster. Need a hard-throwing lefty in the starting rotation.* The coach's face held no discernible expression. He didn't look upset, or sympathetic. Nothing. Maybe that's the way he had to play it. Maybe it wasn't even his decision. Maybe that's where the expression "taking one for the team" had come from. He paced his small hotel room, hearing the coach's words over and over in his head while the walls tightened around him, and for about the thousandth time in his career he wished he'd said fuck it and joined his friends for a beer.

So he did. The message light on his phone was blinking, but he didn't want to deal with any of it, just grabbed his room card and met his teammates at the bar. A whoop rose from the crowd of guys around a table in the back, and Tim couldn't help but smile. He grabbed a chair, nodded and grinned at the shoulder pounds, the catcalls. At least the lefty wasn't there. The thing was, the new pitcher wasn't a bad guy. He wanted a chance to play, like everyone else. When Tim had been called up to the majors, he'd displaced a guy in the rotation, so he knew what it was like to be the interloper. He'd gotten a few cold shoulders, at first. And yeah, he'd been pissed about that. So he didn't want to do that to the lefty.

A big cold draft landed in front of him, and Tim gulped, slapped the glass back on the table. "So," he said. "Least I'm not getting sent to the minors."

There was a round of sympathetic noises and high fives. The last thing he wanted to do was bring the team down. The energy was like a living thing. In the clubhouse, on the field.

"It's still fucked," one of his catchers said. He was about the best he'd worked with since Dan Monroe.

Tim's face softened, staring at the catcher, loving his loyalty. Then he smiled. "Thanks, man," he said. "But if they think it's better for the team, I'm in. Besides, bullpen doesn't totally suck." His mind flashed on an image of his father, the noise he made when he lowered himself into his easy chair, the ever-present bottle of painkillers he needed help opening.

"Bullpen is fuckin' amazing," one of the guys said. The others agreed, calling out names of big-time relievers, pitching lights-out saves.

"Oblonsky's gonna be savin' our bacon."

The catcher ordered another round, and some shots.

"Hell, yeah," Tim said. "That's what I'm gonna do."

* * *

Tim didn't call back, and Margie couldn't sleep. She stood in the kitchen, staring at the water spots on the ceiling tiles, and itched with the urge to tear it all apart. But she didn't want to wake her mother. So she made a pot of coffee and sat down at the table with a pad and a pencil, trying to remember everything that Abernathy had told her. That French had told her. That Durning had told her. It all started swirling together into one voice telling her she didn't belong. That she wasn't playing the game. Or at least not the one they wanted. Her brain was swirling; her eyes felt sticky. She dropped her head in her hands and let the tears come. She didn't remember the last time she cried, like more than a sniff or two. Maybe it was the night Timmy left for Washington. She'd done everything she could to keep busy that night—cleaned her room, did some laundry, pressed her ball girl uniform and hung it neatly in the closet. She'd plopped onto her bed and stared over at it, all crisp and neat, the sparkling white and pinstripes, the navy blue panels running down the sides. She'd imagined Tim on a plane ride to his future and had sensed his awe and excitement and trepidation through their weird twin-link, and then she'd started crying like a damn baby.

Now seated at her mother's kitchen table, the coffee growing cold, the chicken-scratchy notes on her pad barely legible through the tears, she snatched a few napkins from the holder next to the salt and pepper shakers and mopped herself up. The sky was growing lighter; the birds were singing. Margie stood, then walked to the window that looked out onto their backyard. The reflected glow from the looming sunrise painted the clouds gentle shades of pink and yellow.

She refilled her coffee and took it outside. She knew what she had to do.

* * *

Whatever kept her mother from doing anything about the leaking kitchen ceiling was also the thing that had stayed her hand from cleaning out the shed. The mower sat up front, about the only object in the prefab structure that had seen any recent action. Everything else was shrouded in spiderwebs and dust. Margie eyeballed the garage sale fodder, looking for the familiar orange-painted metal tubing. Then she found it. It took some doing to wrestle it free, as it was lodged between the leaf-blowing and vacuuming equipment. The pitch-back had definitely seen better days. Rust was creeping across the orange paint and some of the strings were loose, a couple broken, but she imagined it worked well enough. She set it up in the backyard and started throwing. If she hit it in the wrong place, the ball stuck and she had to go retrieve it, but it was good enough for her needs.

Over and over she threw, and with each pitch the knots cramping her shoulders began to loosen. It was a good thing a whole lot of trees separated the Oblonskys' house from their nearest neighbor; with each release, Margie cursed out her frustration. She'd worked up a good sweat, too. She'd missed that, and made a mental note to take up running again in the off-season. She gripped the ball, imagining Dolph Edwards's smug face painted on the sagging strings. Then Donofrio. Durning. French. Abernathy. All the other people who said she couldn't do this, who called her horrible names and said she should go back to the kitchen. It was kind of fun, and that bothered her a little. She never considered herself a violent, vengeful sort of person. She didn't like being told what to do and had a mouthy temper, but physically hurting someone? She didn't want to think about what it would take to see if she had that in her.

She barely noticed the sky brightening. Her coffee was long forgotten, still perched on the fence post next to the shed, where they'd often hang their sweatshirts if they got too warm while tossing the ball around or doing yardwork. At one point she glanced in that direction, the rising sun sparkling on the shiny porcelain cup, and she could almost see her father's Yankees sweatshirt draped over the post. An involuntary sob rose from her chest. Her mother had sent the sweatshirt to the Baseball Hall of Fame in Cooperstown, along with his uniforms, his gear, and his World Series rings. Margie and her mother had had a battle royal over that one, with a lot of shouting and tears and Tim retreating to his room. Margie had been so pissed at him for leaving her to fight on her own, like he was betraying her, betraying their father's memory. It was more important, her mother had tried to explain, that the world know her father was somebody once. That in Cooperstown, his memory would be kept alive, as opposed to shoving his belongings into some dusty, forgotten closet. Margie thought giving his things away was like a slap in the face. Still in shock over his death, she didn't know how to ask for something to remember him by. There were personal items Margie got to keep—his shaving brush, a watch, and his favorite flannel shirt, which smelled like woodsmoke and Old Spice aftershave. But it wasn't what she really craved. She wanted to keep the baseball part of him. After a lot of arguing and more tears, Mom let her choose one item from the box. She'd kept his catcher's mitt. One day, shortly after they got their driver's licenses, feeling heady with freedom, she and Tim drove up to Cooperstown. After paying homage to their heroes, Tim spending extra time with his favorite pitchers, Margie got up her nerve to talk to one of the curators. She asked about her father and what happens to the donations. She knew he was not actually going to be inducted into the Hall of Fame, but he was part of the game in his own right. The man stammered for a while and said he'd check into it. Sensing that Margie was about to lose it, maybe, Timmy took her arm and tried to get her to go look at another exhibit. They had a long talk in the parking lot.

"It's not fair," Margie said.

"Yeah, Barge, but sometimes things happen for a reason."

Margie knew, even back then, that on some level the discussion wasn't about their father's possessions. He explained why he thought Mom had gotten rid of his things so quickly, why she'd been so adamant about the baseball memorabilia going to Cooperstown.

"To hear her talk," Margie said, "she hated that he played. All that shit about stuck in the bullpen, that they didn't give him any respect, that baseball took the best years of his life. You'd think she'd want to stack all his gear up and build a bonfire."

"You don't get it, do you?" Tim shook his head. "She was pissed, yeah. But she wanted them to see it. She wanted to rub it in Major League Baseball's face that here was this devoted, loyal guy who loved the game so much that he'd play wherever they let him, even if that meant being stuck in the bullpen for most of his career. The unsung hero, more or less."

It sort of helped, as did Tim's gentle voice and manner that could usually talk her off whatever ledge she'd crawled out on, but part of her had still been pissed. In her mind, she saw that big, brown box of her father's life moldering away in some basement in an annex of the hall.

"We're not asking for it back," Tim said. It was creepy how he sometimes knew what she was thinking. "Look." He sighed. "At least you got his mitt. That's something."

She eyeballed him a moment. "Did you get anything?" He hadn't seemed interested in the box or in any of Dad's personal items. After the funeral, Margie even offered him his watch, because it seemed like the sort of thing a son might want from his father, but Tim had shaken his head and walked away.

But at this question, in the parking lot of Cooperstown, leaning against his used Camaro, Tim pursed his lips. He slid his eyes from left to right. It was the guilty look, like he knew who'd broken Dad's favorite coffee mug or how the mess got all over the living room floor. "Promise you won't tell Mom. And promise you won't get pissed."

In that second, Margie knew he'd taken something from the box. He'd taken something big. When he dug into his jeans pocket, she knew what it was. She sucked in a breath when he held out his palm and displayed one of her father's World Series rings.

"Fuck you," she said, grinning at him.

He grinned back.

"Fuck you so hard. So that's why you were all Mr. Polite and Considerate and offered to take the box to the post office for Mom." But she kind of admired him for it.

Tim stuck it back in his pocket. Then a horrible thought occurred to her. "Tim. You're not…giving it to them, are you?"

"Uh, no way. Are you kidding? They'd probably stick it in that box in the basement. Or some anonymous collection." He shrugged. "I just thought he'd like to come visit."

"Aw, John-Boy." She swelled with an urge to fling her arms around him, and he drew his head back and gave her the stink eye, and she laughed.

* * *

The sun was awake in full, and Margie was only peripherally aware of the back door opening and closing. Still, she threw pitches at the netting, but her arm was getting tired and her mother was probably worried about her. And she knew she should get cleaned up, because she wasn't sure exactly what time Fitz was coming. Everyone's "first thing in the morning" was a little different, and he seemed stubborn and irritatingly persistent enough to be one of those early birds.

She nabbed the last rebound from the net and gripped the ball in her hand, fingertips digging into the seams. Then she turned. Her mother was standing on the back porch. She looked smaller than usual, and for a second she looked almost maternal—less the firebrand and more the cuddly mom who might make cookies and play cheering-up games. Until she spoke. "How the frig long have you been out here. Chrissakes, you probably woke all the neighbors."

But all the exercise, and maybe the sleep deprivation, had quenched some of Margie's fire. "Good morning, Mother. I hope you had a pleasant night's sleep."

Mom gave her a squint, and her gaze followed Margie up the porch stairs and probably into the house.

Stephen "Fitz" Fitzgerald was sitting at their kitchen table in his rumpled shirtsleeves, his tie loosened, hanging around his neck.

"How's the arm?" he said.

Margie slid him the side eye and poured herself a cup of coffee, remembering the forgotten mug on the fence post. "Nolan Ryan's got nothing to worry about, but it keeps me from wanting to bust someone's skull." Crap. "That's off the record."

He laughed. The son of a bitch laughed.

Margie sank into an empty chair—Tim's chair, since Fitz was in hers—and only as an afterthought did she realize that her mother had left the room.

Margie stared into the oily film on the coffee's surface, tapping an index finger against the mug. She kind of wished she'd held on to the ball. He gave her the creeps, a shiver through her belly at the way he sat there, mentally dissecting her.

"Look," he finally said, his shoulders sagging forward. "None of this has to be on the record. We can just talk, here. Okay, I apologize for what I did before. I can see how that pissed you off, how that might have led some people to see you in the wrong light. So maybe I jumped the gun a little. If I could take it back, I would."

Words were cheap. Cheap weapons used by bullies and blowhards and cowards. She should know. She'd used a few herself.

"Show me." Margie leaned back in her chair, crossing her arms over her chest.

"Beg pardon?" Fitz said.

"Actions talk louder than words. Isn't that what everyone says?"

Fitz looked amused. Was he making fun of her?

"I was goddamn serious."

"I know," he said, his voice a little softer. "I was wondering how I could possibly show you that. It's too late for a retraction."

She rolled her eyes. "Do I gotta do all your thinking for you? Jeez. Okay, here. I'll tell you my side of the story. Since that's all I basically know to be true. If it comes out in the newspaper still my side of the story, nothing twisted around? That's how."

Fitz nodded.

"What do you guys call that?" Margie tapped the table. "Editorializing?"

Fitz nodded. He spread his fingers wide on the table in front of him. "Okay. Okay, we'll do that."

"I can get you some evidence," she said.

"Complaint forms?" Fitz grinned and extracted a folder from his bag.

Margie stared as he plopped it onto the table. It knocked against her coffee mug and the surface sloshed then settled.

Did she want to know how he'd gotten them?

She didn't know when her mother had come back close enough to hear. Damn, that woman was stealthy. "Lemme see those."

Margie drew them from her grasp. "Mom."

She held her hands up as if she'd been caught raiding the collection box, her cheeks coloring.

"Mrs. Oblonsky, if you'd be so kind, I'd like to ask you a few questions, too."

Here we go. Margie inwardly rolled her eyes.

The index finger pointed. "You, I'm not talking to," Mom said.

A smile crinkled Fitz's eyes. "I can see where you get it from, Margie."

* * *

Mom didn't talk. But she hovered, putting up more coffee, doing laundry, making scoffing noises under her breath that would not be dissuaded by Margie's gentle and not-so-gentle suggestions that she get out of the house for a while. She thought about grabbing Fitz and heading to the diner, but she wasn't ready to face the world. Granted, the world would only be the village of Saugerties, but almost everybody knew her there. She didn't want to talk about how the season had gone.

At first, he asked her some gimmes that seemed safe enough. About her father, about growing up in a baseball family, playing softball during school. How she got the bug to be an umpire, how she'd applied to get into the academy. Margie made a point of not talking to Fitz about her suspicions why Big Al pushed for her. That, she learned from her mother, was called *conjecture*, which had gotten her into trouble last time. So she didn't want to do any conjecturing. *Just tell him the facts and let him write the story.* It wasn't as hard as she'd thought. Once he settled in, he had less of a bug-eyed look; he asked smart questions then did more listening than talking. He took a lot of notes and made sure to ask her how to spell names and which cities different things happened in.

He asked her about Wes.

"He's a great guy, a great ump." She missed him and still felt guilty for sneaking out of Binghamton without talking to him. Well, there was something she could do to fill her off-season. Connecticut wasn't too far away.

Fitz tapped his pencil against his pad. Then he looked up at her, his lips squinching to the side. "Think he'd talk to me?"

Margie shrugged. "He's a big boy, he can decide that for himself."

He tapped the pencil again, eyes searching the ceiling as if deciding what to ask next. But she had a feeling he knew exactly what he planned to say. A tiny voice in her gut told her that talking to him wasn't such a great idea. But what could she say now? Tell him all of it was off the record? She mentally reviewed what she'd told him so far. She hadn't offered her two cents; she wasn't conjecturing about who was at fault; she'd been very careful not to put forth personal information about anyone but herself.

Mom came back in, as if she'd been listening in the pantry. "Are we done here, or do you want another pot of coffee?"

She turned to Fitz, lifting her eyebrows in question.

"Nah, I think I got about everything I need." He tapped the eraser against his lower lip, apparently realized he was doing it—maybe a habit he was trying to quit—then said, "One of my sources thinks Edwards is gonna beat the suspension."

Margie's breath seized. That fucking son of a bitch. She'd filed her paperwork. A copy of the video had been sent to Abernathy's office, according to Fitz. She didn't know what was on the tape, but Fitz said it was damn incriminating. How could anyone look at that and call Edwards innocent? The interference was legit. He'd argued. She'd ejected him. He wouldn't leave the field. She'd seen him pick up a bat and walk toward her. He hadn't looked like he was about to take a few warm-up swings.

A sly smile worked its way across Fitz's narrow face.

"No," Margie said. There was still hope. Abernathy did tell her to be patient. That maybe they were waiting for the brouhaha to die down a little. So far, there was no official letter telling her she'd been released, so maybe there still would be a place for her next season. If she said anything to Fitzgerald on record now—even off record—she could be closing the door on that. "No," she repeated, shaking her head. "No. I'm not going there with you about that."

Fitzgerald watched her for a moment, as if in that span of time she might change her mind.

Then he apparently decided to stop waiting. He scribbled a couple numbers on his notepad, tore off the page, and slid it across the table. "Call anytime you want," he said. Then he thanked her, thanked her mother, and Margie stayed in her chair, staring at the piece of paper, as the door slapped behind him.

When the car rumbled into the distance and disappeared, her mother began to speak. Something about not trusting him. Something about not liking the way he was looking at her. "I know that game," her mother said. "He's working you. If I were you, I'd call those numbers right now, tell him not to print a damn word of what you just said." Margie didn't want to hear it. She got up, put her mug in the sink, and went back to her pitching.

After she'd calmed down some, she flopped into the grass. It was warm beneath her fingers, the dew drying in the sun. The backyard looked like shit. It needed a good mowing, in parts, and reseeding. She should probably wait until spring. She thought about the long, long winter.

She thought about never being allowed to work another game. Ever.

And it pissed her off. But maybe she was going about this all wrong.

Maybe she needed to pull in reinforcements.

29

THE BACKSLIDE

Tim missed Dan Monroe. He worked to Tim's strengths and strengthened his weaknesses and could call one hell of a game. He also made sure Tim never stayed in the bar alone. Even after the other guys drifted out, back to their hotel rooms or scattered to various parties or girlfriends or family in the area, Dan would clap one of those big hands to Tim's shoulder and order them another round. He'd talk about the finer points of squatting behind home plate. He'd talk about the greats: Yogi Berra and Johnny Bench and some guy named Oblonsky. Yes, Dan knew about Tim's father. Tim barely knew about Tim's father. Aside from the All-Star Game in Atlanta and a few other choice memories of going to the ballpark, Tim saw the old man as an old man: a groan as he landed in his chair, a bottle of painkillers on the end table next to the remote, and an always-open can of cheap beer. His cane leaning against the wall. Sometimes he could be convinced to come outside and throw the ball around, and when he did, Mom barked her worries over the porch railing. "Not too much now, Marty. You know what the doctor said." And on and on, their father grumbling: *Patsy, you're taking all the fun out of it, and what's the world coming to when a man can't toss the ball around the backyard with his kids?* It was like they were putting on a show, like a couple of old vaudeville comedians. Sometimes Margie called them George and Gracie. In his heart, Tim knew they loved each other, but sometimes he wished his mother would leave his father the hell alone. At least he didn't hit her. He had friends whose fathers would have a few and slap the kids around. He glowered into the beer that sat alone on his table. Wondering when he'd set the bar of his childhood memories so low.

Alcohol is a depressant. He remembered that from some long-ago high school health class; no wonder it made him think back to his childhood and pluck out the bad memories like ticks from a dog's back. Examine them from all angles, then crush them. Maybe that's why doing blow seemed so natural. You go drinking, you get a little down, and you need something to pick you back up again. And it was just...there. Always there.

He could really go for a few lines now. Yeah, he was taking one for the team. Yeah, if it would mean a better outcome, he'd sit in the bullpen. He'd work on becoming a specialist, like the pitching coach talked about. It sounded wacky to him at first. You had your starters; you had your closers. Occasionally, an extra pitcher on the roster would be called in for long relief, if the starter crapped out. But according to his coaches, the game was changing. He was depressed as hell to learn about it at first, thinking he was doomed to his father's fate, and he could just hear his mother railing on about how it had ruined Dad's life and how she wasn't about to sit idle while they tried to destroy her son, too. But he was starting to wrap his brain around the possibilities. That might be something Dan would say to him, if he were still here, if he were clapping that big hand to his shoulder. "Look on the bright side," he'd begin, and then spin his tale of sunshine and lollipops. He always had a smile. Sometimes Tim wondered what it hid. Everyone had something, he'd learned. Some just knew how to cover it up better than others. His silver lining, the one Dan might dream up for him, was that short-relief guys played more. You only played every fifth game as a starter. Depending on the specialty, depending on how many batters they needed you to face, a reliever might come in every two or three games. If you came in with guys on base, you could earn a save and be the hero. Tim liked the idea of being the hero.

A girl came over. Dark hair, cute, big smile, vaguely familiar. He smiled back. She said a few words, something about glad he was back in town. It bothered him that he didn't remember her name. But he liked the way she touched his arm when she spoke; he liked her laugh. It soothed him, reached inside him, and connected with a memory of pleasure. Maybe if he spent a little time with her, he'd remember.

* * *

Tim's hand shook as he reached for the phone to call his pitching coach. The call he swore he would never make again. But the bed was spinning. He'd tried getting up to take a piss and damn near fell down. No way could he pitch. Even from the pen.

"Well, get off the goddamn phone and get some sleep," the voice growled. After a pause, it softened. "Get some fluids in you, Tim. Call the trainer if you need more."

Tim eased the receiver back on the cradle. His stomach knotted with guilt, making his nausea worse. He curled into a ball and pulled the blanket over his head. It was too easy. It had been too easy. Soft arms went around him; soft, bare skin kissed his back. He'd remembered her name, three lines in, when she began unbuttoning her shirt. Eileen. She wasn't like the other girls, all giggly and fake and giving off mixed messages. How could he not have remembered her name?

The phone rang. He cringed at the loud noise. He considered not answering. If the team sent someone over to check on him, they'd know it was no goddamn stomach flu. His eyes skittered around the room, from the empty whiskey bottle to the plastic baggie to the remnants of room service. But if it was Margie... He wanted to talk to Margie. The news hadn't been good, and he'd been unable to reach her. He cleared his throat, hoping he wouldn't sound sick. Hoping she wouldn't ask questions. But even that noise made his head ring. So he let the machine get it.

"You okay, Tim?" Eileen's soft voice was like a hand stroking his brow. His mouth felt so dry, and his head throbbed. No doubt she was hurting, too. She wanted coffee and asked if he needed anything. Twenty minutes later, she was back with food, orange juice, and aspirin, and an hour after that he'd fallen asleep in her arms.

When he woke next, she smiled and called him sleepyhead and touched his cheek.

He never wanted to leave this room, this moment. But then her smile fell. "You supposed to play today?"

He shook his head. "Called in sick."

"Players can do that?"

He shrugged. "If they're sick. I don't do it that much."

He didn't like to lie. But he didn't want her to feel responsible for him. He tried to be careful about when he partied. He never did it the night before a start. At first. But then he did, and he was able to pitch fine. Maybe he got a little cocky. Or maybe he'd gone over his limit last night. It didn't usually affect him this bad.

There was that one time over the winter, though. He'd gone to Cabo with a few of his buddies for New Year's Eve. Everyone got hammered, and when he woke up the next morning—actually, it was afternoon—he couldn't remember what he'd done. That scared the ever-loving-mother out of him. Anything could have happened. He might have been with a girl without using a condom. Or done something to end up in the sports headlines. He wasn't much for praying, but he prayed, then hoped to God he hadn't done something stupid; prayed for the wisdom not to fuck up like that again.

During spring training, a counselor had come in to talk to the team about drugs and the temptations a baseball player might face. He supposed it was part of their campaign to keep young guys clean. Tim squirmed in his chair while the guy talked. Heat feathered up his neck; sweat formed at his hairline. He itched to bolt from the room. But he didn't want to look weak. All the other guys were muttering jokes under their breath and nudging each other. So he made jokes, too.

Most of them met up after games, had a few beers, smoked a little, snorted a little. But they had it under control. They had to. They knew how.

He wanted to know how.

Underneath the jokes and the nudges and the feigned attention, a small voice inside Tim was screaming. That he couldn't do this alone. He couldn't play naked. He couldn't stand on a pitcher's mound in a major league game, forty thousand pairs of eyes on him, without a little something starching up his nerve.

Already, he was having nightmares. He'd be on the mound, holding the ball, and suddenly he'd forget how to pitch. He'd wake up in a panic—sweating, panting.

He'd never told anyone about the nightmares. Not even Eileen.

She stayed most of the day, napping and watching bad TV, and after she left he took a shower then talked to his mother, because it was the time of the week when he promised to call. She raised holy hell if he didn't call.

"So when should I expect to see you?" she said.

But he couldn't go home. He couldn't go home, and wake up like this, in her house.

* * *

Back in Cincinnati, Alejandro the catcher set, waiting for him. He looked so damn small. Is that why they stuck him out in the pen? He was decent. Tim had seen him catch a few games; he was a workhorse, dependable, did a passable stretch when their starter was out having ACL surgery and their backup went down with a groin pull. *Catchers, man.* Tim shook his head. He didn't know how they did it, stressing out their knees, their backs, how they lasted so many years.

"Are you gonna throw the damn ball or stand around letting the wind ruffle your pretty, pretty hair?" The smile was big and bright behind his mask.

"Sorry, man." Tim liked his accent. It reminded him of Enrique, the famous, ageless Enrique from Cuba who liked to tease Tim for being a white boy afraid of a little blow.

Tim wailed one in. It smacked against the mitt. A chorus of female voices cheered from the bleachers.

The catcher lobbed it back. "Don't be even thinking of poaching my fan club." Alejandro flashed the girls a grin. "Betty, you're lookin' fine with that new haircut."

Tim grimaced. The girls were all looking damn fine, but how long did this dude stay out here, that he knew all the girls' names? He wondered if his father did things like this, to keep from going crazy out here in the pen all those years. Flirted with girls. Listened to other games on the radio. Or did he simply enjoy the freedom of being away from home, the glory of being part of the game.

Tim pitched another one that went wide. Catcher-man grabbed it and trotted up to him. "What's got you so tight? You're not going in today. Lefty's still throwing and they say he looks pretty fresh, could go the distance. Coach just wanted to work you a little."

Tim sagged. Fuck this. He could be in the clubhouse having a beer. "So what's the point?"

"The point," Alejandro said, "is to keep you loose. Keep you ready. Work that goddamn stick out of your ass."

"I don't have…what you said."

The catcher laughed. "Oblondie, you're so stiff I could hang my laundry on you."

He threw the ball back and Tim snagged it, held it in his hands, found the seams. He was throwing too hard. He did that when he was nervous, but he couldn't stop it. He did that when he didn't have his good stuff. Like throwing harder would compensate for it. He tried to remember what the coach told him about holding the ball a little looser. "You don't want to choke the damn thing to death," he'd said. He'd talked about mechanics, and how it caused his arm muscles to shorten, which caused his shoulder muscles to compensate. The knee bone connected to the hipbone. With maps and graphs and those diagrams of muscles and bones.

He eased off a little, but the ball still didn't land where he wanted.

The catcher shook his head, nodded at a girl in a red tank top. "Teresita, tell my boy here to relax."

She gave him a show of cleavage and white teeth and long lashes. "I'll help him relax."

"Oh, I know you will."

"Alejandro, how's your mother?" the girl said.

"Missing her baby boy, as usual."

Teresita leaned over the railing and gave Tim an appraising eye. "I bet your mama misses you around the house, big strong guy like you."

And so it went. Pitch, flirt. Pitch, flirt. Alejandro was working all the girls like it was a big game for him, something to do to pass the time.

When they got a beer after the game, Tim giving the excuse that he wanted some feedback on the new sinker he'd been testing out, he asked if he was actually seeing any of those girls.

"Why, you interested? I could hook you up."

Tim shook his head and Alejandro's eyebrows popped up, as if he were the big brother taking umbrage, like his girls weren't good enough. "They seem nice. And, uh, personable."

Alejandro nodded, grinning. "Ah. You got a girl."

Immediately he saw Eileen's face. He never thought someone could get into his head like that. He didn't see her much, only when his team was in LA. But it was hard sometimes to stop thinking about her. She had a way about her, so gentle and understanding. Different from the other girls. Some of them expected him to be a walking credit card, taking them out for dinner, showing them off. He knew guys like that. Going around with models, actresses. They'd get their pictures in the paper. Tim didn't want a life like that. He wanted normal. But he had a hard enough time pitching lately, keeping his head in the game, keeping that head above water, without the distraction of a relationship.

There was a lull in the conversation, and Alejandro motioned him closer. "So how's that arm?" he said. "You playing hurt?"

Tim shrugged. "Not bad. Most days."

He lowered his voice. "You visiting the jar?"

The back of Tim's neck prickled. He'd heard about the jar. It was in the clubhouse. Uppers and pain pills, mostly, a whole fruit salad of them. The starting lineup—position players, mostly—dipped in. A hundred and sixty-two games made for a damn long season, and some of his teammates swore by a little help now and then. It had taken Tim a good long time to figure out how much partying he could take and still be decent the next day, and sometimes he even miscalculated that. He couldn't imagine what these things might do to him.

Alejandro tapped the table. "Ain't no shame in getting a little help, brother. We're all in the same boat here, just trying to put on a show. Give the people what they want, right? Now who wants to pay good money to take the wife and kids to the ballpark, especially late in the season, and see a bunch of us draggin' around like old men?"

Tim smirked. He certainly felt older some days than others. The day after a tough start. Around the middle of August, he started dragging a little. He'd powered through the single-A short seasons, but he'd been seventeen, eighteen then. He wasn't exactly an old duffer, but he felt it sometimes. And he knew some of the older guys. They lived on painkillers, they got shots, they toughed it out. Season-ending injury was a term that set teeth clenching. Some of those happened around the end of August, when the fatigue started setting in good. "You have a point," Tim said. "You do 'em?"

He nodded. "You ease into it." Alejandro glided his hand like a plane taking off. He went over a little plan, how Tim could try one after a hard outing, get accustomed to the feel when they'd be most likely to rest him the next day.

Tim thought about that. Maybe it would save him. Maybe if he had some kind of backup plan, he wouldn't worry so much, wouldn't get so nervous on the mound, wouldn't try to power the ball. Then he could focus. Just focus on his control and forget about the rest of it.

30

THE TRUTH

It took two phone calls and the promise of Tim's autograph to find out that Wes was working a tough stretch in Scranton, Pennsylvania. Margie dialed the front desk of his motel from the road and claimed to be his sister—a lie that jumped off her tongue way too easily—and the receptionist put her through.

He said nothing at first, and maybe that was just post-game fatigue, but he had a right to be angry. She blurted an apology. The silence, the crackling of the line made her head throb. She rested her left temple against the glass pane of the phone booth at a truck stop somewhere off Interstate 84. The glass was cool; an earlier shower had drained the heat from the air and the clouds chased each other across the night sky.

Finally, voice flat, he said, "Meet me on the roof."

"Why, you gonna push me off?"

He laughed, and her body sighed with relief. If she could still make him laugh, how could he hate her forever?

By the time she pulled into the lot, the clouds had cleared. She immediately got why he wanted to meet her on the roof. It was a running joke in the academy that if you couldn't find Wes after dark, he was probably outside looking at the stars, not in some dive swilling dollar beers like the rest of the guys. And it was August. Something about August and stargazing tapped a memory from last season. Some kind of meteor shower? She wondered if, when he was done with baseball or it was done with him, he'd go back to school like he'd often talked about, get his master's degree in astronomy.

Margie found the stairwell leading up. The motel had the balls to call it a penthouse, but it was nothing more than a plain old tar roof with some deck loungers and rusty old tables. He was seated in a sagging lawn chair as far away from the flood lamp as he could drag it; its twin sat next to him, waiting for her.

He was the same old Wes—a whippet-tight nerdy guy with pale skin and wild red curls. Waitresses, especially the older ones, went nuts over his freckles and pouty lips. It made them all maternal and usually inspired free refills, a slice of pie, and then teasing from Margie all the way to their next destination.

She slipped in next to him, and they watched the stars.

After a while, a white blur streaked across the sky.

"Do I get a wish?" she said.

He didn't answer.

"I wish I could go back in time," she said. "I wish that as soon as I got that phone call from Mack, I went over to talk to you, told you what was going on. I was a horrible, sucky partner. A suckier friend. I should have done better by you. You had my back. I know about guys who don't have your back and you do." She sniffed. "Did."

"Life happens," he said finally.

"I let my emotions get the better of me, and that was wrong. I know that now."

"It's okay, Margie."

His voice sounded odd. Strained. A little higher than usual. He wasn't telling her the truth. Or at least not the whole truth.

He sighed. "I called Mr. Abernathy."

Margie's shoulders tensed. "Before or after I was reassigned?"

His silence fell like a boulder on her chest. Wes shifted his weight, the cheesy webbed chair squeaking beneath him. "Margie."

The floodlight glinted on his glasses. He wore contacts during the games so assholes wouldn't make blind umpire jokes. "It felt like the best decision for both of us," he said. "I like working with you, but maybe it was making us a little complacent."

She'd sometimes thought the same thing, although she didn't want to think about it. And definitely didn't want to be thinking the next thing that popped into her head. "Mack told me French's partner bailed—that's why he wanted me in Erie. Is that even true?"

He didn't answer.

"You thought I was holding you back."

He didn't answer.

"You thought whoever got stuck with *the girl* wouldn't get to move up."

"Margie, no. That's not the reason."

"Then what? 'Cause that's the only explanation I can come up with for why you'd ditch me."

Another meteor streaked across the sky. Margie squeezed her eyes shut and tried to rein in her emotions. Yelling at Wes wouldn't accomplish anything.

"My head wasn't in the game." His voice broke. He cleared his throat and, soft but deliberate, said, "I didn't want to be an anchor around your neck. So I asked Mr. Abernathy for some time off, and to set you up with someone from the call-up list. Someone who would challenge you."

Margie could only stare at him.

He tugged in another deep breath. "Because Julia was sick."

"Wes—"

He held up a hand. "She's okay, now, the baby's going to be fine, but for a while, we weren't sure. I had to be with them."

"Wes." Her eyebrows scrunched together. Family was everything to him. Crap, and she'd told that lie to the front desk about being his sister so the receptionist would let her talk to him. No wonder he sounded kind of stunned when he answered.

"Honestly, I wanted to stay in Connecticut. But Julia convinced me to call Mr. Abernathy and ask him if I could finish the season. She made a great point that if I didn't, I'd regret it, and maybe I'd even lose my spot. He was of the same mind, I guess, because he said that when I was ready, he'd try to set me up with a few games." He waved a hand across the night sky of Scranton. "And here I am."

"Why didn't you tell me?" But who was she to ask that, when she'd done the same to him—cut and run without a word? "Wait. How long had you known about Julia?"

"A while. It was the night before we were supposed to go to Hartford. You know she loves that bakery outside Albany. The drive takes ten minutes longer going that way, rather than heading south over 84 through Newburgh, but their lemon crumb cake is her favorite. I called to see if she wanted anything else. That's when she told me how bad it was. She'd planned to wait until we got there, but then she started crying, and..." He shook his head. "Margie, I made one phone call after that. I know I should have made another, to you, and I know I should have told you earlier, but I wasn't thinking straight."

She pressed a hand over his arm. If Tim or her mother were that sick, she might have done the same. "Don't worry about it, Star Man."

A meteor trailed across the horizon, and they sat for a while in silence.

"Tell me about Holyoke," Wes said.

Margie wished she had a beer. "Real cute little city. Not too far from Connecticut. I'm surprised you'd ask me."

Even in the dim light, she knew the look he was giving her. Many a batter who said the call should have gone his way had been the recipient of that look. Wes's expression was more amused and irritated than mean, but it did the trick. Margie sighed and sank deeper into the webbing of her rusted chair.

"You heard."

"Everybody heard. Did you make the official call for the forfeit, or was that Doug French?"

"French wasn't doing shit. It was damn near a riot zone out there. Players were screaming at me, fans were throwing stuff on the field, and the home team was given fair warning to vacate or they would forfeit the game. Them's the rules. I was working the plate, so as umpire-in-chief, I called it."

He whistled low. "Wow. I wish I'd seen it."

She examined a fingernail. "I got video."

He sat up straight. "You do? Seriously? Did you bring it? Please tell me you brought it."

Margie grinned.

* * *

Ten minutes later, the night manager was setting up a VCR in Wes's room. Wes tipped him with two tickets to the next day's game. "Two more tickets and he might have gotten us beer," Margie said after he left. "Well, gotten me beer, anyway."

"I take what I can get."

She watched him fiddle with the remote until the picture came up. "Thanks," she said. "I haven't had the guts to watch it yet."

"I figured," Wes said. "You look tense. You don't usually look tense."

"Yeah. There's a reason I'm tense."

The reason had a good lead off first base, threatening to steal. She knew what came next. Her throat tightened as the batter hit what was supposed to have been an easy double-play ball. Wes leaned closer to the screen when Edwards went into his slide.

"What a jerk." His upper lip lifted into a sneer. "I didn't see the news tonight. Did they uphold his suspension?"

"Don't know." She checked her watch and wondered if she should call Fitz. He had his ear to the ground about things like that. Then she had a better idea. "You got a radio in here?"

Still staring at the TV and the circus that followed her call— which she didn't care to relive—he gestured toward the nightstand.

She turned the dial to Fitz's station. It was a little staticky, but she could just make out his voice. He sounded impatient as he talked to a caller about why a player wore his socks a certain way.

"Oh. I know that guy," Wes said. "I listened to his show a few times, while I was driving through the southern part of the league. Usually I get the best reception along 84 between Newburgh and Danbury. He's a little cranky, but he knows his baseball."

Margie hooked a thumb toward the radio. "That guy is Fitz. Stephen Fitzgerald."

Wes's eyes bugged, looking even huger behind his glasses. "The reporter. The guy in Helena who implied you thought Edwards was cheating? That guy?"

"Yep. That guy."

Brow furrowed, Wes plucked a slip of paper from the top of the bureau and handed it to Margie. "Maybe that's why he called. This came in while I was at the ballpark. I haven't called him back yet. What do you think he's looking for?"

Margie shrugged and handed Fitz's message back to Wes. "I'm still figuring that out." Wes probably assumed she'd been temporarily benched following the melee in Holyoke, maybe to restore order or for her own safety, or else why would she be in Scranton instead of at her own game? But she didn't want to tell him the rest of it. Mack apparently respected her former partner well enough to act on his suggestion; God knows what Wes would try to do if he learned she'd been unofficially suspended for the rest of the season, or if he knew about the stack of complaints against her. She didn't want him to do something stupid and noble in the name of protecting her.

She didn't want them to take him down, too.

"His angle, from what I can tell, is to make a name for himself. He's also got a stick up his ass about cheating players. Ruins the purity of the game, bad role models for the kids, blah blah blah. Can't say I disagree with him there, but honestly, I don't know what good it's gonna do. Wes, I'm starting to think the system's rigged seven ways to Sunday against a woman trying to make it up to the majors. That I should just keep my head down and do my job. Assuming they want me back."

He spun toward her. "Do you think they'd pull your contract over this?"

"At this point? I don't know which way is up anymore." She worried the cassette's plastic case between her fingers, again wishing for a beer. "Can I talk to you about something? Off the record?"

"Anything."

"What do you know about Doug French?"

* * *

Wes told her the baseball card basics, most of which Margie already knew. Doug French served two tours in Vietnam, so he came to umpiring later than most and was slowly working his way up the ranks. "It was a lucky break for him, I guess," Wes said, "that when I left, you needed a partner."

"I don't know what kind of lucky he thought it was." Margie recalled the day they met. The scowl on his puss at having to work with *the girl*. "He told me that if I fucked this up for him...oh, shit." She grabbed Wes's arm; what he'd said before finally connected. "Abernathy lied to me. Said his partner had to leave suddenly, which is why he needed me to go to Erie. But French was from the call-up list."

Wes's eyes widened. "Huh. I thought he would have told you that. Maybe it was a point of pride. Nobody likes getting put on the shelf."

"Someone offered him a deal."

"What?"

"I overheard him talking to someone about Edwards. The night before we left for Holyoke. The guy said if French looked the other way, he'd make it worth his while."

Wes whistled through his teeth. "Did the guy say what he was offering?"

"They didn't get into specifics. But it sounded like a bribe. From what you just said, maybe they were offering to move him up, give him a regular slot." Margie thought a minute. She'd told Mack, and he'd stonewalled her. No. Mack wasn't in on this too, was he? She didn't want to think that about him. That was crazy. Some kind of multilevel machine designed to look the other way on this guy? Was Edwards really that important to baseball?

"And if I keep going after Edwards, I'm done."

Nothing. She spun on him. "You knew that, too?"

He threw up his hands. "Hey. That's not fair. I've been on your side since we met. If you don't know that about me by now, then maybe you should leave."

She snatched up her keys. "Fine. Maybe I should."

She was halfway to the door when he called her name.

"What? You got more secrets about me that I should be aware of?"

"I'm calling him."

"Him. Which him?"

He pointed toward the radio. "Fitzgerald. If it'll help your cause, I'll talk to him." He paused a moment, took a breath that sounded labored. "You can't let them win, Margie."

She took three steps toward him and sat with a heavy thump on the twin bed next to his.

He picked up the remote.

"Seriously," she said. "You're gonna make me watch that thing again?"

"Yes. Yes, I am. For two reasons. One, when I talk to him, I want to make sure I have all the facts. And two…" A little-boy grin snuck through. "I want another look at how those calls went down."

* * *

179

Margie crashed in Wes's room and left first thing in the morning. He was all shiny-eyed and smiling and wanted to hit the local diner with her, eat pancakes and bacon like old times. But Margie was starting to worry that they shouldn't be seen together. She didn't want the stink of her trouble to rub off on him. So he'd just shrugged, wished her well, and told her to be careful.

She thought about the look on his face all the way back to the highway. Like he knew about the death threats, the complaint reports, the things she hadn't told Fitz. The things she hadn't even told Dan. Then she thought about her mother. She'd had a case of the guilts at about two in the morning. When they were in high school, Timmy called that moment "the point of no return." When you know you're bunking in at somebody else's place for the night but it's too late to call Mom. Timmy got away with it, almost always. Golden boy. Margie never thought that was fair. But now, feeling guilty for not calling, she pulled off at the first rest stop and checked in.

"Holy frig, Margaret Elizabeth, I was worried sick. And the phone calls." She heard the suck of her mother's cigarette.

Margie's stomach dipped south, her mind skipping past the apologies to "What phone calls?"

"Press." Her mother spat the word. "They all want to talk to you. Don't worry, I told 'em to piss up a rope."

Margie's face pinched. For most people, this would be taken as a metaphor. But that's probably the exact wording she'd used. Or worse.

A pregnant pause followed. Margie imagined the finger of smoke, the coffee going cold, the mop and bucket set out with intent. Always a clean kitchen floor. It covered a multitude of sins. "And I had an interesting conversation with a guy named Al."

"Al."

"From the umpire school."

"Yeah. I know which Al." Margie clunked her head against the side of the phone booth. Crap. She guessed it was only a matter of time before he got word. It was humiliating. She'd always tried to do him proud. Every tough decision, every ejection report she wrote, she'd wonder what Big Al would do. What he'd advise her to do. Sometimes she thought of calling him but held that in her pocket as her last resort. She didn't want to look like she couldn't figure it out for herself. And she imagined that was what he would have told her, if she'd called him before the Holyoke game. "You're a smart kid," he'd say. "You'll do the right thing when the time comes."

Did he tell everyone that? Was it faith, or did he simply not want to get involved?

"Did he sound pissed?" Margie said.

"Worried, more like."

"Mom, I'm sorry. I should have called you. I got talking with Wes, and I didn't want to wake you."

"Figured, since you were going all the way to Scranton that you'd be...spending the night somewhere," she added, raising Margie's hackles that she'd even think anything funny was going on with her and Wes. "It would have been nice to hear you weren't dead in a ditch somewhere."

Margie let out a long, steady breath. "He wants me to call him, I guess?"

"Sooner rather than later."

"He said that?"

"No, actually he said, 'Please ask Margie to call me,' but it felt like the 'sooner rather than later' was implied."

She gathered up all the quarters she could find in her car, and the next call she placed was to the number her mother had given her.

Al answered on the sixth ring, sounding out of breath.

His gruff tone softened when he heard her voice.

"Hiya, kiddo. Heard you've been having a rough time."

She forced her mouth into a smile as she kicked the toe of her sneaker against the base of the glass booth, avoiding a wad of gum and about a dozen cigarette butts. "Yeah, well. Goes with the job, doesn't it?"

His silence told her a few things. It reminded her of their last conversation, across his crappy desk at the academy. When he predicted she'd get knocked around. When he asked her if she was prepared to take it.

"Your ma tells me reporters are calling day and night. Talk to any of 'em?"

Her stomach sank into her shoes.

"Margie. I see over three hundred trainees through that academy every year. To be honest, I don't remember more than a handful of 'em. Most don't remember me. Don't even get a Christmas card. You, I've been watching. Not because you're a girl. Because you're good. You got the best eye I've seen in a damn long time, best instinct on the field. Off the field...well, we all got something to learn. You're blunt and you got a temper, and from talking to your ma I see you come by it honest. So, that's always gonna be your cross to bear. I'm not one for advice once you're out of my hands, but I just want to float one thing by you. Right now—and I know it isn't fair, I'm not speaking to fairness right now and I won't—but you got a bunch of guys in the umpire development office weighing in on your future. From what I've seen, a future could go one of two ways depending on the behavior of that individual in question. You gettin' me so far?"

"That if I'm making baseball look bad I could be out."

"Basically. Some of these guys, they claim to want baseball to move with the times, to be egalitarian and opportunities for all and the rest of that flag-waving apple-pie stuff. But I've seen different. I've seen some guys in high places who don't like change. Don't think baseball is ready for a woman. I know, it's not fair and I said I'm not talking about fair. Just what is. You want in this game, they hold the cards. It's their deck and their dice and their casino."

Margie took that in for a moment.

"While they're looking at whatever they're looking at, you might want to avoid giving them a reason to look harder." He blew out a breath. "Margie. A long time ago you asked me a question. I still believe in that answer. Maybe I took you on partly because you're a girl, but in my opinion, you're the right girl, and what you do from here on in determines if you stay."

Margie sniffed and pinched the bridge of her nose.

"Hey. Kid. You all right?"

"Never better, Big Al. You know that." She tapped a finger against the glass. "Sorry, but there's a call I gotta make."

"I won't hold you up then. But maybe you'll want to keep in touch."

"I'll send you a Christmas card."

After she disconnected, she stood for a while, leaning her head back against the glass, replaying his words in her mind. Telling the world what she'd seen and heard could make baseball look bad. Which could mean losing her job. But wouldn't it be worse in the long run for the game to give guys like Edwards and French a pass? She let out a long exhale. Maybe baseball owned the casino, but she was out there representing them. If she said nothing, she'd have to live with that. With the knowledge that she could have helped stop it. With the knowledge that keeping mum was like giving them approval.

She picked up the receiver and put it down. Picked it up. Put it down.

There could be another way to play this.

She popped a couple of quarters in the slot and dialed his number. With a click and a whir, his answering machine started talking to her in that smooth, radio-guy voice. After the beep, she told him he could run the story. But only if he left her name out of it.

31

THE SCOOP

Stephen "Fitz" Fitzgerald played the answering machine message a third time. She was not one to equivocate, to be so careful in choosing her language. Each time he got to the main event—leave her name out of it—he listened again, trying to hear beyond the syllables in that flat upstate New York accent. Trying to parse out the ingredients in that verbal stew, picking out the subtle flavoring in the stock, the notes of the spices, and, most importantly, whose influence had seeped into her to turn the determined "let's go get the fuckers" he'd heard in her voice last night to this. To him, it felt like the difference between the liquid courage after leaving the bar and the regrets in the morning. Only, Margie hadn't been drinking.

He listened again. Nonna waddled in, offered tea and biscotti, and he waved her off. The scowl was one he'd have to apologize for later. But he was missing something, and until he figured it out, he'd never get any peace. In the breath between "I've thought it over" and "here's the thing," he thought he knew the thing.

Either the league president's office was dangling a reprieve, or she was protecting someone.

He didn't know the shape of that reprieve. The first thing they teach you in journalism school, after "you're not the story" and "never use two words when one will do," is "follow the money." Margie didn't seem the type to be mollified by a buyout. She didn't want to lose her job, but for her it was more about sticking with it and moving up rather than the payout. Umpires got paid shit; she wasn't in it for the golden handcuffs. She didn't have kids or a house or a gambling problem or a drug habit, and while they weren't dining on lobster and caviar at the modest house in Saugerties, they weren't exactly eating cat food, either.

Did that reprieve come in a suggestion to look the other way in order to keep her job? If that were true, then he'd pegged Margie Oblonsky all wrong. He rarely pegged anyone wrong.

So who was she protecting?

He looked over his notes while tapping a finger on the table. Then it hit him. Guilt by association. If someone was betting on taking Margie down, he could also be implicating those closest to her. Who had the most to lose? Who was named in those complaint reports? The boyfriend? The brother? He made a note to check their stats, their contract status. For some reason, Wes Osterhaus came niggling back at him. He still hadn't returned Fitz's call.

Maybe the soft, beating heart of this story had something to do with all of them. He snapped up from his chair and grabbed his keys.

"Going out, Nonna," he said. "Work."

* * *

Fitz slid into the booth and ordered two espressos. Late as usual, Joey Q strutted in, straight up and cocky like he owned the neighborhood. He'd been like that since high school, when he got drafted by the Yankees. The career was short, thanks to a bum hip, but he'd stayed in the game, in the front office. Once in a while, when he couldn't sleep, Joey would make a pity call to Fitz's show, but there was always a price to pay—run a puff piece on one of his players, stop saying shit about the lineup or about George Steinbrenner firing managers as often as he changed his socks. "You guys start winning in October," Fitz had said, grinning at him, "and I'll stop saying shit."

This would be a big ask. It might take some good scotch. Or a favor to be named later. "What do you know about Tim Oblonsky?"

Joey's eyebrows hitched up as he slid into the booth. "What, that big righty kid? Looked like lightning in a bottle when Cincinnati called him up, yeah? That kid?"

"The same," Fitz said.

Fitz got a metz-a-metz shrug. "Kid's in trouble, what I see. Word was they were gonna send him down, he couldn't take the pressure, couldn't find the plate, breaker just hung up there. Then I hear they put him in the pen instead."

That smelled all kinds of wrong. "The bullpen? If he can't take the pressure, what's he doing in the pen?"

Joey sniffed and drummed his fingers on the table. He slid an appreciative look at the waitress's ass then back to Fitz. "I got a theory. But you didn't hear this from me."

Fitz waited.

"They're parking him. I've seen teams do that when a kid's got, you know, a confidence problem. Coach likes a pitcher, sees potential...sending him down's the logical step, and maybe you'd do that with a fielder, a guy whose bat's gone cold. But a pitcher, maybe one that's a bit of a show pony? That's gonna crush his morale. And if he's already on the edge...?"

Fitz thought about that a moment. It made sense. Pitchers were a different breed.

"I know a guy who knows a guy." He gave Fitz a squint. "Don't be writin' this down. Says the kid has a reoccurring case of the pinstripe flu."

Fitz barked a laugh. "You Yankees. Think the baseball world revolves around you. You're even coopting the language. And it's recurring, by the way."

"Whatever."

Fitz leaned in. "You think it's a dodge. You think they're protecting something bigger than a 'confidence problem.'"

Joey tapped the side of one nostril and made a theatrical sniff. "I got my suspicions. Don't have proof the bonus baby's putting the bonus up his nose, but he does like the nightlife. That, pretty much anyone can tell you about." He leaned back in the booth and touched his spread fingers to his chest. "Now, myself, I don't give two shits what a guy does in town after the game, as long as when he steps onto the field, he's good to go. It's when he starts taking it onto the field that we're gonna have a problem. Especially if it's fucking with the money my team spent on him or if the virus is spreading to the other guys."

Fitz nodded, resting his long chin on his fingers. "So they stick him out in the pen until he gets the message?"

"I don't know what they're doing with him out there. It could be 'out of sight, out of mind,' for all I know, and at the end of the season they'll decide to keep him or dump him. I don't know what's

187

left on his contract. I can make a few casual inquiries, if you're interested."

Fitz wondered what that would cost him. "Nah, I'm good. But I appreciate letting me bounce this off you."

"Hey, it's my day off and you're picking up the check. What do I care?" He sipped at his espresso, watched the waitress for a while, then sat back again, a look of recognition sharpening his eyes. "Oblonsky. His sister's that umpire just got herself suspended, right?"

"The same."

He grinned. "Aw, hell then. Now we got ourselves a ball game."

Fitz's stomach double-clutched. It was all coming together, what was between the lines of those complaint reports, those halting words on his answering machine.

Miss O wanted her name out of it. But was it to protect her brother's career or her own?

* * *

Fitz liked hats. He was partial to fedoras, like his newspaperman heroes, something he could tip and squash and peer up from under, depending on his mood. A hat gave him the gravitas that his too-young face and cartoonishly long chin did not. It gave him confidence back in high school, a sports fan with no athletic skill, one leg compromised from a bout of childhood polio. He was the stat keeper, not the quarterback. The sportswriter, not the star. He sat on more bleachers than any person had a right to, pushing up his shirtsleeves like the old guys. He even wore old-man suits that hung baggy on his spindly frame. Guys called him "Stevie the Hat." Girls smiled and whispered to each other when he passed by. They thought him exotic and sophisticated, and asked where he got his "cool" vintage look. "I got my sources," he'd say, but really, they were from his grandpa's steamer trunk in the attic. Grandpa was one natty dresser—that was the word his father used—and family rumor said he ran numbers for the mob. Fitz didn't believe it. He just liked his clothes. And his pictures. Clean-shaven, freshly barbered, a dare in his eye. Sometimes Fitz would imagine himself in those pictures, dream himself onto the set of an old gangster movie. He'd be the brains of the operation. Wearing a hat. Maybe a straw boater, like a guy who sold Gatsby his booze.

"It's bad luck to wear the clothes of the dead," his nonna had told him.

"So why'd you save them?"

A wistful curtain fell over her own too-long face. "It keeps him alive." Then, pinching his narrow cheek, she'd say that they looked better on Fitz.

Then a tap on the glass captured his attention. His producer was signaling that he was going to take a leak.

Trevor the vampire could probably go out for a movie and a pizza and nobody would be the wiser. Fitz's show was getting maybe four, five legitimate calls a night. He waved a hand, dismissing the kid, and slumped back in his chair.

His thoughts returned to his column and what, if anything, he should do about it. Take Margie's angle out of it, and the thing had no legs. Keep her in and it was a damn good story, even without a quote from the league president's office ("We don't comment on issues under investigation") and no return calls from Dolph Edwards, his agent, his manager, or Oblonsky's partner, Doug French.

The silence puzzled him. Usually after a good donnybrook, everyone involved wanted to weigh in, get his side of the story out, point some fingers.

But all he could see were turtles pulling back in their shells and ostriches sticking their heads in the sand.

And the "why" about that intrigued him more than the original story.

He'd hoped to talk to Osterhaus. The kid was smart, had worked with Margie on and off since umpire school, and could have been a font of information and background for the story. But he hadn't called Fitz back, either.

Which left him with a bunch of poorly sourced accusations, or a puff piece about Margie Oblonsky trying to make good in a man's game. As puff pieces went, it wasn't horrible. It would be good enough for the *Flushing Shopper*. But not enough for the *Post* or the *Daily News*, and he knew in his gut that this was where the story should go. He knew in his soul that this went deeper than the establishment circling their wagons against a lady ump. It was bigger than Margie Oblonsky and whomever she was trying to protect. It was about cheating players and the infrastructure that let them get away with it. And that was even bigger than baseball.

Trevor slipped back into the booth. Before he could slouch into his chair, Fitz called him over and slapped the two pages of typed copy onto the desk.

"Yeah?" the kid said.

"Read that. Tell me if it's any good."

The kid read. Nothing.

"So?"

The kid shrugged. "It's all right."

"But…?"

"I don't know. What do you wanna hear?"

"Would anyone give a shit?"

"If she made it to the majors, you mean?"

"For one."

He shrugged. "That would be cool." He scanned over the pages again. "I don't know. It kinda sounds like… I don't know. Puffy."

Shit. A hard knot punched his stomach. "Shut up and go back to work," Fitz said.

When Trevor was at one with his comic books, Fitz crumpled up his copy and hurled it into the trash. For a long time, during a stretch of unringing phones and canned interviews, he stared at it. Then it hit him. He could write the story as an editorial. He could make the noise he needed to make, poke the sleeping bear, and do it all without Margie. He leaned back in his chair, popped his fedora on his too-long head, and smiled.

32

THE ELBOW

Tim's elbow bothered him sometimes. Usually the morning after he'd gone a few innings. It was only a little tightness, a little ache, nothing a couple aspirin and an ice pack couldn't fix, then he was good to go. No way was he telling the trainer. Doc would probably pull Tim from the roster, make him get tests, go on the disabled list. That was the death knell for pitchers, he'd heard. The elbow, or the rotator cuff. Some had surgery, but the rehab was long and painful. Sometimes you came out of it okay. But from what he'd seen, these guys were never quite the same. No way was he going to let that happen to him. So he did the protocol. He sat in his apartment with the ice pack strapped to his right elbow, a beer in his left hand. Funny, he'd never been injury prone before. He could pitch a full game, go out partying half the night, get up early and feel like he could do it all again. Had three seasons taken so much out of him already?

He blamed it on September. Alejandro's voice was getting into his head: *By the end of the season, we're dragging around like old men, and who wants to spend their money taking the wife and kids to the ballpark to see that?*

Fuckin' nobody. He was better than this. He wasn't his father. He wasn't going to waste his glory years in the goddamn pen.

He smacked his beer bottle on the glass-topped coffee table and called Alejandro. "Tell me what I gotta do," he said. "Tell me what I gotta do to finish the season."

* * *

They agreed to meet in the bullpen before batting practice.

Alejandro pushed up Tim's sleeve, pressed here and there, nodding like an old-world sage. "Doesn't feel like the joint. Could be just the tendon acting up."

"That's good, right?" Tim said. "I mean, better than the joint."

"I guess. Tendonitis isn't the end of the world, but it could take a while to heal. Trainer Carl will want to give you a shot."

"I gotta tell him?" Tim rolled down his sleeve.

The catcher shrugged, pulling on his mask. "Unless you want to deal with the pain."

Tim thought about that a minute.

"Here's the deal on that," Alejandro said. "Carl and the pitching coach will tell you the same. If you got a blister on your toe when you're pitching, your whole body is gonna compensate for wanting to protect you from the pain when you land on that foot. Compensate and you could be calling on all kinds of muscles that aren't used to working that hard. Because you didn't treat a blister, you could strain a lat, a trap. Hell, you could piss off your rotator cuff. One of those deep suckers. You want to talk pain? You want to talk going on the DL, maybe getting surgery, spending a whole season rehabbing that? Yeah. Don't get a goddamn blister."

Tim thought about that a minute longer. "What would you do?"

"Shit. I'm an old man. I got aches on my aches. I just make a side trip to the salad bowl in the clubhouse and go on with my day, y'know? Then I sit in the hot tub all winter with my ladies. It still aches, but I don't care."

Alejandro flipped him the ball. Before Tim walked over to the pitching rubber at the other end of the pen, he said, "Any of...you know, these other guys out here...hitting the salad bowl?"

"A few. Like I said. Do what you gotta do to get through the season. They spent a lot of money on you, Oblondie, so they'll patch you up good after."

* * *

Margie called that evening, while he was icing his elbow and getting high on whatever he happened to have around his apartment. It was a bad connection; she sounded like she was underwater. From what he could hear, the suspension was hard on her. He wanted to make it go away, but he didn't know how. She'd already told him not to talk to reporters. No problem. He was having enough trouble keeping his focus, staying under the radar, without talking to the press. Fortunately, Cincinnati was kicking ass, at least that week, and his teammates were lighting up the place, so the press gave them all their attention, instead of asking why Oblonsky wasn't pulling his weight. If it was a mistake to put him in the bullpen. If there was talk of him going down to the minors. And he would go home and get buzzed and ice his elbow.

"So what are you doing?" she asked.

He hesitated a moment. "Icing down."

"Timmy. You hurt?"

"Nah. Routine. They had me up and throwing this afternoon but didn't put me in, so that's the recovery protocol."

"Recovery protocol. Huh. You guys in the bigs got a whole bunch of fancy-pants words."

At least part of her was still above water, and that made him smile. For a moment. Silence spread over the phone line, and he reached for something to say to her. "How's Mom?"

"Crazy, as usual."

"You think about getting out of there?"

"Every damn minute." She sighed. "But I'd feel bad. Leaving her alone out here." The pause was infinitesimal. "Oh, I didn't mean…well, fuck. Maybe I did mean that. You could come home once in a while, you know?"

"When the season's over, I swear."

"Tim…"

"Yeah. I know. I said that last year. And I'll do it! Just get off my back, okay?"

"Fine. Don't want to put any pressure on the goddamn *show pony*."

"What the hell's that supposed to mean?"

"Nothin'."

"Margie, you got something to say to me?"

She blew out a breath. "Yeah. I got something to say to you." The pause made his elbow throb. "Keep your fastball down."

"Bite me."

"Right back at you."

And she hung up. Damn it, he hated that. Mostly because she'd beaten him to it. He ripped off the Velcro ice bandage and threw it across the couch. Then called one of the guys from his team, to see where he could find a party. He needed to get his buzz back on. He needed to get laid. He needed to forget about the bullpen. And he needed to lose the thought that kept racing through his head that he would die a little out there every day, just like his father.

33

THE BARGAIN

The phone rang while Nonna was telling Fitz where she wanted the coffee table. At the sound, she stopped directing him midsentence, her face beaming with an impish smile. Even though she'd had a telephone in her Brooklyn apartment for decades, she still acted like it was a miracle that she could pick up the receiver and talk to nearly anyone she wanted. He came home once and found that she'd been engrossed in conversation with a wrong number for twenty minutes. By the end, she already had Fitz marrying the woman's daughter, and he had to gently explain to her that this wasn't the old country, and he wasn't interested in spending the rest of his life with a total stranger. "She's not a stranger," Nonna protested. "Her mother is a lovely woman, and the apple doesn't fall far from the tree."

Nonna plucked up the receiver and sang out, "Good evening, Lastorino residence. This is Maria speaking." As if they'd suddenly been transported to Fifth Avenue. "Oh, yes. That's my grandson, he lives here, he's a wonderful boy…"

"Nonna, for God's sake—"

She waved him off. "He's moving my furniture. You need to talk to him right now?"

"Nonna—"

She nodded and shushed him. "Whom shall I say is calling?"

Like she'd rehearsed it from the movies. She might have curtsied, but that was probably his imagination.

"From where? Did you say the *Post*? The *New York Post* wants to talk to my Stephen?"

Fitz sprang up so fast his bad leg nearly buckled.

"Oh, here he comes now."

Fitz took the receiver from her hands. "This is Stephen Fitzgerald."

"Pete McGill." The sports editor of the *New York Post*. The goddamn sports editor of the *New York Post*. Fitz just about pissed his pants. "Interesting secretary you got there."

He glanced over at Nonna, who was hovering nearby, wringing her hands, her eyebrows expectantly high on her wrinkled forehead. He turned away. "We like her. She works cheap and makes sure I never go hungry. How can I help you?"

"Mr. Fitzgerald—"

"You can call me Fitz. Everybody does. Everybody who doesn't hate me, anyway."

"I like it," he said. "I also like this piece you wrote. It's an angle we've been eyeballing for a while now. Tell you what, *Fitz*. I'd like to print this as a guest column. Maybe use it as a jumping-off point to dig a little deeper."

Fitz's heart damn near stopped.

"But I have a few questions. Poking this bear could have consequences. You got the goods to back this up? Names, dates...?"

He straightened. "I went to journalism school," he said. "I do my homework."

"We'll protect your sources," McGill said. "Standard operating procedure. If I'm putting the *Post* behind this, I need to know who you talked to."

"With all due respect, Mr. McGill. There's only one 'she' in umpiring these days."

There was a pause on the line. Presumably, he was scanning over Fitz's article again. "Huh. Should have seen that pronoun. Must be cross-eyed from editing all day. She on record with this?"

A sweat broke out on the back of Fitz's neck. "What I wrote there is true. What she saw, what she did, the official interference call on Edwards, the forfeit, how the league president's office put her on the shelf. Any number of people could corroborate that."

"But you know more."

He hesitated. "Off the record, a hell of a lot more."

"Well, then. Fitz. We should have a conversation about that. And about your future. We could use a sharp writer around here." He laughed. "Unless you like it too much at the *Shopper*."

Fitz heard the sound of typewriters. The groan of McGill's chair. He imagined the smell of the place: ink, coffee, cigarette smoke. It made his skin tingle.

"I won't lie, they've been good to me. But I'm ready for a challenge. Thank you, Mr. McGill. Sir."

He laughed again. "If we're gonna poke a bear, Fitz, I think you should call me Pete."

* * *

Too amped to sit on the bench with the other relievers, Tim watched the final innings of the game while standing behind the bullpen wall. Alejandro slouched beside him, in a cloud of Juicy Fruit gum and aftershave, drumming his ugly catcher's thumbs against the wire mesh. Each thump and flutter jangled up Tim's nerves even more.

"Will you cut that the hell out?"

Alejandro gave him a slow smile, all white teeth and arching eyebrows. "You're gonna miss me this winter, admit it. You're gonna be sitting at home watching soap operas with your momma, wishing old Alejo was entertaining your ass."

Tim blew out a breath, started to say something about the bullpen catcher's old ass, but then the crack of the bat stopped time. It was the sound everyone who knew fact one about baseball knew, from the kid working his first summer selling hot dogs in the bleachers to the announcers in the booth to the crusty lifer folding towels in the clubhouse. Not a single man in the pen had to watch the ball arc across the sky. Everyone knew it was gone.

"Dude's done," Alejandro said.

Tim nodded. Their starter, a big left-hander, had come out blazing with his best stuff, strong and precise, through the first six innings. He made some of the league's best hitters look stupid. They swung at fastballs that tailed away at the last second, sliders that broke so suddenly it was like they were being redirected by an unseen hand. But he'd lost his control. He'd lost his speed and power. Only by sheer luck had those last few hanging curveballs not been hit downtown.

His luck had just run dry.

About this time during a game, he and Alejandro and the other guys in the pen usually percolated with chatter. They'd be waiting for the phone call from the dugout, telling them who the manager wanted up throwing, whose turn it was to save the day.

But the silence. The silence among them was louder than that crack of the bat, louder than the drunk Mets fans yelling "Reds suck" from the bleachers. Alejandro smacked his gum. Then he nudged Tim's arm. "Gonna be you, Oblondie."

Tim gulped. He didn't want it to be him. He wasn't feeling right. At the end of the third inning, he'd thought it was simply his normal game-day jitters. Alejandro offered him a pill and he refused, a little freaked about what it could do to his pitching. But maybe he should have taken it. There was something loud and rattling about the tension now, a voice in his trembling gut saying *no no no*. His elbow didn't hurt too much, but his arm felt stiff and heavy, and something large had parked itself on his chest.

Off the field, the remedy was so simple. Get smashed and lose himself. A few drinks, a girl, a line or four. It didn't make the pain or the terror go away, but he cared about it less, at least for a while. But now, he worried. "I need to work," Tim said.

Alejandro peered over his shoulder at the bench. The assistant pitching coach was deep in conversation with another reliever, but he looked up and nodded.

"Yeah, okay, Oblondie, let's go."

Sometimes getting a guy throwing in the bullpen was like a show for the other team. It was psychological. It said, "We're about to shut you down." But it could also tip their hand. Now the Mets' manager might rethink his lineup, put in a pinch-hitter. It was all part of the chess game. Tim never had much patience for that. Waiting around made his skin crawl.

Tell me when to throw, and I'll throw.

The phone rang: another sound that gave Tim nightmares. The assistant pitching coach sidled over, picked up the receiver, nodded, set it back in the cradle. Tim held his breath. The smell of the catcher's gum roiled his stomach. Maybe he should have eaten something before the game.

"Oblonsky." Tim nearly pissed his cup. The coach eyeballed him, then the corner of his mouth crooked. "Siddown."

They wanted the lefty. Tim knew better than to show he was

relieved. So he gave the coach a nod and moved aside and let Alejandro warm the guy up.

The lefty got the batter to pop up on one pitch, and Tim's shoulders lowered a few inches. The next one got lucky on a bloop single that fell between the outfielders. He struck the next dude out. Then walked the next two to load the bases.

The thing on Tim's chest doubled in size.

And then the phone rang.

* * *

Tim hated the stupid little car that ferried the relievers onto the field. Like he was some kind of fancy-ass celebrity, being driven in from the bullpen in a tricked-out golf cart wearing a giant plastic baseball cap for a roof. Thirty thousand people staring at him. Alejandro made fun of him every time. Called him Secretariat. Called him show pony. "Show pony, your ride's here." Tim laughed him off, but it was mortifying to get into that thing.

He kept his eyes closed the whole trip in from the pen, his cap pulled down tight, trying to stem the panic. The feeling that he was floating above his body like one of those Goodyear blimps, watching the ridiculous car, watching the show pony losing his nerve.

The mound loomed like the edge of a cliff. As he began the slow walk to the pitching rubber, his stomach lurched straight up to his throat and his fingers began to tingle. He ticked through the routine they'd taught him, to battle the stress and help him focus. They'd tried so many things with him: meditation, deep breathing, creative visualization. All kinds of "be the ball" crap. A sports therapist even came into the clubhouse, gave a talk about intention and attitude. Frankly it put Tim to sleep. It was all because of that guy who wrote a book about using Zen philosophy to be more successful at tennis, and then it got applied to everything—business, music, baseball. Right now, Tim wanted to smack the author with his own book.

But mainly he wanted to run.

All pitchers had their little routines, the things they did to settle in, get comfortable, get focused. Tim dug his cleats into the dirt, scuffing the mound the way he liked it, so he could anchor his left toe. He moved the rosin bag to where it was handy but wouldn't distract him. Then set up to throw a few pitches to Elton. His name was really Mike, but they already had a catcher named Mike and Elton Mike liked to dress flashy when they went out, so hence the nickname.

The catcher was tight. His throws back were quick, compact. When they were going well, Elton was all loosey-goosey like Alejandro. They weren't going well. *Jeez, do I look like that? No. Can't let that get in my head. Damn, the crowd. It's like being underwater, waves crashing over my head. What did that guru guy say about being one with the crowd, being one with the moment, one with the ball?* It was all jumbling up. His mouth went dry. A cold sweat cooled the back of his neck. He should have had another cup of water before going out. Dehydration is the enemy, coach told him. Muscles and joints want to be lubricated. Gotta stop partying so much. *There's your dehydration, bonehead. Gaa. Just fuckin' throw. Jeez.*

Shut the fuck up and throw.

He was allowed eight warm-up pitches before the batter stepped in. The umpire watched him like a hawk, a tall slab of a guy, arms crossed over his chest. Maybe he was acclimating himself to the rhythms of a new pitcher. Or taking a welcome break from being crouched behind Elton over a long, long inning.

"That's enough, son," the umpire said. Tim's stomach tightened. A muscle in his neck pulled taut. He sucked in a deep breath, or as deep as his constricted lungs would allow, then let it out slow, clutched the ball in his right hand, pounded it into the webbing of his glove a couple of times. Said a prayer to his dad for good luck.

The batter who stepped in was a guy Tim had faced in the minors. He was huge and strong and knew how to hit him and had the nerve to smile.

Before he could even throw one pitch, Elton called time and trotted up.

"Okay, Timbo," he said. "Nice and easy now. Just get this guy to chase it. We got this."

Tim eyeballed him. Not helpful. And he hated being called Timbo.

"Yeah, thanks," Tim said.

Elton signaled for a slider. Tim wanted a fastball. He thought about shaking him off, then reconsidered. *Be a good show pony. One pitch at a time.*

That mother sailed in nice. The umpire pumped his fist—strike one—and Tim bit back the urge to howl with pleasure. Damn, it felt good to get one in. It felt right. Like his old self. Maybe he could turn this around. He was half in love with the way the ball felt in his hand, and his arm started loosening up, and he could breathe a little easier. And the ball. The ball had landed with a good solid *thwock* in Elton's mitt.

But he knew he had no business congratulating himself. Not with a job to do.

One pitch at a time.

Slider inside. Strike two.

The crowd and his heartbeat thundered in his ears, in his blood.

Thirty thousand pairs of eyeballs. Thirty thousand pairs of lungs, breath held, waiting for what he'd do next.

The thing on his chest began to squeeze. In his bones he felt the pain of his last outing. The mistakes he'd made. The batters who'd smashed his mistakes over the fence.

Shake it off.

Shake it off.

He tried to picture Margie's face. That smirk, the way she looked when she was about to call him John-Boy.

Keep your fastball down.

Damn it. Get the hell out of my head.

Nerves jumped down his arms, tingling his fingers. He crushed the ball tighter.

Elton called time.

He flipped up his mask and came out. The shortstop came in. The manager came in. They stood too close, hemming him in, all those eyes and moving lips and expectations.

Someone asked if he was okay.

No. He wasn't okay. He was burning up and freezing at the same time. He couldn't breathe. He couldn't feel his fingertips. He couldn't feel anything. Maybe he was having a heart attack. Or he was losing his mind. The stadium began to spin. A hand came out, tightened around his upper arm. And then his legs began to melt away beneath him, the roar of the crowd and the infielder's voices swirling into a tunnel of white noise.

* * *

Tim couldn't tell if the low buzz was coming from inside or outside his head, and that distressed him. The air felt cool, the lights dim.

He swallowed, his throat dry, and licked his parched lips.

Trainer Carl stood over him, taking a calm appraisal. "Evening, Mr. Tim. You gave us a little scare, but your color's looking better."

"Did we win?" Tim said. His voice cracked.

"Let's worry about that later." Carl pressed the cold circle of the stethoscope to his bare chest, moved it around, listening. "You just rest now, you were pretty dehydrated when they brought you in here."

That was the tug he felt on his arm. An IV taped to the crook of his elbow, the plastic tube running up to a bag of clear fluid on a metal stand.

"Did we win?"

Carl laughed softly. "Yessir. It was a real nail-biter, but you boys pulled it off. You rest now, though. I'm sure folks'll fill you in on that later."

Carl's soft Southern accent flowed over the hum, telling him to breathe deep and stop and breathe again. Tim's lungs felt puny and tight, the ghost of the giant monster still sitting atop him.

Then a new voice joined in. It sounded far away, but the words were distinct: "You gotta let me see him. We're like family."

Tim blinked and again tried to sit up. *Dan? Big Dan Monroe? What the hell—?* Surprise shifted to dread and shame and anger, and his body had already decided it wanted to bolt.

"Stay there." Trainer Carl was stronger than he looked. Or Tim was weaker than he knew. "This someone you want in here?"

"No, but...hell, let him in." Tim breathed hard, surprised at the effort those words took.

The door clicked shut, Carl making a discreet exit. The big man blocked out what little light shone overhead.

Two beats later the voice came again, softer, flavored with flat prairie tones and a touch of humor. "Ya knucklehead, if you didn't want to pitch today, you coulda just said so."

Tim blinked up at him. Fucking pity in his eyes. Fucking pity behind that goddamn corn-fed smile. He blinked again to keep the tears from sliding down his cheeks. "Get the fuck out of here."

"Timmy."

He jerked up, pain searing his arm where the IV pulled and the tape sheared off. He grabbed the nearest thing and hurled it toward Dan's voice. "Get. The. Fuck. Out. Of. Here."

Dan dodged the incoming; Tim still didn't know what he'd thrown. Carl's fast footsteps drew close. Tim squeezed his eyes shut. He felt the big man's presence, heard his loud breathing, the quiet murmurs exchanged between the catcher and the trainer. Then there only was one man standing in the doorway. A big slab of a man, breathing in and out through his mouth.

"Are you done?" Dan said. "Can we be grown-ups now?"

"Fuck off. I don't need your goddamn pity."

"Man. I just wanted to see if you were all right. That looked pretty serious out there. Thought they were gonna have to shoot you for a second."

"I'm fine." Tim spread his hands wide; his arm burned from where he'd pulled the IV. "See? Perfectly fine." He forced a smile that made his temples throb. "I got dehydrated from some kind of bug and I'm getting my saline and I'll be good to go for tomorrow. Good little soldier in the bullpen. Happy now? Or do you want to rub it in that I'm a total goddamn loser following in my old man's footsteps?"

Dan shook his head. His lips were a tight line. "Timmy."

"Don't fucking call me that." Tim narrowed his eyes. "Did Margie send you?"

The big man glared. "No. I came to see my old friend's team play. Thought we could grab dinner after, catch up. Then I saw that friend go down. So I came back here. I've been waiting out there for a goddamn hour. But now I'm thinking I was wasting my time."

Tim couldn't think of what to say for a long moment. Dan just stood there. The urge to cry was punching the inside of his head and he punched back.

"I'm in the pen, Dan. I'm in the fucking pen."

"Yeah, so? There are a lot of great guys in the pen. Tug McGraw's in the pen."

"Fuck Tug McGraw. The pen's where you go to fucking die."

Dan shook his head again. His eyes boring into him. His words were eerily calm, laced with controlled anger. "I thought you were better than that. Well, guess I'm oh-for-two today. Wasting my time and wrong about you."

"The fuck you talking about?"

"Timmy." He glared, daring Tim to rebut him. "Word I hear is they wanted you sent down, work your *issues* out with us regular slobs in the minors. The pen, yeah. I get your history with it. But it's a chance. And you're crapping all over it. But, you know? Maybe there is no going back for you. Maybe your head's gotten too big to fit back out the door."

Tim cast his eyes around for something else to throw.

Dan raised his palms. "Fine. I'm leaving. Don't want you to hurt your arm throwing a hissy fit."

"Fuck you."

"In your dreams, boy." He started for the door, then hesitated. "You even know what's going on with Margie?"

"Of course I know what's going on with my own sister. Some kind of bullshit suspension. She's had 'em before. She can handle it."

Dan shook his head. "Try returning her calls once in a while."

And then he was gone.

34

THE DOWNFALL

The word in Pat Oblonsky's kitchen that Wednesday afternoon in early September was tomatoes. Fat, ripe tomatoes, freckled with dirt from the farmers' market, covered their table and nearly every square inch of their countertops. With Margie in for the winter, trying not to think about the phone call that might never come, and the hope that Tim might stick a pin in his inflated ego and spend part of the off-season at home, the answer for both women was to fill the pantry with a ridiculous amount of food.

They prepped and blanched and sterilized canning jars while they listened to the ball game on Dad's old radio, which was balanced on the windowsill for better reception. Tim and the Reds were in New York, playing the Mets in the last game of a three-game series. The Mets had looked like contenders early in the season but had been stinking up the place with a vengeance since June or so. Pat boycotted the Yankees on principle, because she believed they killed her husband. And she only paid attention to the Mets when they were winning or when they were playing Cincinnati. So for the last two games, which they'd watched on television, they'd waited for glimpses of Tim warming up in the bullpen. The manager hadn't needed him, or any relievers, in game one of the series. They brought him in for the seventh inning of the second game because the starting pitcher was getting tired; Tim gave up two back-to-back home runs and they took him right back out again.

His fastball was high.

Mom thought he looked too thin.

Margie felt bad for not calling him. She knew those low moments hit him hard. But he'd been such an asshole the last time they spoke, and maybe that's why she'd provoked him into their

LAURIE BORIS

argument. She hadn't told her mother about that, her mother who thought he walked on golden clouds sprinkling fairy dust in his wake. She sighed and poked at a just-blanched tomato to see if it was cool enough to handle. Maybe he'd been a dick to her because he needed some space to deal with the bullpen thing.

Maybe it was time to let him have what he wanted. She hated the distance growing between them. Even if he did come home, she had a bad feeling it would only be out of guilt. He'd rather be living in some beach house with his buddies or playing winter ball and dreaming about what next season might bring, what the rest of his life might bring. Their parents' siblings hadn't remained close when they'd left home and started their families; Margie rarely saw her aunts and uncles. So why would she and Timmy be any different? It was a story as old as the dirt on the tomatoes. You grow up, you move out, you move on. And she hated the hell out of it.

After a lackluster inning, the Reds' best hitter launched a two-run homer into the right field bleachers. Even over their tinny radio, Margie heard the crowd at Shea deflating.

"I don't think they're gonna put him in today," Margie's mother said. Her voice pinched with outrage as she plunked a skinned tomato into a bowl. "And it's not friggin' fair. The Mets got lucky on him yesterday, so what. You put him right back on that horse after. Everybody knows that. I'm gonna call their pitching coach, give him a piece of my mind."

"Mom. You can't go calling his pitching coach every time… He's gotta work with the coaches, figure this out for himself."

The sigh was long and wounded.

"He didn't look right yesterday," Pat said. "Too thin. Maybe they're working him too hard. I read about that in *Sports Illustrated.* They train these young kids too hard and they get injured."

"Yeah, maybe, but they got all this new science now. They got all these new recovery protocols." Jeez, had she just said that? "Mom, they know what they're doing. It's not like in Dad's time. Tim and Dan and the guys now…they play smart, they ice down, they stay fit. They're like investments or something, and the owners don't want to screw with that."

Mom calmed down, and they worked together in silence for a while. Tomatoes were dunked and canned; the Mets chipped away at

206

the Reds' lead.

Then the Mets radio announcer Bob Murphy said, "Looks like they're getting Oblonsky up in the bullpen…"

Both women's heads popped up like prairie dogs.

Margie darted to the TV. But Channel 9 wasn't showing the game.

Cursing the stupid schedule, she returned to the kitchen, staring at the tomatoes as they listened to the play-by-play.

"Nope," Bob Murphy said. "Looks like the Reds manager is signaling for the lefty."

Margie sighed her relief. Part of her didn't want Timmy pitching today. He needed a day off to recover from whatever was grinding his gears. He'd been like that since they were kids. Frustration only made Margie throw herself at something harder. Tim liked to back off, think about it, and then he usually returned stronger and more determined.

But the lefty wasn't cutting it, the bases were loaded, and when Murphy announced another pitching change, Margie held her breath until he spoke again.

"The two homers Oblonsky gave up in yesterday's game weren't ultimately a deciding factor in the Mets' loss, but that kind of performance has to shake a young pitcher's confidence, don't you think, Steve?"

"No doubt, Bob, but the Reds organization sees something in this kid, to bring him in with the score tied and the bases loaded and two out…"

The two women merely went through the motions after that, both riveted by the voices coming from the radio. Margie tried to picture the strike zone, and Timmy bearing down on the pitch, going into his windup. She closed her eyes, the steam from the boiling pot heating her face as she tried to will magic back into his arm. *You got this, John-Boy…*

"Strike one on a beauty of a fastball low and inside!"

Margie grinned. Her mother hooted and nearly dropped a tomato.

"Mom, quit it, I can't hear."

"Oblonsky sets up again…lets it fly…*strike two* on a sinker. Quick return. Oblonsky readies to throw… He shakes off the sign…wait. Catcher Mike Maneri is calling time. He wants to talk this over… And… Oh, that's not good."

"What? What's not good?" Pat darted over and turned up the volume.

"Oblonsky is down," Murphy said.

"Down?" Pat squeaked. "What do they mean, down?"

Margie's chest ached.

"They're calling out medical. Tim Oblonsky is down."

Pain and concern flashed across her face. "What? Is he hurt? Is Tim hurt?"

"Mom." Margie could barely talk. "I don't know."

The radio crackled with static. Margie's breaths were short and punchy. Nobody was saying anything. Bob Murphy came back and talked about nothing with his partner. She didn't notice until her skin was burning that the tomato bath had boiled over onto the stove, over her hands.

"Shea Stadium," Pat Oblonsky yelled at the operator. Margie hadn't seen her mother going for the phone. "I want Shea Stadium front office. Whaddya mean there's no number? Whaddya mean there's only the ticket office? They got phones, they gotta have numbers. This is a friggin' emergency!"

The first of many cigarettes were lit as Pat continued to bark and fume and eventually gave up. Margie ran her tomato-flesh hands under cool water and listened for updates on the radio. She picked a few words out of the static. Stretcher. Unconscious. Waiting for news about Tim Oblonsky's condition. Play will continue.

* * *

On the six o'clock news, they said he got dizzy and light-headed from food poisoning, and that he'd be fine, but the video clip of Tim crumpling on the mound split Margie's heart. She'd called his hotel room. He was there, thank God, and the team hadn't had to rush him to the hospital, but the front desk was holding his calls. "Mom, I can't reach him."

"Oh, give me that friggin' phone. Hello? Yeah. I'm Timothy Oblonsky's mother. What? He said WHAT? *Especially* his mother?" Pat Oblonsky's lips pursed; her cheeks paled. She set the receiver into the cradle with a quiet click.

Her voice was so small Margie barely recognized it. "He doesn't want to talk to me."

"I'm sorry, Mom. Maybe you just gotta let him…you know, be for a while. You know how Tim can get. Especially when he's sick."

But Margie had a feeling Timmy wasn't sick.

Her mother nodded, then something Margie didn't trust lit her eyes. Mom grabbed up the receiver. "I'm callin' his manager."

"Mom, you can't call a guy's manager and—"

"The hell I can't. Your father knew him when. He could do us a favor."

"Mom." Margie gently took the phone away. "Mom. Stop. Look at me. He wants us to know what's going on, he'll get in touch. Until then…" She glanced over at the tomatoes. "Maybe we should put up the rest of these. You know how much Tim likes your spaghetti and meatballs."

* * *

When Carl finally released him, all Tim wanted was for the driver to get him away from the stadium as fast as possible. Locked in his hotel room felt like the away he needed. At first. But then the walls started crashing in on him, as tight as the fences in the bullpen alley. Like he could die from the walls being so close, the air molecules being so close together, no space to breathe. His heart raced. The cold sweat again prickled the back of his neck. Tim wiped a hand across it. *Fuck Dan Monroe. Who asked him to come here, anyway?*

The minibar called to him. Tim cracked the seal on another bottle of he'd-stopped-caring-what. It went down easy, and hearing his mother's voice in his head that he should use a glass like a human, he poured the next bottle into a plastic tumbler. He stared at it, and his lower lip quivered with guilt. They had to have seen the game. She and Margie were probably worrying about him. Hopefully someone told them the food poisoning thing. Because if he called them now, he'd totally lose his mind. He didn't want to think anymore. The shame of failure hurt like a thousand tiny paper cuts all over his body. He threw down the shot to kill the pain. Sat back in the chair and tried to breathe. But the walls started humming again. So did his head. He was jumpy, his skin itched, he couldn't get enough air in his lungs. Trainer Carl had called it an anxiety attack. The words alone had paralyzed him, and as Carl went on with the explanation of what it was, Tim had mentally checked out, freaking about what it could mean for his career. Freaked about what could happen if word got out. He'd look weak, like he couldn't handle the pressure. His eyes latched onto the phone.

Talk to Margie at least.

He couldn't. He couldn't face her now. It was too humiliating. Especially after what she'd said about him the last time they'd talked. Called him show pony, said he'd changed. Maybe Margie and Dan were right. Or they were jealous. Maybe Margie was just bitter that she wasn't born a boy. He couldn't change that. His lips pressed together.

It wasn't his fault he'd made it to the majors.

But he couldn't stop staring at the phone.

He pulled the little address book from his bag, and then he was dialing, rationalizing with the small, wounded animal in his brain that this was what he needed to do to feel better. And that if he felt better, at least for a moment, it would be enough to handle the rest of it.

* * *

Theresa's hair was a miracle. He played with a long, springy lock as she dozed, her head against his bare chest. He wound the strands around his index finger, picking out the red, gold, and brown. He loved how it tickled his skin as it trailed along his body. Imagining that made him want her again, and their second time was slower, deeper; all the crap in his life evaporated in the kiss of their intertwined limbs. Wrapped in her, he felt powerful, infallible, her sighs as sweet and thrilling as getting a called third strike with two outs and the bases loaded. Better. So much better.

When they finally parted, she smiled at him, pushed a sweaty tangle of hair off his forehead and said, "Nice to see you again."

He'd been about to laugh, but something pinged in his gut. The smile looked a little forced, a little sad, her eyes wide and watchful. Did she know? She said she didn't follow baseball. He liked that about her from the start. He'd let her pick him up in a bar after a game earlier in the season; he'd pitched lights out, helping the team to a big win against the Mets, and he'd wanted to celebrate. She'd been easy company ever since, asking no more from him than a good time whenever he was in town. They didn't talk much about their lives, but he had a hunch she was escaping something, and after assuring himself that that something wasn't a husband, he was more than happy to help. He had some standards, after all. He always used protection, and he never messed around with another guy's woman.

"I brought us a party." She winked and rolled toward the nightstand and her purse, giving him a shot of her gorgeous ass. His hand curved around it almost of its own accord, and she giggled. "Later, hot stuff. And it'll blow your mind. Trust me."

"Why?" he said. "Whatcha got?"

She came back with a plastic bag, grinning like a kid showing off her Halloween goodies. A little weed, a little coke, a bunch of pills. The pills were new to him. She explained what they were, how they were supposed to make you feel. Tim latched onto a few words that interested him. Euphoric was one he liked, although he couldn't imagine feeling any more euphoric than when he was lost in her body. She was one of the many reasons he loved New York. But the idea of sex with her lasting longer…yeah, he liked that, too. They downed a few pills with what was left in the minibar and then lay back, watching bad TV and waiting.

Tim felt nothing at first. That wasn't unusual for him. Nothing, nothing, nothing, and then whatever he'd taken would hit him like a locomotive.

He was still in the nothing stage when she slid her smooth calf up and down his leg and said, "I'm going to miss you."

"What?"

Her pupils were huge; almost nothing remained of the pale green iris. "You're so beautiful. Like one of those Norse gods."

"Okay, you're so high. And what the hell are you talking about? Where are you going?"

"I just wanted one more wild night before…" She gestured with one hand, a futile circling, and giving up, she spread her palm against his lower belly, letting it drift down to his cock.

He stopped her. Not like his cock was interested anymore, anyway. "What, you're breaking it off with me?"

"You're a fun guy, Tim. But…"

"Oh. You want a boyfriend." She didn't answer right away. That wasn't good. Shit. "You already got a boyfriend."

She didn't answer.

"You know, maybe you'd better leave." The hand made another grab for him. "Theresa."

"We're already here," she whispered, sliding on top of him. "Naked." She raked her nails up his chest and he responded despite himself, which annoyed him. "Don't you feel it? Isn't it the best high? I could fuck you all night."

A tempting thought, but… "So you're using me. Why, is your boyfriend busy?"

"Aw, don't be a drag. Touch me." She tried to put one of his hands on her breast.

"Stop it." He moved her off of him.

She pouted.

"Were you using me this whole time?" he asked. "Just having fun until you could meet Mr. Right?"

Her mouth rounded. "Like you weren't using me?" With the dilated pupils, the sudden anger made her look like some kind of demon. The ones that slither into men's dreams and steal their souls. "Like I wasn't just your New York fuck toy?"

She began to cry.

"Hey." He smoothed a hand along her arm. "I'm sorry, I thought we both got what this was. I thought you were okay with it, I didn't think you… I never meant to hurt you…"

The room began to tilt then. In the back of his mind, the paranoia crept in, the pesky pull hitter batting seventh who could blow your game wide open with one swing of his bat. And the thought that this had all been too easy.

She swiped away her tears as if they were the cause of her fury, as if her own eyes had betrayed her.

Then she left, slamming the bedroom door.

The silence settled, and he stared at the place where she had been, and he swore he could still feel the heat of her soft body atop his. As it dissipated, the paranoia rushed in to fill the void. The thing on his chest had returned, pressing down hard, choking him. Tim needed to kill it. He inched the long fingers of his pitching hand toward the bag of pills she'd left behind.

35

THE DISTANCE

Even while she was still working with Doug French, Margie had a sense deep in her bones that something had been seriously wrong with Tim. When he bothered to return her calls, he swore he was fine. But it was a bullshit kind of fine—his words clipped, his silences long. She had a pretty good idea of how he must have felt about getting sent to the bullpen, but she didn't have words to make it better. It only made her think about her own situation, which she didn't want to think about. The irony made her sick. That both of them wanted this dream so bad; it was about all they could talk about when they were kids. How sweet it would feel to run onto the field of a real ballpark, to be like one of their heroes one day. To be like Dad. Now both of them had been given a shot and both were in danger of losing it all, and their conversations about the game were nonexistent. Something wasn't right.

Tim and Margie didn't talk about it, probably because that would make the impending ax seem too real, too close and shiny, but her mother, as usual, was the one to point out the big fat elephant in the room. When she saw the news about Tim's reassignment on the sports page—as a hometown boy in the big leagues, Tim couldn't fart without the local paper reporting on it—she lit the first of many cigarettes, flailing out cuss words with each plume of smoke. Or at least Margie imagined the plumes of smoke. She'd heard the tirade from a motel room when she was working a game somewhere in the Adirondacks.

"Stuck out in the bullpen like your friggin' father." There were a lot of other words, but these were the ones that came out most frequently. Margie tried to talk her off the ledge. She tried, in her calmest voice, to tell her mother that this didn't necessarily mean the end of Tim's career. She'd tell Tim the same thing if he'd return her damn calls.

"Mom. Lots of pitchers are moved back and forth. Sometimes they need to fix problems with their pitching or it's a better fit for a team's lineup. It doesn't always mean the guy's a crap pitcher. Just like me getting moved around doesn't mean I'm a crap umpire." She hoped. "Some things are bigger than one guy." Margie knew that all too well.

Her mother sighed, long and heavy. "My boy. My boy acts like it doesn't bother him, but really, he takes things so hard."

Margie knew that, too. Tim had sulked for a week when he was moved off the mound to second base in junior varsity. Mom had vibrated with outrage and, despite Margie's pleas, huffed over to the school to see the coach. Tim wouldn't come out of his room for two days.

No wonder Tim didn't like to talk about it when things didn't go his way. Margie finally had to hang up on her mother before she could finish her tirade about how stupid the pitching coach was to stick Tim out there, that her boy should be starting, that putting him out there would ruin him.

But now, Margie had a sick feeling that the fourteen-year-old kid in Tim's head was stuck in a room somewhere, listening to Led Zeppelin, and quietly dying inside, and she couldn't do one friggin' thing about it.

She picked up the phone again and dialed the hotel. Again she got the chipper receptionist with the Long Island accent.

Margie identified herself and got the usual spiel about calls being held. "Look," she said. "You gotta put me through. It's a family emergency." She thought for all of five seconds. "It's my mother. She's having apoplexy over here. Do you really want to give someone's mother a heart attack?" She lowered her voice. "Yeah. I know. She's kind of a pain in the ass. I promise I won't put her on the line. But we're twins, you know? I got an awful feeling, and I gotta know if he's okay."

"Margie. I'm not supposed to, but...well, okay." The wires clicked and crackled, and in the distance, it sounded like a phone was ringing. After five rings, someone picked up.

"Dan?"

He let his breath out in a whoosh. "Lemme call you back."

Margie set the receiver down. Stunned. Staring at the phone, wondering what just happened, while anxiety punched her in the stomach.

"Did you talk to him?" her mother said from the hall. "He's okay?"

"I think. Dan's there. He's calling me back."

Mom's shoulders sank. Still she hovered in the doorway. "Standing there isn't going to make him call back faster," Margie said. But her mother didn't move.

Finally the phone trilled and Margie snapped it up. "Look, he's okay," Dan said. From the noise, it sounded like he was at a pay phone, maybe one in the lobby. "He's sleeping now, and the team trainer is in the room with him, but I think we got this. No need to worry your mom."

Margie sank into a kitchen chair. Worry her mom? What about freaking *her* the hell out? "What happened?"

"You saw the video on the news, I guess?"

"Yeah. They said he had food poisoning. I think that's bullshit, myself, but I tried calling him and nobody would put me through."

In the long pause that followed, Margie began to hyperventilate. "The team's story is that a little while ago, he had a relapse." Dan said he'd been at the game, didn't like what he saw of Tim in the trainer's room, so he went back to the hotel later to check on him. "The place was boiling with EMTs. They'd gotten an anonymous tip that Timmy was unconscious." Dan's voice broke. Margie leapt out of her seat.

"I'm comin' down there." She spun toward her mother, who was standing in the doorway, white as a ghost.

"Margie." Dan said it like a plea. Margie got it. Mom, the tornado, would only make things worse. In her mind, she worked through a bunch of ways to get her to stay home. Dan's voice softened when he said her name again. "I don't think... Margie, I know my boy. Swear to God I'll keep you updated, but I think it's better for Tim if the two of you stay put right now."

The *two* of them? Margie's head snapped back as if he'd struck her. Then she pulled herself up taller. "I know my boy, too. And I'm comin' down."

* * *

It was a two-hour trip to Manhattan. Margie didn't trust her mother behind the wheel, so she drove the Cadillac while Pat hunched into a tight knot in the passenger seat, chain-smoking all the way down the New York State Thruway, muttering to herself about the evils of baseball and the raw deal given to her father and how she was going to put the hurt on Tim's manager for all of it.

"Mom. It's not the manager's fault."

"It damn sure is somebody's fault. He's a young, spirited, good-looking boy. You don't plunk a young boy into that kind of environment and give him that kind of money without some kind of guidance."

"Mom."

"It's a girl. I know it's a girl. Some baseball groupie got her claws in him—"

"Oh, Mom, for God's sake. I know it's hard for you to hear, but Tim's all grown up now. He's always had a lot of girlfriends."

"Cheap little floozies treating him like a trophy."

"Mom. Can we have some quiet time now?" She flicked on the radio, and Fitz was in her ear. "Oh, for fuck's sake... Mom, you listen to him?"

"Sometimes, if I'm up late." She shrugged. "He has a nice voice."

He did, but he was talking with a caller about who was going to the playoffs, and she really wasn't in the mood to think about baseball right now. She needed to think about getting them safely to Manhattan, and then to find the hotel, and then to figure out how to keep Mom out of Tim's room while she made sure he was okay.

But then it all became too much to think about, and she drifted into the soothing cadence of Stephen Fitzgerald's voice.

"Yeah, the Reds don't totally stink," Fitzgerald said. "They got some solid performances out of—"

"Their bullpen's crap, though. They gotta dump Oblonsky, he's—"

Margie snapped the radio off.

* * *

Dan met them in the lobby. He looked like he'd aged ten years since the last time she'd seen him. Putting aside her anger that he'd kept her in the dark, Margie allowed him to hug her. "You I'll deal with later," she whispered in his ear. "Talk to me about Tim."

He led them to a quiet corner, sat them down, and began to explain. He went over the thing about the food poisoning, and the EMTs, and Margie stopped him.

"What did he take?"

"Margie!"

"Mom."

"My Timmy doesn't do drugs. I taught him better than that."

Silence.

Her mother sprang to her feet, wobbling a little, and Dan caught her arm. "I wanna see him."

"He's asleep. Carl said he needs to rest now."

"He should be in the hospital," her mother said, returning to her seat with a huff. "Not some hotel room."

"Carl's a professional," Dan said. "He knows his stuff, he's monitoring Tim's vitals, and if God forbid anything goes south, he can have the EMTs back in a snap."

Through her teeth, Margie said, "What. Did. He. Take?"

Dan sighed, a tired old-man sound. "What didn't he take, is the question." His fists tightened against the tops of his muscular thighs. "I never should have left him alone, I should have stuck around, made sure he got back here okay..."

"Not your fault," Margie said.

"He was hurting. My boy was hurting, and I let him chase me out because of my own stupid pride."

"Hey." Margie leaned close and got an arm around him. Big Dan even cried a little; she held him tighter.

Her mother cleared her throat. "Well, if nobody's gonna let me see him, I'm gonna go see if they got some coffee around here that ain't swill. You want?"

Margie shook her head and Mom took off. She stroked Dan's hair, and when he finally got himself under control and looked back up at her, he seemed a little lighter, a little younger.

"The anonymous tip," Margie said, then cleared the emotion from her throat. "I'm guessing he had a girl in his room?"

Dan shifted in his chair. "They said the voice was female. Young. And kind of out of it. The call was traced to a pay phone a couple blocks from here."

Anger boxed its way up Margie's chest. "We won't tell my mother."

Dan nodded. "Good call, ump."

* * *

Margie lay awake while two feet away her mother snored in time with the death-rattling wheeze of the air conditioning unit, which seemed to be set on ice cube and was giving her wicked post-nasal drip. Adding to the symphony was the elevator going up and down. As if she could even sleep if she wanted to, worried about Timmy, still haunted by the TV footage of her twin brother collapsing on the mound like a puppet with no strings. Still, it was sweet of Dan to get them a room. She could read the conflict all over his face as he tapped his credit card on the counter and asked the receptionist if they might have two rooms. He'd wanted to bunk in with Tim, keep an eye on him, but they'd had a big fight in the trainer's room after the game and Tim had told him to get lost. Dan never swore, at least in front of her, but Margie imagined that in the moment, John-Boy might have phrased that a little differently.

Still dressed in her tomato-prepping clothes—an old tank top and denim cutoffs—she slipped out of the blankets, grabbed her room key, and went off in search of Tim. It couldn't be that hard. Reporters and ugly notes found her all the time. Girls figured out where players were staying; she'd heard the stories. And, as she thought, a quick, impassioned conversation with the night manager got her what she wanted. It probably didn't hurt that he kept looking at her legs and her bed-tossed blond hair. She wasn't thrilled about using her femininity to get her way, but if it could get her Tim's room number, she could suck it up a little and flirt.

When she got off on the tenth floor and turned the corner, she saw that he already had company.

* * *

He shot to his feet when he saw her, mouth rehearsing excuses like a little boy caught with his hand in the cookie jar.

"Couldn't sleep either?" Margie said.

Dan shook his head and pressed a big catcher's hand over her bare shoulder. She wanted to fall into his arms, draw in some strength. Baseball old-timers called the catcher-pitcher combination the battery, and Margie thought about Dan like that. That just talking to him was like recharging her battery, giving her the power to keep going when her spirit was falling flat. Spending time with the full battery—Tim and Dan—was a special kind of charge. It made her ache that Tim and Dan were fighting, like the bond was broken. The prospect of losing her brother, in that future she didn't want to think about, was hard enough without Tim losing his best friend. Even though, according to Dan, Tim was doing his best to shove him away.

She stared at the door.

Dan pulled in a long breath and rubbed her shoulder. "He can't throw us both out," he said. Then, giving Margie a firm nod, he rapped on the door.

Nothing happened.

"Try again."

Dan tapped. Margie called in a loud whisper. "Timmy. You up?"

Stupid question, Margie thought, but Dan nodded. "I heard the toilet flush about five minutes ago, so I doubt he's asleep already."

Margie's eyes bulged with the obvious question. "Yeah, I know," Dan said. "I was weighing my options about whether to go in or not. Then you came along."

She rapped on the door again. "Timmy. Come on. Let me in. Mom's not with me, promise."

And they heard the footsteps cross the room.

* * *

Margie sucked air through her teeth. Tim looked like hell. Drawn, pale, like an extra from a vampire movie.

"Don't," Tim said, his voice a rasp. Dan said they'd pumped his stomach, put a tube down his esophagus, and made him throw up. Margie's own innards ached just thinking about that, and her hand went to her throat as they followed his shambling walk through the living room into the master suite that contained two queen-size beds. Tim collapsed into one of them and pulled the covers over his head. The other bed looked like it had been used as a medical staging area. Some wrappings and tubes and stuff still remained. Margie carefully piled the goods on the opposite side and sat.

"So, what?" Margie said. "Are we five again? This just a new blanket fort?"

"Margie, don't," Dan said.

"No." She squeezed her eyes shut to keep from screaming. Or bursting into tears. "I had to sit home with my thumb up my ass for six hours not knowing what was going on. I had to run interference with Mom. I had to keep her from calling the friggin' riot police. I get to ask some questions."

"Where is she, anyway?" Tim said, his voice muffled.

"Snoring like a logging camp, as if you care."

"I care. I told the trainer to get you guys a message. He didn't?"

"No." Dan's hand landed on Margie's shoulder and rubbed in small circles. "He didn't." The comfort of Dan's touch gave her some strength.

"Shit," Tim mumbled. "I'm sorry."

Dan cleared his throat. The hand moving against her skin stopped, tensed. "Should I, uh, do something? Get coffee?"

Tim stuck his spider-fingered pitching hand out the blanket and waved toward the living room. "Room service menu's out there, get what you want."

"I'll do it," Dan said. Margie could almost smell his relief at being able to feel useful. Or maybe to have an excuse to get out of the room.

"Shove over, John-Boy," Margie said.

"Whaah?"

"You heard me. Shove over. You smell like a friggin' dumpster, but I'm used to it by now."

"You smell like cigarettes."

"Really? I hardly smell it anymore."

"Secondhand smoke. Bad for your health. Especially for an athlete."

Tim didn't have to look at her to know what was on Margie's face.

"Shut up," he said.

But he didn't tell her to leave. She didn't get under the blanket, because God knows what kind of cooties his lady friend had left behind. But he didn't make Margie leave.

* * *

When the food came, Dan called Margie into the living room to help him sort it out. She hadn't eaten since lunch, and her mouth was watering at the smells, but Dan tugged her into the farthest alcove of the suite and lowered his voice. "You know what's gonna happen in the morning, don't you? Newspapers. We can't let him see that."

"Right. I'll go down to the front desk, give the word."

"Tell them thanks but no thanks on the housekeeping, also."

She shuddered. "Although someone needs to change those sheets pretty soon."

* * *

Thanks to his sister's umpire-trained voice, Tim had heard everything Margie said, and after the door clicked closed, he feigned sleep. After his outburst in the trainer's room, and...well, this, the last thing Tim wanted was to talk to Dan Monroe. And if he tried to get in the bed with him, there would be hell to pay.

"Don't even fucking think about it," he growled, just in case.

"Hey. We're trying to help you. If you're going to be an asshole about it, all I'm gonna do is lock you in here, run up your tab, and leave."

"Promise?"

"Try me. I got a sudden craving for champagne and lobster."

Tim let out a long breath. It was uncomfortable, inside his brain. Under his skin. Like ants were crawling all over him. Had he been doing so much that he was suffering withdrawal? He tried to remember what Alejandro had told him about that.

And where the fuck was Alejo? He'd called the dude three times, no answer.

"Assuming you're not playing today?" Dan said.

"Travel day."

"Lucky break."

"Fuck off."

"You need to expand your vocabulary."

"I got a few more words."

Tim rolled over and tugged the blanket tighter around his head. He didn't give a flying fuck if Dan ordered food for the entire hotel. He just wanted him to go away. Margie too. He needed to be alone. To think this through. He'd been "invited" to a meeting with the coach when they got back to Cincinnati. He had a good idea what that meeting was going to be about. Part of him was falling in love with the idea of disappearing. He'd let everyone down. His mother, his father's memory, Margie. Shit. Margie had enough problems of her own. She didn't need his, too. What would he do if he couldn't play anymore? It was all he'd trained for, all he'd ever really wanted.

Now he'd fucked it all to hell.

He was about to tell Dan to get out and never come back when he heard the front door click open again.

He peeked out of the covers. Margie was standing in the bedroom doorway, holding a newspaper. Crap. What story had they run with? Did they have pictures? How bad was it? Did they go with the food poisoning thing? Or did they—

Tim shot up. "Bargie. Don't look at that. Don't—"

Her head moved slowly from side to side as she dropped to the mattress. Dan rushed to her, taking the papers away, getting an arm around her.

"I'm dead," she muttered. "It's over."

"What's she talking about?" he asked Dan. "Margie. What…?"

"The *Post*," Margie said.

Dan snatched it up. From where Tim was sitting, he had a good bead on Dan Monroe. The big catcher's cheeks reddened. His eyes bulged with anger. The edges of the paper crushed in his fingers. "That son of a bitch. That goddamn son of a bitch!"

"Lemme see that." Tim made a grab for the *Post*. Dan flipped it onto the bed and, still red in the face, stalked over to the window and stood there like a mountain, arms crossed over his chest. Tim's eyes didn't quite focus, and he felt slow and sluggy, and he wasn't sure he was getting all the words right. The headline was "Foul Ball" and he caught "Oblonsky" and "Edwards" and "illegal slide" and "forfeit." And "scandal." "Margie? This true? French is the guy you worked with in Holyoke, right?"

Dan spun toward him and pointed. "If you got your head out of your ass once in a while, you'd know what was going on."

"That's not helping, Dan." Margie checked her watch, then grabbed her purse from the side table, fumbled through. "Shit. What would help is if one of you had a bunch of quarters. I gotta get some answers."

"Now?" Dan said.

"Yes, now."

"Use my phone." Tim's voice cracked. "Long distance, the team pays for it all."

The look on her face, like he'd disappointed her, like she was angry with herself for not preventing this, like her whole world was caving in, was like another punch in the stomach. She said softly, "Maybe you got enough trouble with the team right now, Timmy. They don't need me running up their bills even more."

The breath leaked out of him like a punctured balloon.

"Besides. It's not long distance. It's just, like, Brooklyn, I think."

The boys rifled their pockets and gave her a handful of change. "What if Mom comes up here?" Tim said.

Margie shook her head, let out an exasperated huff. That was the sister he knew. "For God's sake. Do I gotta do everything around here? She's your mother, too. Figure it out."

* * *

She tromped down to the lobby, to the bank of pay phones. She chose one with a phone number stamped on the dial. If he didn't hang up on her, maybe he could call her back and save her the pain in the ass of pumping coins into the slot.

After nine rings, a tired young voice said, *"New York Sports Overnight."*

"Yeah. Can I talk to Fitz?" Even the sound of his name coming off her lips made her want to spit.

"Name and town."

"Why, this some kind of inquisition?"

"For the show." He sounded like he was starting to wake up.

"Margie from Saugerties."

"Yeah, okay, hold on. Turn down your radio."

"I don't got a friggin' radio."

"Then how are you listening to the show?"

"I pick it up through the fillings in my teeth."

"You sound cute," he said. "What are you wearing?"

"I am in no mood for you. Fuck off and put Fitz on, you asshole."

Static crackled on the line, and she heard Fitzgerald talking to some guy with the thickest Brooklyn accent she'd ever heard. After more crackling, Fitz said, like a kid who'd been caught at hide-and-seek, "Margie?"

"Your call screener is an asshole. Crap. I'm not on the air, am I?"

"Not anymore, you're not. What's up?"

"What's up? What's *up*? You have the fucking balls to ask me what's up? You might have just blown the rest of my career and you're asking *what the fuck is up!*"

The kid at the front counter raised his head and froze. "Shit," she muttered. Then waved to him and forced a smile. "Everything's fine."

"Where are you?" Fitz asked. "Sounds like a hotel. How's Tim? We had three calls asking about him tonight after he was on the news—"

"Like I'm telling you about my brother. So you can print that in your paper and ruin his life, too?"

"Margie. I didn't mean to...what I mean is... Look, can we talk about this? Somewhere we don't have to scream and I don't have to come back from commercial in thirty seconds?"

"Somewhere I can kick your ass from here to Hoboken?"

"I'd hope you wouldn't, but I'd like the opportunity to tell you my thoughts on the matter over a cup of coffee or five."

Margie scrubbed a hand over her face. Maybe she still had a chance to pull her ass from the fire. If she could get him to print one of those statements about having his facts wrong—what was that called, a retraction?—she could take that to Abernathy or even the umpire development office and confirm that she'd tried to keep her name out of it. She checked her watch. "It better be good. I gave up room service on the Cincinnati Reds tonight, so you better be buying."

36

THE USUAL

He sent a cab to her hotel. It was the least the putz could do. Margie left a note for her mother, with Timmy's room number, and said she had to take care of something important and she'd be back before Tim had to catch the team bus to the airport. It was a quick ride to the studio. Some twerpy kid with a punk haircut let her in. Probably the call screener. He looked like he'd been given a dressing-down for being an asshole to her on the phone, and he studied his trendy black boots damn near the whole time he mumbled about the show being almost done and where she should go in and wait.

Nice play, Fitz. Making her cool her jets in what the kid called the "green room" while he was safe behind a Plexiglas window. She paced and fumed while listening to the show through the speakers. He was talking to a truck driver on the Long Island Expressway about how the Mets should trade in their whole team over the winter. Fitz listed a few players he thought should stay, and basically Margie agreed with him, which pissed her off. But if there were a phone in that lounge, or waiting room, or whatever the hell eight square feet of crap lined with pleather furniture and Pat Benatar posters was, she would have disagreed with him on principle.

After his show ended, he exited the booth, positioning his dumb hat just so. Cocky bastard probably studied that in a mirror. "I know a little place in Brooklyn," he said. "Decent food, good people. Won't take long this time of night. I'll make sure you get back quick and safe, so you can look in on your brother. Margie, don't worry. It's gonna be okay."

She glared long and hard. She had no good reason to trust him. But she wanted this done. For her, for Timmy, for that look on her mother's face. But to do that, she'd have to play this game right.

* * *

A middle-aged waitress poured them coffee. "Fitz, the usual? And for your friend?"

"We're not friends," Margie said. Then bit back her words. It wasn't the waitress's fault. "Sorry. Grilled cheese with bacon and…" She decided to skip the tomato. "And fries, please."

He settled back in the booth and gave her a crooked grin.

"What?"

"Frankly, I'm kind of surprised you'd want to be seen in public with me. From the look on your face before, I thought you'd kick down the booth and take a chunk out of my face."

"It's been a long day."

"I'm sure it has. How's Tim?"

"He's fine. He had a little food poisoning, he'll live."

His eyebrows danced up. "Quite the loyalty in the Oblonsky clan. Coming all the way down here in the middle of the night for a little food poisoning."

Crap. What had he heard? "We're not talking about my brother."

He leaned forward, elbows on the table. "Okay, let's talk about you."

Was he actually trying to get out of this by being charming?

"No," she said. "Let's talk about you." Her eyes narrowed. "Was it good for you? Seeing your name in the *Post*? Was that worth it to you, what it's gonna do to a bunch of people's lives?"

His eyebrows jumped higher on his forehead. "What? You want Edwards and French to get away with this? Where's all your flag-waving about fair play and justice and nobody being bigger than the game?"

"My flag's at half-mast right now. I meant what it could do to—"

"You," he said. "You meant what it could do to your career." He looked like he was about to reach across the table and touch her. She inched back, crossing her arms over her chest.

"Margie. I get it. Your reputation's on the line, you wanted to keep your brother out of it, you wanted out of that story." He paused, and the left side of his mouth lifted a hair. "So…I wrote a different one."

She bolted up straight. "Which still made me look like I was suspicious of those guys from the start."

"That goes to conjecture, counselor," he said. "And besides, you weren't the only one whose curiosity got piqued when they saw things that weren't kosher."

She was too tired to work all that through, and she sucked down more coffee. "So, what, is that like the argument that if everyone's speeding the cops can't catch all of us?"

"Well, sort of."

"How is that different than if everyone's cheating, nobody's gonna get caught?"

That appeared to give Fitz pause. "We're investigating this. Why people are looking the other way on Edwards. And other players. Rumors about drug use on the field. We think we can connect the dots."

She leveled a gaze at him. "Who's 'we'?"

"My new colleagues at the *Post*."

"Must be nice. Having people you work with back you up."

"Well, it's not a done deal yet, but sounds a hell of a lot better than twisting out in the wind on my own."

"Like what I'm doing now."

"I can help you."

"Right." She drew out the word. The league president who told her to stay away from the press was going to love hearing that a reporter intended to clear her name.

"I'm serious. Give me a little time. I'll prove to you there's a groundswell for taking action here. That the story goes deeper than one shady player. And then, maybe then, you'll want to go on record with what you heard in that locker room."

Like hell. I'll be let go for sure. She checked her watch. If she wanted to see Timmy off, she had to go now. Already, she'd been away from him for too long. She signaled the waitress to make her order to go, then stood.

Fitz stood with her. "At least let me see you to a cab."

"I got this," she said. "I don't think I wanna take any more favors from you. Maybe this was a big mistake." She slammed down one of the two ten-dollar bills she'd borrowed from her mother's purse.

"Margie." His hand was on her arm. She stared it off.

* * *

Margie could see on Tim's face that he didn't want his mother, sister, and best bud out there with the rest of the team when they boarded the bus for the airport. She didn't blame him. So they exchanged a few quick hugs in the lobby. Margie couldn't bear the sight of her twin's broad but sagging shoulders as he turned away. "Timmy."

He stopped, one hand on the door.

"Call me," she said.

He nodded, eyes not meeting hers. "Yeah. Yeah, okay." Then he was gone.

They watched player after player climb the narrow stairs. They watched the driver make one last circle, securing the cargo doors, then the bus pulled into traffic.

That left the three of them looking at each other. Margie's mother slid her a knowing glance, then excused herself to powder her nose.

"Subtle," Dan said.

"That's her trademark." Margie blinked sticky eyes. She could have fallen down on one of the fussy couches in the lobby and slept for sixteen hours.

"I'd be happy to drive you guys back north," Dan said. "My flight doesn't leave until tonight."

Margie thought long and hard about that. It would be nice to have Dan around. And Mom seemed to like him. But it would be like prolonging the inevitable. All the goodbyes were starting to wear on her. A day here, a weekend there. Late-night phone calls when neither wanted to hang up. He still had a future in baseball, a contract for next season, the potential to catch someone's eye in spring training and get moved up. If anyone got word they were together...

"Margie." He put both hands on her shoulders and she turned to face him.

She sucked in a breath. "It could look bad for you. Being seen with me. This thing...with the umpires...it could get ugly."

His eyes narrowed. "Because of what that reporter wrote."

"I can deal with him," she said.

232

Dan looked skeptical.

"You trust me, Big Dan?"

"You know I do. It's them I don't trust. I don't like the position they put you in."

Margie didn't answer.

He pushed a lock of hair behind her ear. "What do you need? What can I do to make this better for you?"

Always the good catcher, having everyone else's back. She couldn't help but smile. The smile quickly faded.

"Margie. Margie, I know I don't have the right to ask, and we haven't, you know, known each other all that long...but I want a life with you. If we have to wait a little longer, I can do that."

Margie's brow crumpled. She was exhausted as all hell, and she didn't know if she'd heard him right. "Dan, did you just ask me to marry you?"

He grinned. That goofy grin that crinkled his eyes, showed his big white teeth. "Yeah. I guess I did."

She had no idea how to answer him. Life was way too confusing at the moment, and she was afraid that if she opened her yap in her state, she'd say something that would end up hurting his feelings.

All she could think of saying was, "Ask me again."

"Right now?" He slipped a glance around the lobby. "You want me down on one knee?"

"Dan."

He let out a long breath. "Yeah. Okay. I hear you."

She very badly wanted to touch him. The angle of his jaw. The hard muscle of his forearm. "But I liked that you asked." Then she spied her mother coming back from the ladies' room, her eyes questioning.

"What? What did he ask?"

Dan blushed. Fortunately he was facing away, so Pat hadn't seen him. Margie gave his shoulder a quick squeeze. "He asked if he could take two hot babes to lunch before he had to catch his flight. I said I didn't know where he intended to find them—"

"Speak for yourself." Pat looped her arm through Dan's. "I could eat a horse. Where are we going?"

* * *

233

"Take a seat, kid. Thanks for stopping by. You all right, want some water?"

"I'm good." The fluorescent lights in the manager's office were making Tim's head pound even more than it already did, but he tried not to show it.

"Suze, give us a few minutes, okay?"

The manager's assistant nodded and pulled the door closed behind her. Tim ground his teeth as it clicked shut. He was superstitious about closing doors in ballparks. Like something bad would happen behind them.

The lights buzzed. The air conditioning whirred on and off. Tim scuffed his shoes against the carpet. The pattern made him dizzy. He looked back up.

"Have you seen Carl since you got back?" the manager asked him.

Tim's mouth dropped open. "I didn't know I was supposed to... The message said come to your office." He hooked his thumb over his shoulder. "Should—should I go now?"

"Nah. Later's fine. Let's just chat for a while, you and me."

A pall of silence fell over them. The coach came around the front of the desk, perched on the edge, clasped his hands over his knee. It was a paternal pose. His own father never did such a thing, but his other coaches had. Often when they were about to say things he didn't want to hear.

Tim swallowed. The squirmy thing on his chest—he figured it had been around so long, he might as well give it a name—sank its claws into his skin.

"There's no shame in it, Tim."

Tim looked up. Swallowed again. Feeling too soft and tender in the places where the claws dug in. "What?" He sniffed, forced a smile that didn't take. "It was food poisoning, Coach, I must have eaten something bad in New York, that's what..."

The manager shook his head. "Sell that shit to your mother. Not me."

Tim gulped.

But the expression on the older man's face wasn't one that said he had Tim by the balls. It held compassion that Tim didn't feel he deserved, given the crap job he'd been doing on the mound this season. Given that he'd just lied to his coach. "I'm guessing you might want that water now?"

"Yes, sir."

The coach hit a button on his phone, then resettled himself against the desk. Suze came in, deposited a tray beside him, and briskly departed. The click of the door resonated in his gut. Coach handed him a glass. Tim tightened his grip around the base to keep his muscles from shaking.

"You think you're the only pitcher ever had a bad case of nerves on the mound?"

Compassion or no, any answer Tim might give felt like a trap. The guys he knew made it look so easy. He was supposed to be fearless when the coach handed him the ball. Professional. Nobody in the clubhouse talked much about nerves. You went out, you sucked it up, you played, you got the job done. If you didn't get the job done that day, you forgot about it. You let it roll off your back.

"Look," the coach said. "I gotta be straight with you here. We made an investment in your future with this team. We like to take care of our investments. When we take care of each other, when we trust each other, everybody wins. If you got a problem, and you tell us about it, we have ways to solve that problem. If you're playing hurt, we can patch you up or put you on the DL until you're cleared. If you need to work on your delivery, on your mechanics, we'll give you more time with the pitching coaches. But if you break that trust, we got a problem." He pointed toward the field. "I got a team to worry about out there. A team full of other guys we've also made an investment in. Now, I'm a realist. I know this job comes with…challenges. Pressures. Not everybody handles those challenges the same. I was a young player myself, once, after all."

He'd been a damn fine player, too. Everybody knew how many Gold Gloves the coach had, how many batting titles, how many World Series rings. Tim grew up hearing stories about him from his dad. He was pretty sure he was supposed to compliment his coach about that glowing past, but he didn't know how to do it at that moment without sounding like a suck-up. Or like he was trying to skirt the issue of why he'd freaked out on the mound and then later, sort-of-on-purpose taken too many pills and woke up with a tube down his throat.

The manager continued. "But I got a lot on my agenda and you didn't haul your ass all the way up here to listen to my war stories. So, let's get down to business, Mr. Oblonsky."

Tim's stomach shrank.

"I'm putting you on the DL. For the rest of the season or until Carl clears you to play again."

"Coach…"

The coach raised a hand. "You'd prefer to be sent down next year? Because I can make that happen, too. In fact, I fought long and hard to keep that from happening. I got a guy who wants to send you packing right now, frankly."

They'd wanted him sent to the minors? They'd wanted him gone? "DL's fine, sir. Thank you, sir. I—I want to do what's right for the team, sir."

"Good." The coach smiled and patted Tim's arm. "See? Now we're trusting each other."

37

THE FALLOUT

Fitz grinned at the remaining ten copies of the *New York Post* Nonna had purchased and put on the hallway table for the neighbors. He felt a few inches taller as he plopped his fedora on his overly long head and headed out the door, bound for a meeting with his new boss. Now he had steak to go with his sizzle. He'd made a few inquiries about Mr. Douglas French. He'd talked to a few people about the night Margie overheard the deal Fitz had started calling the Hullabaloo in Holyoke. Someone gave him a reliable tip that there was another witness. The Binghamton clubhouse man, an older fellow beloved by damn near the whole city, had been gathering towels well within earshot of the conversation and was willing to speak to Fitz on record because, in the man's own words, "What I heard made me sick to my stomach." Even better, because of connections Fitz had lovingly cultivated during his years on the road, he had eyeballs in the minor league commissioner's office who hinted at a paper trail of complaints against French and why he had been quietly moved from a regular slot to the call-up list.

Personal issues, said one report. Another suggested a gambling problem, started to remedy his alimony and child support debts, but the limb of that tree was shakier.

It was not yet an ironclad case, and would require more digging to corroborate the sources, but Fitz felt confident that it was a hell of a lot stronger than what Margie alone had offered. In fact, if he could nail down one more source, maybe he wouldn't need Margie or Osterhaus at all.

Fitz checked his watch. He'd planned to meet his editor at a neighborhood bar before heading to the station for his overnight shift, and during the walk he went over the pieces in his puzzle.

The sidewalks tended to roll up after hours in this part of Brooklyn, and he was glad for it, and for the pleasant weather. He did his best thinking while he wandered the city, soaking in the atmosphere, the familiar neighborhoods, the streets he'd been walking since he was old enough to venture out on his own.

He passed the barbershop, closed for the night. He stopped to check his reflection in the mirror and admired the figure he cut. Maybe with the next check he got from the *Post*, he'd buy a new suit, one of those custom-tailored jobs. Nonna would be heartbroken, but she'd get over it when she saw how smart he looked. But what he had was working so far. In his grandfather's rumpled suits or shirtsleeves, he had that average joe on the next barstool appeal. Would a potential source be put off if he looked too slick? Maybe the dapper don thing worked for Tom Wolfe, but he was no Tom Wolfe.

But one day…one day he might be the Tom Wolfe of the sporting world. One day he might—

Movement flashed across the window. Fitz turned in time to see the barrel of a bat, aiming to hit him out of the park. And then he was looking at concrete.

* * *

When Fitz walked into the studio, Vampire Trevor just stared.

"Whazzamatter," Fitz said to him. "You never seen a good-lookin' guy before?"

"You're, um, bleeding?"

He pushed out his lower jaw, touched his lip, felt the slick heat, the swelling, the pain. It must have split when his face met the pavement. No wonder it hurt like hell to smile. Hurt to breathe, too. Maybe he'd landed on a rib.

"You see someone about that?"

He sailed his fedora onto the couch.

"I didn't see him. That's my problem. Chickenshit bastard whiffed, then took off at a dead run before I could get a look at him." Of course, Fitz was on the ground with the wind knocked out of him at the time. He couldn't have given chase to save his life.

The kid still gaped.

"Close your mouth, you're catching flies."

"You need ice or something, boss?"

Fitz waved a hand as he went into the booth and sat heavily in his chair. He pulled a handkerchief from his pocket and dabbed at his lower lip. It wasn't as bad as the kid was making out, but maybe that ice would be a good idea. He talked for a living—or at least part of his living—and a fat lip and a bruised rib wouldn't help matters any.

"We got new filler." The kid held up a cartridge. "Interviews and stuff. I could load that up and, you know, take the phones for a while?"

"Sure."

The kid smiled. "No shit?"

"No shit. Don't tell the union." He hauled his ass out of the chair. "But get me that ice first."

* * *

The kid did a decent job. It was good to know he wasn't a total waste of oxygen, sitting in the producers' booth reading comic books when he wasn't futzing around with the equipment Fitz wasn't allowed to touch. He started thinking about the asshole who'd taken a swing at him. He should have seen that coming. Getting a byline in the *Post*, working on a radio show...he should have expected that a crazy or two would come out of the weeds at some point. Diehards are passionate about their sports. But he hadn't expected this. Someone yelling at him on the subway about his views on the Yankees starting lineup, someone buttonholing him on the street about how a monkey with a typewriter could write a sports column...that kind of thing he might have predicted.

Not someone trying to take him out with a Louisville Slugger.

The timing of it prickled under his skin. Just a few days after his column was in the *Post*. Right before he was supposed to meet with his editor to discuss his new angles.

He drummed his fingers against the producer's desk as he thought. A few ideas wiggled around, sparked his interest, but the connections were hazy. He needed more information. He needed to take a ride up to Binghamton, get into that ballpark, talk to some people. Maybe on the way back he could look in on Margie. It wasn't that far out of the way. All right, it was about an hour out of the way.

But it was a nice part of the state, and he'd seen tomorrow's weather report. It looked like a good day for a drive.

* * *

Fitz stood with his hands on his hips, staring at the sign in front of the stadium: "Thanks for a great season, see you in the spring!"

The main entrance was locked.

Fortunately, there was a number for security on a small placard near the door.

He found a nearby pay phone and called. The guy who answered sounded pissed to be disturbed, but with a few smooth words and that magic *New York Post* cred, Fitz was promised the keys to the kingdom. Or at least a guy who'd be there in fifteen minutes and who'd give him an hour to do whatever he needed.

Fitz waited, armed with coffee and donuts.

A car pulled up out front. A clean-cut guy in his midforties hauled out, shook his hand. The shake was enough to show Fitz he was still in fighting trim, not so firm that he was trying to establish dominance. It was enough information to show that he was willing to work with Fitz, or at least give him the benefit of the doubt. He was grateful for the coffee, but passed on the donuts, patting his gut as if to say he was watching his waistline.

"So, *New York Post*, huh?"

Fitz flashed his credentials—so new the plastic holder was still factory-fresh. The guy nodded and worked open the door.

"Where do you need to go?"

Fitz thought about that. Margie said she'd been changing in some kind of equipment room near the clubhouse when she overheard her mystery man talking to Doug French. "You might think this is a little weird," he said. "But I wouldn't mind a look at the laundry room."

It was a long walk from the front entrance, deep in the bowels of the old stadium, and Fitz made baseball small talk on the way. They jawed about playoff possibilities. The security guy was a Mets fan, which meant he hated their division rivals on general principle, but he had grudging respect for the Braves' chances.

"You catch that last game, when the Reds were in town?"

Fitz shook his head. He'd had to take Nonna to a doctor's appointment, so he'd missed most of it. He'd gotten to the pressroom just after Tim Oblonsky had to be taken out, then he tried to get a quote but nothing doing, nobody was talking about that.

"It was a close one," Fitz said.

They'd turned a few corners and finally Fitz saw the big machines. He took a mental measure of the distance between where he was standing and the clubhouse. "Humor me a sec," Fitz said. He nodded toward a corner of the clubhouse. "Stand over there and say something."

The guy gave Fitz the hairy eyeball. "Seriously, man?"

Fitz let his shoulders relax. Then he had a better idea.

"You work at the games," he said, "or do you just lock up after?"

The guy pulled himself up taller. "They got a game, I'm here."

"You were here when the Rockhoppers were in town?"

"Which time?"

"Couple weeks back?"

"Yeah. Yeah, I remember. Nice day. Big crowd."

"Margie Oblonsky was in the ump crew. You saw her here?"

The smile said it all. "Yeah. Margie. She's a pistol. They don't have, you know, equal facilities for ladies, so when she comes in I unlock the equipment room for her, so she can change somewhere private. I'm working on 'em to put a regular locker in there for her, for next season."

Something inside Fitz did a happy dance. "Maybe you could show me that room?"

"Sure." He gestured. "It's on the other side of that wall."

The happy dance became a jig. If French and his friend were talking in the clubhouse, Margie could have caught damn near every word.

"You don't want me to go over there anymore? Recite 'Mary Had a Little Lamb' or something?"

"Maybe later." Fitz connected a dot. "Tell me, if you'd be so kind. There was an older gentleman collecting the towels in the clubhouse that night. You know him?"

He nodded. "Sure do. Eddie Johnson. He's been with the organization since... Well, I can't remember when he wasn't."

That was indeed the name on the slip of paper in his pocket. "Good man?"

"One of the best I know." His eyes narrowed slightly. "Is he okay?"

"Sure, sure. Just covering my bases. So to speak."

"If you don't mind my asking? Why would the *Post* send someone all the way up here? I mean, not that the owner would mind the publicity. He loves his publicity. Just seems a little out of your purview."

Fitz's lower lip throbbed, reminding him of the gentleman he'd run into last night. Maybe he should be a little more circumspect about what he was after.

"Background," he said quickly. "I like setting the scene, painting a picture. Tell you the truth, my editor wants a puff piece on Miss Oblonsky." He mugged a face that said he wasn't thrilled with the idea. "I hope to round it out a little, you know, talk to some of the people who met her, add some color."

"Margie's plenty colorful all on her own," he said. "Don't know what I could add to your story, but I got a few minutes to talk."

38

THE NERVE

In the interest of safety, you are suspended until further notice.

Margie was about to ball the letter up and wing it across the room, but her mother eased it from her hand. "This is evidence," she said, her voice freakishly soft and gentle. "We gotta keep a record."

Margie felt as if the top of her head was going to blow off in a geyser of steam, like in the cartoons. "Whose safety?" she screamed. "Mine? Theirs?"

"Honey." Mom's spindly hand landed on Margie's shoulder. "Maybe you should go out for a run or something. Then we'll talk about what we're gonna do about this."

Margie tried to take deep, slow breaths, but the air felt ragged going in and out of her lungs. If she went for a run, she was afraid she'd never come back. She'd run from here to Portland and bust some skulls in the boss's office. Starting with Mack Abernathy.

Instead, she slammed out the back door, hauled Tim's pitch-back net from the shed and took her frustrations out on it. She broke three of the strings and had to poke through the pricker bushes to find the ball. Then she tied the strings as best she could and tested her work. Fine and dandy. She hurled fastballs, curves, sliders, until she was out of breath and soaked with sweat. Then she flopped down in the grass, cursing Abernathy. The Eastern League. Doug French. Dolph Edwards, Chip Donofrio, Warren Durning, and every asshole who ever looked at her sideways.

Cursing herself, for even thinking that baseball would let a woman stay.

And Stephen Fitzgerald. Every other pitch she'd thrown was aimed at his big stupid head.

Hats. Who the hell wears hats anymore? And making everyone call him

Fitz, like he thinks he's some old-time reporter from the movies. Asshole.

She didn't know how long she lay there fuming, watching the stupid puffy clouds float over her head. She wanted to punch them, too.

* * *

Eventually Margie caught the aroma of meat searing on a grill. Steak, probably.

Her mother was trying to tempt her back inside, and it was working.

Her mouth began to water and she opened her eyes, surprised by how late it was getting, the sun skirting the tops of the trees. She must have fallen asleep. The last thing she remembered was lying down on the grass in the backyard, thinking about her future.

Now it all came rushing back to her.

She got up, brushed dirt from her jeans, and started toward the house. Margie considered that maybe the suspension was one of those blessings in disguise. Like fate's tap on the shoulder, telling her that she'd tried her hardest, maybe harder than anybody ever thought she could, harder than she thought she was able, and it wasn't meant to be. The letter was like a giant rubber stamp on the whole thing that it was okay to stop now.

Maybe she was meant to do something else with her time on this planet.

Dan Monroe wanted to marry her. She smiled at how cute and goofy he'd looked when he thought she wanted him to get down on one knee in the hotel lobby. He was just about the best man she'd ever met. So if a good guy like Dan wanted to marry her, she wasn't a total loser at life, right? Maybe she loved him, too.

But that didn't feel like enough for her. What was she going to do, stay home while he traveled all over the place playing ball, keep the house clean and cook and have a bunch of babies? Or be like those girls in the rooming houses and the bars, hanging like jewelry around the players' necks?

That might have been okay for some girls; her mom always said that her Women's Lib things were about having choices. Working if you wanted to work, being a housewife if you wanted that, but not because someone said that's what you had to do.

Maybe Margie would be good with staying home and having kids. Someday. But she couldn't even imagine that at the moment.

"Oh, there you are," her mother said. Right. As if she hadn't known exactly where Margie was, and exactly what it would take to get her back inside. "You want to put up some water for the corn?"

"Sure." She stopped by the stove. "That's a lot of corn. We having company?"

Her mother's lack of response was making Margie nervous. She didn't want company. She just wanted to be left alone.

"Mom. Who's coming over? Shit. Is it Tim?" The season wasn't over yet. That would mean he'd been cut. Or worse. "Is Tim coming home?"

"Honey. Relax." Mom got the butter out of the fridge. "It's not Tim."

"Crap. It's not some reporter, is it? I'm not ready to talk to anyone, I don't—"

Then she saw the outline of the hat in the driver's seat of the car that was pulling up to their house.

"No." She set the pot down and backed away. "No, no, no. He is not coming in here."

"Margie. Honey."

"Don't you 'honey' me. I am not talking to him." She snatched her keys from the hook near the door. And a fat lot of good it would do her, because he was blocking her in. "Ugh! I can't believe you...you...invited him here! You know what he did. You saw what he wrote. No. I am not talking to that...that...asshole."

She stormed out and made a beeline in the other direction, putting as much asphalt as she could between herself and the opening and closing of that man's car door.

"Margie."

"Fuck off." She kept walking. "Just fuck off and disappear."

He was following her. Bad leg and everything, she could hear him huffing to keep up, and in the same way she knew the steak was meant to lure her back inside, she knew the act was meant to get her to stop.

"That's not right," she said over her shoulder.

"If you'd stop, I wouldn't have to chase you."

"I don't know why you're even here. Leave me alone. I wish I'd just told you to leave me alone from the start."

He laughed. The jerk actually laughed. "You did. Quite colorfully, if I remember right."

"Do I gotta say it again? You got a memory problem?"

"I want to help you. Okay? I want to help you, so slow down a goddamn minute and let me explain."

She stopped and spun toward him. "What? Okay, what? You got me suspended. What could you possibly say that will make me want to hear anything you got to offer me?"

He tugged in a couple breaths, like he was having trouble getting air. Then she noticed his face. "Holy shit. Someone finally have enough of you and pop you one?"

He grinned, then winced. "He missed, actually. The sidewalk, however, did not. Also, I may have bruised one of my ribs, and the painkillers are wearing off."

She narrowed her eyes at him. Crossed her arms over her chest. "Talk. You got thirty seconds. If I don't like it, I'll bruise another one."

"I don't doubt you would."

"You're wasting time."

"We can nail French."

"Talk slower."

"I thought I had thirty seconds."

"You said the magic word. I'll give you a minute."

"I got a reliable witness." He wheezed for a couple breaths, pressing a hand to his rib cage. "Heard French in the clubhouse taking a deal to look the other way in Holyoke."

Margie couldn't speak for a moment. "So you wouldn't have to use my name."

"It would add more weight to my argument," he wheezed again, "but I probably won't need to."

She thought that over.

"I also got"—he sucked in another breath—"motive."

"French wanted a regular slot. That's not any kind of big secret around the league."

"There's more."

"He hated me and wanted me gone. That's not a secret, either.

Now that he got his way and I'm done, probably everybody's gonna know about that, soon. Thanks a heap."

"It's official? They cut you?"

"You want to see the letter? It looked pretty damn official to me."

"Letter... Those goddamn sons of bitches."

"Thanks for the sympathy vote. Too little, too late, hat boy."

"We can stop it. We can tell them—"

"We? There's no 'we' in this. There's you, trying to make a name for yourself as the big New York sports guy, and there's me, screwed over and my only chance to make it to the majors blown to kingdom come."

"You think I haven't taken my lumps for that? From you, and"—he pointed to his face—"whoever tried to turn me into hamburger with a baseball bat last night."

Margie couldn't talk for a second. "You said it was the sidewalk."

"Yeah. The designated hitter missed."

Her gaze dropped from his damaged face, to his chest, and back up again. Had he really dodged the bat, or was that a lie to save his pride?

"Let me say this once more." His voice was soft, even. "I can stop this. I don't need to use your name. I can dig deeper, and with the new evidence I have from my contact in the commissioner's office, French will be history. Then we'll go to work on whatever Edwards and his friends are up to."

Margie squinted at him.

"I'm serious, Margie. I want to do right by you."

"I don't know why, but I'm starting to think you mean that. Maybe that *sidewalk* knocked some sense into you."

"So you'll hear me out?"

Margie turned on her heel and headed back toward the house. He followed.

"You'll hear me out?"

"I didn't say that," she said over her shoulder. Then took three more steps and stopped. "You coming?"

"You're inviting me?"

"I think my mother already did that. I just hate the idea of all that food going to waste."

* * *

She never thought the sound of three people eating could be so loud. Her mother bit into her corn in a way that set Margie's nerves on edge, as if with each chomp she was giving her daughter secret signals.

Finally Margie put down her fork. Maybe Fitz took that as a cue that she was ready for his pitch, because he stopped eating, too, pushed a lank crop of hair back from his forehead—thankfully, he'd taken his hat off once he came through the door—and cleared his throat.

"Thank you for dinner, Mrs. Oblonsky," he said. "Best steak I've had in years."

Margie eyeballed him. Like he never had steak in New York, among all those sports guys he rubbed elbows with. They probably lived on steak. She would, if she had the money.

"It's the marinating," Margie's mother said. "A little teriyaki sauce, a little lemon…easy-peasy. I could write it down for you."

"That would be great." He gave her a smile that looked halfway sincere and set his napkin on the table. "Hey, I got an idea. Why don't you go relax and Margie and I will clean up?"

"Forget it. Guests don't clean. Not in my house." She passed him a shifty glance. "Unless you're trying to get rid of me."

"See?" Margie said to Fitz. "Nothin' gets by her."

"To be honest, Mrs. O"—Margie was secretly pleased that her mother did not suggest he call her Pat—"I got a little business to discuss with your daughter."

"Yeah, yeah. I figured." She peered out the window. "Might be a good time to give that garden a little spritz. Now that it's cooling off some."

When the door closed, Fitz leaned toward her but didn't start talking. Like he was waiting for Margie to jump in. She eased back, watching him. After she'd let him hang long enough, she said, "You really got someone. You got someone who heard the whole thing in Binghamton."

"Not only that, but I talked to him this afternoon. Said he's willing to go on record. Said it was the right thing to do."

She knew he wanted her to go along and think if she went on record it would also be "the right thing to do," but Margie didn't bite. At least not until she heard more from him.

"We got French," he said.

Margie waited for him to explain.

"He wanted the deal because he needed the money."

"That bad?" Margie asked. Sure, she made do on a tiny per diem during the season. She ate macaroni and cheese, was a fixture at dollar beer night, and washed her clothes in the boarding house sink to save her quarters—mostly for dollar beer night and phone calls. Her mother had taken a few jobs defending some clients she didn't like that much, back in the day, because she had two young teenagers and a late husband with five World Series rings and no pension. You do what you have to do, whether that's taking care of the people you love or staying in the game you've devoted your life to; Margie understood that more than most. But why would you risk blowing up what remained of that career you loved—and maybe other people's, too—over money?

"Man's got a gambling problem," Fitz said, looking altogether smug, an expression that unsettled Margie's stomach. "Among other bad habits not proper to talk about in front of mixed company, if you get my drift."

Margie's eyes narrowed. "And you know that how?"

"My contact in the commissioner's office. Saw some private correspondence from last year expressing concern over his unseemly behavior. With a suggestion he take the off-season to think about it. I got a strong hunch he had himself a guardian angel who kept it out of his official records. For a price."

"Damn," Margie said. "That price could have been going easy on some guys."

"With the reward of a regular slot and, potentially, paying off his debts."

"That's why he warned me not to fuck it up for him."

"And fuck it up for him you did." Fitz nodded toward the living room. "Or maybe that guardian angel's goodwill plum ran out. French just got the kiss-off letter, same as you."

"We were both suspended over this?"

Fitz nodded.

Margie sat back again. "So, how does this work, now? You can print whatever you learned about French in your story?"

"I can and I will."

"And the *New York Post* is okay with that?"

"Hey. You're the one who got burned here, Margie. Don't tell me you're going soft."

"Fuck you, I'm going soft. I'm pissed six ways to Sunday over what he did. I just…"

He pushed his plate aside and leaned back.

She lowered her voice. "If a guy's got personal problems like that, and it was, like you said, *private correspondence*, I don't know that it's fair to report it without giving him a chance to respond."

His mouth quirked. "Well, God bless us, everyone. Truth, justice, and the American way."

"You makin' fun of me?"

"No." He stood. "I think it's goddamn admirable. Everybody should be like you."

She stood, glaring at him. "Look. *Mister* Fitzgerald. I'm damn well aware that no matter what I say, you're gonna do whatever the hell you—"

"Hey, I didn't run with that first article. I merely rewrote it so—"

"Didn't anyone ever tell you not to interrupt a lady when she's talking?"

"If I see one of those around here, I'll be sure not to interrupt her."

"I think we're done. Don't let the door hit you in the ass on the way out."

"But I so rudely interrupted you. Please, Miss Oblonsky, continue."

She gave him a good stare, but something in his damaged face made her think he wasn't being totally sarcastic, and she softened her tone. "Let him know, at least. Let him know so his family doesn't have to find out about it on the front page of the newspaper." She couldn't believe she was saying that. But she didn't think she could live with herself, otherwise. Stooping to that level would make her as bad as they were. And she had Tim to think about. Would she want some reporter digging up his problems, blasting them all over the sports pages? It would ruin Tim's career and break her mother's heart.

"Maybe I'll think about that." Fitz put on his hat and gave her a crooked grin. "See you in the funny papers."

* * *

Margie stood at the window, watching him go. The back door slapped open and closed, and eventually her mother came up behind her.

"You did a good thing there," Mom said.

"Hurt like hell, though."

"The hard decisions often do."

She was transfixed by their reflection. The differences between them, the similarities.

"You'll see," her mother said. "He'll come around, do the right thing."

"Are you kidding me?"

Her mother laughed. "I got ice cream. The good kind. I wasn't about to offer it to him. You want?"

"Maybe." She followed her mother into the kitchen, watching her hands as she fussed with this and that, putting the plates in the sink, getting out the bowls and the spoons and the big pewter ice cream scoop that had been her grandmother's.

"Mom?"

"Yeah, Margie, what?"

She tried the words in her head: *Mom, we gotta talk about Timmy.* "We have any whipped cream?"

39

THE ASK

After a few days Margie got antsy, so she decided to go visit Wes. The season was over, and he'd been on her mind since his latest nephew's birth announcement came in the mail. Maybe it would lift her spirits to see a friendly face.

Junior looked kind of squishy, had red curls on top of his head, and smelled like talcum powder. His eyes were huge, and they followed her around the room. She'd brought a big stuffed dog. Maybe that was what he was looking at. She put it on a chair.

"He's just a baby, he's not going to bite you," Wes said.

"You say that now."

"You want to hold him?"

Margie panicked a little. She'd never held a baby. But Wes coached her through it, telling her where to put her hands and how to support his head. He kept squirming around, and when she sat on a chair in the living room, next to Wes and his sister Julia on the sofa, the baby started playing with a lock of Margie's hair.

"I don't think he's ever seen a blonde before," Wes said. He came from a family of redheads, and Julia's husband had dark hair. The baby stared at her like she was some kind of alien.

They sat for a while, talking about baby things, and eventually Julia took the baby away for changing and then said she was going to try to get him down for a nap.

"So how's everybody doing?" Margie asked Wes.

"Good," he said with a smile. "Everybody's healthy and the doctors are giving us good reports." He talked about percentiles and the landmarks of baby development, and he spoke quickly, which meant it was a subject he was well acquainted with, which meant he was happy. He talked about baseball and astronomy with equal enthusiasm and confidence.

Then he stopped and said, "Margie, how are you doing?"

She sighed. "How many weeks you got?"

"Twenty-two until spring training."

She told him about Fitzgerald printing the story with her name in it even though she said not to—Wes had read the story—and that someone tried to hit him with a bat.

"But he's okay," Margie said, because she knew Wes would ask. "And nobody knows who did it, although anybody who'd ever met him would have a good idea why."

He nodded, his fingers steepled under his chin, which usually meant he was thinking. The silence made her nervous and she kept talking, telling him her theories and what Fitz said about French and how Margie didn't think it was fair to print any of that without at least telling him first. Then she started talking about Tim, how freaked out she'd been when they drove down to his hotel in Manhattan, how she almost lost her shit when she saw him looking so pale and sick, thinking that he could have died. "And then..." She was sniffling at this point, trying to stem the full-on waterworks, but losing the battle. "In the middle of all that, Dan Monroe asked me to marry him."

"Aw, that's great, Margie! He's a real nice guy, real polite." Wes grinned, but then his face softened. "Wait. Can you still be an umpire if you marry a player?"

"Moot point." Margie shrugged. "On top of all of it, I got a letter from the league. I've been benched until further notice."

"Just like that?"

She handed him the letter. He took it from her and frowned into the text as if he was taking the words apart, letter by letter.

"You're appealing this, right?"

Margie sat up taller. "I can appeal?"

"I don't see why you can't at least ask about it. It's not a dismissal. Dismissals aren't issued until November, when our evaluations come in. This is only a suspension. Players appeal suspensions all the time. Dolph Edwards did it. It didn't work for him, but I guess the officials agreed that his role in Holyoke was really blatant. You were just doing your job."

"What the... They upheld Edwards's suspension?"

"Yes. It's really not looking good for him. I thought someone would have told you."

"I've been a little busy." Frankly, she'd been avoiding the news. At least Edwards didn't get away scot-free, and that helped somewhat. It kind of made her smile.

"Call him."

"What?"

"Call Abernathy's office. See if you can talk to him."

Margie's mouth opened and closed. "I can't just..." The last time she saw him, he'd had a whole bunch of complaints against her. Before that, she'd called his office to accuse a man of taking a bribe. And Abernathy had told her to drop it.

"I have Rosemary's phone number. That's the best way to find out his schedule. It's more efficient than calling him direct. And she's really friendly. She always asks about the kids."

Yeah. Rosemary was awesome. But Margie was afraid she'd come off like some big whiner who couldn't solve her own problems. Couldn't take the heat.

"Look," Wes said. "This is like a learning opportunity. The letter is not very clear. It doesn't have any dates on it, and it doesn't specify what you're being charged with. They're supposed to include the pertinent information. You're calling for clarification. There's nothing wrong with that."

"You're right."

Rosemary answered on the third ring, her greeting chipper until Margie said hello. Then she dropped her voice like Margie was someone she wasn't supposed to be talking to. It sent chills down Margie's back. She swallowed and asked if she could talk to Mr. Abernathy.

"Actually, he's out your way," Rosemary said. "He has a few meetings in Rhode Island this week."

"Maybe you can help me then. I got this letter, and I'm not sure what it means."

Pause. "Yeah, hon. You're gonna have to talk to him about that." Pause. "I can see if I can get you on his schedule for the winter meetings."

Margie's stomach dropped at the idea of waiting that long. What if she went all the way down to Florida and then found out she had no job? That would suck big time.

Perhaps Rosemary sensed Margie's worry. She dropped her tone again and said, "Hang on a sec. Let me get him on the other line and see if he's got an open slot during this trip."

* * *

Wes stood when she came back into the living room.

"I got a meeting," she said. "I gotta go to Providence, like, right now, but I got a meeting."

"I'm going with you."

"Wes."

He grabbed some keys from a table near the door. "We'll go to Fenway afterward. The Red Sox are playing Cleveland. It's been way too long since we watched a game together. Maybe Yaz will hit a few out for us."

Margie finally relented. How could she turn that down?

During the trip, they talked about babies, mostly. How Wes could sit for hours and stare at little Mitchell, as he learned about the world. He couldn't wait until he was old enough to play baseball, or find shooting stars, or look through the telescope. It was nice to watch the scenery fly by and listen to Wes for a while. Like old times. And it gave her mind a vacation from the spiral of crap it had been serving up lately.

But as soon as they crossed the state line, Margie's nerves started peppering her with doubts. If she walked into the meeting with Wes, it might look like she didn't have the confidence to do this herself. Worse, it could look like she'd put Wes up to it. If they were still gunning for her, she didn't want him to take the heat for being on her side, at least publicly.

"When we get there," Margie said, scooting down a little in her seat. "I want to go in alone."

He glanced over at her.

"Not that I don't really, really appreciate that you have my back. I always have. But I'm worried about how it's gonna look if I don't do this on my own. Like, look at the little girl, she can't take the heat."

He nodded. "I understand how you might want to avoid that

256

perception. But think about this, Margie. There's a reason there's more than one umpire on the field. If you didn't get the best angle on the play, you can ask your partner for another opinion."

Margie thought about that as she watched the mile markers go by.

"Right after we drove through Hartford," Wes said, "you were talking about how you hoped Tim would get help."

"That's different. Addiction, it's physical. It's like…a disease, once you get hooked."

"How is this different, when you get right down to it? Look. No matter what people think about you, nobody can say that you aren't working as hard as you can to be a good umpire. And I'm sorry, but I think somewhere along the way you've been losing sight of the fact that we're not meant to do this alone. Okay, maybe we *can*, technically. But just like you talk about how crazy it's making you that Tim won't get help? It makes me crazy that you don't, either. And before you yell at me, it won't make him or you look weak, not to the people who matter. You have to stop being so stubborn and afraid and *ask*. If you don't *ask*, you're hanging yourself out to dry like you were in Holyoke."

Margie couldn't find the right words to yell at him at that moment. Then she turned toward the window and slumped down, her chin resting in the palm of her hand. "You're just saying all that stuff because you got me trapped in the car."

"Maybe. Maybe it's the only time I really get to. At the risk of making you angrier, did you actually ask Doug French for backup in the Holyoke game? Or did you assume he was going to jump in because he was your partner?"

Her mouth opened and closed like a fish. "He…he told me that I was on my own! I wouldn't ease off on Edwards, so he told me I was on my own. His exact words. So I didn't even think about asking. Whose side are you on here, anyway?"

"Well, yours, ultimately. But you and me, we've always been about the learning opportunities."

"Gaah. I am sick to death of the *learning opportunities*."

"No, you're not," he said gently. "Maybe you're getting them a little faster than you think you can manage them at the moment, but same as me, you live for them. You need them. You're smart and

257

curious, and whenever you stop learning and growing, you get really grouchy."

"Fine. Let's get down to it. What did I do wrong?"

"I told you. You didn't *ask*."

"And if I *asked*, you think he would have backed me up?"

"I think he might have helped you restore order instead of leaving you to struggle through that alone. Even if he'd made some kind of deal to give Dolph Edwards special treatment and you refused to go along with it, I don't think he'd want to put the safety of that many fans and players at risk just to prove a point."

Margie smirked. "I love how you can always find the good in anyone. If you ever meet the devil, you'll probably think, 'Oh, great, I was feeling a little chilly.'"

"Maybe I would."

She turned back toward the window.

"Margie, I'll do whatever you want in Providence. I'll help plead your case with you. I'll sit there and say nothing, and you can pull me in if you need another opinion. Or I'll drop you off and go find something else to do for a while. It's your call."

She thought about that for another few mile markers.

When they pulled up to the address Rosemary had given her, Wes left the engine running. It was a modest building, a colonial two-story converted into a series of office suites. It didn't look especially intimidating, but she knew appearances could be deceiving.

And two thoughts hit her in that moment.

One, this would probably be the last time she'd ever see Mack Abernathy.

Two, while Wes was a saint for getting her here, and for offering to come in, for being one of the few people she'd met over the last few years who truly had her back, this was her fight. She had to walk up those stairs alone.

* * *

"I really appreciate that you took the time to see me."

Abernathy's quick nod made her think the feeling wasn't mutual. That he'd rather be focusing on his other meetings. He shuffled some papers on his desk. *Okay. You're going to make this hard.* She cleared her throat and tried to get the words right in her head.

"About that article in the *Post*. I wasn't looking for publicity. I wasn't looking to make trouble. Okay, I talked to the reporter. I'll take my lumps for that. I was steamed over what happened in Holyoke, and in the moment, talking to a reporter seemed like a good way to get someone to hear my side of things. But then I thought better of it and told him to leave me out of it. I didn't want to be the story. I never wanted to be the story. I was just doing my job."

"So I read," Abernathy muttered.

"And I meant it," Margie said. "I was doing the job you and the umpire academy and everyone who was good enough to hire me wanted me to do. Then you asked me to stand down until the dust settled, and I've been doing that...but then I got this letter."

She passed it across to him. He slipped on a pair of reading glasses and gave it a looking over. She didn't understand why it was taking him so long to respond. It was only a couple sentences, and it had been from his own office. Maybe he was buying time to think of a good answer. Or else it was one of those offices where one person didn't know what the other was doing, like in her mother's law firm.

"See, there's no details, Mr. Abernathy. Mack. Sorry. Maybe you can see why I had some questions."

He frowned and rubbed his forehead, as if he could press the wrinkles out of it. "We could have done this on the phone." He tossed the letter onto the desk. "This is just a formal statement. It's essentially what I told you. That we're sitting you out until the situation settles down some. For your own safety, for—"

"See, I get that," Margie said. "I saw what happened to Fitzgerald after the article ran, so I get why you'd be concerned enough for my safety to want to sit me down. But I can take care of myself, Mr. Abernathy, I—"

"Back up there a minute," he said. "What happened to Fitzgerald?"

She thought for sure word would have gotten around by now. "Someone tried taking him out with a bat."

Abernathy's eyes bulged. "You saw this?"

"Just the consequences. I don't know all the whys and wherefores, and he said he didn't see the guy, but from reading the article, it's pretty clear Fitzgerald ticked someone off enough to take a swing at him. Have you ever met him, though? Half of baseball probably would have cheered. But you didn't hear that from me."

"He tried talking to you again after this?"

"I didn't give him squat," she said.

"I don't want to read one more word in the newspaper about you and this. You already have enough strikes against you, and I don't know how long I can keep defending you."

"You've...been defending me?"

One side of his mouth tipped into a smile. "Among others. But you didn't hear that from me."

"So, I could get cut."

"What happens next is out of my hands. The evaluations come in, and then we decide on the assignments for next season. And then there are the complaints. We look carefully at those."

Margie sat up straighter. "Those complaints, they aren't right. Most of them are from guys who didn't like that I tossed them. Just look at my record. I don't give a damn who won or lost those games. I don't care who's on which team. I call the plays. I treat everyone fair. I don't let my personal feelings get in the way of the calls, I don't—"

"Margie. You say you don't want special treatment? Then you'll have to go home and wait it out like everyone else."

"Fine." She started to stand up. Then stopped. "No. I'm not done yet. Yeah, okay, you guys are gonna get all your information and make whatever decisions you think are right for baseball. I can't change that. But I've been good at what I do. I've been working hard to improve, putting myself in situations where I can have...*learning opportunities.* I take a good hard look at each ejection report I write, seeing if I can analyze the situation and do a better job the next time, if need be. So all I can do is ask, Mr. Abernathy. I want to ask if I can keep getting a chance to do that job."

Margie stopped. Her heart beating hard against her chest. The air around her seemed to vibrate with the echo of her words. And yet the silence. The silence from that desk sucked it all away. Finally, he spoke. "It's been...a *learning opportunity* working with you. But we'll have to let you know."

* * *

Wes passed her a hot dog and a tall soda. A beer would have been more welcome—in fact she wanted a whole tray of them—but she had to stay clear in case Wes needed her to share the driving on the way home.

"So tell me something," Margie said. "If I wanted to go back to college…one day. How would you do that?"

"Okay. First, you need to decide what you want to study. Then you can do some research to find out what schools teach it, then—"

"Miss Oblonsky?"

Margie turned toward the small, squeaky voice.

"Oh, my God, I told you, Becky, it's her, I told you it was her!"

Two little girls were practically quivering in the aisle. They couldn't have been more than nine, ten. And they were shoving their programs at her. "Can we have your autograph, Miss Oblonsky? Please, please, please?"

Margie glanced toward Wes. He just shrugged and smiled at the girls.

"Please, call me Margie," she said. "You two play ball?"

They both nodded enthusiastically. "She plays second base, but I want to be an umpire," one of the girls said, and thrust out a fist. "See, I can already call a strike!"

"That's very good." Margie winked at Wes. "But try to remember to keep your thumb tucked into your fingers. It's way more professional that way."

She signed autographs while the girls practiced their strike fists, and they chatted for a while, and one of their mothers came to fetch them and apologized to Margie if the girls were bothering her.

After they left, Margie excused herself to the ladies' room and cried.

40

THE REHAB

Even though Tim's brain wasn't operating at full capacity during his meeting with the team's manager, he understood his choices: get clean or get out. So he'd let Carl book him into a rehab center in Vermont that some other ballplayers had gone to. He'd been too hungover to deal with the shame of telling his family—that he was checking into this place, that he needed separation from the rest of his life in order to do it—so Carl agreed to make the call for him. Tim knew it was a weasel move, but he rationalized himself into believing they'd understand. Or at least Margie would, and she'd explain it to Mom.

The place wasn't too bad. The mountain views and rolling green meadows made for a comforting backdrop. After detox, he started private and group sessions. He heard a lot about triggers and codependence and performance anxiety. Talking with his counselor one-on-one was weird at first, but the idea of sharing his problems with total strangers made him want to bolt. Gradually he warmed to it. When he finally screwed up enough nerve to say something about the pressure, the thing sitting on his chest when he took the mound, he saw a lot of heads nodding.

He had been feeling mostly good, or at least somewhat better, and strong enough to believe that he might be able to do this—if he could either stay away from or learn how to manage situations that triggered him. But on the last day of his program, during the last scheduled appointment for that afternoon, he sat in his private counselor's office, palms sweating, one heel bouncing against the floor, thoughts spinning around in his mind: *Is this really gonna work in the real world? What happens when I leave? What happens when I have to pitch again? If I have a crap outing, what will I do to shake it off?*

"What's going on, Tim?"

It took him a full thirty seconds of staring at the golden leaves raining down on the big green lawn to come up with the words. Because in that moment, the place was reminding him too much of home, and his legs twitched with the urge to run. He could easily imagine him and Margie and his dad out there, tossing a ball around, and it choked him up a little. He took one of the slow, deep breaths they'd instructed him to do when he was feeling anxious. "I just— this place… Everybody's been great. I'm getting a lot of support. But out there… I don't know." Tim's voice went small, tight. "I'm not gonna be able to call time and spend five minutes doing creative visualization when I'm on the mound with the bases loaded."

The counselor's smile was patient. "Well, no. And basically, you're right. The real hard work begins after you leave. Our job is to help prepare you with tools you can call on to make the best decisions for you in the moment. One choice at a time."

Somehow that didn't comfort him.

The counselor opened Tim's file. He scrutinized a piece of paper and frowned. "We don't have a follow-up therapist listed. Your team's doctor made that a condition of your release. He recommended someone, but if there's a professional you'd rather go to, that's okay, too. I just need a name."

Tim shook his head and pointed at the form. "Whoever you have there's fine."

And the next morning, armed with his treatment plan and his release paperwork and the name of his appointed stranger with whom he'd been ordered to share the intimate workings of his mind, he returned to Cincinnati.

But the thing on his chest was still breathing.

* * *

October used to be Margie's favorite month. The leaves turned red and gold and crunchy. She and Mom made apple pies that became for her the taste of autumn in the Hudson Valley. And, before he left baseball, it was the month her father came home. The Yankees were in a post-season drought back then, before the George Steinbrenner years, but Dad still returned in a good mood, full of plans for his time off. Some of her fondest memories were when she, Dad, and Timmy piled onto the sofa to watch the playoffs and the World Series. She and Tim went wide-eyed with awe when Dad told funny stories about the players they'd only seen on television. They made mock bets with each other about which teams would win, and in how many games. Margie usually got it right, her only prize the satisfaction that she'd called it and Timmy hadn't.

Then Margie turned fourteen and October gave the Oblonsky family the cold shoulder. On the Friday before the start of the 1975 American League playoffs, Margie waited for her father to return from work, eager to tell him she had looked at all the stats and predicted that the Red Sox would take the Oakland A's in three games. But he never came home. She didn't want to watch the playoffs that year, but Timmy turned on the TV anyway, mumbling, "It's what Dad would have wanted." Neither of them paid much attention. Even though Margie's prediction had been spot on, the play-by-play became white noise, a backdrop for their shock and grief.

Eventually, Margie stopped avoiding the things she loved because they reminded her of him and started needing them because they kept him alive in her heart.

But October was never the same for her again.

That year, home alone with her mother after her second season in baseball, October woke her at three in the morning with a coil of dread in her stomach.

She couldn't stop thinking about Tim. She sort of got why he wanted to go to ground for his rehab, but it still hurt that he'd shut them out, hadn't even told them where he was going. And she had the strongest feeling that he was hurting, too.

Part of her wanted to call that goddamn trainer, browbeat the information out of him, and drive to wherever they'd stashed her brother. She'd make sure he was okay first and then give him hell for making their mother cry. She was also furious with herself that she'd sensed something had been off with Tim for a while and she hadn't made the connection earlier.

Instead, she called Dan.

He answered on the second ring. "Timmy?"

The way he said her brother's name damn near broke her heart.

"Sorry, it's the other Oblonsky. So, you couldn't sleep, either?"

"Not a wink," he said. "I'm starting to wonder that if you catch for a guy, you form some kind of mental connection. Like twins."

"Makes sense. Have you heard anything from him at all?"

"Not a word, Margie." She could tell how much that hurt him, too. "Although last night the phone rang a couple times, maybe two, three in the morning, but then it stopped."

Her insides ached, just imagining Tim at the phone, wanting to reach out but changing his mind. "You think he'll be okay?"

The silence made the October claws sink in deeper. "I don't know, hon. You know how Timmy is with pressure. Once he gets settled down, he usually gets the job done fine. The problem lies in the settling down part. I hope they're teaching him ways to handle that. And I hope like hell they're saying that he should trust the people who have his back, instead of shoving them away."

Margie wanted to be comforted by that. After she and her mom found Tim in New York, after what happened to Doug French, she'd read about addiction. That it was a disease and that the potential to crawl back into it—or substitute one addiction for another—was always there. Could Tim stay clean? Or, if he was stressed out, had a bad game, even if he was bored, would he cave at the first whiff of temptation? If he went back next season and his teammates were still using, how would Tim handle that? Would their pregame phone conversations be enough to talk him off the ledge, or would he opt for a different kind of courage? She highly doubted that offering to live with him in Cincinnati would go over very well. He was a grown man; she couldn't watch him day and night. Nor would he want her to. Maybe part of that reason he had to get away and do this alone was about her. She'd always been his pregame security blanket. She never thought that was a bad thing. Helping him made her feel good, useful. Talking to him before his games made her believe that even though they were grown and mostly out of the house, they wouldn't drift apart like Mom's and Dad's siblings had.

Maybe he realized that, too, and wanted to see if he could handle the tough spots on his own.

"I'm so worried about him, Dan. I don't know where he is, where he's going... It's a long way to pitchers and catchers reporting. A long time to get himself into trouble."

"I hear you big time."

She lifted her gaze from the kitchen table to the calendar on the wall. The week she'd planned to visit Dan was too far away. "You mind if I come out a little earlier? Like, tomorrow?"

"Margie. You can come out whenever you want."

* * *

Earlier in the year, when he'd felt confident that Cincinnati was going to keep him for the season, Tim had rented a furnished apartment in one of the nicer neighborhoods. It always felt like he was living in someone else's place. There was way too much black leather, glass, and chrome for his taste, but he didn't spend a lot of time there so he hadn't bothered to do anything about it.

When he walked back in after his long absence, Tim wondered if he should make a few changes. Warm the place up a bit. Maybe even move. He'd learned in one of his rehab classes that avoiding things he associated with using could improve his chances of success. Like the glass-topped coffee table in his living room, for one, where he'd set up and snorted more lines than he could count. And the swirling pattern on the ceiling over his bed, where many mornings he woke, hungover, and swore the whirls were spinning faster. But there were associations in the city, too. Clubs where he'd met various people in the bathroom and taken whatever. Neighborhoods where he'd gone to parties he barely remembered.

The first night home, he covered the coffee table with a big towel and tried to sleep on the living room sofa, but that wasn't happening.

Twice, he picked up the phone, wanting to call Dan Monroe. Twice, he lost his nerve and set the receiver down. He took a few more deep breaths and dialed the number. After two rings, he slammed it back into the cradle. What would he say, anyhow? "Sorry I was such an asshole in New York"? "Sorry I cut my best friend out of my life"? He didn't want to be a weasel anymore. He knew it was only right to say those things face-to-face. To him. To his mother. To Margie.

The demon on his chest squeezed hard. This place, the apartment that looked like a stockbroker should live in it, felt suddenly icy cold and sent a shiver down his spine.

He had to get out.

He had to get out now.

* * *

Conscious of her mother hovering in the bedroom doorway, Margie zipped her duffel closed. "Yes, Mom. I have a map. Yes, Mom, I have gas money. And yes, Mom, I'll call you when I get there."

"I didn't ask. Did I ask?" She took another puff of her cigarette.

"You didn't. I'm just saying, is all."

"Okay. Fine. You don't have to jump down my throat about it."

Margie had just hoisted the strap to her shoulder, but she set it down on the bed and turned to face her mother. She let out a long, deep exhale. "I can't... I'm going a little crazy, with everything that's going on. I hate the idea of leaving you alone, but I can't sit here and wait and wonder when and if he's gonna contact us. Do you get that even a little bit?"

Her mother's eyes blazed, and she streamed smoke out both nostrils. "Yes, *Margaret*. I get that. I get that more than you'll ever realize."

Margie's mouth softened. Of course she should have known her mother would get it. Pat Oblonsky had been a baseball wife, a baseball mother, husband and kids going in and out of her house, not always calling regularly to check in, not always showing up when they'd promised.

"I'll be back Monday night," Margie said. Her mother nodded. "He'll call, Mom. I know he will. You know how Timmy gets."

Her mother nodded again. "I wish..." Her voice broke, and she stubbed her cigarette out in an empty coffee cup on Margie's desk. "Even when you two were little, you were the stronger one. Emotionally. The tougher one. I never really worried much about you on that score. It was him I was worried about. So fragile sometimes. I wish he was more like you."

Margie didn't know whether to smile because her mother was proud of her or fall into a quivering mess worried about Tim. She crossed the room and took her mother into her arms. After they'd both cried for a while, Margie sniffed and said, "Okay. I'll be home on Sunday."

Her mother pulled back, eyebrows drawn together. "The hell you will. You got a good man waiting for you who thinks you're the answer to all his prayers. I had that once, and let me tell you, it doesn't come along every day and it doesn't last forever. So go. Let him make you happy. And if and when your brother decides to get in touch, I'll let you know."

* * *

Margie stopped for lunch and a bathroom break at a diner somewhere near the Pennsylvania/Ohio border. While she was swilling coffee, she consulted her road atlas. Ten hours until Des Moines. Her plan was to get as far as Chicago then sack out in a motel and finish the trip the next morning. She'd already mentioned to Dan that she might break the trip up, so he wasn't expecting her at any particular time. But then she noticed something interesting on her map and dragged her finger along the route. If she exited I-80 and dipped south onto 71, she could get to Cincinnati, and it wouldn't take her that far out of her way.

Tim wasn't answering his phone, but she had his address.

It was worth a try.

She paid her bill, gave the waitress a huge tip, and got back in the car.

The drive through Ohio wasn't bad. Lots of highways and rolling hills. It was like a bunch of other places she'd been, so she stopped noticing after a while. There was too much on her mind to sightsee. She thought about what she'd say to Tim, if he was there. She tried to think logically, because at the moment she was so mad she was sure she'd start yelling, and that was exactly what she didn't want. Or, who knows, maybe he needed someone to yell at him. Maybe everybody else in his life had walked around him on eggshells. Maybe it had made him soft. She didn't know.

When she got to Cincinnati, she found Tim's neighborhood fairly easily. It was a pretty chichi place, close to Riverfront Stadium. He'd told her at one point that he actually had to buy his parking space, which was irritating and strange, but handy because it was in the lot right next to his building and he had a guaranteed space every time he came home. That's how she knew where to find his car. You'd think it'd be easy to spot a black Trans Am with a flame painted on the hood. But she wasn't finding one. The security guy was starting to look at her funny, so she ducked out and thought she'd try her luck with the front desk.

She hoped her face looked troubled enough to get some sympathy. If it matched the way she felt, she'd be golden. "Hi," she told the man behind the counter. "I'm Margie Oblonsky. This is kinda weird, I know, but I had to be in town, unexpected, and my twin brother, Tim, lives in this building. Someone swiped my purse out of my car while I was getting gas, and it had my address book and everything in it. Including his phone number. D'ya think it might be possible to, I don't know, buzz his apartment or something, see if he's around?"

He took a long squint at her face. "You do kinda look like him." He called into a back room. "Hey, Lenny. Come out here."

Another man, shorter and balding, came through the door. "Yeah?"

"This young lady—Margie, right?—is looking for Tim Oblonsky. They're twins."

"Twins, huh?" He also scrutinized her, and it was beginning to really piss her off. "Sorry. I haven't seen him. He's still on vacation, I think." He hooked a thumb over his shoulder. "I got a whole heap of his mail in the back."

"Damn." She pushed a hand through her hair. "I was really hoping...maybe you could just let me in? Then I could crash here, and call my mom and have her wire me some money so I could get home."

The taller man looked the more sympathetic of the two. "Honey, I hate to even ask, but you wouldn't believe the girls who come around here with all kinds of wild stories about why they gotta be let in. If you had ID or something..."

"Which is in my purse, of course." Damn, she hated lying. She'd locked said purse in her trunk. She rustled through her coat pockets. Car keys. Tissues. Her last pay stub from umpiring, a little crumpled. She grinned and spread it out across the counter. "There. My name's right on it."

Lenny went agog. "You're *that* Margie Oblonsky? Chuck, this here's *the* Margie Oblonsky. Tim Oblonsky's sister's the umpire!" He swung around the counter and pumped her hand. "Margie Oblonsky. Wow. I read about you. What you did. They gave you a bum deal, a real bum deal. That call took major guts. I totally agree with you about Edwards. It's making baseball look bad, having guys like that around. And now some jackass stole your purse, too? Man. Chuckie. Give the woman the key already."

Chuck grinned. "Well. If you can't trust an umpire with someone's apartment key, who can you trust?"

* * *

Tim had been home. That much Margie knew for sure. One of his suitcases was open on the floor near the foyer, stuff dribbling out of it. For some reason, a giant bath towel was spread over the coffee table. A pillow and blanket adorned the sofa. A small black address book sat next to the phone.

"Timmy," she said under her breath. "You're gonna be the death of me. What have you been up to?"

She tried to give him the benefit of the doubt. Maybe he came home, felt restless being alone, and called a friend, wanted to change into a favorite shirt that was in his suitcase, and the two of them were out right now having a burger or something. But why did it look like he'd made camp in his living room?

She flopped onto the sofa and pulled the blanket over her, staring out the picture window at the twinkling lights of the city. It still wasn't adding up. She could hardly call her mother and say she'd basically broken into Tim's apartment and found a bunch of weird clues she didn't understand. And she was so tired. Well, she did say she was going to crash somewhere. This place was as good as any.

* * *

She woke in a cold sweat in the middle of the night. Again, the October claws doing their worst. Three o'clock, right on schedule. And still, no sign of Tim.

She called Dan.

"Margie? Where are you? You okay?"

"Dan. Dan, stop. I'm fine. Stop talking until you can promise me one thing. That you won't tell my mother where I am."

"Uh, all right. I promise. Where are you?"

"I'm at Tim's place. His car wasn't here and the front desk guy let me in and it looks like he's been home recently but left again, and he hasn't come home yet and—"

"Margie." His voice was soft and patient and it made her take a breath. "That's because he's here."

He said Tim was okay but sleeping, and Margie didn't have the heart to ask Dan to wake him. Dan suggested Margie get some shut-eye, too, and leave fresh in the morning. But that sleep business wasn't happening. She fiddled around with his many remote controls until she found something sort of entertaining on his giant television and fell into a haze. The next thing she knew, light was streaming through the big windows and she got the heck out of there as fast as she could fly. On her way out, she thanked Chuck and Lenny for their kindness and promised that Tim would give them both a really big tip the next time he was in town.

It was the least her brother could do for making her chase him halfway across the Midwest.

* * *

Eight hours later she was pulling into Dan's driveway.

Dan was down the front porch stairs before she could get out of her car. His face looked more worried than happy to see her. This puzzled her. When she'd called from Cincinnati, he'd told her Tim was okay. More likely, Dan was concerned about what she might say to her brother. That her temper would get the better of her. Maybe he was right. She welcomed Dan's hug with a sigh and rested her aching head on his shoulder. She was grateful that Tim had run to him. Grateful that Dan understood her well enough and loved her brother enough to give her this time out.

With his arms still around her, he said, "Before you go in there, there's some things you should know."

"Talk to me, Dan," she said against his soft flannel shirt.

"He was in a real bad way when he showed up here last night."

Margie stiffened.

"No. No, Margie. He wasn't high or anything. Least I didn't think so. Look, you gotta promise me you won't tell him I told you this—he was kind of emotionally wrecked. I don't know what happened when he returned to Cincy, he hasn't talked about that yet, but apparently it was bad enough to drive him straight here. So maybe... Well, he's your brother and you know him better than anyone, but from what I saw, maybe you'll want to go a little easy on him to start." He pulled back and met her eyes. "You'll do that?"

Margie nodded, and feeling like her legs had turned to wood, she let him lead her up the stairs.

* * *

Tim had been wrapped in an afghan on the sofa, but when the door opened, he scrambled out and got to his feet. Margie's heart squeezed tight, the claws digging deeper. With his hair mussed and his eyes huge and wet, he looked so young, so vulnerable—and scared. The last time she could recall him looking so broken was probably at their father's funeral. Fucking October. She didn't know what they'd helped him with in that rehab place, but she knew one thing. Damn sure he hadn't talked about Dad. The one thing they should have helped him with. That was when he'd started drinking beer and getting high, almost every weekend. Maybe it wasn't the rehab people's fault. Maybe Tim didn't want to talk about it. Or he'd forced himself not to remember.

Tim stood, arms floppy at his sides and lower lip wobbling as he waited for her judgment.

She knew she had to go to him, make her legs move, say something. She wanted to drown him in hugs. She wanted to slap some sense into him. She wanted to comfort him. She wanted to yell at him until his eardrums bled. But it wasn't all his fault, and it wasn't all hers. It was too much to think about. So she let her heart guide her. It took her across the room and grabbed on to him so fast and fierce he stumbled backward to keep both of them from tumbling over.

Dan might have said something about giving them some space, but about all she could focus on was her brother. Soon he gave her shoulder a couple of firm pats and leaned away, signaling that she should let up on him. She stepped back. His eyes were wet and he quickly swiped at the tears with the back of his hand and shot her a grin, one she knew so well.

"Man, Barge. You look like shit."

"Ha. No wonder you get so many girls, with sweet talk like that."

"I suppose you already told Mom...you know, that I'm still alive and everything?"

"No way, John-Boy. That's your story to tell. Call it my gift to you."

He sighed and sank back onto the sofa. She kicked off her shoes and sat cross-legged on the other end.

"I'll call her," he said. "In a little while. I just wanna..." He sniffed, but she heard the effort in his voice not to cry. "Margie Bargie. I'm sorry. I should have told you. I should have done a lot of things. You got every right to be pissed as hell. I should have told you. But I needed—they were gonna let me go if I didn't...and I needed to do the rehab thing on my own. I had to prove to myself, you know, that I could."

She nodded, then said softly, "Timmy. What happened in Cincinnati?"

He looked at her blankly.

She let out a quick exhale. "I stopped by your apartment and got your doorman to let me in."

His cheeks colored. "You busted into my place?"

"What can I say? I was worried that my brother had disappeared off the face of the earth. So I may have taken advantage of my celebrity status to get a key and see if I could find any clues. Lenny's a fan."

"Remind me to thank him later," he grumbled.

"Timmy." She touched his arm. His muscle tensed but he didn't move away. "What happened?"

He closed his eyes and took a slow, deep breath and let it out. "It was stupid. It was so stupid."

"Take your time, then. I'm not going anywhere. Or don't tell me. Up to you."

"No. I want to. I got back to my place and... Margie, it was like the walls were closing in on me. Like, reminding me of all the times I got high there, who I was with, what kind of game it had been. I went into full panic mode, and I knew I had to get out of there. And not be alone. So I called a girl I knew. I always felt better when I was with her. I was halfway to her place when I remembered why I always felt that way with her. Because before we, uh…" His blush returned. "We'd, you know, get a good buzz on. And when I remembered that, I slammed on the brakes so hard someone almost ran right into me. I chucked a U-turn right in the middle of the main drag and booked it back to my place. Only I didn't go in. I never made it past the parking lot. I knew if I went in there, what I would do. Who I would call. There's a guy in my building, always has a little stash for me. So I got on the highway west and kept going till I found that big lug and begged him to take me in."

Margie leaned her head against his arm. "That was a good decision." Her mother had been right. Dan was a definite keeper. "So which part are you gonna tell Mom?"

He took another couple of deep breaths like before. "All of it." He paused. "Eventually." Another breath. "And I will. I'll tell you the rest of it, too. I really want to hear what's up with you. I've been such a lousy brother, Bargie, and you've been going through your own hell, and I'm so sorry—"

"Hey," she said. "We don't gotta do that now."

She felt him relax with relief. "Okay. Okay, good. So maybe for now we can just…be. You know. Just hang out, like we used to."

She nodded, then looked up at her twin. "Did you bring your glove?"

He snorted a laugh. "I always got my glove. You got your mitt?"

"No, but I'm pretty sure I can sweet-talk a certain catcher into letting me borrow his."

* * *

The sun hung low over the afternoon, giving the blanket of fallen leaves an ethereal golden glow. As Margie set for Tim's pitch, a shiver of memory went through her. There were no mountains standing watch over them like at home; although the working class suburb of Des Moines where Dan lived was almost as flat as Florida and the air felt sharper, crisper, in one blink she could place Dad on the other side of the yard, where he'd be scuffing a booted foot into the leaves while saying, "Okay, you two, five more minutes then let's get the rakes."

Tim stood by an old red maple and twirled the ball in his pitching hand. "You ready, Barge? Think you can handle the heat?"

She set. "Bring it on, John-Boy."

He looked good out there. Strong. Tall. Tim Oblonsky was not the same sagging, broken boy she'd hugged in the living room. Margie didn't know what made the change—their talk, the fresh air, holding a baseball again—but she didn't much care. If she could still see her Timmy, then she had hope. The rest was details. And time.

The first pitch was a pretty one—a by-the-numbers fastball, not his usual blazing speed but hard enough. She caught it clean and winged it back, and he delivered another one, just as nice.

After so much driving over the last couple days, her body sang with relief from the exercise, from the stretch through her arm and back as she returned the ball to Tim. Ten pitches later they slipped into an easy game of catch, like old times.

Dan must have been standing out on the back porch, because Tim held on to the ball after Margie tossed it back; then he turned toward the house and said, "Hey, you want in?"

Big Dan's laugh made Margie smile. "Why," he said. "You tossing the umpire out of the game?"

"Nah. I'm sending myself to the showers. It's been a long couple of days. Guess it's catching up with me."

Margie watched her brother shuffle through the crunchy leaves. His eyes moved across the yard like he expected to see the ghost of October. Dan met him halfway; he clapped Tim on the back and whispered something in his ear as Tim handed him the ball and glove then disappeared through the sliding glass door.

"What did you tell him?"

Dan grinned as he slipped his catcher's mitt off Margie's hand and gave her the glove and ball. "I promised I'd go easy on you."

"Bite me," Margie said.

"Ha. There's my girl."

"You're never gonna let me forget I tossed you out of that game, are you?"

"Nope. Never." He winked at her. "Hey, it gave me a good excuse to buy you dinner, didn't it?"

"Only because I liked your stats."

"Oh, I think you liked more than my stats."

She moved closer. He smelled so good, like autumn leaves and woodsmoke. "Maybe I did."

He was still smiling when their lips met, but they quickly softened into hers and he pulled her tight against him. The mitt and glove thumped to the ground, one after the other. She'd never kissed a man in a rain of falling leaves, surrounded by the ghost of October. The claws eased their pressure on her chest and, one by one, began slipping away.

But one stuck, and stuck hard, when a thought of Tim intruded. She had one of those twin senses that he was hurting. That he was remembering something he didn't want to remember. Part of her wanted to run to him. Part of her knew that there were some things he had to wrestle with on his own.

She broke the kiss but not the circle of his arms. Couldn't do it if she tried. "Okay, Mr. Monroe. Back to your position."

"I kinda like this one." He tilted his head and kissed her neck.

She kinda liked that one, too, but Tim could be looking out that window and she wasn't so keen on her brother watching his best friend and his twin sister make out. "You wanna see what happens when you keep arguing my calls?"

"Actually, I wouldn't mind arguing about this one for a while."

"Just get over there." She poked him in the side.

He raised his hands in resignation. "Fine, fine. I'm going." He plucked up the gear they'd dropped and handed her the glove and ball. "But this is a new one for me. I never caught a girl before. Chased a few, maybe. But never caught one."

She grinned at him as he took a spot near a sturdy oak and set into a crouch. He'd caught one now.

Margie had been the catcher for her softball team, and other than winging a ball into Tim's pitch-back in frustration, it had been a few years since she'd pitched for real. Her muscle memory was set to handle the size of a softball, the fast-pitch windup and delivery. The first few bounced short, went wide. Then she fell into a nice groove—her body remembered at about the same time that Dan caught on to the slightly different skill required to catch a softball pitcher. Then they too slipped into an easy game of catch. After a few rounds, Dan asked what they should do about dinner.

"Considering you got the two of us here, now, maybe we should get something delivered?"

He liked that idea and said there were a few places nearby that were pretty good. He held on to the ball she'd just thrown, and they went inside to check out their options.

Tim was on the phone. From his body language—there were lines around his tear-reddened eyes, but his shoulders weren't as high as she'd seen them in other tense situations—Margie had a feeling it had been a difficult conversation so far but it was beginning to turn a corner. When she and Dan came in, Tim put a finger to his lips and mouthed "Mom," then flashed her a thumbs-up sign.

Margie nodded, tried to send him a mental wave of strength, and led Dan to the front door. "Maybe let's go into town instead? Bring something back? Give him some time?"

Dan considered that. "Tell you what. I'll go. You stick here in case."

"Tell you what. Lemme go see what Tim wants me to do."

She went back into the kitchen to get the takeout menus she'd seen on the counter. Tim was still on the phone, doing more listening than talking, but he looked lighter, somehow. When his eyes met hers, she whispered, "You want some privacy?"

He shook his head and tugged her toward him, giving her a quick one-armed side hug and a kiss on her temple. "Yeah, Mom," he said. "Yeah. Margie's been awesome. I'd put her on, but she and Dan are heading out the door to get us some dinner. And you know how grouchy she gets when she doesn't eat. Yeah. You'll see us both real soon." During the pause that followed, Margie held up the menus. "Sure," Tim said, pointing to the Chinese one. "I don't know about Dan's work schedule, but if he wants, we'll bring him, too."

As Tim continued to listen and nod, he made a little shooing motion with his fingers. Margie understood. That at least for now, Timmy had this covered. And now was about all she could ask for.

* * *

It was early Sunday evening. After a late breakfast of pancakes, eggs, sausage, and bacon, they'd spent most of the afternoon watching football and raking leaves. The second half of the four o'clock game turned into a blowout by a team none of them liked. Tim groaned when yet another touchdown was scored, and he announced he was going to take a shower.

"About time, too," Dan said, grinning, and Tim raised a middle finger behind his back as he walked up the stairs. Still chuckling, Dan switched over to some random program and Margie curled up next to him on the sofa, his big arm slung around her shoulders. His chest made a fine pillow, and she listened to the strong, sure beat of his heart. If she were a cat, she'd be purring. She didn't remember feeling this peaceful in a long time, especially in October.

She didn't even remember falling asleep, but the next thing she knew, the National League playoff game was starting. Al Michaels was rattling off the highlights from the first two games. And Tim was coming back down the stairs.

"Turn that off," she snapped at Dan as she fumbled around for the remote. He looked at her like she was nuts.

"Margie, what the—?"

"It's okay, Barge." Tim flopped into the easy chair next to the sofa. "I told him I wanted to watch."

But she didn't feel like it was okay. With his hair wet and in a floppy T-shirt he'd borrowed from Dan, he looked so young. About the same age he'd been when he defiantly switched on the playoffs after Dad died. She could still remember the tension in his fourteen-year-old face as he stood there, straight as a fence post, making himself watch, proclaiming that Dad would have wanted it that way.

Her chest suddenly tightened; the October beast sharpened its claws. Dan caressed her upper arm, as if trying to reassure her everything would be all right. That October would be all right.

"See that, Timmy Boy?" Dan pointed to the TV. "That's gonna be us next season."

Tim snorted. "Keep dreaming."

"Nah. You gotta think positive. It could happen. I mean, look at the Braves. Yeah, they're probably going down like a sack of potatoes tonight, but look how far they made it. And you, my friend, pitched their goddamn lights out. You. Pitched a division-leading batting order stupid in their own house. In that stadium right there. Man, I wish I'd been there to see it."

When Tim smiled, Margie felt the claws retract. But only for a second.

Something wasn't right with him. The smile looked like it was being propped up by sheer will alone. The corners quivered a little.

"Timmy? What is it?" Margie ducked out from under Dan's arm as he released her.

Tim shook his head like he was shaking off a pitch. Before he turned away from her, she saw his face. Eyes big and wet, the blue in them glassy. The smile collapsing under the weight of those unshed tears.

And then, even those began to fall.

Dan picked up the remote. "Don't!" Tim cried out, so loud that Margie jumped back, nearly crashing into the coffee table.

"Don't," he said, softer, his voice strangled with tears. "I want to watch. I want to remember. He was there that night. I know he was. And I just...I just want to remember."

So they sat with him, Margie on one side and Dan on the other. It was a short game, and the Braves went without much of a fight, but Margie spent most of it remembering their father with Tim, in their silent twin language.

It was a long time until Tim spoke again.

After the last player was interviewed, after the last unsuspecting reporter was doused with champagne, after Dan put another log on the fire. Tim laid his head on Margie's shoulder, let out an old man's sigh, and said, "They were right. In the rehab place. If I'm gonna pitch next season, I need to get, you know, a therapist. You know, where I can talk about Dad and stuff and how I can deal with the pressure. In the real world. Maybe I'll go to those meetings, too. Where you get a sponsor."

Dan nodded slowly, and said, "We could make some calls in the morning. There's gotta be places like that around here."

Tim raised his head. Scrubbed a hand across his face. "No, you don't have to... What I mean is... I love you like a brother, man. You know that. But I need to go home."

41

THE WAIT

1983

Margie woke at three in the morning to sleet peppering her bedroom window. She tried to let the sound of it comfort her back to dreamland, like the rain often did, but the staccato *tink-tink-tink* only joined the other static crackling through her head.

The first spark started when Wes told her about his letter. As he'd suspected, Umpire Development decided to give him another season in double-A ball, this time in the Southern League. "You'll see, Margie. You'll get one, too, and I'll see you at the winter meeting. Maybe your mail distribution route is slower than mine."

That was three days ago. Still no letter. Then Dan had called. The Orioles wanted to bring him up, and he was to report to Miami for spring training in February with the other pitchers and catchers. She'd been thrilled for him, of course. And for Wes and for Tim. They all knew what they'd be doing when the season started. Each had a letter confirming where they were supposed to be and when.

She still had no idea. Baseball hadn't taken her back—even though her performance evaluation was pretty decent, considering—but they hadn't outright rejected her, either. "That could be a good thing," Tim had said earlier that day, when they were driving home after his meeting. He'd started inviting her along, and she was so proud of the progress he was making. She even talked a little, about how tough it was finding the right balance between helping Tim and letting him figure things out for himself. "I mean, with players," Tim added, "there's a lot of shaking up during spring training. Probably it works the same with umpires."

"It kind of doesn't, but thanks for the thought."

He reached over and patted her arm. "They'll find something for you, Barge. I read that evaluation. Quick footwork around the bases, good eye, snappy with your calls, a higher level of skill, and that thing they said about you displaying more confidence and leadership than last season? I mean, come on. You're too good to sit on the shelf for long." After a pause, he'd said, "Hey, here's an idea. If for some idiotic reason they're too stupid to pick you up, come to Tampa and hang out with me during spring training. Maybe they'll let you catch."

She laughed at the old family joke, but at least she had one invitation.

It still didn't help her get back to sleep.

Maybe a cup of tea or some warm milk might help. She tossed on her robe and headed down to the kitchen. Her mother was sitting at the table, doing the *New York Post* crossword puzzle and listening to the radio. A low-key commercial for some kind of insurance company droned on. Maybe that was the only advertiser they could get so late at night.

"Ten letters, starts with an R," Mom said. "Nineteen eighty-two American League Rookie of the Year."

"Robin Yount." Margie tugged open the refrigerator.

The commercial ended and a familiar voice came on.

Margie rolled her eyes into the frosty void. "Mom. You still listen to him? After everything?"

She shrugged. "He talks baseball and he's got a nice voice. It's very soothing."

"You think so? Maybe he'll help me sleep."

"Make fun all you want, missy. He's doing some good things."

"Yeah, like what? Ruining people's careers? Getting himself beat up?"

Her mother gestured to the radio. "Like this."

Margie caught the words "...*pervasive drug use even during games...don't know where the dots connect or how high up it goes, but trust me, we're looking into that and we're looking into that hard...*"

"He's been like a dog with a bone lately. Talkin' about those, whadyacallit, *performance-enhancing substances.* Asking why nobody's testing the players for them. Calling for a special investigation. On and on about how it's bad for baseball."

282

Margie's stomach clutched. "He didn't mention anything about Tim, did he?"

"You think I'd let him go on living if he had?"

"Remind me not to piss you off."

"Ha. And here's the kicker." She flipped the paper around and showed Margie the sports page. Below the main story was a smaller headline: Baseball Bad Boy Busted; MLB Future Uncertain.

"Holy shit." A quick scan told her a cop broke up a bar fight instigated by an out-of-his-mind-high Dolph Edwards, who was arrested for drug possession and for beating the crap out of another patron; the victim happened to be a lower-level minor league suit Edwards had a beef with following the infamous Holyoke game. One witness reported that Edwards yelled, "This is for not doing what you were paid to do" while he rained punches on the guy's head. An official investigation of the incident would follow. The California Angels' management would not comment. It didn't take much of a stretch for Margie to imagine the poor schlub was one of the guys she'd overheard leaning on French to get her to look the other way on Edwards. It also seemed pretty obvious that the Angels might think twice about whether Edwards's moneymaking potential was worth putting up with his crap any longer.

"I read the whole article." Mom tipped her chin toward the radio. "Turns out those 'reliable sources' Fitz credited were pretty darn reliable."

Margie set the milk on the counter and grabbed the phone. "What's his number?"

"Oh, for frig's sake. You aiming to dig yourself in deeper?"

"No." As if he'd heard their conversation, Fitzgerald repeated the station's call-in number in that easy, guy-on-the-next-barstool voice. "I want to thank him."

Trevor the call screener picked up after eight rings. "Yo. Name and town."

"Yo to you. Margie Oblonsky. Can I just talk to the man, please?"

"Name and town."

"Seriously?"

"Name and town."

"Fine. Margie from Saugerties."

There was a pause.

"He says wait a minute."

A minute was more like four—enough time to heat some milk and pour it into a mug.

"Margie?" Fitz said.

"Anyone try to rearrange your face lately?"

"It would only be an improvement. Wow. Margie from Saugerties. How's my favorite umpire?"

"Yeah, we don't have to talk about that. I just... I wanted to say... It's a good thing, what you're doing."

The pause made the back of her neck itch. "Good enough that you'll maybe go on record with your story? Help us see how high up the ladder these shenanigans are going?"

"One day. Maybe. It's a little complicated for me now."

"With you being on the shelf, you mean? Or were you dumped like French?"

Margie's eyes widened. "French got dumped?"

"Dumped and dumped hard. There's talk that just this afternoon, Edwards was singing like a canary to get his charges knocked down. So far, he's tagged another ump and a couple of suits. Then he mentioned he had help from some guy named Donofrio. Whose hobby was trying to intimidate umpires who wouldn't play."

No kidding. "Sportswriters, too?"

"Nah. He's a noisy little punk. Swinging a bat off the field doesn't seem like his style. But he's in enough trouble. I'd imagine the league might be taking another look at the fat, juicy paper trail in your ejection reports. Could mean a suspension, to start. But you didn't hear any of that from me. Like I said. I got friends on the inside. Ones that say there's a few more fish that need frying. I just have to reel them in. If you have anything else to contribute to the cause, I'm always open."

Maybe she would ask him about those friends. Someday. "I'm considering a few offers, so I think I'd rather stay out of the papers for now."

"Loud and clear. Just don't forget about me, you hear?"

"I don't know how that would ever be possible. You and your stupid hats."

"So you gonna marry that big ol' farm boy, or what? Now that he's going to the majors, that catcher is one fine catch, or at least the ladies tell me so."

"What? How the hell did you—?"

He laughed. "Like I said. Friends on the inside."

"Goodbye, Fitz."

"Aw. I guess you're not gonna stick around to take questions from my infinitesimally small audience, are you?"

"*Goodbye*, Fitz."

He was still chuckling when she hung up.

42

THE SPRING

Margie slapped her trunk closed and dusted off her hands. "So, I set it up with the oil company and they're coming to fill the tank tomorrow. That should take you through the middle of March or so. And you got at least a half-cord of wood left."

Mom dragged deep from what she swore was her last cigarette. "I'll probably use less since I won't have you two around, turning up the heat every five minutes. What, you've been practicing for the Florida weather?"

"Aw, admit it, Mom." Tim shot her a big white grin as he loaded up the back of his Trans Am. "You're gonna miss us like crazy."

"You bet your asses I will. And you darn well better pick up that phone once in a while."

"We'll call you when we get to Tampa," Margie said. "Or, you know, here's an idea—you could get on a plane and come visit."

"I'll think about it."

Tim shook his head. "You still hate Florida that much that you won't come visit your own kids? Man, that's harsh."

"I said, I'll think about it."

"Don't strain anything thinking about it," Margie said, then turned to her brother. "You ready to blow this place, John-Boy?"

"Me? I was born ready."

Mom, eyebrows drawing together, took two steps down the stairs and waggled a finger at them. "No drag racing, you two. If anything happens to you, I'll kill you, I swear."

Margie laughed. Before she popped the car out of park, Mom still watching them, Margie gunned her engine, just to get a rise out of her.

She followed Tim, smiling all the way to the Thruway. She hadn't gotten anything from Umpire Development except for her performance evaluation back in November, but for the moment, she was almost okay with that. She was even looking forward to being a spring-training groupie, with Tim on one side of Florida and Dan on the other.

Maybe she'd find a cheap rooming house somewhere in between, and be like those baseball girls she'd met in Montana and Binghamton. She thought Dan would find that funny, but when she told him, he didn't laugh.

"Margie, I'm behind whatever you decide to do, and it would be a real kick to see you up in the stands, but I'm not ready to count you out. Even on spec."

Truth be told, Margie hadn't really counted herself out yet, either.

But a good umpire is always prepared.

* * *

Camping out in the stands under the hot sun reminded Margie of her teen years, going to various places with her mother to watch Tim pitch. Little League. High school ball. College. All she needed to complete the memory was a bottle of Coppertone, a warm can of Tab, and a soggy American cheese sandwich on Wonder Bread. Tim said he'd reserved a seat for her near some of the other families. Margie figured she was in the right place when she saw the gaggle of red-capped people in the box seats down front, and immediately felt every inch the spectator rookie she was. No cooler. All the other families had coolers. Why hadn't she thought to bring one? *Well, it's all about the learning opportunities.* She grinned, thinking about Wes.

She'd touched base with him before she and Tim left New York. He was excited about his new assignment. He probably assumed she hadn't gotten a letter, or she would have told him, so he didn't ask. But he encouraged her to come to the preseason meeting anyway. "You could still get on the waiting list for a call-up spot," he said. "Sometimes call-ups become regulars, which you've already seen."

Yep. She'd seen that. And she supposed he had a point. But she'd also watched Doug French self-destruct from being on the shelf too long.

Then she became aware that a woman was trying to get her attention. Margie focused on the woman, who was dressed like she was going on safari rather than sitting at a ballpark. A pocket for everything in that vest.

"Hi," she said, perky as anything. "You're new! Which one's yours?"

"Uh, hi. Well, he's not mine, exactly, but Tim Oblonsky's my brother."

She and another woman squealed. "You're Margie! Oh. My. God. I was so hoping we'd get to meet you!"

"Uh, thanks?"

They fussed over her and got her a cold soda and a Reds cap and told her their names. Apparently she was now part of some sort of tribe, and she didn't know how she felt about that, but it was kind of nice to belong somewhere.

* * *

In what must have been the eighth sign of the apocalypse, Pat Oblonsky came to Florida. She was welcomed to the Reds' family section like the baseball royalty she'd always wanted to be. They cooed about her talented children, especially her strong, handsome son, who was now on the mound for an inning of exercise during an exhibition game with the St. Louis Cardinals.

"He looks good, Pat," one of them said. "He's going to have a fine season, I can feel it."

"From your mouth to God's ear," Mom said. "But your young man there"—she gestured toward third base—"mark my words, he's Gold Glove material."

And on they went. Talking about their husbands and boyfriends and sons and nephews, speculating on what the owners should do to help the team finish higher in the standings this season. Margie figured Mom had this handled for Team Oblonsky, so she went off to stretch her legs. The stadium was packed, and no wonder. Most had come to watch St. Louis, since they were the World Series champs. Maybe some scouts were there, too. She was thrilled and grateful that Cincinnati had taken Tim back with open arms, but she couldn't help but wonder if he might do better with a team that wasn't slumping so hard. Or one that would put him back in the starting rotation.

She was coming out of the ladies' room when she spotted a familiar face: Buddy Jones. Other than Big Al, Buddy had been her favorite instructor at the Umpire Academy. She felt bad that she hadn't kept in touch. When he recognized her, he smiled at first, but then frowned in confusion.

"Margie? No game today?"

"What? Oh. No." She pointed to her cap. "Just here to support my brother."

"Tim. Gotcha. He's looking pretty fit out there."

"Yep. That he is."

People wove around them, getting snacks, chattering about the game, the players.

When she couldn't take the awkward silence any longer, she blurted, "Okay. I don't have an assignment. I never got my letter."

He nodded, his face growing serious. "Aw, Margie. That stinks. You were one of our best trainees. I can't imagine why they wouldn't..." He raised an index finger. "Hold that thought; I need to make a call. You'll be here for a while?"

She shrugged. "I'm Team Oblonsky. We're playin' the Cards. Where else am I gonna go?"

* * *

A couple more innings went by. Tim was done for the day. He visited their box to say hi, and Margie swore three girls in the general area damn near exploded. He signed a couple autographs and let some fans take a picture with him. Then he insisted they take one of him and Margie. "'Cause she looks so cute in that cap," he said, flicking the bill with a finger. They goofed around for a while, posing for the camera, talking to the kids and the other players' families. She was having so much fun, she didn't notice that Buddy had returned until her mother tugged her sleeve and said a guy wanted to talk to her.

Buddy was smiling. "This is what I love about spring training. You can get up close and personal with the players."

Something about that smile was making her uneasy. She thought she knew what he was going to tell her, and she didn't want him to start talking to her yet. "Buddy, have you met my brother? Tim, this is Buddy. He teaches at the Umpire Academy."

Tim's grin broadened as they shook hands. "I think we've met. Think you called one of my starts last season."

"Think you're right. Margie, got a minute?"

Crap. No avoiding it now. She followed him up the aisle, very much aware of her mother's stare burning into her back.

* * *

"Don't tell me you turned him down."

Margie didn't answer.

"You *turned him down?* Margie. For frig's sake, what the hell is wrong with you?"

Margie put her hands over her ears. "Stop. Stop screaming at me. Oh my God. Stop."

Her mother stopped. Right in the middle of the stadium parking lot. With Tim and half of Florida there and everything. She almost looked like she was about to slap Margie across the face. Pat Oblonsky shook her head, lit a cigarette, then resumed walking toward Tim's car. "You're crazy. I can't believe you turned him down."

"I didn't turn him down. Yet. And hey, aren't you the same lady who yelled a blue streak at me for accepting my first offer?"

"That was different. It was friggin' Montana. This could be your way back in. When we get back to Tim's, you call him."

"No."

"No. Why the hell not?"

"Mom." How could she even explain this? "It would be for a place on the call-up list. In Double A, yet. Like, they'd call you to come in if someone got sick or whatever. Since my last assignment was as a regular crew member in Double A, being a call-up would be like going backward. You don't want to go backward in umpiring. If you're not moving forward, the league above you stops looking."

Her mother exhaled out the side of her mouth, then smirked. "If you're not even working, I'd imagine they'd stop looking even faster."

"I read my evaluation. I've been upping my game, and I'm worth better than this. I want a regular slot."

"Timmy. Tell your sister she's lost her friggin' mind. Maybe you were out in the sun too long."

He laughed. "Aw, that's too easy. I already know Bargie's crazy." She elbowed him in the ribs. "Seriously, Mom. She's right, what she said about umpires. For the great job she's been doing, and the crap she had to deal with last season, they need to do better by her."

"Thanks, John-Boy."

"Team Oblonsky," he said, offering up a high five.

As they settled into the car to drive back to Tim's place, the consequences of the choice that awaited her hit Margie hard. She wanted more than a call-up spot. But if nobody bit... No. She refused to think about that.

* * *

Tim had to go to Orlando for two days of exhibition games, and their mother was needed back at work, so after Margie dropped her at the airport—under the condition that there would be no more discussion about Margie's career—she continued on to Sarasota, where Dan's team had a one o'clock start.

She'd hoped to get there earlier—Dan had left a ticket for her at the gate—but thanks to road construction detours and a lot of traffic, it was already the fourth inning by the time she pulled into the lot. She started walking toward the box seats on the third-base side, and already spied the gaggle of coolers and Orioles caps, under which she assumed were the players' families, but she felt a little hinky about rushing over there and introducing herself as Team Monroe. She was still nervous about too many people knowing they were together. The item on the complaint report about "making calls favorable to her boyfriend's team" still nagged at her.

She took an empty seat a good few rows away from the party people and settled in to watch what was left of the game.

Dan was behind the plate.

It had been a long time since she'd seen him in uniform, and damn, he looked good. Even behind a mask and a chest protector.

A pitch went way outside. Dan snagged it, called time, and jogged out to the mound. She imagined what he was telling the young pitcher. Tim said when Dan came out to meet with him, he'd tell a joke or something to get him to loosen up.

The pitcher nodded, Dan clapped him on the shoulder with his mitt, and he trotted back to the plate.

But not before he saw her. He smiled. That smile made her think things she shouldn't be thinking at a family-friendly venue. Maybe she should be sitting in the team boxes. Maybe she should get an Orioles cap and a cooler and maybe even one of those stupid little umbrellas that kept the sun off your face.

If Umpire Development showed her the door, maybe she could be happy bouncing around Florida for a while, rooting for her guys, being careful to make sure she was wearing the right cap at the right stadium. Then she'd think about the rest of her life.

Whatever Dan had said to the pitcher worked, because he struck the guy out. He had an 0-and-2 count on the next one, but the pitch that followed was a hanging breaker and the batter jumped all over it. It bounced off the outfield wall, and the left fielder played it well. He rocketed the ball to the third baseman as the runner was diving in headfirst. She saw herself as that third-base ump, setting to eyeball the impending play. The tag was late, and the ump called him safe.

But one of the umpires had overlooked something. The runner hadn't touched second base. Margie leapt from her seat, but oh, the restraint it took for her not to yell, "He's out! He missed second!"

As if the Orioles manager had heard her thoughts, he jumped out of the dugout and asked for an appeal.

After a brief consultation among the umpires, the crew chief called the runner out.

Much arguing ensued. Margie's heart was beating so damn hard. Last season, she'd be there, getting those guys off the field, warning or tossing the ones who wouldn't let up.

Finally everyone simmered down. Margie checked her watch and swore under her breath. If she didn't leave now, she'd be late for her meeting. Warring thoughts raced through her head as she booked out of there and navigated the Florida highways toward Umpire Development headquarters in St. Petersburg. Her heart was still pounding from that play. If the execs didn't bite at what she had in mind, how could she possibly walk away from something that made her feel so alive?

* * *

Mack Abernathy stood when the big boss's secretary let Margie into the conference room. He didn't look unhappy to see her, which she took as a good sign. Two men she didn't recognize were also there. Abernathy introduced her first to the boss, a tall guy with a crew cut who was the head of the whole Umpire Development program, then to a silver fox of a dude who was the president of the Southern League. It was pretty damn impressive that they were available on such short notice for this meeting. In her mind, that was either a good sign or a really, really bad one.

After some preliminary chitchat, they got down to business.

The big boss let Abernathy start the conversation. He tented his hands on the table, atop a folder in which, she presumed, were her various complaint reports and performance reviews and whatever else that could determine—or undermine—her future.

"After all the rankings came in last November," Abernathy said, "the evaluation committee recommended that you were to be provisional for the Eastern League, pending crew assignments for this season. I don't know where the mix-up occurred that you didn't get a letter, but I apologize for that. Things do go amiss, every once in a while."

Margie pulled in a deep breath. "So it's true, then." She was careful to keep her voice calm and professional. "I was never officially dismissed."

"That would be true, yes. You were not. One of our committee members fought for you and fought hard. But we don't have a crew assignment for you in the Eastern League, Margie. Everything there's buttoned up tight for now. However, there's one slot open on the call-in roster for the Southern League." He then deferred to the good-looking guy sitting next to him.

The Southern League guy leaned back in his chair and said, "We have you penciled in, if you want it."

The room went silent. The air conditioner clicked on. The water in the cooler bubbled. She really wanted a drink, and regretted not having taken the one the secretary offered when she first came in. Margie swallowed.

Here goes nothing. Or maybe everything. "I'm really grateful for your offer," she said. "I've been giving it very serious consideration. And I would like to accept, with one condition." She wiped her sweating palms against her pant legs under the table. "I've done my job, and my overall season evaluations have been pretty good. I'm always looking for ways to improve and get more experience. I love this game, and I have great respect for its integrity. I hope you've seen that, too. So, I want an opportunity to work in as many games as you need me. I'm happy to be on that call-up list, but only if I get your word that I'll be first in line for your next regular crew assignment."

She wanted to say more but held her tongue.

It was time to let the silence do her talking.

After a god-awful number of heartbeats, Abernathy nodded. So did the Southern League guy and the big boss. "Margie," Abernathy said, "would you mind giving us a few minutes?" He buzzed for the secretary and she was escorted back to the lobby, where she paced, nearly hyperventilating from nerves, then picked up last week's *Sports Illustrated* but wasn't able to focus on a damn thing. She'd started to put it back on the table when she noticed the *USA Today* sports section that had been sitting underneath. She caught a small headline and froze.

"Angels Cut Edwards Loose."

Margie sat. The article was merely a statement that he'd been released from his contract, but she knew the story behind those few carefully chosen words, and there was probably a lot more to it that she didn't know. Undoubtedly Fitz would publish whatever lurid details he could find, gloating about it, then setting his sights on the other fish he'd promised to fry. But at the moment, this was enough for Margie.

Finally, she'd gotten her vindication. That she'd been right about this guy all along, and finally, someone was doing the right thing about it.

She stared at the door, her chest tightening again. *Oh, crap. Is this what they're talking about?* The story was from that day's paper. With the fresh reminder that Margie had played a part in shining a light on that cockroach, were they reevaluating bringing her back, to possibly give baseball another public relations nightmare? No. She refused to look at it that way. She'd just been doing her job. It wasn't always neat and tidy, and people sometimes didn't like her for it, but that was okay. If she had a hope of sticking around, it would have to be okay.

Maybe fifteen minutes later, which felt like three hours, she heard footsteps. The door clicked. The big boss stepped into the room and nodded at her. Margie stood. The newspaper slipped to the table. She was trying to read his face, his body language. He wasn't giving her too many clues, but nothing about him said "call security," so she considered that a mark in her favor.

"Miss Oblonsky. We've been looking over your files, taking everything into account, and we just had a brief consultation with another member of the committee. Now we have a counter offer. We'll put you on the call-up list, guaranteed at the very least until the All-Star break. After that, if a regular crew spot opens up, while we can't absolutely guarantee you'll be first in line, we'll revisit your performance reviews and make every effort to give you serious consideration. But it won't be in the Southern League. We want to try you out in the International League, see if you're good enough to stay."

Margie blinked. And blinked again. Had she heard that right? They still wanted her on call but in Triple A? Damn. In her head she did some quick math. Three umps to a crew in Triple A, more teams, more chances to work. More chances for a regular spot. She fought hard to suppress a huge grin and the urge to hug him and dance around the room. *Cool it, Margie. You got this. You got this hard.*

She stood a little taller. "I find those terms acceptable. May I get that in writing?"

43

THE BOYS

Part of Margie's job as Tim's spring training mascot was to scope out restaurants both of them would like—places that served good southern home cooking and plenty of it. If they had seven kinds of fried fish on the menu, kept the sweet tea coming, and offered key lime pie for dessert, she was there. A view of the water also helped.

So she knew exactly where she wanted Tim and Dan to meet her for dinner. Tim was back from Orlando and Dan's game tomorrow was in Clearwater, so the opportunity was perfect.

The rough-hewn tables were covered with white butcher's paper. The shrimp was right off the boat. The chicken wings would melt the enamel off your teeth. And all the waitresses knew them. They were so nice that Margie didn't even care that the serving staff was far more interested in Tim than in her.

"You here on your own tonight, hon?" her favorite waitress asked when Margie came through the door.

"Nope. We're gonna be three."

The waitress grinned. "Tim bringin' one of his baseball friends?"

"You might say that."

"Well, then I'll get our best table ready for y'all."

She crossed to the back, swept a grease-spotted runner of white butcher's paper off a table and rolled another length across it.

Yep. My kind of place.

Tim and Dan must have met up in the parking lot, because they both came in together.

Tim had stopped to flirt with the waitress, so Dan reached Margie first, all smiles. "There she is." He drew her into a hug, then kissed her on the cheek as they disengaged. "I finally get my first groupie and she doesn't stick around long enough to bat her eyelashes at me and beg for my autograph? What's up with that? You got another guy stashed away down here?"

"Ha. I can barely keep up with you two. That's one of the reasons I'm glad you're both playing in the same county right now. So I get a chance to treat you guys to dinner."

Dan began to protest at the same moment Tim returned and flopped into a chair across from the two of them. "Nope," her brother said. "No way."

"Yes way," Margie said. "And it's about damn time, too. I've sponged off you long enough."

Tim gave her an accusatory stare. "Something's up with you. You're way too happy."

"They got catfish and hush puppies on the menu. What's not to be happy about?"

"Spill, *Margaret*. You went to Saint Pete while I was gone, didn't you?"

"Fine." She paused while the waitress brought over frosty mason jars of sweet tea. Waited until she left. Waited until she picked up one of those jars and took a long, long mouthful, swallowed it, and put it down. "Yes. I went to Saint Pete. And yadda yadda yadda, I'm in the International League now."

Margie had never heard two men whoop that loud. Tim practically leapt across the table to give her a hug. Dan grabbed her and danced her around the restaurant. Tim broke in and gave her a twirl. Then he ordered extra hush puppies for everyone.

When they finally settled back at their table, Margie explained the deal she'd struck. "You should have seen how smooth I was. I strutted right in there and told them I was worth better than what they were offering. Then I sat back and waited. They even huddled up and talked it over. Well, okay, it's on the call-up list, but it's still Triple A." She stuck a hand up and high-fived Dan.

"It's an in," Tim said. "When they see how good you are, they're gonna boot someone's ass up to the majors just to make room for you."

"Only thing is, I'll probably be living out of a suitcase for a while. I got spoiled in Montana and Binghamton, having a place that was sort of centrally located. The International League is spread out pretty good."

"Wait a sec." Dan's face set in pondering mode, and he snapped his fingers as if that would help him remember better. "Timmy. International League, they got a bunch of teams mid-Atlantic, right?"

"Yeah, I think. Virginia, North Carolina…"

Dan grinned. "And there I'll be in Baltimore. Margie Oblonsky, you can park your hot pot and that god-awful Genny Cream Ale at my place and crash whenever you want. I'll even let you wash your delicates in my sink." His smile faltered, but only for a second. "I don't actually have a place to live yet, but when I get one, you're welcome any time."

Tim let his mouth fall open, giving his usual John-Boy innocent look extra oomph. "Say. Dan, that sounds an awful lot like some kind of indecent proposal. Exactly what are your intentions toward my sister?"

Dan's goofy grin was completely adorable. "I dunno. Maybe play hard to get? Let her chase me for around a while?"

Margie shoved her shoulder into Dan's giant arm. "Shaddap, both of you." The sun was melting into the bay, rippling gold across the water. The sight stopped her. She wanted to freeze this moment. It might be a long time before the three of them could get together again like this. The regular season would be starting in just over a week. Tim in the National League, Dan in the American League, and Margie bouncing all over the East Coast. She imagined all the games she'd get to work, all the new *learning opportunities* she'd have. That was its own kind of wonderful. But this… The moment felt so perfect, she couldn't stop smiling.

"Yeah, I think Mom was right," Tim said. "Maybe you have been out in the sun too long."

"I'm just happy, damn it. I'm out on the town with my two favorite guys, watching the sun set over Tampa Bay, eating food Mom wouldn't approve of, and the baseball gods have given me a second chance. What's not to be happy about?"

"You got a point there, Bargie." Tim grinned and called the waitress over. "But I think our happiness could be vastly improved if there was some key lime pie on the table."

* * *

299

Margie had been happy. But as she followed Tim back to the house, a familiar curl of dread began waking up. It tapped a claw against her stomach, and by the time they pulled into side-by-side parking spaces, it was making her regret that second slice of pie. She grabbed his arm before he reached the front door. He looked back, his blue eyes questioning.

"I'm worried about leaving you," she said.

His mouth relaxed and he tilted his head, an expression that always made him look like a little kid. "Margie Bargie..."

"I know. You've been doing so well and you're a grown-up and I can't..."

"You're right. You've been awesome. I can't tell you how grateful I am that you came down here. But I'm gonna be okay. Yeah, I guess I'll have to deal with some pressure sometimes, but so far, I'm handling it."

Her eyes dropped to his hands, fussing with his ring of keys.

His voice was as soft as the night air. "I can't... You've got your own life. A second chance. And Big Dan's nuts about you. I can't, I won't ask you to give any of that up. Not to take care of me, that's for sure."

Crickets chirped. A gecko scurried across the sidewalk.

He continued. "I'm already working on lining up a support system in Cincinnati, and Carl's gonna get me a whole notebook of when and where there are meetings in pretty much every city we're playing in. So I think I'm covered."

"But you're still gonna call me?"

He grinned. "I'll call you before every game if you want."

"Only when you need to."

"Deal."

* * *

Before they went to bed, Tim told Margie that the next day's schedule—basically workouts and meetings—might be boring for spectators. He suggested she drive over to Clearwater and watch Dan play. Much as that tempted her, it had been a long time since she'd had a day completely to herself. And there was someone she wanted to visit.

She didn't even know if Big Al would be there. Umpire training had officially ended a few weeks earlier, but off-season it was still a ballpark, so somebody might be around who could tell her how to find him. If she totally struck out, she'd call it a good day for a beautiful drive up the east coast along A1A. Maybe she'd even stop at one of those surf shops, buy a cheap bathing suit, and sweet-talk someone into giving her a few lessons. She always wanted to learn how to surf.

After the three-hours-and-change drive, she pulled into the stadium parking lot but only saw a handful of cars. She took a chance that one might be his. The white van with the license plate "BIG AL 1" looked like a safe bet, although that might have been a company vehicle, maybe the one they used to shuttle recruits to and from the local airports and exhibition games at other stadiums.

She wandered inside. The place hadn't changed a bit. Part of her cringed, remembering how nervous she'd been her first day, when Rocky Anderson told her where to set up the coffee.

Maybe he's learned how to make his own by now.

She heard footsteps to her left and saw a man in a Big Al's Umpire Academy golf shirt pushing a mop-and-bucket cart toward her.

"Help you find something, miss?" He squinted. "Margie? That really you?"

She met him halfway. "It's really me."

"Sorry, I'm a mess, or I'd shake your hand. Young lady, you are a sight for sore eyes, if you don't mind my saying. How you doin'? You up in the majors yet?"

"Workin' on it," she said.

"You come here for a little nostalgia? Or is there something you need?"

"Well, I might be on a wild goose chase, but would the big man happen to be around?"

Hector checked his watch. "About now, probably in his office. You remember where that is?"

Margie laughed. "I wore out the floor tiles going to his office. I think I can find it."

* * *

His door was open. His head was bent over some paperwork. A deli sandwich and a bottle of Coke sat beside him. Not wanting to startle him, she gave him the courtesy of a knock.

He looked up. "Hiya, kiddo." His smile was warm, with a hint of something in it that made her think he'd been expecting her.

"Did Hector rat me out?"

"Nah. Just had a feeling I'd be seeing you one of these days soon."

"And why would that be? Other than the fact that you were always my favorite instructor?"

He gave her a cockeyed smirk. "Flattery will get you everywhere. Have a seat. Want something to drink? I remember you were particularly fond of the god-awful water in this place. But if you've grown some sense, there's another Coke in the fridge."

She grabbed it from the cube in the corner and sat in his guest chair, rolling the cold bottle between her palms.

"So, a little bird told me a rumor about you and a new assignment. That true?"

"As if you didn't know."

"Know what?" he said.

"Oh, please. You had something to do with recommending me for the triple-A call-up list, didn't you?"

"Hey," he said, putting up his hand. "I saw a qualified candidate who was getting a bum rap."

"And you helped that qualified candidate get back in the door." Her gaze drifted to the papers on his desk before returning to his. "Thank you."

He grinned. "My pleasure. But don't make a liar out of me, Margie Oblonsky."

She leaned back and twisted open her soda. "Wouldn't dream of it."

"You owe me, though."

"For you, anything."

He tapped his pencil against the desk. "Did you read in the papers that we had three women in this year's training class?"

"Really?"

"Yes, ma'am. Things are changing out there for baseball; I can feel it. I already got a few good prospects on the waiting list for next year. So if you don't have anything on your dance card come January, maybe you'd like to be a guest instructor. Class the joint up a bit. Might even pay you."

She would do it for nothing, but she wasn't about to tell him that. "You still make them do laps for getting their calls wrong?"

"Yeah. Why?"

"You ever read anything about the benefits of positive reinforcement?"

"Not that I'm aware of."

"Then today's your lucky day. I'm about to offer you a learning opportunity."

44

THE FUTURE

Three months later

The visiting team brought in a relief pitcher, but his delivery didn't look right. From everything Margie knew about physics and baseball, curves didn't break that hard without artificial means. In case she was wrong, she let him throw another one. Again, it acted the same. She signaled for time, stepped away from her position near third base and gestured that she wanted to meet Dave Spelling, her crew chief, on the mound. She also wanted to see the ball.

He took the ball from the catcher and jogged in from behind the plate. "What's up, Margie?"

Meanwhile, the first-base ump and the visiting team's manager had joined them. Margie eyed the pitcher. His face might as well have been made of stone.

Margie said, "Feel something funny about that ball, Dave?"

Dave turned it around in his fingers, and his expression alone said he knew what Margie was after. "Sam, you mind letting us have a look at your cap?"

"He don't have to show you nothing," the manager said.

Dave ignored him. "Sam. The cap, please?"

The pitcher let out a huge sigh and plucked it off his head.

Margie took it and examined the underside of the brim. Yep. Just like she thought. "Pretty creative place to store your lip balm, Sam."

"It's not even my cap," he whined. "It's—"

"All over your pitching hand, too, I'd imagine," Dave said. "If it's anything like this ball."

Then Dave threw the pitcher out of the game. The manager started kicking up a fuss and using unbecoming language. Dave tossed him, too.

* * *

Dave was one of the best crew chiefs Margie had ever seen, and she'd seen quite a few of them while she worked her International League fill-ins—a game here, a game there. She liked his style. He believed in giving everyone a fair shot, but anyone who thought he was a pushover would be making a big mistake. Over a round of beers after a game in Richmond, Virginia, Dave handed out praise to Margie and to Joe, the other member of their crew. Margie felt bad about how she'd gotten this assignment—an ump went out on six weeks of medical leave after a serious car accident—but she counted herself lucky. Dave and Joe were nice guys and excellent umpires. It only took one game to know they had her back; after five she'd already learned a ton from them; now three weeks in, they felt like family. More and more, she was grateful for having worked with Warren Durning and Doug French, to show her what bad partnering looked like, to show her by comparison how great it could be to not only work in the game she loved but really like and respect the people she got to work with.

Joe got her attention. "Margie, how'd you know he was putting Vaseline on the ball?"

"I wasn't sure it was Vaseline, but I had a good hunch it was something. Curveballs don't break like that without help." She reminded herself to thank Tim for that tip next time they spoke.

"Great eye," Dave said. "And once again I have to say we're damn glad you were available when Mike was taken out. I mean, God bless him and I pray for his recovery, but between us and these four walls, you had the best creds of anyone on the call-up list."

"Thanks," Margie said. "Glad to be here. Actually, I'm glad to be anywhere."

They traded a few stories about other illegal things they'd seen in games, and a short while later, Joe said he was going back to the hotel to call his wife. Dave watched him leave, then gestured for Margie to lean closer. "Can I get something out in the open with you?"

"Uh. Sure."

"Are you a call-up by choice, or are you looking for regular work?"

Margie didn't know what to say to that. "Are there actually umps who are call-ups by choice?"

"Well, yes. Some have other things going on. They work in independent leagues, or have other jobs… So it does sound like you're looking for regular work."

"Yes!" She got hold of herself. "I mean, yes. I am in the market for a regular slot, when and if one opens up. Why, you know of any?"

He nodded. "See, here's the thing. Joe's moving up. He got the call a few days ago that he'll be starting after the All-Star break. He's a humble, classy guy. As you've no doubt already noticed. That's probably why he's not running around crowing about it. And Mike… I got a message right after the game that his doctors are saying he'll need more time. The rest of the season, it looks like. Maybe more. That's why I asked you. I wanted to know if I'd be looking for one ump or two."

The large winged things in Margie's gut began doing a happy dance. "Sounds like one, Dave. If you want me, I'm all in." Then a thought struck her. "I hope this isn't out of line, because I know it's your choice as crew chief. But if you're looking for a name to fill that third spot, I know one very qualified candidate."

Dave stroked his chin, nodding. "Actually, Umpire Development said they were sending someone to meet with me"—he checked his watch—"in about ten minutes. They said he's the best they've got. But if he doesn't work out, I'd be happy to hear who you have in mind."

"Ten minutes?" She started getting out of her chair. "You want me to make myself scarce?"

He held out a hand. "No, stay, if you don't mind. I'd like to get your take on him. Since we might all be working together."

She peered over her shoulder at the hotel bar. It was getting kind of crowded. "Hope he can find us. It's a little thick in here."

Dave chuckled. "Well, if he's not smart enough to find us, he probably wouldn't make that great an umpire, would he?"

"Ha. You're probably right."

Then a voice said, "You must be Dave Spelling."

It was a familiar voice. At first Margie thought her brain was playing tricks on her, then Dave got up, rounded the table, and stuck out his hand. "You must be Wes Osterhaus. Great to meet you."

Thank you for reading!

Thank you for reading *The Call*. Won't you please take a moment to leave a short review on Amazon or Goodreads? It really does make a difference—your thoughts can help other readers decide if a book is worth their time.

Want to hear about new book releases, special offers, and events? Please sign up for my mailing list at http://laurieboris.com/mailing-list/.

ACKNOWLEDGMENTS

I'm all alone in my little pink room while I'm writing a novel, but it takes teamwork to publish one. As always, I'm grateful to Tom DePoto for the first look and the hard truth. You make me want to be a better writer. As do Bette Moskowitz, Mare Leonard, and Anne McGrath, who helped me with some early feedback. Beta readers are gold, so a big thank you to Melissa Bowersock, Leland Dirks, Lynne Cantwell, Erin McGowan, LB Clark, and Jeff Dawson. Thank you to Rita Dybdhal Cline, for answering my many questions about umpire rulings, and to the fabulous Perry Barber for her enthusiasm and some perspective about what the climate was like for female umpires during Margie's time. Off the field, mad love to David Antrobus of Be Write There Editing.

Thank you to my blended, extended family for always being on my team. And last but never least, I'm grateful to my husband for still not running away screaming after all these years of being married to a writer.

A LITTLE ABOUT LAURIE

Laurie Boris has been writing fiction for over twenty-five years and is the award-winning author of seven novels. When not playing with the universe of imaginary people in her head, she's a freelance copyeditor and enjoys baseball, reading, and avoiding housework. She lives in New York's lovely Hudson Valley with her husband, Paul Blumstein, a commercial illustrator and web designer.

Connect with me online:
Website: http://laurieboris.com
Amazon Author Page: http://www.amazon.com/author/laurieboris
Facebook: http://www.facebook.com/laurie.boris.author
Twitter: http://www.twitter.com/LaurieBoris

LAURIE'S OTHER FICTION

Catering Girl (women's fiction, novella)
Frankie Goldberg, struggling actress and stand-up comic in Los Angeles, can't keep her day jobs, thanks to her smart mouth and a lot of other bad habits. Now a thirty-something catering assistant on a movie set, she reluctantly agrees to bring a cappuccino to the resident diva. The young star Anastasia Cole is in tears, distraught about disturbing changes in the script. Frankie serves a side of common sense with the coffee, and excited to have an ally, Anastasia offers her the role of a lifetime. It's not what Frankie had in mind—but being needed might be exactly what she needs. (*Catering Girl* is a prequel novella to the romantic comedy *The Joke's on Me.*)

A Sudden Gust of Gravity (romantic suspense)
Waitress Christina Davenport lands in a world of trouble when she accepts a job as an assistant to a charming street performer. She'd wanted to be a magician and vowed to never again stand in the background holding some guy's props, but Christina has a score to settle—with her traumatic family history, with people telling her she can't hack it on her own. Reynaldo the Magnificent is more than a little full of himself and has a dark side, but to Christina, he could be her second chance, her redemption, her ticket to something bigger. If only she can learn from him before he discovers her secrets. (Finalist, 2016 Next Generation Indie Book Awards and an indieBRAG medallion recipient.)

In the Name of Love: Stories about Revenge, Redemption, and Rebirth (flash-fiction anthology)
A lonely neighbor tries to melt a widow's reluctant heart. Bullying brothers threaten to spoil a young girl's Halloween. Left at the altar once, a woman takes a gamble on a second chance. These are just a few in a collection of thirty short and shorter stories about growing up, growing older, moving out, moving on, revenge, redemption, and love in all its shades of bittersweet pain and joy.

The Picture of Cool (Book One, Trager Family Secrets)

Television producer Charlie Trager spends his days working with beautiful women on a daytime talk show. But underneath his cool façade, there's a hollow spot in his heart, waiting for the right man to ease his loneliness. Then he meets the show's next guest, a handsome young politician with a bad case of nerves—and a secret that could turn both their lives upside down. (Short novella: 14,000 words)

Don't Tell Anyone (Book Two, Trager Family Secrets)

Liza's mother-in-law once called her a godless hippie raised by wolves. Now, after five years of marriage to her elder son, five years of disapproval and spite, the family accidentally learns that Estelle has a fatal illness. And Estelle comes to her with an impossible request. A horrified Liza refuses but keeps the question from her husband and his brother. As the three children urge Estelle to consider treatment, their complicated weave of family secrets and lies begins to unravel. Can they hold their own lives together long enough to help Estelle with hers? (Winner, The Kindle Book Review's 2013 Best Indie Books Award and indieBRAG medallion recipient. May be read as a standalone story.)

Playing Charlie Cool (Book Three, Trager Family Secrets)

Television producer Charlie Trager knows he's lucky to have a successful career and good friends and family who support him. The man he loves, however, is not so lucky. Joshua Goldberg suffers the spite of an ex-wife gunning to keep him from their two children...and maybe Charlie. Determined not to let Joshua go, Charlie crafts a scheme that could remove the obstacles to their relationship...or destroy their love forever. (Note: May be read as a standalone story, but if you'd like to know how Joshua and Charlie met, you might want to read *The Picture of Cool* first.)

Sliding Past Vertical (women's/literary fiction)

Sarah loves Boston. The feeling isn't mutual. After a run of bad luck, she moves back to the college town where best friend Emerson lives. Still in love with her, he'd dreamed of her return. But well-meaning Sarah's hasty decisions often end in disaster, so Emerson's dream may become a nightmare.

Drawing Breath (contemporary/literary fiction)
Art teacher Daniel Benedetto has cystic fibrosis. At thirty-four, he's already outlived his doctor's "expiration date," but that doesn't stop him from giving all he can to his students and his work. When he takes on Caitlin, his landlady's daughter, as a private student, the budding teen painter watches in torment as other people, especially women, treat Daniel like a freak because of his condition. To Caitlin, Daniel is not a disease, not someone to pity or take care of but someone to care for, a friend, and her first real crush. Convinced one of those women is about to hurt him, Caitlin makes one very bad decision. (Finalist, 2013 Next Generation Indie Book Awards.)

The Joke's on Me (romantic comedy)
When a mudslide plummets her hopes, her home, and her entire collection of impractical footwear into the Pacific, former actress and stand-up comic Frankie Goldberg takes the only possession she has left—a cherry red Corvette convertible—and drives east to her family's bed and breakfast in Woodstock, New York. This begins a journey into the family she left behind, the family she joked about in her act. But the joke's on Frankie. While she was doing impressions of her slightly menopausal Jewish mother and her sister the serial divorcee, her family was slowly leaving her. And maybe that joke is just too new to be funny. Travel along with fearless Frankie as she puzzles through the eternal dilemma of coming back home to find that nothing is where you left it. (Finalist, 2012 Beach Books Festival.)

LAURIE'S OTHER BOOKS

First Chapters (Contributing Author)
Indies Unlimited: Author's Snarkopaedia Volume 1 (Contributing Author)
Indies Unlimited: Tutorials and Tools for Prospering in a Digital World (Contributing Author)
Indies Unlimited: 2012 Flash Fiction Anthology (Contributing Author)
Indies Unlimited: 2014 Flash Fiction Anthology (Contributing Author)
Boo! (Contributing Author)
Boo! Volume Two (Contributing Author)
Boo! Volume Three (Contributing Author)